A WOMAN MADE FOR SIN

Reece said nothing. He only folded his arms and glared at Aimee.

Aimee glared back. "I am tired of letting you dictate the terms of our relationship, Reece Hamilton."

Reece could listen to no more. "We don't have a relationship, damn it! I am simply a childhood fantasy of yours! It's time you got over me, grew up, and sought a man who wants you in return."

"You *were* a childhood fantasy; and last Christmas, I *did* grow up. I was no longer dreaming of love—I was *in* love with you, and after the kiss we just shared, don't bother denying that you love me. I won't believe you . . ."

Books by Michele Sinclair

THE HIGHLANDER'S BRIDE

TO WED A HIGHLANDER

DESIRING THE HIGHLANDER

THE CHRISTMAS KNIGHT

TEMPTING THE HIGHLANDER

A WOMAN MADE FOR PLEASURE

SEDUCING THE HIGHLANDER

A WOMAN MADE FOR SIN

HIGHLAND HUNGER
(with Hannah Howell and Jackie Ivie)

Published by Kensington Publishing Corporation

A WOMAN MADE FOR SIN

MICHELE SINCLAIR

ZEBRA BOOKS
KENSINGTON PUBLISHING CORP.
http://www.kensingtonbooks.com

ZEBRA BOOKS are published by

Kensington Publishing Corp.
119 West 40th Street
New York, NY 10018

All Kensington titles, imprints, and distributed lines are available at special quantity discounts for bulk purchases for sales promotion, premiums, fund-raising, educational, or institutional use.

Special book excerpts or customized printings can also be created to fit specific needs. For details, write or phone the office of the Kensington Special Sales Manager: Attn. Special Sales Department. Kensington Publishing Corp., 119 West 40th Street, New York, NY 10018. Phone: 1-800-221-2647.

Zebra and the Z logo Reg. U.S. Pat. & TM Off.

First Printing: August 2014
ISBN-13: 978-1-4201-2653-2
ISBN-10: 1-4201-2653-9

First Electronic Edition: August 2014
eISBN-13: 978-1-4201-2654-9
eISBN-10: 1-4201-2654-7

10 9 8 7 6 5 4 3 2 1

Printed in the United States of America

Prologue

Buckfast Abbey, Summer, 1816

He had tasted death. Rolled it around on his tongue and licked its dry, cracked lips. He had drunk from death's dark soul and then done the impossible. He had survived.

Fate's plans for him had not included an untimely and disgraceful demise, but something profoundly more meaningful. Revenge. Its sweet flavor would mix with death's, and he would know satisfaction at last.

He turned the final corner down the dank stairwell and entered the oval space filled with the scent of old vellum. Only this room prevented the long days from becoming a living nightmare of pain and torture. In this small area lived the past. Written on countless aged scrolls were the lives of once-powerful leaders, who, like he, had seen their lofty attempts at fulfilling fate's decree hampered by lesser men. But death had determined those men unworthy to walk these lands of promised power. *They* were the ones who deserved his sentence of physical damnation, not he.

Time, the monks said. Time to heal his wounds. Time to reflect on past indiscretions and do penance. He, of course, complied and joined their devotions. And his reward was this room of solace, quiet, and promise. Fate had drawn him here. The answer to his future lay somewhere in these cool stone walls along with a promise that not all was lost. That all he aspired to be and have was still within his grasp.

He moved over to remove a small marker in one of the numerous carved openings used for storage. Placing it on the small wooden desk, he turned, pulled out the next scroll, and uncurled the sheet of vellum. Carefully, he secured the ends with heavy rocks. He sat down slowly to avoid any more pain than necessary, and began to read aloud.

"I, your servant, am unable to show you, noble lady, anything worthy in my deeds, and I do not know how I can be acceptable to you . . ."

The words of the manuscript filled him, flowing over him like a balm on his raw wounds. He had been wrong. It was not a king's secrets he was searching for, but a queen's. He continued on.

Hours passed, and though no natural light could shine into the small enclave, he knew it was dark outside. The single candle that had been lighting the room was nearly gone. The monks would be searching for him, telling him it was time for another devotion, solemn ceremony, or some mysterious rite in dedication to God.

A debate began to play out in his head as he continued to read. He knew he should return. Tomorrow would come and the scrolls would still be here. But fate was with him tonight. If he chose to leave, it would surely forsake him, leaving him scarred, ruined, and powerless for his remaining days. Here beneath his fingertips was the answer for which he had been searching. He could not abandon fate's gift. It might not come again.

He flipped to the final page and read the end.

Nothing was revealed. No secrets. No messages. And yet he knew his destiny was intertwined with this woman's story.

How this ancient manuscript had made its way into the

abbey's dark walls was a mystery. He could spend years trying to find out whose hands had held this scroll, only to discover the hard-gained knowledge was meaningless. So why had fate placed such words in his grasp? Why was his soul so affected by this woman's inexplicable victory?

He knew if he did not find the answer, he would be forsaken once again. Fate had little time for fools. It certainly did not deliver enemies and resurrect kingdoms to unworthy men.

"Hallo?" called a voice whose accent spoke of a life lived in a variety of places. "Son? Are you down there? You have missed the divine reading, and supper is nearly finished. Are you well?"

He sighed deeply and returned, "Yes, Father, I am coming. I am afraid in my studies I lost track of time."

Crunching footsteps echoed against the walls. An old man dressed in black robes appeared. "What is it that had your attention for so long today? What did the Lord bring to you?"

He stifled another sigh and brought his hood farther up to shade the majority of his face, though he knew the old monk had seen the monstrosity that lay underneath the brown folds. The man had found him washed up from the sea and had brought him to the abbey to tend his wounds.

He should have died. And though the monk might believe it was his God that had revived his nearly dead carcass, he knew better. Something the old man would never understand.

A withered hand poked out from the arm of the black cape and glided down the vellum outstretched on the table. "You are reading the *Encomium Emmae Reginae*. It is very old, written many years ago by a monk of St. Omer in praise of his Queen Emma. Few take interest in that which occurred so far in the past. So little history was captured then. It is difficult to tell the truth from fiction." The aged monk paused to cough violently into his hand. His remaining days were few. Consumption was taking him, slowly and painfully.

"My apologies, Father. The staleness of the room makes it hard to breathe," he said, and then waited patiently for the monk to continue, for the man was one of the few in the abbey who had studied any writings that were not directly related to scripture.

"This accounting, while biased, is believed to be true, unlike others."

His heart momentarily stopped. "Are there other stories of the queen? I mean here, at the abbey?" he asked the old monk, hoping his tone reflected his eagerness rather than the apprehension he felt. For he was close. He knew he was.

The monk rolled his eyes upward and began to nod his head. "There is indeed more text written about the queen. But such legends are too elaborate to be believed. We had another visitor to the abbey who was also much interested in the monarch. I will tell you what I told them: The accounting is highly questionable and cannot be considered reliable. Its value is in understanding how stories were embellished back then . . ."

The old monk stretched his head back and surveyed the dusty scrolls stacked in various-sized cubicles within the walls. After a minute, he stretched out his arm until the tips of his gnarled fingers touched a single scroll nestled in a group.

As he watched the monk slip the document out of its resting place, he realized it would have taken many more months at his present pace before he had read the item. The monk gave it to him and he laid it out, anchoring the corners. His heart began pounding with renewed hope. He heard the old man's opinion of the story, that it was an allegory and not one of truth.

But he knew differently.

Fate had not deserted him.

Fate had been with him all along, as it was with all great men.

Bending over, he read the simple legend. Unlike the other manuscripts, the handwriting was jagged and the scattered drops of ink indicated it had been quickly scribed. He gnashed his teeth and calmed his suddenly tumultuous emotions. Any doubt of the importance of today's find completely and resolutely vanished.

"You said only one other had studied these, Father. Please, tell me. Just who was that person?"

Chapter 1

London, October 6, 1816

"Millie, do not shake your head at me! I absolutely insist that you come! Of the three of us, you know the area the best. And, Jennelle, do not think because you are sitting behind me I am unaware that you are at this very moment rolling your eyes and signaling Millie to refuse," Aimee added as she glanced back, affirming her guess. "Millie fled through those alleys just a few months ago."

Millie felt her jaw tense and tried again to make her best friend see reason. "It was at night and you must remember, Charles was with me, Aimee. It was *your* brother who knew where to go, not me, when he managed to save me from—"

"And since then you have gone with him a dozen times or more when he has needed to visit one of his ships," Aimee interrupted. She knelt down and clutched her oldest friend's fingers in her own. "This is my one opportunity, Millie. Charles will be busy with his dinner meeting, which he made clear that none of us were invited to, and—"

"And *we* have already accepted the invitation to Lady Shackleton's card party," Jennelle chimed in.

Aimee continued to clutch Millie's hand but faced Jennelle, giving her an angry stare that she hoped would singe her friend's red hair. "I can recall numerous occasions where you demonstrated just how easily we can and will send our regrets." Standing back up, she said more forcefully, "I not only want but *need* your help, but know that if you both refuse, it will not sway me from going. Tonight is my last chance, and I *am* going. Even if I have to go by myself."

Aimee's voice was soft but emphatic. It was completely out of character for the tall, willowy blonde, who was typically very sweet and gentle. But today, her bright green eyes snapped with a compelling urgency that conveyed her threat was not an empty one.

Jennelle was about to offer a word of caution when Aimee cut her off. "It is a *brilliant* plan. Millie, tell her," Aimee said to the most adventurous of their group.

Nicknamed the Daring Three when they were just children, the three girls were best friends and nearly inseparable. Even Millie's recent marriage to Aimee's elder brother had not separated them. Aimee was positive that if she could just get Millie to agree with her plan, the ever-so-logical Jennelle would follow. She would be compelled to, from sheer friendship.

Millie, now sorry that she ever mentioned her husband's mysterious thief, laid a hand on her agitated friend's arm. "It is a bold plan, Aimee, but I am unsure why you would want to get involved. I think Chase has his own ideas about routing out the thief. Should we not just wait . . . ?"

"My brother may be your husband, Millie. And you may find him intriguing and his tediousness an adventure, but since you became Lady Chaselton . . . well, I must finally tell you the truth. You have turned into quite a bore!" Aimee huffed and began pacing. "Four months ago, it would have been *you* planning this night raid, and it would have been Jennelle and I holding *you* back."

Millie opened and closed her mouth, unable to deny her friend's accusation. "I expect you are correct, Aimee. I have tempered my inclinations a bit, but you must understand that as the Marchioness of Chaselton, I cannot continue to act as I once did," Millie declared, adding underneath her breath, "Not to mention, Charlie would kill me if he found out." Then realizing Aimee had heard her, she looked down, tucking an escaped dark lock of consistently errant, thick, wavy hair behind her ear.

Her husband was called Charles by his sister, his mother, and Jennelle, but never by her. She normally referred to him as Chase, like most did. Only when he was particularly aggravating did she call him Charlie, a pet name she had given him when they were younger, knowing how much he detested it. But since they had married, Millie used the term more and more often in her private thoughts. It was her name for him. Hers alone.

"You are shamming it, Mildred," Aimee stated unequivocally, "and you know it. Charles would be upset, but he has caught you in many a more provocative situation, and he still fell in love with you *despite* your ways. I am asking you for one small favor, one small adventure, and suddenly you turn prim and proper. It is unfair, I tell you! After all the crazy exploits Jennelle and I have joined you on."

Jennelle's dark red eyebrows popped up at the mention of her name. "It is not a small favor, Aimee. Dressing up like men and leaving in the middle of the night in an attempt to stow aboard Charles's ship to catch a thief, is *not* a small favor." Despite her red hair and flashing blue eyes that hinted of her Irish ancestry, of the three of them, Jennelle was the one who was most able to remain calm and cool in even the direst of situations. As the years came and went, Millie and Aimee wondered what, if anything, could break that cool composure, and secretly hoped to be around if it ever did.

Aimee walked over and sat across from her two friends, deciding honesty was the only way she would get them to understand and agree. "Please, please do this. Reece has been in town for nearly a month and has refused to see me. No matter what I do, he avoids my company. Can you imagine, Millie, what it would be like if Charles suddenly no longer wanted to see you or speak to you?"

Millie bit her bottom lip. She could not imagine the pain Aimee just described, but the mere thought of not being able to talk with Chase, even when they disagreed, was horrifying. Aimee had been in love with Reece Hamilton, Charles's best friend, since she first saw him when she was six years old. Almost nine years Aimee's senior, Reece had been amused by her infatuation, but it was not until last Christmas that their relationship changed—significantly.

During the war, Reece's and Charles's visits home were infrequent. Consequently, it was customary for Reece to pay Lady Chaselton and her daughter a visit whenever he returned. He would relay any news of the war and the well-being of her son, just as it was expected that Charles would visit Reece's family. Last December, it had been three years since Reece had seen Aimee. It must have made a difference, because this time he kissed her. And according to Aimee, the kiss had been no ordinary one. She was now certain Reece was the only man for her and that her destiny was tied to his.

Millie sighed. "Tell me your plan one more time. All of it, from the beginning. And, Jennelle, pay attention for probable difficulties, for I believe we are going on an adventure tonight."

Jennelle rolled her eyes but knew all was lost. Millie had acquiesced. But what had she expected? For marriage to change her petite, excitement-seeking friend into a paragon of the gentle sex? For Aimee to suddenly stop seizing every opportunity to convince the one man she had ever pined for to love her? Jennelle held her breath and then exhaled long and soft, realizing she was the only sane one of the bunch. And a sane person really *should* be accompanying her two friends during this crazy escapade.

"I'm unsure as to the intelligence of this idea, Aimee, but tell it to us once again."

Aimee felt alive and excited all over. The rented hack hit a large cobblestone and her fingers fluttered to Millie's for support. "I cannot believe I am finally going to see him again, Millie. It has been so long. If I have to endure another Season of pretentious old men or even worse, loquacious, overly eager *young* men and their tittering marriage-focused mothers, I really shall perish. You have no idea how fortunate you are, Jennelle, that your father is not compelled to see you advantageously married. And, Millie, you are the luckiest of us all to have convinced Charles he was in love with you and to ask for your hand. If only Reece would do the same."

Millie took a deep breath and blew a wayward strand of her dark hair away from her eye. If they were caught, it was highly doubtful she would be able to convince her husband of anything again. She glanced out the window. They were just about to cross into Shadwell at Thames, the main entrance to the London Docks. "I want your promise, Aimee, that *if* we stumble across the thief, you will not make a single move until all three of us are sure that he is indeed Reece. Chase is still not positive this latest event is a simple prank."

"But you said the thief was only taking some papers that were of little value and of interest only to Reece and Charles. Besides we three and Mother, who else would know what Reece and my brother really value?"

Millie moistened her dry lips, uncomfortable that Aimee

refused to consider the possibility of there being a *real* thief. "I said that it was the randomness that made Chase wonder if it really was a thief or Reece playing a practical joke."

"Ah, but you also said *only* Reece would be interested in the papers that were taken. So, it *has* to be him. And when I catch Reece in the act, he will have no choice but to speak to me. All I need is five minutes. Five minutes and I will know whether what happened between us at Christmas was real or *a passing moment of passion*," Aimee countered, contemptuously gritting out Reece's words that had haunted her for months.

Millie again glanced out the window and tried to dismiss the ill feeling pressing on her chest. "I hope so, Aimee. I really hope so. Now, when the carriage stops, refrain from speaking unless absolutely necessary. Use the hand signals we discussed and stick to the shadows. I went with Chase to visit the *Zephyr* a couple of days ago, just after it arrived. They had a lot of cargo and there is a good chance Charles's ship is still moored." Millie began praying but stopped when she realized her prayers were in conflict. She did not know whether she wished for the *Zephyr* to be inaccessible, thereby ending this insane quest, or for Aimee to be happy.

The carriage rolled to a dead stop. Once more, they agreed to follow the plan and then proceeded out of the hack. It was difficult to see, but dressed in male attire and wearing the dark cloaks Aimee had pilfered from some of the younger footmen, it would be just as difficult for a passerby to see them.

Moving down one of the narrow alleys, they edged along until they could see Pennington Street. On the other side were the large warehouses of the north quay. The ground and lower floors stored mostly sugar in various forms, but it was the upper floors that filled the air with scents of coffee and cocoa.

"This way," Millie whispered and moved farther east

before crossing the street in order to avoid the buildings on the western portion of the docks, where the ships' officers often stayed.

Aimee followed with Jennelle alongside, each watching out for the other as they returned to the relative safety of the shadows. Only a sliver of the moon peeked through amassing clouds to light the narrow alleys between the large buildings.

The London Docks had been built to augment the river wharves with much-needed dock capacity. Two canal-like basins connected the River Thames to a body of water in the shape of a square, which was surrounded by warehouses and dock slips. Ships entered via the basins to load and unload their cargo, choosing a dock based on commodity type. Everything from tobacco, ivory, wines, and spices was stored and shipped from these docks. And right now, the *Zephyr* was moored at the north quay.

Aimee fought the instinct to pinch her nose. She had heard about the strong odors around the docks, but nothing could have prepared her for the overpowering aromas coming from the buildings they were skirting. One smelled of tobacco, another of wine. There were the unmistakable scents of fish and brandy, and many more. On their own they could be endurable, even pleasant, but together, the stench overwhelmed the senses.

Millie stopped short and Aimee and Jennelle very quickly saw why. Dock laborers, watermen, and others who made a living by the riverside were still roaming the network of docks where the ships were secured. "This has to be the craziest, most insane thing we have ever done," Millie hissed, ignoring her own rule of complete silence. "I cannot believe that I actually let you talk me into it."

"I didn't *talk* you into it," Aimee scoffed. "I *threatened* you into coming with me. And I would have made good on my threat too—that's why you are here. Besides, I thought you had done this before."

"*I was with your brother*, Aimee, and that makes all the difference. In case you have not noticed, this harbor is quite large and the number of docks that support all these ships is vast. Chase knows this area, not I," Millie argued. "Scrambling around here in the dark, praying to God that we are not caught, is not what I call a well-thought-out plan. Aimee, I really think we should return."

Jennelle was about to voice her wholehearted agreement with Millie's assessment of their precarious position when Aimee piped, "Look, isn't that Charles's ship, the *Zephyr*?"

Millie followed the tip of Aimee's finger and grimaced. Several hundred yards away, rocking against the wharf, was one of five ships her husband and Reece owned in a small but very profitable shipping company. While Chase preferred to remain in England to oversee the accounts and assist with cargo decisions, Reece elected to remain at sea primarily aboard the *Sea Emerald*, a unique ship he had built to move light cargo with exceptional speed.

"See, Millie! The ship is still at the dock! And there is hardly anyone near it! This is destiny. My plan just has to work. Reece intends to sail out tomorrow. He would find it irresistible to sneak aboard and pinch something before he left."

Jennelle glanced back and forth from Millie's wan, uneasy expression to Aimee's expectant and determined one. "She is going to do this, with or without us, Millie," she whispered.

"I know, I know. I also know that we could stop her if we really wanted to."

"True, but she would never forgive us, and then she would only try again with a plan even more dangerous. But next time she would not ask for our input, help, or even let us know."

"Jennelle, sometimes your reasoning leads to the most dreadful conclusions," Millie grunted. She turned to Aimee and pointed to a newly emptied wagon. "I'm going to move toward the *Zephyr*. When I give the signal, follow my lead. And watch out for the laborers. There seem to be several out tonight."

Jennelle trailed Millie as they advanced around the wagon and slowly crept up to the *Zephyr*. A minute later, they verified the entry was clear and began to tread softly up the wooden planks. Aimee followed, stepping past an unconscious man posted as a guard. Charles would be angry if he knew the men were asleep, allowing any thief easy entry. She slipped by the sprawled figure and located the hiding spot Millie and Jennelle were crouching behind. Quietly, she hunkered down with them and waited for what she knew her friends hoped would never come.

But it did.

After a half hour of waiting, Jennelle snaked out her finger and pointed to a dark, lone figure crouching low. At first Aimee thought he might be a sailor, but his movements were those of someone unfamiliar with the ship as he moved in and out of view. Then he began peering into boxes and containers that had not yet been stowed below. Aimee elbowed Millie and pointed. Millie nodded to indicate that she and Jennelle were also witnessing what was happening in the shadows.

The figure neared, hunched over as if trying to mask his height with a limp. Then, he leaned into the faint moonlight, unrolled the paper he was holding and briefly scanned the parchment before curling it back up and putting it in the bag he was carrying. Regrettably, in those few seconds, Aimee realized that the skulking man was not Reece playing a prank on her brother. Not only was Reece much bigger than the creeping thief, but unlike the dark, unruly strands she was seeing, Reece's hair was the color of sand kissed by the sun. More than that, Reece was tall—incredibly tall—which was initially why Aimee had been drawn to him as a child. She had inherited her unusual height from her mother, and Reece had always made her feel petite and beautiful rather than tall and awkward. Now, at one and twenty, she possessed a slender figure, pale gold tresses, and large green eyes every Society matron wished her unwed daughter possessed. And yet, around most men, Aimee retained the uncomfortable feeling that she just did not quite belong.

"That's definitely not Reece," Jennelle whispered. "As soon as he is gone and it is safe, we need to leave." Aimee nodded, saddened to know her plan, which had been going so well up until now, was not going to work.

They waited almost another half hour, watching the man as he hobbled in and out of the shadows. Then, hearing a noise that sounded as if it could be an approaching dinghy, he turned around swiftly, and in doing so was unaware that the paper he had looked at earlier fell out of the bag he was carrying. Millie was afraid he was going to lean over and pick it up, and in doing so, see them, but instead he quickly slinked away, finally enabling them to vacate their niche.

"Follow me," Millie murmured, indicating the direction to disembark, and exited their secluded hole.

Leading the way, she slowly crept alongside the same containers the thief had hid behind in an effort not to capture any attention. She paused only to pick up the dropped document and glance back to verify her friends were not far behind. Jennelle trailed carefully, tracing her friend's footsteps and quiet manner. But as soon as Millie was past the warehouse, she began to run. Jennelle cursed under her breath. Millie might possess the shortest legs of the three of them, but Jennelle tended to forget that she also possessed the fastest. "Come on, or we will lose her," Jennelle hissed, and sprinted after Millie's shadow.

Aimee was about to follow when she spied someone

coming over the bow. The moonlight briefly caught a bright blue-and-gold scarf before it was hidden again behind a cloak in the shadows. Aimee recognized that scarf. It was the one she had given Reece at Christmas. Later she had overheard him telling her mother that he never wore such items and would give it to one of his men. And the lucky man who had received her scarf was currently weaving his way around the deck. He might not be Reece, but Aimee had no doubt that the man worked aboard his ship.

Quickly, she improvised a new plan, wishing she had the opportunity to at least relay it to her friends, but by tomorrow they would have discovered it for themselves. Jennelle might not understand, but Aimee was positive Millie would support her decision to seize the opportunity to confront the man she loved.

And with that last thought, Aimee did the unthinkable and deliberately got herself captured.

Millie stopped suddenly, aware that something was amiss. She spun around and grabbed Jennelle's shoulders. "Where is Aimee?"

Jennelle's blue eyes grew large at the alarm registered on her friend's face. "Bloody hell," she replied, using one of Millie's standard phrases. "I don't know. She was right behind me."

Millie whipped past her, heading back to the ship. "Come on, we have to find her. Some men were still on the ship, just on the other side. I thought we could sneak out without their noticing. Hopefully, Aimee is just hiding from them."

Jennelle heard the worry laced in Millie's low voice and it frightened her. Millie rarely became flustered in tight situations. She was courageous and *always* had a plan. "What are we to do if they did see her?"

Millie swallowed. "Stay here and hide. If anyone—and I

mean *anyone*—comes near you, Jennelle, scream as loud as you can. I'll whistle twice, just like we used to as kids, when I return."

Jennelle's eyes grew wide when Millie pulled out a small pistol and checked it to make sure it was ready to fire. She adjusted the hood of her cloak, and two seconds later she was gone. Jennelle watched in awe as the petite figure moved silently with such speed, darting in and out of view as she moved around the ship. For twenty minutes, Jennelle waited, wondering what could have happened to her friends.

Two low-pitched whistles came from nowhere and then Millie appeared, lines of fury and panic etched in her face. "She's gone, Jennelle. They took her in a small boat and she is now far offshore, headed for one of the ships anchored in the Thames."

"But you said there are a hundred ships out there!"

Millie looked down at the miniature gun still clutched in her hand and murmured, "I could have stopped them. But I was afraid. It was so hard to see. They were so close together. I was afraid I might hit her, but now I don't know." Looking back up, her large lavender eyes had grown dark with fear. "I'm to blame. I should never have agreed to come. She would not have if I had refused."

Jennelle shook her head vehemently and swallowed. "No, Millie, she was coming anyway. You and I both knew it. And deep in our hearts *that* is why we came."

Millie squeezed her eyes shut. "I led her straight into danger. I was the one who decided when to leave, and then I went first instead of watching out for you both. I was unprepared, and if *anything* happens to her I will never forgive myself, Jennelle. Never."

Jennelle took a deep breath and forced calm into her voice. "There must be something we can do."

"There is. I can tell the only person with the speed and the resources needed to find Aimee." Tears began to fall

18 *Michele Sinclair*

down Millie's cheeks. "Good God, Jennelle! What am I going to do? Charlie will never forgive me for putting his sister in danger. How could he?"

Aimee heard the splash of oars and wondered again at the wisdom of her decision. *No, this is the only way*, she told herself for the umpteenth time and braced her legs as the pinnace cut through the choppy water. The man on her right passed gas and the smell was even worse than the stink of the sack over her head. She rested against the side of the small boat and tried to think about anything other than where she was.

Her mind floated to Reece.

If all went well, she would be standing in front of him within the hour. Oh, she would have to do some explaining. And of course, Millie would most likely get a stern lecture from Charles when he found out, but it would be worth it.

If she could just *talk* with Reece—and if possible throw herself in his arms—he could not deny her. She had never told her friends just how serious a kiss Reece and she had shared last winter.

On that fateful day, she had not even been looking for him when she found him alone, sleeping. They had just exchanged Christmas gifts. Aimee gave him a rich blue scarf, on which she had embroidered with gold floss a ship sailing on the windy seas. She thought he could wear it when aboard his ship, and possibly think of her. He accepted it graciously and then gave her and her mother matching pearl combs from some island he had visited. Aimee wished Reece well, knowing he would soon depart again, and excused herself to go and enjoy some time painting before dinner. Aimee was not yet out of earshot when she heard him mention the gift she'd given him. The next words she would never forget.

"Aimee spent hours designing and sewing that for you,

Reece," her mother had explained, educating him on just how much energy was spent on a gift meant specifically for him.

"I can tell. That is why I didn't tell her that I don't wear scarves. Never have. I find them a nuisance whipping at my neck, and I prefer my hat when wearing something on my head. But many of my men enjoy a nice scarf. Maybe I'll give it to one of them."

Aimee had no idea how the conversation ended. She rushed up the stairs and into her room so that no one could witness her tears. After several hours, Aimee decided that Reece Hamilton was a silly little girl's dream, and that dreams were seldom realized. She rose and donned a new dress, a simple light green frock that was not nearly heavy enough for the winter cold but made her feel pretty and confident. Whenever she wore it, men always turned and stared. Of course, she pretended not to notice—but she did. Aimee smoothed the silk, added some pearls, and gazed at the lovely woman in the mirror. "You can go back to your sea, Mr. Reece Hamilton. If you cannot appreciate me as a woman, then I shall no longer look at you as a man."

Realizing that she still had over an hour until dinner would be called, she had decided to adhere to the original plan and paint. Aimee entered one of the unused bedrooms that had large windows and captured the afternoon sun, but realized immediately that she would have to paint elsewhere. She had forgotten to ask one of the servants to light the fireplace, and the room was frigid. She decided to move her paints and canvas downstairs to what she had termed the "indigo" salon as a child.

The room was decorated in various rich shades of blue, ranging from dark to the color of bright sapphires, including indigo—her favorite color. As a child, whenever she did not want to be found or interrupted, she would collect her things and closet herself in the back, out-of-the-way room in the house.

As she descended the staircase, Aimee had heard her
mother leave to visit a friend. She had hoped Reece had
departed at the same time and was on his way to Southamp-
ton, where the ship he owned and captained was anchored.
She never dreamed she would find him asleep on the large
settee in the indigo salon.

Every night since finding him there, Aimee had relived
the moments, from when she entered the salon until the
moment Reece left. Unaware of his presence at first, she
had strolled in, propped open her easel, and placed her
paints on a nearby table. It was when she turned to go back
and retrieve her brushes and canvas that she saw him.

Reece was stretched out, sleeping. He had stripped off his
coat and waistcoat, so that he wore just a white linen shirt,
breeches, and boots. His arm was thrown casually above his
head and the other lay comfortably across his stomach. His
legs were crossed at the ankles, stretching the tan fabric of
his breeches so that it outlined every muscle, every bulge,
every part of his lean and powerful lower body.

Aimee stood still and stared at Reece, letting her eyes
slowly wander up his hard, rippled stomach to the dark
hair poking out from the opening of his shirt. His face was
perfect. Not the pretty bone structure of the men who flirted
with her in Town or at the country dances, but rugged,
bronzed by the wind and the sun. It spoke of strength and
stamina and a passion that Aimee longed to experience. Her
eyes reached his lips, pausing to remember his smile and
how it reached his sky-blue eyes.

It had not been a conscious decision to kiss him. It had
been compulsion. A need to end her childhood fantasies.
She had intended it to be brief, soft, and exploratory—to
know what his mouth would feel like under hers. Never did
Aimee dream that he would awake and kiss her back.

At first, his lips had moved lightly across hers, urging her
to do the same. They were warm and worked an instant

magic as Reece cupped her cheek and whispered, "Ahh, Aimee. My beautiful Aimee, how you torment me. Open your lips and remind me what a fool I am for going back to sea."

Instantly Aimee complied and felt his tongue probe her mouth as he slid his hands slowly up and down her spine. He deftly shifted to a sitting position and lifted her onto his lap, never letting her lips be free of his. Her arms found their way around his neck and he deepened the kiss, searing her mouth forever to his. Aware of her violently racing pulse, Aimee held on, praying Reece would not realize what he was doing and pull away. But he did know.

Reece's powder-blue eyes burned as he caught her face between his palms. "God, how could I help but fall in love with you? You are like an angel, soft and perfect. If only you weren't Charles's sister," he whispered, stroking her cheek.

Warmth welled up inside Aimee, mingled with a sense of love that was so acute it brought tears to her eyes. "Reece, don't send me away. Please don't send me away. You have to leave so soon, but not yet. Let me stay with you for a little while," Aimee pleaded as she reached up and twined her fingers in his thick hair.

"God, Aimee, how I have fought to keep myself away from you, but I don't think I have the strength to send you away now." And then he kissed her again. But this time hard and deliberately, letting her feel the need and desire she had aroused in him.

Aimee felt his arms pull her even closer. They were strong and secure and she never wanted to leave them. His hot, sweet, sensuous lips moved against hers, creating a growing, aching need for more. She felt her hair tumble out its pins as Reece's strong hands dived in. Her lower lip trembled as he moaned aloud. Suddenly she needed to be even closer to him. Feel his skin on her palms. Tentatively she slid one hand under the freed hem of his shirt and felt his warmth permeate her fingertips. Tingling with the sensation, she sought more as his tongue slipped away from her mouth and down her nape to her shoulder.

Aimee could still feel his hot breath trailing down her arm as his mouth slid down the light green sleeve of her dress. When he cupped her soft breast, she knew then that no other man would ever touch her like that again. If she could not be with Reece, she would be with no other. She gasped as his thumb drew lightly across her nipple, causing it to harden instantly. But the inexplicable sensation only grew when he bent his head and took the firm fruit into his mouth.

"Perfect," he moaned, flicking his tongue over the sensitive flesh. When he began to suckle, Aimee thought she would expire from pleasure as her senses started spinning out of control.

"Reece, what is happening to me?" she managed to ask as his mouth began to lathe her other nipple. She shivered. His touch was everything and more than she had dreamed it would be. She could feel his hand on her leg and wondered how it got there, but she didn't care.

Slowly his fingers caressed her soft skin, moving up her leg with each stroke. "God, Aimee, you are so soft. Nothing in the world can be as good as you. Are you even real?" he whispered into her mouth before she could answer affirmatively and that she felt the same way about him.

Never had she imagined being with a man could make her feel so alive, so wanted, so beautiful. But the sensations Reece was causing continued to build, making her want only more. Involuntarily her body began to writhe with unknown need. She thrust her tongue into his warm mouth and kissed him with an almost violent demand, unconsciously flexing and arching her hips as his hands drew closer to her heat.

Slowly his fingers closed around the heart of her fire.

Aimee cried out softly as a deep tremor shook her. She could hear Reece calling to her, pleading for her to forgive him. "Stay with me, Aimee, and don't be afraid. I would never hurt you. I just want for one brief moment to know what heaven is like. Can you remember that later and forgive me?"

Aimee nodded and tried to remember how to breathe. His fingers were moving in a gentle rhythm, and when she thought she could stand no more, he parted her and slid a finger into her warmth. He had groaned in what seemed to be part pain, part pleasure, and began to create a magic Aimee could never have dreamed existed. He was touching her, and it felt wonderful. Better than wonderful, it felt like what he wanted to find. It felt like heaven.

He moved his finger gently within her, easing it slowly out of her tight passage. He added another finger and entered her again, caressing the tiny mound of sensitive flesh that was concealed by her mass of soft curls. Again and again, he entered her, massaging and stroking and building a force within her that soon exploded into a million stars. Aimee heard herself gasp and he immediately reclaimed her mouth, swallowing her moans and searing her forever to him as uncontrollable waves of pleasure rippled through her body.

He held her for a long time afterwards, kissing her forehead, stroking her brow. She remembered his every touch, whether on her arm, neck, or cheek; each was a tender caress showing that he loved her. They had not said a single word the rest of the afternoon. They had just sat and held on to each other, knowing he had to leave later that day.

Then he had left and she had not seen or spoken to him since. He had had opportunities. She had provided him multiple chances and ways to speak with her and even meet privately, but he had intentionally avoided all of them. That was why she had jumped in front of Reece's man. The fool had stood dumbfounded for a moment, and Aimee wondered

if he was going to take her with him or if she was going to
have to throw herself into his boat. But then, as if he could
read her thoughts, he had grabbed her and hauled her close,
quickly binding her hands behind her back.

Aimee had been about to announce that she was not
going to fight him, that she would willingly go with him if
he would allow her to see his captain, when a rotten-
smelling bag was thrown over her head. Suddenly she was
being roughly manhandled and then hauled over the side of
the ship.

"That 'im, Petey? Pretty skinny, isn't he?"

"Be careful with 'im. Had to track 'im careful-like and sneak
up on the feller to catch 'im unawares. Fought me terrible
for a time."

Aimee had almost laughed aloud at the lie when she felt
herself being lowered down into something rather unstable.
She was shoved down and made to lie on something wet.
When she heard the oars splash down, she realized immediately where she was—in the bottom of a pinnace heading
toward Reece's ship.

The man nearest to her passed gas again and Aimee decided she had had enough. She sat up as best she could, but
before she could announce who she was and again offer to
go with them willingly, a gag was tied behind her head over
the foul bag. This was *not* at all going according to plan.

"There, that'll keep 'im quiet. Don't want nobody knowin'
what we did till we tell the cap'n. I'm still not positive that
he's goin' to be happy about your plan, Petey."

"Gus, I caught 'im! I caught the bastard that's been stealin'
the cap'n's things. Right from the boss's own cabin. He'll
give us a bonus for sure for bringin' the thief in."

Aimee heard Gus snort. "Well, maybe yer right and maybe
yer wrong, but you better 'ide 'im below for a day or two
until we think up a real good way tae let the cap'n know."

"Good plan, mate. Good plan. That's what we'll do. We'll

hide the bloke below. Tell no one, mind ye. Don't want no one else gettin' the credit for our find. This one's mine."

Aimee felt her heart race. She was to be held for two days before she got to see Reece! This was *not at all* what she had planned. She had to get back, now. *What would Millie do?* Aimee asked herself. *She would fight.* Aimee started kicking and writhing and twisting and doing anything she could to get them to let her go.

"Ow!" she heard someone yell. The same voice turned mean. "Stop that or I'll throw ye overboard, and tied up like ye are, I doubt you'd go far."

Hearing the threat, Aimee immediately stopped fighting, but she could not stop her racing heart. *Don't panic, Aimee,* she told herself. *Don't panic. When they move you, wherever down below is, they will remove your gag and you can tell them who you are.* It was not ideal, but it was still possible that in less than an hour she would be sitting across from Reece, trying to convince him not to kill her two kidnappers, Peter and Gus.

The oars stopped and a minute later Aimee felt the small boat bang on the side of a much larger object. She hoped it was Reece's boat, the *Sea Emerald*.

Another minute went by when she heard a bunch of scuffling. Suddenly, one of her two captors was leaning over her, pressing her farther down into the pinnace. It was then that she heard a different voice, this time from far above.

"Petey, you should thank your sorry arse you showed up. Hurry up now and get aboard. The boss wants to pull up anchor and leave—now."

"Now?" Gus asked, punching Aimee's leg as she tried to maneuver to a less painful position.

"Yes, now," the deep voice replied in hushed tones. "Seems that a few boats are leaving on the morrow to catch the winds, and Captain Hamilton wants to beat them out of the harbor. Remember last time we had to wait?"

"Aye, I remember," Gus replied in a huff. "The cap'n was in a foul mood for days. Fairly destroyed all of our leftover Christmas cheer."

"Well, he's going to be in a high dudgeon if he finds out you and Petey left the ship so close to us pullin' up anchor. Hurry and get up here."

Aimee felt like this might be her last opportunity to stop this nightmare, and began to kick and fight as best she could against the bindings. "He better be worth it, Petey," were the last words she heard before pain shot through her jaw and darkness swallowed all thought.

Chapter 2

October 7, 1816

The Marquess of Chaselton sat behind his desk and quietly prepared himself for Millie's arrival. Though most peers and associates had shortened his title to Chase, his family and close childhood friends whom he had known before he inherited his title called him Charles. His wife had several names for him, depending on her mood, but his favorite would always be Charlie, an old, and once despised, childhood name. It seemed whenever she used it, he found himself agreeing to whatever desire flittered through her mind.

But not tonight, he promised himself. *I refuse to be vulnerable to any form of persuasion. Whatever mess you have found yourself in, Mildred, I will not get you out of it. This time, you will have to learn your lesson.*

The moment when Millie's very dour but cherished maid, Elda Mae, had interrupted his biweekly dinner with his shipping company's investors, he had known something was wrong and that Millie was at its center. Thankfully, the hour had been late and it was possible for him to suggest that he and his business associates continue their conversations during their next meeting. He had an uncomfortable feeling that it would be best if no one learned of Millie's indiscretion.

He drummed his fingers on his father's old writing desk, repeating to himself the need to remain calm and that he had known this moment had been coming for some time. In fact, it was overdue, for he had been expecting Millie to become ensnared in some uncomfortable predicament since the moment his sister and her other best friend arrived in London for a visit. For more than two weeks, the Daring Three had been together, chatting about whatever nonsense women do and going to see whatever women wanted to see. And during the entire time, he had been awaiting news of a mishap.

Married for only a few short months, Chase recognized that the expectations of a wife and marchioness would be foreign to Millie, and therefore he continually pressed upon her the weight of her new responsibilities. He had hoped that as Millie became adjusted to her role, she would realize that it was now time for her to adopt a more mature and sensible attitude and overcome her seemingly constant desire to seek out reckless adventures.

It was not that he desired to squelch her spirit—far from it. Millie's exuberance for life filled him in a way nothing or no one could. But he never would admit it to anyone, especially her. Despite wishing he were otherwise, Chase was well aware that he was far too pragmatic for a man of his age. He might be only thirty, but the last ten years of his life had been oftentimes brutal, hardening him in countless ways.

As the Chaselton heir, he had been raised to be practical and outwardly sedate. As a war spy, he had learned to suppress every emotion while cultivating caution and vigilance as constant companions. As a result, most people believed him indifferent to the people and events around him, thinking him cold, calculating, and unfeeling. And while he often was just as others saw him, little Mildred Aldon—the bane of his childhood—had somehow broken through every shell he had built around his heart. It amazed him how she continually found ways to remind him of what a sheer joy it was just to be alive.

Not long after they were married, he realized his need for her was growing in intensity, and it frightened him. As a result, he had an overwhelming desire not just to make her happy but to keep her safe, secure, and away from the dangers with which he had too long been associated.

This past spring he had almost lost her, and though Chase knew the men behind the ordeal were dead, he could not stop the nagging feeling that something had been left undone. Too many questions had yet to be answered.

Sir Edward Lutton—the treasonous mastermind—had drowned near the rocky cliffs of the Chaselton country estate. And though the violent waves had pummeled his body into fish food, Sir Edward's death had not ended the ordeal. The aftermath of dealing with a treasonous plot led by a key intelligence officer was long and arduous. It would be several more months before the full extent of the damage his one-time mentor had caused would be known.

Thankfully, nothing found so far had been determined to be permanently harmful to the men serving in uniform or to the homeland and her allies. And yet, Chase remained unsettled. And he was not alone in the feeling and found himself needing to meet somewhat frequently—and discreetly—with those in parliament and the war department. So, when his mother suggested letting his sister Aimee stay with Jennelle while they went to Town for the Little Season, Chase had quickly agreed. Many in Society migrated back to London during the autumn months finding it easier to entertain and be entertained than at their country estates. Because the unofficial Season was much smaller, Chase believed it would provide the perfect opportunity for his mother to educate

Millie on her new role as marchioness. Too late did he realize that his mother had plans of her own.

Soon after they arrived, he and Millie began accepting invitations to meet with those of similar status. As expected, his mother had helped introduce Millie into Society, this time not as a debutante, but as a peer. And while inexperienced, Millie had proven she was quite capable of comporting herself as a marchioness. She had hosted her first party and it was such a success that his mother—Dowager Lady Chaselton—had announced that she was now Millie's largest impediment. She needed to leave in order to give Millie the chance to begin building a legacy of her own. Then, without warning, she promptly left London to visit friends in northern Scotland; a distance he suspected quite intentional as it was too far for him or Millie to reach out for assistance even if they should desire it.

Chase had no illusions then or now that his mother had long been planning the trip north. But if his mother's intentions were to provide Millie and him some time alone, she had an unusual way of going about it. Because at the same time his mother announced her decision to leave, she had also revealed her already-delivered-and-accepted invitation to Aimee and Jennelle. They would join Millie in London, so that both girls could benefit from Millie's station and find a husband. Chase had openly snorted at that comment, for every man and mother in Town knew his sister had no interest in finding a husband. And though hard to believe, Jennelle had also made her disinterest in the state of matrimony quite well known.

He had almost elected to use his rank and refuse the invitations, but seeing the anticipation on Millie's face, he had been unable to make even an empty threat. Long ago, he had offered silent sympathy to the man who would claim Millie's heart, and he had been right to do so. For every day, he battled with himself and every day he lost. His need to constrain his wife's audacious inclinations rarely won over his desire to make her happy. So the moment Aimee and Jennelle arrived, he had been waiting for the inevitable chaos that always followed the Daring Three.

A knock on the door made his head spring up and he straightened in his chair, readying himself for the despair he would see on her beautiful face. He also knew that despite his earlier promises, he would be immediately affected by the expression, needing to right whatever wrong that may have happened. "Come in, Millie, and tell me what happened."

Chapter 3

October 8, 1816

Chase flung the front doors of Hembree Grove wide open and marched down the halls, barking orders for someone to find Lady Chaselton and have her immediately join him in his study, uncaring how openly angry he appeared. When Elda Mae had come in the previous night, her face drained of blood, he had assumed one—if not all—of the Daring Three had been goaded into something innocuous, like gambling, and had lost quite a tidy sum of money in a bet. But upon seeing Millie bedraggled, dressed like some street urchin, her hair askew and tears streaking down her face, he had known something far more serious had occurred.

Entering his study, he tossed his coat onto the couch and wrenched off his cravat. He then rubbed his scalp vigorously, unaware of how it made his chocolate brown hair unruly and his overall appearance fearsome. A large man, with hard, dark features, he was a naturally imposing figure. But when he detached himself from his emotions, his eyes, despite their warm golden color, grew distant and quite cold.

Since last night when Millie haltingly explained how the three of them had gone to catch Reece pretending to be

W & H Shipping's mysterious thief, Chase had continuously berated himself for his naïveté, for it was he who had given Millie the idea. That previous morning, Chase had accused his friend of being the one sneaking around taking odd items from the office and ships. Reece had then cheerfully returned the allegation, thinking the prank a rather unusual one, but deciphering its purpose would have to wait until after his return.

It had been foolish to speak so openly with Millie in the room. Chase and she had been talking about their plans for the day when Reece had arrived and encouraged her to remain, stating his visit was to be short and uninteresting. That night he was leaving on the *Sea Emerald* for Savannah and then a few other places. He had also asked Millie to tell Aimee of his lengthy voyage and that he had meant what he said. Millie had asked "About what?" but Reece said Aimee would understand. Chase had seen that Millie was unsatisfied and was going to probe for more information, so to help out his friend, he asked Reece about the thief—an incredibly shortsighted solution. But Chase's true folly was not having procured from Millie a promise of silence on the subject.

The lack of such a vow had practically been an invitation to gossip. As a result, she had predictably not only disclosed Reece's parting comments to her friends but also all that she had heard concerning the thief. Never could Chase have dreamed what the Daring Three would do, armed with such information. Not a sane man in the world would have anticipated the three of them being so foolish as to venture to the London Docks in the middle of the night, all in the futile hopes of catching his best friend having one last lark before he left for America.

Chase sank down onto one of the padded hearth chairs and fought the inclination to assure his wife that he was almost certain Aimee was safely aboard the *Sea Emerald* and not in immediate danger.

Based on Millie's description of the pinnace and scarf she had seen, he had suspected which ship had his sister. Less than half a dozen ships had left the Hermitage Basin before Chase was able to order it closed for a search. Aimee had not been found, but just two of the ships that had departed prior to the search had pinnaces. Only the ones belonging to the *Sea Emerald* were painted green and white.

He had been talking to the captain of the *Zephyr* when one of the dock managers escorted two night laborers, who had witnessed the abduction but were "too far away to do anything about it," over to see him. They said a thin man was being dragged into a green and white pinnace, but that the man neither fought his captors nor struggled for his freedom. Neither worker could recall hearing any cries for help.

Chase had encountered enough liars to recognize when a man was hiding something, and those men had been too scared to lie convincingly. He believed their story, mostly because he could just see his little sister, with her claims to be madly in love, seizing any opportunity to be with Reece.

So after sending the two workers away, he ordered the *Zephyr*'s captain to quickly remove much of the ship's cargo and leave immediately. Chase knew there was little chance of catching the *Sea Emerald*, despite the *Zephyr*'s lightened load. Reece had his ship especially built by a man in the colonies working on a new design for swifter, more maneuverable ships. So far, the *Sea Emerald* was proving to be one of the fastest on the Atlantic. If pressed, Reece could get to the West Indies and back in less than two months, but Chase expected to see his friend in port long before then. The minute Reece discovered Aimee aboard, the *Sea Emerald* would be on its way back to London.

Until then, Aimee would be uncomfortable without the

luxuries of a soft bed, good food, and servants, but she would be safe. More than likely Reece had locked her in a room for the entire trip, making his younger sister quite repentant by the time her feet touched shore again. It was up to Chase to find a way of making his wife just as repentant and finally willing to end her penchant for being reckless with her life.

It was one thing to be venturesome, daring, bold, and even a little rash, but only the most senseless of people would go out in the middle of the night to the docks with no ability to protect themselves. And yet the Daring Three had done just that and would continue with such foolishness again and again if he did not do something to discourage this behavior immediately.

It has to stop, he told himself as he mentally replayed last night's discourse.

He had spoken to Millie in a way he had never spoken to anyone. Fear unlike any he had ever known had flooded through him, washing away his supposedly perfected self-control. Even so, it was nothing to what it could have been. What Millie did not understand was just how much he loved her; that if any harm ever came to her, he would be a terrifying man to be around. He had gained too many deadly skills in the war and his restraint would cease to exist.

Millie might be smart and resourceful, but she thought herself invincible and she was not. Worse, her ignorance of the world also made her vulnerable. Fortune had watched over the Daring Three last night, and thankfully none of them had been hurt, but if he relayed the good news about his sister's safety, Millie and Jennelle might then see last night's escapade as a success.

When the rap on the door came, he had not yet decided whether or not to tell her. All he knew was that he would do whatever it took to ensure Millie never caused him to fear for her well-being again.

Jennelle entered the study first, letting Millie follow. She knew her presence had not been requested and she should not join a married couple's discussion about a highly private matter, but she did not care. This time she would be at Millie's side and not on the other side of the door, cringing, unable to do anything but listen to the fiercest tongue-lashing Jennelle had ever heard. She had waited for Millie to defend herself, but she had uttered not one word. Jennelle vowed that would not happen again today.

Charles had assumed last night's foray was not only Millie's idea, but a direct result of her recklessness. And with the exception of one scathing comment about how *she*, "Jennelle, the sensible one," should have stopped Aimee or told Chase what Millie was planning, all of his stinging assaults were aimed at his already suffering wife.

He never once considered that Millie might be terrified about losing her best friend. Not one word of comfort did he offer. And though he never raised his voice, never yelled or shouted one word, his low, menacing tones whipped out one harsh statement after another. And based on the barking orders he had just bellowed the moment he came back home, it appeared Millie was about to receive a second serving of the same.

Jennelle practically had to bite her tongue in an effort to keep her promise. Millie had practically forced her into a solemn vow to never correct any of Charles's erroneous assumptions about just who had perpetrated what part of last night's events. Jennelle knew that Millie incorrectly blamed herself for what had happened, but mostly Millie believed she was somehow protecting Aimee by keeping the focus of Charles's rage on her.

Jennelle's royal-blue eyes glared murderously at Chase and it caused him to blink. *After what happened last night, why the hell is she mad at me?* He took a deep breath and watched his wife come in the door to stand next to Jennelle. His heart lurched again in pain and fear, knowing just how fortunate his wife was to have escaped uninjured.

Millie licked her lips. "Were you able to find your sister, my lord?"

Chase's jaw tensed. He wanted to pull her into his arms and plead for her to stop calling him my lord, but even more, he needed to discourage any future reckless behavior. "The boat with Aimee aboard left port before I arrived," he answered honestly.

Millie let go a soft cry. Her hand flew to her mouth and she sank into a nearby chair. "I'm so sorry. I never should have—"

"No, you should not have," Chase began, his voice full of growing reproach. He raked his fingers through his hair. "What were you *thinking*, Mildred?" he asked her for the umpteenth time.

Millie forced herself not to flinch at the bitterness attached to each enunciated word. "I only thought to help." Jennelle went to stand beside Millie's chair and clutched her friend's hand in her own.

Again Chase fought the urge to be the one to give her comfort. His instincts wavered between wrapping his arms comfortingly around her and protecting her. *No, not this time,* he warned himself. *I must be hard if she is to learn that she can never again be so foolish.* "Do you not realize even now the severity of the insult you give me?"

Millie looked up; her eyes, a strange color of lavender, widened, stunned by his accusation. "But I—"

Chase cut her off. "But what, Mildred? Do you ever think about the consequences of your schemes and thrill-seeking exploits? Bloody hell, you are the Marchioness of Chaselton now! How do you think it makes me feel to know that my own wife believes that I am unable to handle an inconsequential thief without her assistance?"

Jennelle squeezed Millie's hand, urging her to argue, to say something, but Millie's back only slumped further. Again anger singed the edges of Jennelle's control. It was near impossible to stand and do nothing as her friend, who was always so full of life, vibrant and diverting, was whittled away by her husband's cruel tongue. And still the man did not stop.

"Not to mention the damage to the Chaselton name. Did you consider my mother, Millie? How is she going to feel when she discovers that you risked, and may have harmed, *her only daughter* in one of your schemes?"

Jennelle could feel Millie recoil and again mentally begged for her to do something—cry and yell that Mother Wentworth had *three* daughters, not just one, and for him to say otherwise was heartless. And yet, Millie refused to defend herself. She just silently absorbed each blow, unable to stop the tears streaming down her cheeks.

Chase squeezed his eyes shut, wishing he could withdraw his last words. Millie's face had become etched with such deep pain and regret, his heart had wrenched. He had not needed Jennelle lancing him with her piercing blue eyes to know he had gone too far. His mother would not have placed blame, and she certainly would have not used the situation as a chance to teach a lesson. There were other ways for reining in his wife's boisterous temperament. This was not the way.

Chase was about to walk around his desk to her side when Millie rose to her feet. Shakily, she extended her hand

and he saw what she clutched—a rolled-up piece of paper. He took it. "What is this?"

Millie raised her chin to answer, not in defiance but in preparation for his next verbal blow. "The real thief dropped it."

"The *real* thief?" he repeated. He unrolled the parchment and saw that it was a map.

"Yes. He was there. We hid until he left. Then when we tried to leave, Aimee was . . ." Millie could not finish the sentence, afraid that if she did she would start crying again, and this time she would not be able to stop.

"Describe him."

Not bound by a promise on this topic, Jennelle answered. "The man was average height. We could not see his face, but he had dark hair that was somewhat long. He also had a limp but was quite agile in spite of it."

As Chase listened to Jennelle, the full implications of what she was saying dawned on him. He had truly believed Reece behind the odd thefts. First, the *Sea Rebel* was rifled, leaving maps and charts everywhere. He and the *Sea Rebel*'s captain had thought a drunken seaman looking for a bottle of whiskey the culprit. Then the W & H Shipping office, by the London Docks, was broken into. After the raid on the *Intrepid*, Reece had identified what had been taken at each site—an old, worthless chart. It was then Chase had suspected his friend was playing a prank. But whoever had been on the *Zephyr* had not been Reece.

Chase studied the map. Part of a large assortment of ship equipment they purchased at an auction, the collection of charts had been buried underneath several items in a chest. They had almost thrown them away because they were old and unlabeled, but Reece had wanted to study them some more. So along with the other items, the charts had been divided among their company ships. Reece's interest in the charts as well and it being his recognition of what had been taken were the two primary reasons why Chase had truly thought his friend was behind the missing items.

Chase laid out the map on his desk and looked at it carefully. What was so important about a useless old map? Was the thief collecting them? Or was it one in particular he was looking for?

"Did he see you?" Chase finally asked.

"I do not believe so, but it is impossible to tell. We were hiding and had not observed him until he was making his way off the ship," Jennelle answered in her typical logical way, but the coldness of her tone was unmistakable.

Chase swallowed. His mind started moving quickly over what he knew about the robberies, this time analyzing the events not as mere pranks but for what they actually were: threats.

Every incident had been obvious, so whoever the thief was, he either did not feel the need to hide his trespassing, or he wanted Chase and Reece to know they were being robbed. More perplexing was that the thefts had happened in locations that were supposedly guarded, and yet the perpetrator had been able to get in. A bold move, unless the thief was skilled at handling any opposition should it arise, *or* was intimately familiar with the owners of W & H Shipping. Chase's mind drifted back to the small group of business associates he'd met with the previous night. He had once thought all those closest to him to be honorable—but he would not be fooled again.

Chase looked down once more at the map in front of him. It made no more sense than any of the others. Several symbols were scattered around and at the bottom there was a legend that was illegible. There was an outline of what could be water, land, or something altogether different. He and Reece had just assumed the drawing represented water, but now he had no clue what it was. However, whoever was stealing the charts most likely did know.

And that combination of facts made Chase very uneasy.

Someone thought the maps of great value and was willing to take great risks to find them. And if he was brazen enough to break into guarded ships and the offices of W & H Shipping, then it was more than probable he would eventually try to burglarize Hembree Grove as well. Many people had been in and out of his home the past few weeks in an effort to ferret out Sir Edward's schemes. Most had met his wife, and with her petite stature, dark hair, and unusual eye color, they would easily recognize her even in men's clothing. Chase could feel his heart tighten. If Jennelle was mistaken and the three of them *had* been seen, they could have been recognized. No longer would the thief be seeking a simple chart, but the opportunity to silence potential witnesses.

Chase balled his hands into fists, frustrated at what he now must do: get Millie and Jennelle away from Town— immediately. He had no doubt that Millie would refuse to leave. Her passionate nature would demand to stay there, with him, despite the danger it put her in. But her staying in Town for even one more night was not an option. Telling her about what he had learned about Aimee's whereabouts, however, was. But it was an option he refused to elect.

Chase took in a deep breath and tried to use a less harsh, but still stern tone. "I need time, Mildred, to find Aimee, and I need . . . not to worry about you." He hated making Millie leave without letting her know the truth about his sister. Worse, he hated using Millie's guilt as a means of compelling her immediate departure. But his self-loathing was nothing compared to his fear if she stayed. "Mother is not due to return from Scotland until after the holidays, and I am not going to send her word about Aimee until I know something definitive. Hopefully, she will have been found and will be once again home and safe. Until then, I think it might be best if you visit your father in Wareham for a while."

Millie nodded, lowering eyes so that they looked at her clasped hands held rigidly in front of her. "When do you want me to leave, my lord?"

Pain shot through him hearing *my lord* yet again. "I think it best if you pack and leave immediately. I will have the post chaise readied to take you and Jennelle to Dorset. I'll have the driver stop at Tarrant Crawford at her father's before taking you the rest of the way to Wareham."

Millie kept her head bowed and replied, "Yes, my lord," before running out of the room.

Jennelle paused for a moment before following. And for the first time in her life, she consciously broke a promise and stepped back into the study to confront Chase.

"You speak of consequences, my lord. Indeed Millie will have to live with hers, and I will have to as well, including being forced to allow these proceedings without interruption or interference. But I wonder, my lord, if you yet comprehend the consequences of *your* actions today. I have my own reasons for believing that Aimee is well, and I judge that you too suspect she is with Mr. Hamilton. So then that leaves me to wonder, why would you intentionally injure your own wife? Revenge? Anger? Are these foul emotions not just as damning as the reckless ones of which you just accused Millie? Why would someone so proud of his self-professed restraint cause such pain? I pray, my lord, you are not telling yourself that it was out of love."

Chase's jaw clenched and his defenses rose. He thought of Jennelle as a younger sister, but he did not have to explain himself to her. "I have my reasons."

Jennelle's royal-blue eyes narrowed. "Well, then I hope those reasons bring you the comfort you seek, for it will be quite lonely here and I predict for much longer than you anticipate. At some point, my dear friend will reflect on all that happened and the accusations you so damningly conveyed, and when she does, I doubt Millie will be inclined to return. As for myself, I am quite certain it will be a significant period of time before our paths cross again."

Chase watched as Jennelle exited the room, her back rigid and her lips thin with fury. It was the first time in his life he had ever witnessed her anger. He sat down and forced himself to dismiss her words, as they were painful and incredibly accurate in their assessment.

No, he promised himself. *Jennelle is wrong. Millie loves me and she will forgive me.* When Aimee returned in a few days, all would be well. Until then, Millie would be safe and protected. She would be angry at first, but she would forgive him.

She had to.

Millie helped Elda Mae fold another garment and place it in a large wooden trunk capable of holding only a fraction of her things. "Just a couple of items from my dressing table and that will be all, Elda Mae."

The older woman, who had taken care of her and then her two best friends since they were children, fidgeted with worry. Never had she seen her missus like this. Her Millie was a fireball, never to be constrained, for to do so would kill her. And that was exactly what she was witnessing now. The slow death of one of the world's most beautiful creatures. How could the master be sending her away now, when she needed him most? Could he not see the cruelty of what he was doing?

"But, my lady, we have yet to pack your gowns or any of your jewels."

Dark-haired ringlets bounced as Millie shook her head. "I will not be needing them. Since I do not plan on doing any entertaining, it will only weigh the carriage down with unnecessary weight. No, it's best they stay here."

Elda Mae turned around several times, searching for something to do. "I'll help Jennelle's maid, my lady, and then go pack my own things."

Millie's eyes brimmed with tears as she clasped the older woman's hands. "Please understand when I ask this of you, Elda Mae, but you must stay here."

Jennelle, who had been sitting in a chair across the room, stewing, popped out of the chair at Millie's words. "Stay here? Millie, you cannot do this! Elda Mae *is* coming."

Tears from Elda Mae's velvet brown eyes spilled onto her cheeks. "But, my lady, I should be with you. You need me . . ."

For the first time since Aimee's abduction, Millie's look was firm and unwavering, hinting that not all of her soul had been crushed with Chase's indictments. "No," she stated forcefully to Jennelle. And then, looking back at her faithful companion, she pleaded softly, "Elda Mae, what I need most is for you to apply those eavesdropping skills you have perfected over the years and discover what Chase knows about Aimee. Send word to me and Jennelle as often as you can. It is important, this thing I ask of you. Please do not turn me down."

"I could never turn you down, my lady. Haven't in all my born days, and I'm not likely to start now. I love you like you was my own flesh and blood. And if you need me to stay, then I will. And don't you worry none on Aimee. She's a delicate-looking thing, but you and I know differently. Our girl's a scrapper and will be back here in England giving her brother what for before you know it."

Millie closed her eyes and looked out the window, watching Chase order another team to be added to the post chaise.

"Your words to God's ears, Elda Mae. For I don't know how I shall go on if harm befalls Aimee because of my thoughtlessness."

Jennelle marched over, grabbed her friend by the shoulders, and swung her around. "Now you will listen to me and all that I say, Millie. I will not hear any more of this. You refused to listen to me last night, but you will do so now." Jennelle was just as much to blame as Millie, and if she could not convince Millie that Aimee was safe with Reece, then she herself would begin to doubt it, and the fragments of composure she was clinging to would disappear.

"I did hear you, Jennelle. That Aimee would have screamed and fought if she were truly captured? That based on what I told you, she intentionally got caught by Reece's men in order to seek him out? Maybe, but there were five ships that left the harbor and four of them were *not* the *Sea Emerald*. If you are correct—and I hope and believe you might be—then Reece is most likely turning around and returning at this very moment. Aimee will be reunited with her brother."

"And all will be forgiven."

Millie sank down onto her bed and closed her eyes. "I do not know. Despite what you heard, Charlie does love me and I so love him. His anger is in many ways justified."

"But it was not your fault! *Aimee* practically made us go, and it was *she* who put herself in danger. Not you and not me. I love her just as much as you, but I will *not* own responsibility for her abduction and neither should you!"

"I agree it was Aimee who made the choice that caused her to be captured. But you cannot deny she would have stayed home if I had stayed firm and refused to go. She could not have made it there safely without us, and I *knew* in my heart that we should not have gone. So it is *my* guilt that weighs heavily on me. Not Charlie's anger."

Jennelle crossed her arms and started pacing. "Aimee will be fine. You and Charles will be fine. We will *all* be fine!"

Millie nodded. She did honestly believe Aimee was safe and with Reece. The more she thought back and considered the events of last night, the more convinced she became. Aimee had not been caught unaware. She had been hidden when the two men walked by and actually had jumped in front of them. She then patiently waited as they got over their shock and finally decided to grab her. Aimee had had ample opportunity to run away, let alone scream for help. But as much as she believed Aimee would return and all would be well, Millie was not convinced that the same could be said of her and Chase.

He was furious with her, and though she was not to blame for much of what he had accused her, there was one point he had made repeatedly that she could not deny—it was her adventurous spirit that created the foundation for what had happened. Chase wanted her to change. And though a piece of her would do anything for him, she was not sure she *could* become someone else.

Even for him.

Even to keep his love, which she so desperately needed.

Chase watched the slim, petite figure dressed in gray enter the post chaise. A second later she was followed by a redheaded figure in dark blue. His wife, the one who in the past four months had brought him more joy than he could remember having in all his life, was leaving him, and by his command. He wanted to kiss her good-bye and tell her how much she meant to him, how much he loved and needed her. But he knew if he took one step outside and felt her soft body against his in a good-bye embrace, he would be unable to let her go.

Never had Chase seen Millie look so defeated or forlorn. So many things had been running through his mind when he had spoken to her, he could barely recall half of what he had said. The only truth he kept coming back to was that he needed her to be safe, to know that she was cared for and away from any danger. As soon as he confirmed Aimee was aboard the *Sea Emerald*, he would go to Millie, tell her the joyful news, and heal whatever pain he might have caused her. Hopefully, his sister might even be back home by then.

Chase calmed his building guilt by reminding himself that Millie was on her way to her father's. He had initially thought to send her to the Wentworth country estate, but with his mother in Scotland, Millie would be all alone there. So he sent her to her father's, where she could enjoy his company and take pleasure in one of her favorite pastimes— riding. Chase would send Hercules, her monstrous black horse, to Wareham first thing tomorrow.

The driver snapped his whip and the horses began to move. He let the thick gold curtain slip through his fingertips and gripped the back of a nearby high-back chair. Millie had not said more than a few words to him since he had announced he was sending her away. She had avoided him whenever possible and had even left without saying goodbye. Normally, that would have been a clear indication of her anger and resentment about his most recent lecture. Yet the few glimpses of her he had stolen had indicated something else entirely. Her cheeks were pale and the light in her eyes had vanished, leaving only a chilling emptiness. Grief tore at her for her friend, and he had only added to that pain.

He looked about the empty room. Never had the world seemed so lonely.

As the carriage began to move, Jennelle watched the house from the window and saw the gold curtain swish back into place. So Charles had at least watched his wife leave, if only from a distance. Was it regret he felt, she wondered, or had he just been ensuring his orders were followed?

Never will I marry, Jennelle silently pledged. She had seen what Millie endured for the sake of love and what Aimee had done to pursue it. Jennelle was positive no man in the world was worth bearing such pain, despite the brief wisps of pleasure she had witnessed. With every passing moment, she became more determined to be the only one of the Daring Three smart enough to stay away from the things that can cause the most pain to a woman.

I vow never to fall in love, and I absolutely will never marry.

Chapter 4

October 9, 1816

Consciousness came back slowly and painfully. Aimee tried to open her eyes, but the world was dark . . . and rolling. She moaned and felt the gag, the rough cloth biting into her lips, which were now dry and cracked. Her head felt like it had been broken into several pieces and then put back together incorrectly. Unfortunately, it did not make her unaware of certain things, like how she was aboard a ship that was continuously rocking back and forth. It also did not obstruct her ability to smell. If possible, the stench was more dreadful than what the sailor had produced. Aimee had no idea where she was or what she was smelling, but she prayed to every saint she could remember for it to end.

Planting a foot down on something solid, she shoved herself to a sitting position and slowly inched along the floor until she felt a sack containing something with large lumps behind her and then leaned back, hoping it would support her.

She had no idea how long she had been on the ship. It could have been just a few hours or a day—maybe even two, according to her stomach. It was possible her captors had left her to starve to death. Her only hope was to free herself.

Aimee fought against the bindings with renewed strength. After several minutes, her skin had become raw and she could feel blood running down her fingertips. The rope, however, had not loosened at all. Tears began to fall.

Millie and Jennelle had been right. No intelligent plan would ever allow this level of failure. Since she'd been separated from her friends, she had experienced practically every emotion except the one she had been seeking. The residual anger, fear, and despair were now morphing into misery.

She was going to die, and only a few feet below the man she loved.

Aimee wondered how Reece would react when he learned she had died trying to reach him. At the very least, she hoped he would regret refusing to see or talk to her.

"Eh, you there. You still alive?"

Aimee awoke with a start at the sound.

Petey witnessed the movement and smiled. It had been just over two days since they put out at sea. Captain Hamilton had been in a fierce mood, keeping his men working until they fell asleep at their posts. The captain was the best of leaders, and Petey, as well as the rest of the crew, would follow him into the pits of hell, knowing that each time, Captain Reece Hamilton would see them to the other side. But not a man on his crew wanted to see the Thames anytime soon. They would go to any port in the world as long as it was not in England. The last two times they had anchored there, it was pure hell for several days afterwards, and this visit had been no different.

Aimee felt rough hands reach behind her head and begin to loosen the knot holding the gag tightly in place. "Now, if you make a noise, I'll be putting the rope back and leavin'. You hear me?"

Aimee nodded her head and her mouth was free seconds later. She licked her lips, knowing she would never again be unappreciative of the ability. Then she felt the rough cloth covering her face being yanked off, allowing her hair to tumble free down her back.

Aimee blinked several times and inhaled deeply, thankful to breathe in what felt like fresh air. The room was dimly lit but it still took her eyes several seconds to adjust. She was finally able to discern that the faint light came from the small doorway adjacent to some stairs across the way. She looked around and realized that she was in some dank hold that contained crates and food—some of which smelled as if it was already rotting.

Petey watched in total shock as the beaten beauty looked around and took in her surroundings. He had kidnapped a bloody *female*! There was no way he was going to tell the captain that this girl was the one thieving their ships. He would skin him alive, even though it was true. The captain came from nobles and took their gentlemen's code to an extreme.

The girl glanced around the dank room, licking her lips, when suddenly her green eyes settled on him and darkened dangerously. Petey held his breath. He had seen plenty of women. Those who worked by the docks or around them were either old and worn ragged from years of hard labor or young and scraggly. This one was neither.

Dirt was smeared on her face and she was wearing men's clothes, but none of it could detract from the beauty that sat bound in front of him. It was as if an angel had come down from heaven. And what had he done? He had taken her prisoner. He was surely going to spend eternity with the devil now.

"Blimey, what've I done?" His question was barely a whisper, mixed with both shock and horror.

Aimee's emerald gaze flashed with anger as she studied
the squat, unshaven man holding on to the doorframe for
support. From his voice, she knew he was not Gus, but Petey.
He had short bowlegs, straggly light brown hair, and blood-
shot eyes that made him look more pitiable than wretched.
He was dressed in ankle-length pants with a pocket on the
side and a dirty, long-sleeved linen shirt that closed in the
front. A well-worn dark wool coat hung open to reveal a
single-button vest that came just below his waistline. His
tarred hat was clutched in his right hand while his left was
attempting to loosen the handkerchief tied around his throat.

"You kidnapped a lady, Peter. That is what you have done,"
Aimee replied crisply and waited for him to repent and move
to release her. After several seconds, she realized the man was
transfixed and unable to move. Petey was never going to stir
until she told him what to do.

"Peter, please untie my hands." As if hypnotized into
doing what he had been told, Petey ran over and cut the
bloody ropes. Spellbound, he watched her gracefully stretch
her fingers as if she had a cramp from doing embroidery.

The golden angel looked up at him—her expression un-
readable as her green eyes assessed him. "Peter, I could use
some water and some food." She saw his bushy brows fly
up and then, with a nod, he dashed out of the room.

Suddenly free and able to see, Aimee waited for the resentment and anger to rise anew but found that every emotion, every bit of loathing, every wish for harm to fall on
those who did this to her was simply gone. Maybe she was
too tired. Maybe she was too hungry to put out the effort, but
whatever it was, all of her immediate desires were focused
on getting a warm meal, fresh air, and, if possible, some
clean clothes.

Aimee looked up as she heard two sets of footsteps approach. She assumed Petey was bringing the same friend
he'd had with him the night of her abduction.

"I hope, Peter, that you were able to fetch some water along with who I assume is Gus," she said, eyeing the much heavier man who appeared to be in his late forties.

Petey nodded in awe before handing her a small bucket with a ladle inside. Aimee took the metal scoop and dipped into the water, bringing the contents to her lips. At first it hurt to drink, but as the cool liquid went down it became easier. She took several more scoopfuls before stopping to study her two captors. They were completely different. One large, the other small. Where Petey had light brown hair, Gus's was dark.

"Gus, is that bread you have in your hand perchance for me?" Aimee asked in a serene voice as if she were a guest at tea.

Gus's hazel eyes grew round with surprise. He had been staring at her bloody wrists, frozen with fear and shock. "Uh, aye, miss, 'ere you go. Cook made it fresh dis morning."

Aimee took a bite, closed her eyes, and smiled. Fresh bread was another thing she would never undervalue again. She finished the whole thing, never moving from the sack of potatoes she had been leaning on. She licked her fingers and said, "If you would both help me to stand, I would like to leave this room and go somewhere a bit more comfortable."

Petey took a tentative step forward. "Miss, we didn't know ya was a . . . a . . . *female* when we took you. I swears I didn't know."

Gus nodded vigorously in agreement. "Ye even fought like a tar, kickin' and movin' all wild and crazy. Never did I dream a girl could move so mean."

Aimee lifted her hands to the men. "I believe you, especially as I was dressed to disguise my gender and aboard a ship at night, hiding in the shadows. Like you, I and two friends were attempting to catch the thief who has been sneaking aboard Wentworth and Hamilton ships while they are in port."

Rising to her feet, Aimee leaned on a large crate for support, happy to see Gus's and Petey's cautious smiles at her unexpected ability to understand their gross blunder. For some odd reason, Aimee felt inclined to put the men at ease, not berate them for the pain she even now felt in her limbs and head. Millie had always ridiculed her for her innate desire to see that everyone around her was comfortable, even if they did wrong by her. Aimee had no doubt that when she saw Millie again and relayed this story, she was sure to receive an "I told you so" from her friend.

Suddenly, the ship lurched and Aimee fought to keep her balance despite holding onto a crate. It was then she heard the waves lapping against the ship's hull and realized such a sound would not be heard if they were still in the harbor—or moving slowly upriver. Aimee's gaze darted from Petey, then to Gus, and then back, not really focusing on either before she closed her eyes and let out a small wail. "Good Lord! I'm at sea!"

Petey and Gus did not know what to do. She had seemed fine, but without warning, her face had become very pale. As she collapsed on a box of tinned beef, Gus blurted out, "This *is* a ship. Where did ye think ye were, miss?"

"Millie! Jennelle! They must be going crazy with worry right now. And Charles . . . oh, he must be apoplectic, sending every ship he has to chase me down." Then capturing Gus's mystified gaze, she asked, "Is there *any* chance we are still in or near London's harbor?"

Gus took a step back as the flurry of questions kept coming from the bedraggled beauty. "I don't know most of what ye said, but we's nowhere near England anymore, miss. This here's the *Sea Emerald*. It's mighty fast, and right now we are headin' to the Americas."

Aimee assimilated that bit of information and came to one conclusion. If no ship was capable of catching up with them, then the *Sea Emerald* would just have to turn around. Reece would be furious, but she would have a day, maybe two, to not only calm him down but force him to see reason about their relationship—though at the moment, she could hardly even call it that.

Aimee was just about to tell Gus that he needed to take her to his captain, when another idea struck her. She might not know how long it took a ship to get to the Americas and back, but Aimee knew she needed far longer than two days to recover her current debacle of a plan. "If this is the *Sea Emerald*, then is Mr. Hamilton aboard?"

Petey's brows furrowed in confusion. "Ya mean the cap'n? Is he aboard 'is own ship? Of course, miss. Where else would 'e be?"

Aimee smiled, relieved to hear at least one objective in her plan was still possible to achieve. She could and would speak with Reece. However, she hoped not to do so looking like a bedraggled mess. "Would it be possible to go somewhere more comfortable, so that I can clean my face and hands? And if possible, would you have something that I could use to wrap my wrists?" she asked, gritting her teeth to hide the pain.

Petey grabbed one arm and Gus the other as they helped her walk until her legs became accustomed to working again. They approached the stairs as the boat rocked one way and then the other. Aimee reached for the wall to steady herself.

"Careful there, miss. Are ya all right?" Petey asked, his voice full of concern. He had seen many cases of seasickness, and in his years of being on the water, only a rare few were naturally immune.

Aimee frowned, not understanding his question. "Yes,

Peter, I am fine. I am just not accustomed to walking on a moving floor."

Gŭs elbowed Petey and whispered, "Why does she keep calling ye Peter?"

Aimee stopped at the top of the stairs to answer the question. "Because that is his Christian name. And am I correct to believe that yours is—Octavius or Augustus?"

Gus grunted, refusing to answer, and marched around her before Petey could ask another question. "This way, miss," Gus grunted. "Follow me and I'll take ye back to Petey's and mine's quarters without anyone seein' ye. Our place is cramped, but it's a sight better than the hold."

Anyplace is a sight better than the hold, Aimee thought to herself as she followed his large but surprisingly nimble body through a narrow hall and up another staircase. She was just about to ask if he was lost, when they went down a few steps and into a very small but livable room containing two bunks that consumed most of the space.

Gus lit a lantern and hung it on a nail protruding from the wall across from the beds. When he turned around, he saw Petey repeatedly making the sign of the cross. Gus glanced in the direction that was causing Petey such alarm and immediately joined him in prayer.

Below, in the hold, the room had been dark and barely lit. Gus could not deny that Petey had captured a girl and that she looked to be fairly pretty. It was hard to miss the long blond hair and large green eyes, but now, in the lamplight, they could truly see the damage they had inflicted two days ago.

Gus immediately thrust a small wooden stool, nestled in the corner, toward her. "Here, miss. Uh, please sit down."

Aimee turned and smiled at him as if he had given her a throne and not the shiner radiating underneath her left eye.

Feeling left out, Petey wanted to give Aimee something

as well. "Is there somethin' else ya need, miss? Anythin' at all, just name it and I'll get it for ya."

Aimee's eyes lightened to the color of soft grass as she watched a familiar look of infatuation overtake their expressions. She almost thought to say something to dismiss any notions they may have, but decided against it. Instead, she would for once follow Millie's suggestion and use their fascination to her advantage. She just wished she knew how.

Aimee took a deep breath. *What would Jennelle tell me to do?* she pondered. *She would tell me to figure out what I wanted most and ask for that.* "Peter, I know this is unlikely, but by chance are there any women's clothes aboard—such as a dress, skirt—anything?"

Gus slapped his hands together and grinned, revealing a missing bottom tooth. "Aye, there is some female clothes in the chief mate's cabin." He poked his friend in the shoulder with his elbow. "Remember, Petey? Remember that old gal Collins brought on board a couple of runs back? She left in such a hurry she forgot a whole trunk of her stuff. I'll go get it."

Petey jumped in front of the small opening, blocking his friend's path. "Eh, she asked *me* to get the clothes. Not ya. *I'll* go get 'em." Petey paused just as he was about to exit. "If ya don't mind me asking, miss, what's yer name?"

"You may call me Aimee."

Petey's face broke into a large grin that showcased his rotten teeth. "That's a pretty name you have there, miss."

Gus kicked him and threatened, "If ye don't get the clothes, I'm gonna fetch 'em."

An hour later, Aimee had fallen asleep on one of the beds, waiting on Petey and Gus to return with some clothes. The sound of heavy footsteps approaching, followed by two more sets of nervous clomps, returned her to consciousness. Peter and Gus had finally returned—but not alone.

Feigning sleep, she tried to assess the newcomer entering the room, through thin slits as she barely opened her eyes. The man was slightly taller than Gus and younger, with bulging shoulders and a chest that matched his muscular arms and thighs. He reminded her of a lion, with his thick brown eyebrows and mass of tawny hair unevenly pulled back into a ponytail. By the way Petey and Gus were standing, whoever the man was, he held at least some authority. Then he moved in closer, stared at her for a moment, and without warning, let go a stream of curses that almost caused Aimee to jump and give herself away.

The man pivoted to glare at Gus and Peter, opening and closing his mouth several times, obviously unable to find any more words to express his anger. Taking a deep breath, he pointed his finger in Aimee's direction. "I don't know how much of what you told me is true, but even if *one morsel* of it is a lie . . ."

Petey and Gus stood there gaping, neither of them able to find the words to assure the man that everything they had said was the gospel truth.

The man shook his head and started rubbing his temples. "I mean, *do you realize what you two have done?*" The large man paced for a second in front of the makeshift bed before pausing. "That woman," he began in a hushed whisper behind clenched teeth, "*is the One.*"

Watching Petey and Gus look at her suspiciously, Aimee could no longer hold her curiosity. She slowly rose to a sitting position. "Who, pray tell, is the One?" she asked. "And who are you?"

The man jumped just a bit before resting his brown gaze unflinchingly upon her. He was even bigger than she had first thought. His brown skin and sun-bleached hair indicated that he had been at sea most of his life. "I am Frank

Collins, the chief mate on this ship. And heaven help us, *you* are the One."

Collins shook his head several times again, wondering what he was going to do. The captain was going to explode . . . no, he was going to do more than just explode. Every man aboard was going to die a miserable death as soon as he found out that his own men had not only kidnapped, beaten, and dragged the woman he loved aboard his ship in the middle of the night but also left her to starve for two days. "Good Lord, of *all the females in England, why you*?" he asked in a croaking voice.

Aimee watched curiously as the large man tried again to pace in the small space. Taking one step, he pivoted and took another in the opposite direction. After about five pointless turns, he stopped and stared at her as she attempted to sit serenely on the bed. He licked his lips and pointed at the left side of her face. It had been painful to lie down on that side, and based on Collins's expression, it must look as swollen and bruised as it felt. Her tongue swiped the nasty cut on her bottom lip and Collins let out a groan. The poor man was at a loss.

Aimee watched patiently as he mumbled to himself the few options he had in dealing with her. Unable to sit and watch the man's anxiety continue to grow, she decided to intervene. "Mr. Collins, perhaps if you could tell me the difficulties you are trying to sort through, I could help. I am quite quick on my feet despite my appearance to the contrary."

Collins snorted. "Have you any idea what you look like, my lady?"

Behind him, Petey elbowed Gus. "Did the chief just say *my lady*?"

Collins whipped around. "You're damn right I did. Neither of you has a clue who is sitting on your bunk, do you? You really don't know the trouble you have brought on us all." He paused, put his hands on his hips, and hissed, "That is

Lady Aimee Wentworth, *little sister* of our captain's best friend and co-owner of this ship, mind you. But more than that—*she is the One.* You should not be worried about *if* you are going to die, but *how*. Hell, I'm worried about joining you because I didn't throw you overboard myself. Pretty soon I'm guessing we all three will wish I had."

Aimee, tired of the threats being bandied about, decided to intervene. "Good lord, Mr. Collins, do you not think that you are exaggerating just a bit? I mean, as soon as I speak with Mr. Hamilton I am sure I can smooth over all of this mess with some far better alternative than death. I must own some blame for the current situation as I intended to be captured. I assure you these men could not have detained me otherwise."

Collins gaped at the daft woman. "Are you trying to tell me you *let* Gus right-hook you across the jaw, my lady?"

"Well, no. That unwelcome experience was not in my plan per se . . ." As soon as she said the words she saw an even greater fear rise in the stout man's eyes, and quickly added, "but I was struggling at the time, and he *did* believe me to be a man as well as a thief."

Collins raked his eyes over her slender figure. Yes, she was in men's clothes, but only a fool would think she was anything other than a woman.

Aimee fluidly rose and went over to place a placating hand on his bulky arm. "Mr. Collins, I am sure my appearance looks to be much worse than it is."

"I doubt it," Collins grumbled. "And if you could see what Gus did to your lovely face, you would not be so agreeable right now."

"You do not know me all that well, Mr. Collins. I suspect I might surprise you."

Collins swallowed and his brown eyes grew round with

appeal. "My lady, my heart can't suffer any more surprises at the moment."

"Well then, let us overcome just one problem at a time. I wager that once I am able to clean up a little and dress into something . . . without an odor, the circumstances that brought about my presence here will not seem as bad."

Collins scowled and mulled over her comment. Cleaning up would not hide the bruises, but at least *some* of the evidence of what she had endured would not be staring the captain straight in the face. "Perhaps you're right, my lady. Come with me to my quarters. I'll see if I can pinch the captain's tub for you to bathe in," Collins added, suspecting she was like the captain, who preferred to bathe en route to their destination and not just upon their arrival. "You probably want the water at least somewhat warm, too."

Aimee blinked a couple of times at the strange comment. Didn't all the men on the ship prefer to bathe in warm water? She decided not to pursue the subject and nodded that she agreed to his plan.

Three hours later, Aimee felt like a new person. After consuming a delicious platter of cheeses, meats, and bread, she had been able to bathe and clean her hair. Now, with the exception of her wrists, which were still raw and angry, she felt wonderful. The chief mate's cabin was not very large, but in comparison to the hold and Gus and Peter's small cabin, Aimee thought it spacious.

In addition, Collins had placed a trunkful of lady's odds and ends on the end of his narrow bed. All of the garments were too large around the bustline, but the extra material made it almost long enough for her tall frame. She had found some dark thread and did a quick seam along the sides of a pale yellow frock so that it hugged her slender figure. It was far from stylish and the inconsistent stitching made it obvious she lacked the skills of a seamstress. However, she did feel at least somewhat feminine once again.

Her hair was still slightly damp, so instead of arranging it she decided to let the waves of blond curls remain free. Aimee was just placing the second comb she found in the trunk to pull the tresses away from her face when she heard a sharp rap at the door.

Collins rapped on the door and waited. He could not ever remember his gut being wound in such tight knots. He would rather face nonstop storms all the way from London to the Americas than have to deal with the problem Gus and Petey had just handed him.

Though she had been covered with filth, her hair matted, and dirt and bruises were smearing her face, any man could have seen that Lady Aimee Wentworth would be a rather pretty woman, once clean. When he first saw her, he had barely recognized her from the faint picture the captain kept in his cabin, but her pale hair, high cheekbones, and long lashes were an unmistakable combination that belonged to only one person. The captain's woman.

When they had left port last Christmas, the captain had been in an extremely foul mood. Nothing had pleased him, and it had taken very little for him to be irritated. After several weeks of such unusual behavior, Collins had caught the captain in his cabin holding a picture of a lady. He had been drinking, a very uncommon indulgence, and told Collins that he had found her—the One. The one woman men searched for all their lives. But she couldn't be his.

Collins had asked why the captain could not marry her, and it was then he learned just how deeply the man felt about Society's rules. He was the second son of a lord, and without a title, she could never be his. Collins did not understand, as the captain was very wealthy, something he would have thought could negate the lack of a title. But when he declared that any woman would be lucky to have a man with such means, the captain had slowly shaken his head.

Money was not enough. Not for her. She was the daughter of a marquess, and more than that, she was the sister of his best friend. Who was he? An ex-soldier who became a mere merchant. Collins said no more, but he noticed that not once since Christmas had the captain even looked at another woman. When at port, he did his business and kept to the ship. He didn't even imbibe with his men. His captain had become a haunted man. Haunted by a woman he referred to as the One.

Collins was about to knock again when he thought he heard a high-pitched sound. A second later he realized that what he heard was singing. It was quiet and soft, but the tune was haunting and he could not help but stand there and listen. Only after several minutes did he realize what he was doing.

Damn woman, he hissed to himself. How much worse could this get? Did the Lord really need to make her a siren too? It did not matter what she looked like; a voice like that could ensnare a man's soul and make him forget just where his loyalty lay.

This time Collins banged on the door. The singing thankfully stopped. As he waited for her to open the door, he rehearsed what he was going to say, for he wanted no arguments about leaving immediately to see the captain. The sooner he turned her and all the problems her presence was going to cause over to someone else, the better.

The moment the door opened and he saw what was on the other side, all thought left him as his jaw fell open. When it came to women, Collins gravitated to those who were curvaceous, dark haired, and dark eyed, but he had never seen an angel before.

Once she was no longer covered in grime and filth, he knew she would be pretty, but nothing had prepared him for the vision standing in his cabin beckoning him to enter. Finally, the captain's strange behavior all made sense, for the woman standing in his cabin was the most beautiful female he had ever seen. Yes, this fairylike vision could indeed drive an eternal seaman to the land.

Aimee smiled at the warm assessment Collins's eyes were giving her. As she suspected, the bath had done much to improve her appearance. "Mr. Collins, thank you so much for the bath and clean clothes. They are greatly appreciated. I can tell you that I shall never again take a fresh gown for granted."

Collins noticeably gulped and he sought to calm his inner voice when she swung her arm wide, indicating for him to come into his own cabin and join her. But as she did, her wrists became visible. Collins's eyes bulged with rage as he stared at the angry red wound. No bath could diminish the raw, painful injury. He looked down at her other arm and saw that it was damaged just as badly, if not worse. "Who did that to you?" Collins demanded, his voice tight with unleashed anger.

Aimee looked down to where his eyes were focused. "My wrists? Unfortunately, that was of my own doing while trying unsuccessfully to wrestle myself to freedom. They still look bad, but they do not hurt nearly like they did when it happened."

Collins heard her voice make light of the injury but knew without a doubt that such wounds were very painful. Unfortunately, he also knew they must be tended to. And the moment he did, he knew the captain, who had temporarily retired to his cabin, would investigate upon hearing her high-pitched yowls. But at least the captain would finally know she was aboard. "My lady, if you would follow me. We need to see the cook."

Puzzled, Aimee followed Collins out into the narrow corridor. Something thumped behind her and she watched how Collins extended an arm around her to hook the latch so that the door did not bang as the ship rolled with the waves.

When they reached the deck, Aimee stopped. Without a word, she stood with her eyes closed, enjoying the wind as it whipped at her face, hair, and gown. It felt wonderful. "Mr. Collins, if you do not mind, can we stay here for just a moment longer? I would so like a chance to view the ocean. While I have felt it beneath my feet, I have not yet actually seen the Atlantic."

Collins looked back in the direction of the captain's cabin and then at the radiant beauty beckoning him to allow her to enjoy his favorite love—the sea. Relenting, Collins nodded. "But just for a minute. We really have to see JP."

"JP?" Aimee repeated, smiling as she walked over to the deck's rails and peered over.

"Jean-Pierre, but everyone calls him JP," Collins said as he spied, from the corner of his eye, Smiley and Red Legs Solomon stop what they were doing to ogle the captain's woman. Soon, more men joined them in an effort to catch a glimpse of "the One" as she stood confidently with her face in the wind. Collins had already known that it would be impossible to keep her presence hidden from the crew, and consequently had done the exact opposite. He had spread the word that the captain's woman was not only on board but had been injured by one of the crew. Hearing the latter, it was not hard to convince the crew to keep quiet about her presence until Collins found the right time to inform the boss. But no one had agreed not to stare at the siren if given a chance.

Grimacing, Collins gestured for her to follow him. "It's time. We need to go now, my lady."

Aimee sighed. Once they were inside where the wind could not smother her words, she asked, "It's time for what?"

Collins did not answer but went down two narrow sets of stairs that led to a small factory of delicious smells. Instantly, Aimee felt like eating again, and this time a meal big enough to satisfy even someone of Mr. Collins's size. "Please say it is time for dinner. Mr. Jean-Pierre? Is that your name?" she asked the man with a twitching mustache. He was shorter than she was by several inches, with thinning dark hair, but unlike most men who could not see eye to eye with her, JP was not in the least intimidated. "It smells absolutely wonderful. I can honestly say that I have never inhaled better scents in my life than what you are creating in here."

JP narrowed his gaze as the tall, trim blonde bent over to peek in his pots. Then, without asking, she used a nearby ladle to sample the contents. Every man aboard the *Sea Emerald* knew to stay away from his kitchen. Step inside and you did not eat. It was a clear and simple rule, and all followed it—including the captain. JP could be mean when crossed, but as one of the most coveted cooks on the seas, he was allowed to be. It had taken Captain Hamilton three years to convince him to move on board the *Sea Emerald*, and JP had only one firm stipulation—stay out of his kitchen.

Collins gave JP a grave look and then introduced them. "Uh, JP, this is . . ." He was about to say "the One" again before changing his mind. He really did not want to explain to the lady just what the term meant and how the captain felt about her. That conversation was for her and the captain, and no one else. ". . . Lady, uh . . ."

"Aimee," she said between sips.

Collins swallowed. "Lady Aimee, this is . . . JP."

Aimee turned, looking chagrined about her miniature

eating foray, and greeted the cook as if he were the most
gifted genius in the world. It completely disarmed the Frenchman. "Mr. Jean-Pierre, you are truly a master. I shamefully
admit to sneaking into many kitchens, but I have never been
in one so cleverly organized. Despite the confined space
allotted to you, you have whipped up dishes that make the
mouth water in anticipation of the next bite."

Aimee paused, taking in the cook's twitching mustache.
"Mr. Collins, I believe we have interrupted this magician at a
critical time and must allow him to continue his work. If we
do not, the carrots will be undercooked," Aimee said, pointing to the diced vegetables on a table against the wall. "And
that would be a shame, for the stew Mr. Jean-Pierre is preparing is one of the best I have ever tasted." She hummed for a
second and pointed to the ladle in the soup. "Mr. Jean-Pierre,
would you mind terribly if I tried just one more sample?"

JP opened his mouth to say many things but nothing
came out. Seeing that the cook was visibly shaken, Collins
grimaced. "We are not here for victuals, JP, and you have
my apologies about the interruption, but we have need of
the whiskey." Collins caught the cook's eye and with his
chin directed JP's gaze to her wrists. He knew exactly when
the Frenchman saw them.

JP gulped, for he knew what the chief mate intended to
do. And it did have to be done. "Should we get zee boss?"
he whispered.

"That is a question I have been struggling with since I
first learned of her and her . . . condition." Collins pressed
his lips together. "Yes, we will get him, but let's wait until
after we wrap her wrists, I think."

Aimee held up her hand. "Just what do you believe will
happen after I meet with Mr. Hamilton?"

"*Captain* Hamilton will no doubt immediately turn us
around and head back to London double speed. And seeing

the condition you're in—pardon me, miss, but your wounds are quite distressing to the eyes—he would most likely fire us all. And that's if we're lucky." Collins rubbed the back of his neck. "To tell you the truth, I wouldn't blame him. But these men are a good bunch and would follow the captain through just about anything. Such trust between a crew and their boss is not quickly developed. It would cost him a lot to fire us. And the men? Most would eventually find work, but nothing as good as the *Sea Emerald*, and they know it."

Aimee had surmised that Collins, even Gus and Petey, would get a lecture. She had even felt guilt at the thought, for she suspected Reece's lectures were something along the line of her brother's—and quite unpleasant. But after hearing Collins's prediction of what would happen, Aimee had no intention of seeing Reece until they were much farther out to sea. She needed enough time to convince him that they belonged together. That his being a second son and his love for the sea made no difference. That she loved only him and he loved her as well. Being happy and in love, he would then harbor no ill feelings toward his crew.

Until then she intended to stay aboard, which was not the horrible experience Society people purported it to be. Strangely enough, she enjoyed being on a ship. The sounds and the motion were both appealing and soothing, and she was not ready to give them up.

Unfortunately, her new plan was doomed unless she convinced Collins that a delay in disclosing her presence would benefit both him and the crew. She delicately shrugged her shoulders and said, "Then why not wait to tell Mr. Hamilton?"

"*Wait?*" Collins barked. The stress of having her around without the captain knowing was already intolerable. Collins doubted he could wait. Barely three days out, it already felt like the longest voyage ever.

Before he unequivocally refused her suggestion, Aimee

explained, "I am already here. The anger Mr. Hamilton might feel at my being aboard will not change. However, if we allow some time to pass for my wounds to heal, the severity of the repercussions might be significantly less. In addition, Mr. Hamilton would have more time for his anger to ease. I would hate to know that men lost their jobs because we were impatient."

The only disadvantage to her proposal was the impact it would have on Millie and Jennelle. Both were undoubtedly upset by her disappearance. But surely by now they had confirmed she was on the *Sea Emerald* and therefore in safe hands. If Aimee could actually talk to them, she had little doubt that they would be encouraging her to take the risk.

The real unknown was her brother. Charles was going to be furious with her; thus, his anger was *another* reason to delay telling Reece. It would give her brother several more weeks to make peace with the idea that his little sister ran away with his best friend.

She sighed and locked pleading green eyes onto Mr. Collins's brown ones until he finally muttered the words she wanted to hear. "We will wait."

Aimee swallowed as she realized what Collins had prescribed for treating her injuries. "You have to be seriously befuddled if you think I am going to allow you to pour that nasty-smelling liquid onto my wrists, Mr. Jean-Pierre."

Frowning, he looked at her. "My name is not *Mister* Jean-Pierre, it is *just* Jean-Pierre. And, *oui*, I must clean your wounds wiz zis nasty-smelling liquid, as you so politely put it."

Aimee ignored his sarcasm and pulled her arms behind her back. "And just how much do you know of wounds, Mr. Jean-Pierre? Do you claim to be a doctor as well as a cook?"

"I know all too much, me lady," JP replied, his French accent thick. "I 'ave been on ships all me life, and too often wounds such as yours are fine one day and foul zee next. Even after we do cleanse your injuries, zey may still not heal right."

Aimee gulped, remembering well the stories Jennelle told Millie and her about how some physicians believed that spirits stopped the flesh from turning bad and causing a man to die. But mostly, she remembered Millie's terrifying account of cleansing her brother's wound and the level of agony it had produced. "I'm sorry, gentlemen. It is not that I am a coward . . . but, well, maybe I am a coward. You see, I am quite aware of the pain that is caused by what you intend, and let me put it this way . . . *there is no way in bloody hell you are going to do that to me.*"

Collins sighed. He wished Lady Aimee was ignorant about the treatment, but that would have meant something had gone right this day. "If you refuse, then I will be forced to notify the captain and *he* can do it," he stated, part of him praying to God that the threat would not work.

Aimee inhaled and stared at Collins. Deciding he was not bluffing, she straightened her shoulders and asked, "Are we to do it here?"

JP looked at Collins and gave him a hostile glare. "My kitchen is for cooking and cooking only. I suggest your cabin."

Collins frowned and shook his head. Pulling JP aside, he whispered, "It's too risky. The captain is next door to my cabin. One female shriek and he would walk in, demanding to know what the hell was going on. Only after we were fish fodder would he realize the right of what we were trying to do, but then it would be too late. I'd rather take *your* wrath."

Aimee had thought Collins's previous comments about his imminent death were jokes, but she was beginning to believe the man truly believed Reece would physically harm them if he saw her injured or in pain. "I can assure you, Mr. Collins, that Mr. Hamilton would never hurt you or Mr. Jean-Pierre."

JP snorted, crossing his arms, and Collins grimaced. "Not unless he had a good reason, my lady. But, aye, he is certainly capable and willing if given adequate motive, and holding down a woman—especially *you*—and causing her to scream in pain . . . well, I can promise you, to him that *would* be a good reason."

"But I would stop him. I would tell him what happened and explain the situation."

Collins inhaled deeply, but his frown remained. "I'm hoping you are going to do exactly that, my lady, but *only* after you heal somewhat. Right now, one look at you and the captain is not going to listen to explanations. As a leader and a sailor, he is as fine as they come, fair and capable. But the captain is also a soldier and a damn good one. It would take very little to trigger his combat training and become one again. Hearing you in pain, seeing your arms and face . . . this time, we," Collins said, waving his finger between himself and JP, "would be his enemies. And I've seen the captain in battle. We would die before you or anyone else could stop him."

Comprehension flooded Aimee's countenance. She had known Reece only in safe, happy surroundings. Yet, Collins was right. For eight years, Reece had been constantly surrounded by danger. His crew had depended upon him. They knew him, and Reece knew them well. But he had been brought up as a noble, and like all gentlemen, his code of honor was nonnegotiable. If Reece believed his men had put her in danger or caused her harm, all the trust between them would be gone instantly. She had not realized how her decision to be abducted would affect others until now. Whatever the pain she had to endure to reduce the potential damage her presence might cause was a very small price to pay.

"Mr. Jean-Pierre, I suggest we do this on deck. *If* I do cry out *and* am overheard by Mr. Hamilton, it would be easier to claim it was one of the crew. Correct?"

The cook nodded in agreement, stray locks falling in front of his eyes. "Would be best. I'll get a calming salve and some clean rags for bandages."

Aimee watched as the two men gathered what they needed. Collins looked at the cook and said, "We best be quick. The captain will rise and be on deck within the hour."

Jean-Pierre stepped past Aimee and out into the small hallway. "Put someone on guard to direct zee captain elsewhere if need be. This way, mademoiselle. No use delaying what must be done."

Aimee swallowed and followed the thin man up the stairs and into the early night air. Clouds covered much of the stars, but there was still enough light to maneuver. She took a deep breath, surprised to discover how much the smell of the warm sea air calmed her. On a crate a few feet away, Collins put down the glass container he carried and began ripping strips of cotton.

Aimee pulled up a smaller box and sat down. It was then she noticed a hushed crowd gathering around them. These were the men whom Reece depended on and who depended on him. Aimee decided then and there that no matter what the pain, she would not scream. Not a single man witnessing what was about to happen would remember their captain's future wife as a weeping female being held down by their chief mate in order to save her life.

Collins had never been so nervous in his life. He would face a battalion of Frenchmen rather than this lone woman, who suddenly appeared relaxed and prepared to face what must be done. If the captain could witness her bravery, he would be incredibly proud. Collins figured on telling him . . . one day . . . but far, far into the future.

Aimee held her wrists in front of her and nodded to JP. Seconds later, what felt to be liquid fire smothered her wounds. Screaming would not have helped. Yelling would not have helped. Nothing would have helped her endure the pain that was consuming her. Tears blinded her eyes and she squeezed them shut. "Is it over?" she choked.

"Aye, my lady, the worst of it is over," she heard Collins reply and then the world went dark and she felt no more.

Chapter 5

October 10, 1816

Aimee blinked twice and tried again to focus on the wood beams above her. She groaned. The last thing she could remember was being out on deck, and it had been dark outside. The bright light streaming through the window indicated she had been out for some time.

Her arms were throbbing, but the pain was at least bearable. Grunting, she looked down at the makeshift bandages and fell back against the surprisingly soft bedding, sapped of energy. Her body seemed to have a mind of its own and was rejecting the idea of doing anything that might touch, move, or disturb her throbbing wrists.

"Aimee Wentworth, you have just survived the worst of it, and you did yourself proud," she said, speaking sternly to herself. "Now unless you want Reece's men thinking you are a sad little pampered creature expecting to be catered to, *sit up*."

Reece glanced at the wall separating his quarters from those of his chief mate. He had been bending over his provisional desk, trying to discern a peculiar riddle regarding one of their navigational charts, when he thought he heard Aimee's voice. He stood up and raked his hand through his hair. Had he actually gone mad?

Distance and time, he had told himself, would enable him to conquer his emotions and physical craving for her, but neither had worked. Instead, they had driven him to insanity. Too often he had imagined her on the boat singing, talking to him, sitting with him, or being out on deck enjoying his beloved wind and sea, but he had always known it was an illusion of his own making. And never did his fantasies include Aimee scolding herself.

Reece froze, listening. When only silence greeted him, he shook his head a few times and went back to the chart. The one on top was one he had made, and yet something about it was different than he remembered.

Hoping that Collins would be able to identify the discrepancies, Reece rolled up the parchment and went out into the narrow hallway to bang on the door to the room next to his. "Collins," Reece bellowed. "Open up, man. There is something wrong with these charts."

At the sound of Reece's voice, Aimee instinctively sat up and hit her head on a low-lying bag of . . . something. A voluble "bloody hell" came out before she could muffle her response.

Reece looked quizzically at the closed door. "Did you just *sing* the words *bloody hell* to me, mate?"

Aimee sat frozen. It *was* Reece on the other side of the door. Worse, because she had said something, he believed Collins was in the cabin. Looking around, she could find nothing sizeable to hide behind or anything to duck under. Two seconds away from pure panic, Aimee heard Collins join Reece in the corridor and sighed with relief.

"Can I help you, Captain?"

Reece looked at his chief mate, puzzled and suspicious.

He then saw the latch on his door was attached from the outside. "Did you bring a woman aboard, Collins?"

Collins looked at Reece, wide-eyed but unblinking. "Not I, Captain," he grunted. "After Rosita, I figured on spending a few cruises *without* female companionship, if you know what I mean."

Reece grimaced and glanced back at the closed door. To pursue the conversation meant talking about certain topics and admitting private thoughts he planned on taking to his watery grave. "Um, I wanted to go over these charts with you," he said, pointing at the wooden door to indicate he wanted to step inside his chief mate's cabin. "I swear we are off course, not by much, but it is difficult to tell with the cloud cover we have been having at night."

"I've been following the course you laid out, sir. We're heading south as you wanted."

Reece frowned. The fastest routes from England to the Americas were not necessarily the most direct. Going south toward the equator before turning toward the Indies allowed them to avoid the strong current that flowed from the Americas across the Atlantic toward Europe. And Reece had a particular route he liked to follow because it shaved at least two days off the trip. "I know, but I sense we're off. Get the log line and chronometer. I want to know exactly where we are and get us back on course. Let's go in and take another look at these charts. I want to—"

Collins very nervously jumped in front of Reece to block the door. "Aye, Captain. But I told Heilsen that I would be returning directly. Let me handle him, then I'll meet you in your quarters."

Reece scowled at Collins. He was tempted to tell him that the second mate could wait, but decided against it. He needed a change, and outside all he could hear was the wind and the noises that actually belonged on a ship. "I'll come with you. I've been down here too long anyway."

Aimee heard heavy footsteps walking away, and was just starting to breathe normally again when she heard the rattle of someone asking to enter the room. Aimee swallowed, but before she could answer, a burly, flaxen-haired man in his midtwenties shuffled in and gave her a wide saucy grin. "Ahh, too bad yer awake, as the boss told me I could throw ye over me shoulder if you weren't."

Aimee blinked at the cheeky sailor smiling at her as if he had just won first prize in some popular event. Then he gave her a very low, showy bow, and she had to bite her bottom lip to keep from laughing. "And just who are you, good sir, and why would you prefer to cart an unconscious female over your shoulder?"

"Name's Hurlee, miss, and it's best not to ask questions when one of the bosses tells ye to do somethin'," he answered with a wink. "But if ye don't mind, we need to leave right away."

Aimee released her bottom lip and nodded. "Of course, Mr. Hurlee."

"Uh, Hurlee's me given name, miss," he clarified as he turned and left the cabin.

Realizing that Hurlee truly meant to leave at that very moment, Aimee scurried off the bed and grabbed the loose slippers Collins had found with the other clothes he had given her. Leaping over the doorjamb, she barely caught up to the surprisingly nimble sailor before he disappeared down a set of stairs. She wanted to ask where they were going, who he was, why they had to leave, and why so fast. But instinct told her the answer to all of her questions was Reece and keeping him from finding her. Silently, she followed the broad-shouldered seaman. It was not long before her nose was able to discern at least one answer to her growing list of questions—they were headed to the kitchen.

As soon as she was safely inside, Hurlee grabbed her hand, performed another awkward low bow, and kissed each of her fingertips. "Ah, if only I could be yer One. Ye really are one beautiful woman, miss."

Aimee shook her head and smiled, unable to be affronted by the man when he was trying so hard to flatter and impress her. But before she could reply, an empty sauce pan whizzed by her head. "Out! Out! Out wiz you, and never come back. I only agreed *la dame* could come in here. Not you, you . . . you . . . obscenely large man. Out!"

Unoffended, Hurlee grinned, shrugged his shoulders, and quickly scooted out of the small room, closing the door before another pan went flying toward his head. From behind her, Aimee could hear angry mutterings mostly in French. "*Imbécile*. Pretty women always make men go crazy." He paused to look at her. "But it's zat man Collins who is *fou* if 'e expects me to 'ide ye 'ere in me kitchen."

Piqued, Aimee replied in English, "Since you feel so strongly, Mr. Jean-Pierre, maybe you should *not* hide me. I have no problem leaving this kitchen and announcing my presence to Mr. Hamilton. Of course, I'll have to explain these." She held up her wrists. "And, of course, just how kind you were in cleaning them."

The cook squinted at Aimee. Her face was bruised and her dress was ill fitting, and yet the woman definitely outshone any female he could recall. Her pale golden tresses and sharp, twinkling eyes could mesmerize the most hardened of men, and JP knew he was far from immune. If only she would be haughty or proud, then he could easily spurn her presence.

Instead, he took in a deep breath and turned back to his pots. "You must love 'im deeply, mademoiselle. And I, being French, know better zan to contend wiz an emotional woman. So stay if you must"—he waved his ladle as if splashing something all around—"but *be quiet*."

Aimee gave him a mock salute and smiled. Finding a narrow, tall stool next to where he was working, she sat down and propped her elbow on a bench, placing her chin on her hand. "Mr. Jean-Pierre, whatever happened to the stew you were preparing?"

Jean-Pierre stood stock-still for a moment and closed his eyes, taking deep breaths. What had he expected from a woman who insisted on calling him *Mister* Jean-Pierre? That she would heed his simple request for silence? "It is *fini*, mademoiselle. Just like everyzing I prepare. I stir and combine and bake zee finest foods in zee world and zose men," he said through gritted teeth, using his ladle as a pointer, this time toward the ceiling, "just gobble it up. No savoring. No enjoyment. Just swallow is all zey do."

"Oh," Aimee replied, not even trying to hide the disappointment in her voice. She had no idea that nothing else could have captured the respect and the loyalty of the thin cook more.

"You really like me stuff, eh?"

"Absolutely!" Aimee proclaimed. "You included paprika, and I have been trying to convince our cook for ages that it would only enhance the flavor."

Jean-Pierre's eyes widened in appreciation and eagerness. "Ah, so you know something about cuisine."

Aimee watched as he moved a large bin of carrots and potatoes over to the table she was sitting beside. "In truth, I know very little. Like you, our cook detests anyone—even other cooks—being in her kitchen. But whenever she is on leave to visit her family, I have been known to sneak into our kitchens and help with the pastries. Tilly, who stands in for her, thinks it's amusing."

"I zought zee, eh, nobles did not like, 'ow do you say? Get zeir 'ands dirty. Cooking can be dirty, eh? Especially zee pastry."

Aimee got up and without thinking, selected a knife and began to assist with the chopping. "It is only a little mess, and pastries are so fun to make. The dough is like a piece of art begging to be molded."

JP jumped as she slammed down the cleaver, cutting a large spud in two. She was right. He did not like anyone— even other cooks—in his kitchen. But it was clear she was not going to leave or just sit quietly. "Mademoiselle, zere is an apron be'ind zat cupboard zere. Yes, zere. I 'ave no use for such zings, but you may want to protect your . . . uh . . . your *robe*, since you insist upon interfering."

Aimee grabbed the thick covering and put her arms through the loops. "As I have only this gown until I can stitch the sides of another, I thank you and will be glad to *help* you in any way I can. Just what pastry are you making?"

JP shook his head. "Never 'eard 'ardtack called a pastry before," he said, handing her the bowl. "Keep adding a spoonful of water until it sticks togezer. Make it into a ball, let it sit, and zen roll it out very zin for baking."

Aimee did as she was told and started to add the water, but her dress was made for a shorter woman, making it difficult for her to maneuver her arms.

JP chuckled. "So Collins gave you Rosita's zings, did 'e, eh? If 'e ever tells you zat you are a burden, just mention 'er name. I promise you zat 'e will immediately be quiet."

"But why? What happened to Rosita? And why did she leave her clothes aboard the *Sea Emerald*?"

"Ah, now, mademoiselle, I will not explain to you ze complexities of a man's world. Just know I 'ave given you ze keys to dealing wiz Collins."

"You are an evil man, Mr. Jean-Pierre," Aimee replied, smiling. "And I am glad that you are my friend."

JP froze for a second and then turned to look at her, twitching his mustache. *Friend?* How could she think that? They most certainly were not friends, and he did not want a single seaman on this ship to think otherwise. Not only was she a woman, but an English woman who, like all women, loved to talk. It was for his benefit—not hers—that he had not thrown her out. He was about to explain all this to her when Collins opened the door.

"My lady, I need you to come with me. You can spend more time with your new *friend* here tomorrow, if you are up to it."

Realizing that Collins must have overheard Aimee and thought to tease him about it, JP was about to remind the chief mate how unwise it would be to tangle with him. But before he could do so, Aimee had leaned over the small cooking table and kissed his unshaven cheek. "*Au revoir*, Mr. Jean-Pierre."

If Collins had a death wish, he would have busted out laughing upon seeing the shock on the old cook's face. He had already pressed his luck by teasing him about his and Aimee's "friendship," but he had not been able to help himself. She and JP had been gabbing like magpies and everyone knew that JP demanded absolute silence when he cooked. Collins had to hold on to the doorframe to keep himself from falling when he realized the buzzard was allowing her to actually help cook! As if a noble lady knew anything about the kitchen besides eating what was prepared there.

Collins maneuvered down one narrow corridor and into another, marching back as quickly as he could to his cabin. Once they were inside and the door was closed, Aimee asked, "Mr. Collins, whatever is the matter with you? You seemed much calmer before. I know it was a little exciting earlier this morning with Mr. Hamilton knocking on the door, but—"

"Exciting, my lady? Did you say *exciting*? No, that was nothing compared to later, when the captain accused me again of bringing someone on board because he could smell her—*your*—scent!"

Tilting her head back, Aimee peered at his face. "But, Mr. Collins, you spoke truthfully. You did not bring anyone on board."

Collins ran his hands roughly over his face. "My lady, I think by the time this is over, I will be ready for sainthood. Half of the men are besotted with you. Bloody hell, you even converted JP! He hates everyone!"

"Mr. Collins, you do exaggerate."

"Do I? Because I don't think I do."

Aimee exhaled. The man was obviously frustrated and needed to unload his burdens, so she moved to sit down and quietly pay attention to his ranting.

"I bet even Kyrk," Collins snapped, throwing his hands up into the air, "who truly despises women being on ships, would take a liking to you given enough time. Maybe I should sprout a few blond curls so that I could bend the crew's will to my every whim."

"Now, Mr. Collins, you know that I am not trying to bend anyone's will, and if I am being such a bother, then perhaps it would be best to take me to Mr. Hamilton right now."

"Oh no!" Collins said, waggling a finger. "It was you who asked to see him *after* you are healed, and that is what's going to happen. But starting now, I'm going to put down some rules, and you will follow them."

Aimee pulled her legs up and under her to give the broad man some room, for it seemed he needed to pace. "I think that is a splendid idea."

Collins stopped for a brief second to see if she was being sincere. Unable to decide, he continued. "Rule One. We work on four-hour shifts, so you will have to be ready to leave any cabin with only a moment's notice. When you hear a double knock, open the door and be prepared to leave. Second rule—"

"Excuse me, Mr. Collins. But what if I am asleep? I am by nature a morning person, and find it difficult to wake in the early evening hours if I'm asleep."

Collins stared at her, dumbfounded, for several seconds. "Aboard this ship, you'll be what you need to be. Now for the second rule."

"And why a double knock? How about a triple or just one solid thump? What made you decide to choose a *double* knock to indicate immediate departure?" Aimee couldn't help it. She knew she was egging the man on, but he reminded her of Charles, who tended to command instead of persuade.

Collins was flummoxed the woman was daring to make light of his . . . her situation. "The *second rule*, my lady, is to never, under any circumstances, go into the captain's quarters."

Aimee scrunched her brows. She had not considered doing such a thing, but now that it was forbidden, she suddenly wanted to.

Collins hurried on before she could ask some silly question as to why. There were more reasons than just the obvious. For if she did go in, she would see pictures of herself, and there was no telling how she would react. "Third rule, unless being escorted to and from the kitchen, you are to remain in this cabin."

That decree caused a dark shadow to pass across Aimee's eyes, and Collins instantly knew that the even-tempered woman was no longer amused by his rules. Her icy expression could freeze the sea. However, he too was not someone easily influenced. Ask Rosita.

Aimee found her voice. "I expect you put some thought into your rules, Mr. Collins, but perhaps they could benefit from a little more consideration. For example, I suggest we revisit your third rule about me being confined *as a prisoner* on this ship."

Collins clenched his jaw. "I did not ask for you to come aboard. My men did not ask for you to come aboard, and *for certain* my captain didn't ask for you to be here. In your own words, you hoodwinked Petey and Gus into capturing you. And since I am the one who is in the uncomfortable position of saving you and my men, the three rules stand!"

Aimee rose fluidly and straightened her back. Collins was taller than she, but somehow she knew how to make her presence formidable. "I assume Mr. Hamilton sleeps predominantly at night?"

Collins felt like he was a puppet on a string, and he doubted he would ever get used to her calling his captain "mister." "Aye, he does. After the night reading," he answered hesitantly.

"Then I shall go above after he descends, Mr. Collins. It is unwise to lock someone up for too long in a small stuffy room, even one as comfortable as yours." Aimee could see she was making little headway and was not close to persuading him. "Perhaps it is time to discuss Rosita."

It sounded ludicrous, but she immediately got a reaction. "What about Rosita?"

Aimee shrugged her shoulders nonchalantly and again sat down on the bed. God bless JP. He had been right. "Simply put, Mr. Jean-Pierre and I were having a lovely discussion when you entered. One of the more interesting topics was Rosita and how—"

Collins threw up his hands. "Fine! You can leave the cabin. But only after you are assured that the captain has retired for the night!" And then quickly added, "*And* it won't be this cabin, but one of the crew's." It would be cramped and it would smell, but he felt no guilt. The lady deserved both.

Aimee's smile was full of satisfaction.

"My lady, you are nothing like you look, all soft and sweet. The captain would be wise to stay clear of you."

Aimee's smile grew, unfazed by his assessment. "I am

honestly not that bad, Mr. Collins. By next week, you might even be glad I was aboard."

Collins shrugged and crossed his arms. "You might want to save all your charm for the bosun." Aimee knew from what she had studied about ships that the boatswain had many jobs, from overseeing maintenance and rigging to foreman of the deck crew. "It's now Carr's responsibility to decide which of the crew is to watch over you and ensure you are never where you shouldn't be."

Aimee rolled her eyes. She suspected that was pretty much everywhere.

"Oh, and one more rule . . . *stop singing.*"

Chapter 6

October 12, 1816

Reece leaned back in his chair and, using the heels of his palms, he vigorously rubbed both eyes. He had been in his cabin for the last couple of hours, studying one of the new nautical charts he had procured in London. Of the latest design, it not only mapped out the current that ran from south of England toward the western coast of Africa, but it more accurately laid out how the current of Atlantic Ocean water moved parallel to the equator. Once across, he used the warm eddies that spun off from the current to push the ship northward along the eastern coast of America. It was the route Reece had used for years, but learning just where and when to turn could add or remove days from a trip.

The map was much larger than the ones he was more familiar with, in that it not only showed the currents, but the depths of the water near the coast, seabed descriptions, details of the coastline, navigational hazards, as well as information on tides and currents. All information he needed if he intended to improve his normal route.

Reece inhaled and rubbed his scalp. Blowing the lungful of air out, he heard the sound of someone singing. It was faint, melodic, and haunting. He closed his eyes and just focused on the sound. It was the one from his dreams. Aimee was on board the *Sea Emerald*, humming wherever she went. And when she stopped singing, the dream always ended with her waking him with a kiss.

Ten months, he muttered to himself. After all this time, it seemed no matter where he was or what he was doing, his thoughts kept coming back to her. Frustrated, he got to his feet and headed to the upper deck to get some fresh air.

The sun was sinking on the horizon. It was always cool on deck without the sun, but they were now close enough to the equator that it was comfortable to be out at night. It also helped that the weather had been agreeable, with scattered clouds and no showers. Although it was rare they were able to get across the ocean without encountering at least one sizeable storm, it did not look like it would happen tonight.

"Collins," Reece said as he stepped onto the afterdeck.

Collins swallowed, gave Reece a brief acknowledging look, and then snapped his brown eyes to the main deck. "Captain." His gaze was focused on the two men staring at each other.

Reece took in the scene. Both seamen were standing, fists clenched, glaring at each other. The dogwatch crew had all stopped their duties and were eagerly waiting to see who was going to strike whom. "What happened?"

Collins pursed his lips. "Nothing much. Gilley was backing up to tighten the brail on the lower sail when he tripped over the ropes Bean was coiling."

Reece nodded in understanding. Bean was mad at having his work ruined and Gilley probably had a mean rope burn after losing control of the brail. Accident or not, the inevitable conclusion of such a mishap was a fight. Upon looking at the two men, Gilley looked to be the more likely winner. He was far taller and had several missing teeth due to years of working—and fighting—on the seas. But Bean was not to be underestimated. Though the shortest on his crew, he was far from the weakest.

Collins started to walk around Reece. "Better go stop it before it gets bad."

Reece held out a hand and stopped him. "Stay. The weather is calm, so it's safe enough for them to have it out. Besides, the men have been too quiet the past couple of days."

In truth, Reece was glad there was about to be a fight. He even hoped some others would join in. Experience had taught him that it was far more dangerous when men could not release their frustrations and pent-up energy. But Bean and Gilley had yet to throw a punch. They were not even cursing. The only thing they did was stare at each other, periodically looking down at their feet.

"What the hell are they doing?" Reece grumbled.

Collins squeezed his jaw shut. He knew exactly why neither man had delivered the punch they both desperately desired to throw. Aimee was belowdecks and her cabin was close to where Gilley and Bean stood. And like every other fool on this ship, they had fallen for her charms. Collins had given up his attempts to prevent it from happening.

He had tried to keep her in her cabin. He had even assigned one of the ordinary seamen to stand guard and make sure she did not leave. But later that night, he found the infuriating woman on the main deck—with Smiley right at her side. Collins had been about to go over there and explain to the man that he had been ordered to be her guard, not her escort, when Collins saw that they were not alone. There, for all to see, was Aimee, sitting and talking with several seamen who were off shift. He had gone over to put a stop to it, knowing how much the crew coveted their free time and sleep, but by the time he got close enough, he realized the seamen not only accepted her presence; they desired it.

Deadeye was playing his violin, something he had not

done in weeks, and all of the men—along with Aimee—
were singing. Softly, but the tune was one with which he
was familiar. It was called "The Wrecked Ship," about a
ship that sank and had no survivors. He had intended to interrupt and remind them that Aimee was not just any
woman but a titled lady, but instead found himself joining
in, helping the others teach her the lyrics to another three or
four sea songs. He probably would have been there all night
if it had not been for the early morning watch coming on
deck to assume their shift.

It was then Collins realized Aimee Wentworth was no
angel. She was a menace, able to remove the good sense God
gave men. It was up to him to put an end to her escapades.
His intentions must have been obvious because Carr had
come to his cabin in the morning and asked Collins to let
things be. The bosun had many responsibilities, but one of
the most important was being the deck crew foreman. And
Carr was one of the best. So when his bosun had explained
how he was getting more work out of the men than ever by
allowing those who completed their duties to go up on deck
at night, Collins had given in, despite his gut telling him that
giving Aimee such freedom was dangerous.

Reece looked over his shoulder at his chief mate. The
damn man had gone just as mute as the two men glaring at
each other on the main deck. The whole crew was acting
strange. It was as if they had all become pacifists while in
London. The curses that could be heard all throughout the
day and night were a fraction of their normal volume and
vulgarity. After a week at sea, he should have heard Collins
threaten bodily injury to at least one of the able-bodied
seamen. And yet nothing.

Reece was about to demand an explanation for why
everyone was acting like their mothers were on board when
he saw Carr step up onto the deck. *Finally*, Reece thought
to himself. Carr was one of those bosuns who knew just

when men needed to be separated and when they needed to be let free to settle things physically.

Reece watched, half anticipating for Carr to order the two men to fight it out. But upon hearing what the bosun did order, Reece lost his balance and would have fallen had he not been holding on to the side rail.

Apologize? Asking a seaman to apologize was about as ludicrous as asking JP to offer lessons in cooking. It was possible but so unlikely it was a waste of time. Reece turned and was about to head for the main deck when he heard Carr again make the demand.

"Ya heard me! Shrug 'er off and get back to what yer supposed to be doin'. And you men, stop your shilly-shallying and help Gilley and Bean get things right and clean before *nightfall* comes." Not until he said *nightfall* did every man in sight perk up and start to work, helping to reset the sail and straighten up the deck.

Reece stopped in his tracks. His mind started to whirl. "Collins, if I didn't know better, I would think my whole damn crew fell in love while we were anchored in the Thames."

Collins took a deep breath and exhaled. "Highly, uh, doubtful, Captain." Reece was about to say that he did not *actually* believe his crew was in love but that something unusual was definitely going on, when Collins nervously stretched his neck and added, "Maybe, uh, Captain, I should just go down there and, um, have a talk with the bosun."

Reece blinked, stunned. His initial concern had been born from puzzlement, but now that Collins was acting just as jittery as the rest, Reece was actually concerned. Normally, his chief mate worried enough about the crew's behavior—explained and unexplained—for the both of them. It was one of the reasons Reece relied on Collins as much as he did.

Reece rocked back on his heels and shook his head,

trying to decide just how to handle his crew, when he heard one of the men on deck begin to hum. Others started to join him—including Carr and Collins. The haunting melody was the same damn tune Reece had been hearing in his dreams!

Squeezing his eyes shut, Reece shook his head back and forth. A large grin overtook his features as the feeling of relief flowed through his veins. He was an idiot. Someone had snuck a woman on board. Now, everything made sense.

He had not *imagined* a woman singing. A woman *had* been singing. It explained why the men acted as though they were in love. It even vindicated the mysterious mood swings Collins had been having. The last time a woman was on the *Sea Emerald*, it had been because of his chief mate. His relationship with Rosita had ended in disaster, just like all the others. First Blackie had tried, and even Jolly George had coaxed a woman on board, thinking himself in love. Most captains banned such activity, but not Reece. While things always started out fine, it was not long before hell of some nature broke out; that, more than any sanction he could impose, kept the women away.

However, Reece would give his men credit. They had been at sea nearly a week, which was the longest time a woman had been aboard without being the cause of some incident. Reece chuckled to himself, wondering just who it was who had smuggled her aboard.

He considered looking for her but immediately decided against the idea. Right now she was not a disruptive presence. In fact, as long as the crew was trying hard to keep her a secret, she was just the opposite. It was unfortunate that such peace and quiet would not last all the way to the Americas. The men would eventually explode and the woman would go from fascinating to annoying everyone around her.

Women were just not made for small spaces. The constant rocking made them dreadfully seasick and they were easily bored. They belonged on land, not at sea. Only there could they enjoy all those things—shopping, walking, stability, visits from friends—they constantly needed. So it was impossible the peace would last, but as long as he delayed "discovering" who she was, it remained Collins's problem to deal with.

Reece turned to go back to his cabin and once again heard the faint musical sound of a woman's voice reach his ears. He sighed. While it was good to know the reason behind his men's bizarre behavior, he just wished the damn woman's singing didn't remind him of Aimee. It was bad enough she plagued his dreams; he did not need her plaguing him while he was awake.

Chapter 7

October 14, 1816

Lord Aldon's heart seized as the enormous horse leaped over the obstacle. It seemed impossible that such a huge animal could hurl itself so high in the air or that such a small person could influence, let alone control it. But his Millie could. She had been able to do so since the day she had brought Hercules home—a present he had unwittingly purchased for her on her sixteenth birthday. That was nearly five years ago and they were still inseparable. The large mammal seemed to understand not only how small and vulnerable his daughter was but how much she adored him.

He watched as she slowed the black beast down and turned toward the stables. Each day she rode longer than the day before in her daily search for some type of relief. He recognized the pain etched in her face. It had been carved into his own the day her mother passed away. Only his Millie and his love for horses seemed to keep part of him anchored in the present. He did not want the same to happen to his daughter.

Lord Aldon sighed and dropped the curtains. It had been

nearly a week since his daughter arrived home unexpectedly and without explanation. Two days later Hercules was delivered with a brief note from Chase stating that Millie should not be without her horse while he remained in London. Lord Aldon never asked his daughter why or for how long she was visiting. In many ways, he did not want to know.

He liked his son-in-law. Liked him a lot. And he suspected that if he became aware of the particulars of Millie's visit and accompanying distress, his estimation of the highly regarded marquess would plummet to an irrecoverable level. Besides, it was not a father's place to interfere in a marriage, and when loved ones knew too much, they oftentimes could not help but interfere.

It was that premise which had kept him silent for nearly seven days. But watching his daughter fall deeper into despair, Lord Aldon had also come to the conclusion that distance and time were not helping. A little parental prodding was needed.

Lord Aldon approached the stables and immediately one of the younger hands rushed to open the doors. "Her ladyship has just returned, my lord. She insisted on brushing down her horse," the lad quickly added as a gentle reminder that Millie insisted on doing a stable hand's job when it came to Hercules.

"Hush, boy. I know my daughter and her peculiarities. Go off now and tend to your other duties." Lord Aldon moved around the numerous apparatuses and stalls, working his way down to the one Millie had selected long ago to house her horse.

Her mother died when Millie was a small child. The three of them had been very close, much closer than typical wealthy families, but then most marriages were for things such as convenience, money, land, and power—not love. So when his wife had been taken from this life, there was a time he had feared that he might never recover. He might not have, if he had not had Millie.

As she grew and her love for horses became as strong as his, he had built himself a matchless horse farm. The Derby, Ascot, and trips to Tattersalls became positive ways to pass the time. But the pleasure of the stables, the horseflesh, and daily rides would never give Millie the solace it gave him. Her problems resided with those who were alive, not dead. Millie needed to face her emotions, and until she did so, her misery would only grow.

"I saw you ride today. He's a mighty fine stepper, your horse."

Millie looked sideways at her father and continued the long, even brush strokes. "You didn't used to think so. In fact, I believe you thought him to be a monster."

Aldon chuckled. "Ah, well, that is because he is one, darling. But when a horse loves you, it makes all the difference." He watched Millie's brief smile retreat and her face become expressionless once again. "Do you remember when he was first delivered and how you begged and pleaded for weeks to ride him?"

"I distinctly remember each and every no."

"I was positive he would kill you, the one precious thing I had left in the world. Of course I said no. It was only later that I realized you would never cease hounding me, that your dogged personality would eventually outlast my protective nature."

Millie shot him a halfhearted smile. "Then I shall endeavor to acquiesce more often."

"You will not. Your tenacity is one of your most endearing qualities and one that too many lack. The more important something is to you, the more risks you are willing to take. You approach challenges directly, becoming *involved* in the solution, not content to stand by and wait for someone else to solve life's difficulties. It is a gift you got from your mother. It can be a frustrating trait for us . . . husbands and fathers, but in the end, such resolve is appreciated. Don't ever forget that," he finished, congratulating himself. It would be difficult for Millie to return to Chase and work out their problems, but based on the little nudge he just gave her, he felt assured she would.

Millie felt her father bend over and kiss the back of her head before leaving the way he came in. It was an unusual caring act, but one that touched her.

Her father clearly had been referring to her and Chase and the reasons behind her unexpected arrival at Abileen Rose. Thankfully, her father had never asked why she had come home or what was behind her growing depression. Yet he had recognized that she needed some guidance and decided to remind her of who she was.

Millie placed the brush down and called over an astonished hand to complete the job of cleaning Hercules. She wiped her hands on her short coat and exited the stables.

Her father was right. She had been waiting for others to take action, in the mistaken belief that Aimee would be quickly delivered back to London. That event had not occurred. From what Elda Mae said in her brief letter, a Bow Street runner had been a regular visitor to the London residence. Chase, however, had yet to write a single word. Why, Millie could only guess, but power and money were what was needed to find Aimee now. Something Chase had, not she.

If she could just *know* for certain that Aimee was on board the *Sea Emerald*, she would be able to better handle the other issues between her and Chase. But even those needed the affirmation that Aimee was safe and not in any danger if they were to be resolved. Sitting around waiting for answers went against every element of Millie's being and it was something she was not going to continue doing. If Chase would not or could not provide answers, then she would seek them herself.

As Millie walked back to the main house to change her clothes, she mulled over how someone would go about investigating an abduction from the London Docks. The answers that readily came to mind—interview dock owners, hire Bow Street runners, speak to those working that night— were no doubt steps that Chase had already taken. And if he had received no answers by now, there were either none to give or, more likely, those who knew something were keeping silent. Unfortunately, only certain women were accepted around the docks, and as a titled woman, Millie knew she would have little chance of success if she tried to obtain information there.

Millie paused midstride as an idea began to crystallize. She was wrong. There was a way to get the answers she was seeking. And it was something that Chase, his power, his money, or even his Bow Street runners could not do. She would need assistance, and her plan was not without risk, but at least she would be helping in the search for her friend.

Picking up her skirts, she ran the rest of the way, feeling something other than powerless for the first time since she saw Aimee being dragged away.

Chapter 8

October 15, 1816

Chase slid open the connecting door and entered Millie's empty bedchambers. After having discovered nothing about the thief and with no return of the *Sea Emerald* and his sister, he yearned for solace. So he sought the one thing that gave him a modicum of relief—the smells and comforts of his beloved wife.

Each night he opened the door and imagined Millie sitting at her dressing table, chattering aimlessly about some odd piece of information she had found amusing. Then he would walk over to the heavily padded leather wing chair she had placed by the hearth just for him. As he dropped into the chair, he would revisit his favorite memories. They were all of Millie.

He would recall her at twelve years of age, hopping around on one foot in her shift with her dark hair draped down over her shoulders and her lavender eyes snapping with fire. He had known then that Millie would become one of the most beautiful women he was ever likely to encounter, but it was only after he kissed her eight years later that he realized he was in danger. She had stirred passions in him he had not thought possible—and he had pushed her away. He had led the life of a spy, and to be with him would put her in danger. So he had struggled to keep her out of his life and away from the complications of his world.

Those closest to him and Millie had discerned their love for each other before they could even admit it to themselves. And the resulting ruse that had brought them together had caused the Season's largest stir, when in a jealous storm he decked Millie's escort, swung her, protesting vehemently, into his arms, and stomped out of a ballroom announcing to everyone that Lady Mildred Aldon was his fiancée. And every night since had been heaven, until six days ago when he had sent her away.

A week without the very person who made life worth living was a week in hell. Chase had not foreseen how difficult it would be. Hourly, he contemplated whether or not to send for her, but each time, he forced himself to shelve the idea. Millie was safer with her father and hopefully happier, away from the constant reminder of Aimee's disappearance.

Chase wished he had some news confirming Aimee's safety. It had been over a week since his ship, the *Zephyr,* had left to chase down the *Sea Emerald.* If Captain Spalding had been able to meet up with Reece and secure his sister, they would have returned by now. It had been a slim chance regardless, but Reece should have turned back anyway upon discovering Aimee aboard. With no sign of either ship, it might be another two months until Aimee was back home. That is, *if* she was aboard Reece's ship.

And until he learned something that either proved or disproved his sister's safety, he could not write to Millie.

Chase heard someone come up the staircase. The light footsteps definitely belonged to a woman. The housekeeper always retired early, and with Millie gone, none of the maids had a reason to come up here at night. He listened as whoever it was made their way down the empty hall, only to stop outside Millie's bedchambers—not his. It had to be Millie. His heart began to pound and his palms trembled with the need to touch her. How had she arrived without him knowing? How had she known to ignore his orders and come home, that he needed her desperately? Did she need him just as much? And suddenly he didn't care and rose from the chair the moment the door eased open and a candle flame lit the room.

Elda Mae entered and Chase immediately went still. He watched as she stole over to the bed, bent down, and opened a large travel trunk. Had the chest been there the whole time? Could it have just arrived? After placing a note on top of the folded items, Elda Mae stood back up, but before she could close the lid, she spied him standing there, watching her. The cold bleakness in her eyes gave him his answer. The chest was intended for Abileen Rose, and from the volume of its contents, it contained the rest of Millie's wardrobe. His wife thought to remain away, and for some time.

"I did not realize you were here, my lord. I shall leave immediately," Elda Mae said in a clipped voice.

Chase was well aware that Millie had asked her old nursemaid to remain at Hembree Grove. Millie trusted the woman implicitly and had undoubtedly asked her to apply her eavesdropping skills and relay any news of Aimee. Elda Mae was an excellent choice for a cohort, mostly because, while she respected Chase and his rank, she did not fear him in the least because they both knew he would not terminate her employment without Millie's consent.

"What is in that chest, Elda Mae?" Chase choked out.

"Exactly what it looks like, my lord. The rest of her ladyship's things."

This time Chase did not miss the coldness in the maid's tone. "And the note?" he asked, pointing at the folded item, waving at her to give it to him.

Elda Mae hesitated. His request was a demand, and they both knew that he was going to read her letter. She leaned over and snatched up the piece of paper. "I have nothing to hide and neither does her ladyship."

Chase took the letter and began to read.

My dearest Elda Mae,
*   Know that as I write this I am well and hope this letter finds you in good health. I must ask you to pack the rest of my things and send them to my father's estate, Abileen Rose. And though I know you will want to resist, I must beg you to remain at Hembree Grove. Please do not be troubled over Aimee. It shall not be long before this terrible wrong is righted.*

*   Dearest regards,*
*   M.*

Just below the signature, within the small amount of room remaining, was Elda Mae's reply.

Lady Chaselton,
*   Enclosed is what you requested. I will remain at Hembree Grove until you ask for my attendance, which I hope will be soon.*

*   E. M.*

Chase held the short message tightly in his grip as a never-ending emptiness threatened to swallow him whole. He watched his hand outstretch as Elda Mae took the letter and returned it to the chest. "I was unaware you know how to write."

Elda Mae grunted. "Most of us servants do. Now, if you will excuse me, my lord."

"Why does her ladyship wish you to stay here?"

Elda Mae stood still, thinking for several seconds before she answered. "I suspect with me around it won't look to the other servants as if you've abandoned your wife like you did."

"That's what you think?" Chase growled. "I didn't *abandon* my wife, Elda Mae. If anything, I am the one who should be pitied. I sent her home to be away from constant reminders. To keep her safe and away from danger. Trust me, Lady Chaselton is much happier at Abileen Rose."

"I don't doubt that she's happier not bein' lectured and held accountable for every thought and action of Lady Aimee's. But I don't think she's seein' your demand for her to leave her home as a compassionate move to keep her safe. I certainly know that I don't see it that way. Now, if you will excuse me, my lord. I have to speak to the footman and make sure this chest is delivered to her ladyship right away." Elda Mae gave a short, perfunctory curtsy and then picked up the candle and headed to the door.

"I'm not going to explain myself to you, old woman . . ."

Elda Mae stopped by the door and pivoted to look Chase directly in the eye. "I didn't suppose you would, as you couldn't even give that small amount of kindness to your wife." Chase glared at her, but Elda Mae's hazel eyes held firm. "You say you acted out of concern for her ladyship's welfare. But have you once looked at the things that happened that night from her ladyship's point of view, my lord? Have you thought about what's going to happen because you didn't?" Elda Mae huffed and turned back around, but before she left the room, she added, "For your sake, I hope you do so soon."

Chase's jaw tightened and he forced himself to relax. Elda Mae had only been protecting Millie. And if it had been anyone else who had hurt his wife, he would have supported the old woman coming to his wife's defense. He wished he could have offered a smooth, simple explanation for his behavior, but he could not chance her telling Millie. For without a doubt, she would.

Chase returned to the chest and retrieved the note. Going back to his room, he sat by the small writing desk and read it again.

It shall not be long before this terrible wrong is righted.

Millie still loved him, believed in him. She was waiting for him to send her good news. Putting the note aside, he dipped the quill in ink and began to write. He explained what he had learned about Aimee and that he truly believed her safe. He wrote about the thief and how he had yet to be seen again, but that Chase suspected he was not yet done. He told her he was still trying to determine just what the thief was after and that he was doing all he could to resolve the situation so he could bring her safely back home. Mostly, he wrote about how much he loved and missed her and that she would only have to wait a little longer. He signed it and returned the quill to its holder.

Standing up, he picked up the sheet, uncaring that the wet ink stained his hands, crumpled the paper, and then tossed it into the fire. The letter was not a kindness. Upon receiving such news—of Aimee's probable well-being, of the thief and the possibility that he would steal again—no threat or entreaty could prevent Millie from coming home.

Chase watched as the white sheet crackled and turned black in the flames. He suspected he would write to her several more times in the days to come, and vowed to put them all into the fire.

Aimee picked up her empty plate and headed to the kitchen. She knocked on the door, and after no response the second time, she walked in, affirming that JP was not inside. Based on the steam rising from one of the pots, he had not been gone long and was most likely on his way to Reece and Mr. Collins with their evening meals.

With a sigh, she placed her plate onto the stack of the other dirty dishes waiting to be washed. She was so bored, she would have cleaned them, but the last time she had volunteered to do so, she had received an emphatic no.

The cook was a complex man. Upon first being introduced, she thought him gruff in manner. Now she realized that compared to the hostility JP showed most of the crew, he was practically fawning over her. It explained why she got a plate when so many others ate from a handkerchief or whatever they could carry. It also explained why the meals were apparently a little more varied than normal. But Aimee suspected that their menu would soon become monotonous. The fruits and vegetables were almost gone. And if Reece had not been in the navy, where canning was first tried and proven a viable way to preserve food, her diet would soon be just meat and hard bread.

Aimee was not deluded to think that she would relish such simple meals, but like the rest of the Daring Three, she was glad that dietary variety was not a requirement for happiness.

Deciding to sneak out rather than risk JP finding her there, Aimee left the kitchen and headed back to the cabin that the men had finally decided would be permanently hers. She took one step inside and plopped down onto the bed. The room was very small, but that was not what bothered her. It was the having nothing to do.

She sat up and looked out the porthole to confirm what she suspected. The sun was nearly down and soon she would hear the whistle for the second dogwatch. Her body was getting attuned to the three- to four-hour watch cycles, and she was now sleeping as the nightshift crew did—in the morning.

Sighing, she lay back down and studied the grain on the

wood slat above her. Remaining hidden was now her choice. In another week her wrists would be healed, but it was clear that she would have scars. And because of that, she suspected Collins would let her remain hidden for as long as she wanted, knowing every day brought them closer to the Americas and delayed Reece's wrath. While she wanted to remain hidden for at least another week, which would ensure they were closer to America than to England, she was unsure she could do it.

Every cabin was now clean. She had even managed to convince the men to let her wash their clothes. She had never done such labor, but then she thought the men probably had never had their clothes cleaned before and would not know if she had done a poor job.

She had tried to convince Jean-Pierre to let her help in the kitchen some more, but it was not long before he began to treat her like the main cook did at home. If she insisted, her presence would be allowed, but her help was absolutely not wanted. And truth was, cooking was fun only if you had more ingredients to use than were available on board.

Over the past few days, the men had snuck by to give her gifts. One had brought her some dyes to use as water paints, another some pencils and paper, and even one crewman called Red Legs Solomon had whittled her a paintbrush as they sat out singing and talking one night. And she had painted, but there were only so many times she could recreate the sea using her porthole as a reference.

The piercing sound of the second mate's whistle calling the next shift broke her self-pitying train of thought. Time was her enemy. At home, she would have painted. Part of her longed to be able to do so again, but what she really needed was to be useful. If Millie were here, she would look around and decide for herself what she could do, and then make it happen. And if Mildred Aldon Wentworth could do it—so could she.

Swinging her legs around so that they hung off the bed, Aimee leaned over and picked up the broken piece of mirror one of the men had given her. Her appearance was nothing close to what her lady's maid could do, but all things considered, she looked quite presentable. It helped that she had convinced Collins to let her bathe again yesterday, so she also smelled better than she had. And tonight she needed to use what few assets she had.

For this was the last afternoon she intended to sit bored in her room with nothing to do.

"Miss! Come 'n' watch us! Tonight we got us a full moon, so we was goin' to play us some cards. Ya can see me teach ol' Swivel Eye Stu a few tricks."

Aimee came closer and dragged a nearby crate over to use as a seat. "Why, I would love to join you, Mr. Stuart, along with Mr. Easter and Mr. Linwood, but not to watch. I would like to join your game."

Skylark Linwood, nicknamed for the tunes he could play, grimaced. Swivel Eye nudged him with his elbow. "Come on, Skylark. 'Twould make it more fun to play with four till the others get up 'ere."

Linwood's frown only grew more severe. Thin and wiry, he had a long neck and a protruding Adam's apple. "I don't mind playin' wid ya, miss, if ya knew da game, but as ya don't, it might be best for ya to watch."

Aimee nodded. "I agree, Mr. Linwood. But it may be that I know how to play, for I am knowledgeable of the rules to several games. My friends and I play them regularly. Of course, I am not the master my best friends are, but I have learned a few of their tricks this past year. I would love to apply them amongst seasoned players."

"Ya don't have any stakes though."

Aimee's green eyes flashed. "You forget that I've seen you play before, Mr. Linwood. You play for duties, not funds."

"Miss, ya have no chores to be givin' us and ya knows that we're not goin' to be givin' you ours," said Swivel Eye Stu.

"True. How about if I lose, then I owe you a portrait." Aimee frowned, pretending to think hard. "And if I win, you have to teach me about what you do."

Tom Easter cocked a brow and folded his arms. "I ain't bloody teachin' anybody a bloody damn thing."

Aimee studied the most normal-looking of all the seamen. He was average size in bulk and height. He even had brown hair and brown eyes. In Town, nothing about him would have made him memorable, but on the ship, his normalcy made him stand out. "Mr. Easter, I thank you for the compliment. You must believe that I will win."

Swivel Eye Stu slapped his knee. A thin man with a wandering left eye, he talked fast, moved fast, and tended to nick himself shaving. "Aw, miss, Bloody Tom might be thinkin' that, but I sure ain't!"

An hour later, Aimee laid down her cards with a smile. More men had joined the games, and she had lost several hands but had won quite a few too. And while she intended to pay her debts, she also intended to collect what was due her.

"Ahh, my lady, you are quite the strategist. It is not often I find someone who can match my skills."

Aimee politely shrugged. The crew called him Englishman, mostly due to his proper speech, but Digby Miller reminded her of Reece a few years ago. He was smart, young, and hardworking. He also aspired to become a captain and like Reece, he intended to remain unmarried. "Mr. Miller, I shall enjoy our lesson."

The group had grown too large to play cards anymore, so Swivel Eye Stu put them away. Aimee leaned back against the side of the ship and asked, "Mr. Solomon, how is it that you were given the name Red Legs? Your pants are dark, like the others."

"That's cuz his name has nothin' to do with his pants," said Skylark Linwood.

Swivel Eye Stu nodded. "Aye, 'ol Red Legs was late one day 'n' wakin' up. He ran so fast he was on deck 'fore he realized he forgot his pants. The bosun refused to let him go get 'em. And so his white legs turned bright red in the sun. You should have seen 'em."

Solomon scowled at Linwood and Swivel Eye. "Hurt like hell, too. Never would've thought the sun could cause a man to feel such pain. Somethin' you might be careful of, miss. The sun on deck can be a mighty powerful thing."

Aimee almost reminded him that she was never up on deck during the day, but decided against it. "Mr. Miller," she said, pointing to the mainmast. "How do you raise those large sails and the ones above them?"

"Different ways. With the capstan, or those"—he pointed to fore-and-aft sails—"the jibs, staysails, and spanker are pulled up using a line that goes up the mast to the halyard— that perpendicular piece of wood. The lines are connected to a sail's corners, which allow the yards to control the sails. We use braces—that rope right there—to set the angle of the yard so we can catch the wind."

Aimee followed everything he said. It was difficult in the dark to see all the details, but the ropes were clear enough in the moonlight, as well as how they were connected to the mast and yard. "What about those? Are those done the same way?"

Bloody Tom scoffed. "'Ardly."

"No, my lady. Those are too high and must be set by climbing into the rigging."

"I am guessing that responsibility is not yours."

The Englishman's eyes grew large. "No, my lady. None of us can do that work. Only the rigger's willing to work that high."

"Only *one* person?" Aimee asked for clarification.

"Both the sailmakers also climb the masts to help when needed, but no one else does."

Aimee sighed, looking up at the sail at the very top, thinking that she could climb that high and not be scared. It was one of the few truly adventurous things that she could do better than Millie or Jennelle.

Chapter 9

October 17, 1816

"Mr. Willnon?" Aimee asked as she poked her head down into the opening that led to the lowest point on the ship. It was also one of the foulest smelling. "Are you in here?"

She saw the flame from the lantern first and then a stooped, round-faced man appeared. His shape and form reminded her of a well-fed nobleman, but unlike those she knew with Dudley's proportions, he had energy and worked hard. Dark hair grew everywhere she could see—his forearms, beard, even his knuckles—just not on his head.

"My lady, you shouldn't be down 'ere."

Aimee smiled. Most of the seamen were gruff with her when she caught them unawares, but she knew it was more an act for their fellow shipmates than real anger. Dudley Willnon was an exception, perhaps because he was happily married and everyone he worked with knew it.

"Mr. Willnon, what is this place?" Aimee asked, continuing to stay just outside the small area.

"The bilge."

"What is it for? And why does it smell . . . so wet and damp?"

Dudley pointed his finger for her to back up, and she did so happily. He closed the hatch and made way to move around her, but Aimee stepped into his path. Realizing she would not move until he answered her question, he grumbled, "What rain don't go off the deck and back into the sea, eventually comes here. The weight can make it safer in rough weather, but too much slows us down."

"So what do you do when too much water collects down here?"

Dudley tensed his jaw. His mother had taught him better than to talk about something like bilges to any female. "Me lady, is there somethin' you need?"

Aimee pursed her lips and decided that she knew enough about the bilge from its smell. Besides, she had other reasons to meet with Dudley, and this was the first opportunity she'd had to observe him at night, for normally he worked the day shifts.

She lifted up her hand so that he could see the two palm-sized ovals she held. Dudley moved the lantern closer and saw that they were portraits of Swivel Eye Stu and Gilley—two of the sorrier-looking men on the *Sea Emerald*.

"I did these this morning. Do you think they will like them?"

Aimee shifted her hand so he could take a better look. Both men looked like who they were, and yet she had drawn them as they would have looked if given the clothes and the funds. They almost looked like gentlemen. Even in the dark shadows of the inner hull, Aimee could see Dudley was not just surprised but impressed.

"Blimey," he muttered. "Do they know? That they look like . . . that . . . ?"

Aimee shook her head. "Not at this time, though I do plan to give them their portraits later. If you recall, I lost a couple of games playing cards with them and this is my payment. I owe you as well, Mr. Willnon. I thought I would create something similar for you to give to your wife."

Dudley's face broke out into a very large grin and she knew that she was on the verge of achieving what she came down here to do. She had purposely started with the two hardest men to draw, but the most willing to talk and teach her. But as ordinary seamen, it had not taken very long before Stu and Gilley had divulged as much as she wanted to know on how to keep the ship clean and in working order. Aimee was far more interested in the rigging, sail-making, and how to work the ship. That was the work of able-bodied seamen.

"Me wife," Dudley repeated aloud, his eyes shining with the idea. "Would you, me lady? Just tell me what I need to do and when. And I'll be there."

Shaking her head, Aimee slipped the two portraits back into the side pocket of her dress. "No need, Mr. Willnon. I can get all I need when I join you on your shift right now."

"Did you say *join* me?"

Aimee nodded. "I'll shadow you, not for the whole time, but just enough for me to get an understanding of what you do."

The line of his mouth tightened a fraction more. "Now what do you want to learn a sailor's job for? Not like you're going to do it."

Aimee stifled the desire to stomp her foot like Millie did in times of frustration. "Your captain and chief mate do not do the things you do either, but they know them."

"That's because they're the captain and the chief. You're . . . a . . . well, a woman. Females shouldn't know such things."

"Mr. Willnon, that is simply a ridiculous statement invented to protect the pride of a man. Besides, we had an agreement when we played cards the other night."

For a long moment, Dudley just looked at Aimee. He had no idea just what all those fancy words meant, but he was fairly certain that she had taken exception to his comment. "How was I supposed to know you was serious?"

"About learning the ship? Yes, I am quite serious. I know very little about ships, and as I am on one, and will be for several more weeks, I would like to end my ignorance. Regardless of my reasons, you are indebted to me to share your knowledge, and as an honorable man, I am sure you will settle this matter by letting me join you on your shift."

Dudley's eyes had grown dark and insolent, and Aimee realized she might have just pushed the kind man too far with her speech. "Mr. Willnon, please help me. Do you never wish that your wife better understood your passion for sailing and the sea?"

Dudley twisted his lips and looked at her enigmatically. Finally, he gave her a single nod.

Aimee's face brightened and she continued. "I have a problem, Mr. Willnon. I suspect everyone aboard the ship has been told about my feelings for Mr. Hamilton, but he still views me as the little girl I once was. He believes I am fragile and soft and come from a life that prevents me from understanding who he is. I need to prove to him that I understand his world—that it is gritty, hard, and oftentimes uncomfortable—and that I appreciate it and even sometimes want to join it. I do not need to be pampered to be happy. And I am not a weak female who needs to be protected. But he will never believe me unless I can prove to him otherwise."

Dudley's eyes shifted from stony to gentle and contemplative. *Damn good argument*, he thought to himself.

No one had to tell him about her feelings for the captain, for it was obvious. She would often look to the place the captain stood when he was on the upper deck. And if she really was the one who created all the consternation whenever they had to go to London, then it was clear the captain loved her in return. And Dudley had no doubt she was indeed that person. Many of the men were falling for her, and he might have too, if he were not already fully enamored of his wife. Regardless, all understood she belonged to the captain—even if he was the only one who did not realize it.

Dudley felt himself giving in. "You won't be interferin'? Slowin' me down? Chatterin' on about nonsense?"

A satisfied light crept into Aimee's green eyes. "I promise."

Dudley grabbed one of her wrists and pulled it into the light. "And these?"

Aimee raised her chin and said nothing.

The skin on her wrists was new and pink, but in a few more days the bright color would dim, leaving white scars. Dudley did not like to think about the captain seeing them. They alone would probably keep Aimee from ever setting another foot on a ship. Though her quest was doomed, Dudley refused to be part of the reason Aimee thought she had failed. "Don't tell any of the other men."

"I won't say a thing," she promised and followed him out of the inner hull.

Before the end of the shift, there was not a seaman—ordinary or able-bodied—who did not know Dudley was telling Aimee all about what he was doing and why. As a result, the men were more willing to not just let her repay what she owed them, but settle their debts as well. It was as if she was the first person to be interested in learning from them rather than telling them how to do their jobs.

Now she just needed to convince the crew members who did not owe her anything to talk to her as well.

Millie sat down and opened the third and last trunk Elda Mae had sent to her. It had taken nearly three days for her maid to get the message and send the items. In truth, it was a remarkably short time, but to Millie it had felt like forever.

Once she had made the decision to stop waiting for Chase to deal with her mistakes, she wanted to begin immediately. She could have gone to her father for funds, but it was likely that he would want explanations—or alert Chase to her unusual request.

One by one Millie pulled out and discarded items. Her old nursemaid had been fastidious and had done exactly as requested. She had packed *everything* Millie had left behind. That was the only way Millie knew to prevent Elda Mae from becoming suspicious. For if she had asked for only the few items she was truly interested in, Elda Mae would have arrived with the trunks, and then there would have been no way Millie could have enacted her plan.

She reached in and sighed with relief as her fingertips clasped the dark burgundy velvet cloak Madame Sasha had made for her last spring when it was still cold at night. She spread it wide over the floor and then reached into the trunk to pull out the last item she needed to venture into a place where a woman of her rank would never be found.

On the bottom was a small, old locked chest with gold filigree roses decorating the cedarwood. Her father had requisitioned it for her mother when they moved to Wareham and purchased Abileen Rose. Her mother had loved roses and had planted them all around the estate. Millie lightly fingered the item before confirming the small revolver was still inside. Then she placed it on the ground beside her cloak.

Starting at one end, she pressed the hem, feeling for bulk. Finding none, she continued along the edge until she heard a soft crumpling sound. She grabbed the scissors on her dressing table and carefully cut the thread that hid the concealed papers. At the snap of the last string, out flew nearly a hundred pounds. Only a tiny fraction of that was needed to get her to London, but she may need more for her plan to work.

Every*thing* she needed was here. Now she just needed every*one*—each in their own way.

Anxious to get started, Millie laid out a traveling outfit and threw together a light trunk of personal items along with her plainest garments. Next, she sat down and quickly scribed three notes. The first was to Jennelle, telling her to expect her arrival. The second was to her father, explaining that he was indeed right. Sitting and waiting when she could take action to solve her problems would only bring her unhappiness. She just hoped Chase would understand and eventually accept that for her to be happy, she had to be free to be herself.

The last note was an entreaty to the one person who might understand and support her idea—Madame Sasha, who was much more than just a gifted modiste.

"Damn Chaselton, damn his title, damn his wife, and damn everything he holds dear," muttered a deformed figure looming over what turned out to be an incomplete replica of the first map in the series. He should have known when he grabbed the item that the vellum felt much too pliable to be a relic nearly eight hundred years old.

His warped hand crumpled the reproduction and threw it into the hearth, snarling at the smell of burning animal skin. He had been followed tonight and had almost been caught. The runner was more skilled than most of his kind, but he had not been trained by someone like him—a master in lies, deception, and spying. He had trained Chaselton himself, and should have predicted that his one-time protégé would make such a clever move.

Tonight's misstep had just confirmed what the marquess probably had only suspected—that the targets were the unusual maps purchased by chance last year. Then again, the withered man thought as he tapped a finger against his chin, maybe it was not chance that placed the maps in his enemy's hands, but fate. He wanted it to be Chaselton. Who better to provide the means to destroy him?

Chaselton might have been lucky and thwarted him once, but he would not do so a second time. He had no doubt that one, maybe two, of the nine maps were on the *Sea Emerald*. He had the one from the offices of W & H Shipping near the docks, as well as the ones off the *Intrepid* and the *Sea Rebel*. Last night, he had successfully found another in Reece Hamilton's empty townhome. That left three more, which were most likely hidden away at Hembree Grove. And while Chaselton might now know that the maps were being stolen, he still had no idea why they were of value. Both he and his partner, Reece Hamilton, still thought they were related to sea navigation and would continue along the path of such misguidance until it was too late.

"Ah, Chaselton. You may be aware that you have an unusual thief on your hands. You even now know what is being stolen, but you do not know *why*. This time, only I have the answer."

Chapter 10

October 18, 1816

"Aye, my lord. That's the way of it. I followed him meself, but he musta known 'cause he disappeared like he ne'er was there. Mighty strange that."

Chase eyed the odd-looking man in front of him. He was of average height, muscular from years of hard labor, with thin brown hair that was turning gray around his temples. Chase had used the Bow Street runner before because he was discreet, smart, and capable for someone who had learned everything from the streets. With training, he could have made an excellent spy except for one thing—the man had a memorable face.

His mouth was small, which was made to look even more so with wide cheeks and bushy dark brown eyebrows. A somewhat bulbous nose conflicted with close-set eyes, making them look smaller than they were. Not any one feature was in itself remarkable, but put together, it made Randall Greery quite unforgettable. "Where did you lose him, Mr. Greery?"

"Out on the docks. He was moving along the Thames, leaving Blackwall and heading toward Bugsby's Reach when I lost him. I didn't believe anyone knew the East India Docks better than me, but he moved like a native to the waterfront," Greery said, still puzzled how the man had simply vanished rounding a small crate of tinned meat.

Unfortunately, that told Chase very little. "Were you able to at least verify that the thief got what he was after?" Chase asked, half expecting another negative answer.

"Yes, my lord." Greery coughed and frowned. Depending on the job—and the pay—he would often employ one or two others he trusted to assist with a case. Tonight had been one of those times. "One of me men, Roberts, put the map you gave us in with the others, like you asked. It's gone, along with the case to your telescope, my lord."

"Just the case?"

Greery bobbed his head. "Yes, my lord. Roberts found the telescope lying under the table as if it were thrown aside."

Chase leaned back in his chair and thought for a second. "And have you been able to determine if any other ships are missing charts, maps, or drawings of some sort?"

This time Greery grimaced. "None, my lord. There've been the normal robberies and skirmishes around the docks—food, money, and the like—but nothing on any of the ships. With the exception of W & H Shipping, the rest have been left alone."

Chase drummed his fingers noiselessly on the map in front of him. On the surface, he was dealing with a simple burglar who was doing nothing more nefarious than taking some worthless pieces of paper. But the moment Millie told him about her encounter, his gut had twisted. His every instinct said this thief was far from harmless. The man had been too good slipping in and out of guarded places. And based on Greery's feedback, he was also skilled at evading being seen and disappearing when being tailed. That level of skill required practice. This thief was not going to be found unless he was lured into a trap.

So when the *Tempest* came into port, Chase had moved quickly. The forgery had been decent—good enough to fool someone as they quickly located and absconded with it, but its primary purpose was to goad the man into making another move sooner versus later.

"Mr. Greery," Chase began in a tone that indicated a change in topic. "Were you able to discover anything on the pinnace?"

"Aye, my lord, good news. I was able to track down the models of all five ships that left port that night. Three of them definitely did not have pinnaces at all. One may have had them, but crewmen that had worked aboard her several times said they only used the jolly boats, and they were painted blue. That leaves only the *Sea Emerald,* whose pinnaces we know for certain are painted green and white. I got some of my less reputable men to talk to a few laborers on the docks that night, and they confirmed what the workers already told you. They thought the boy being grabbed was a drunken shipmate, for he did not fight or cry out for help."

Chase nodded, relieved to learn that his original conclusions were most likely correct despite the fact that the *Sea Emerald* had yet to return to London. Aimee was most likely with Reece, which meant the most likely reason his friend had not yet turned around was that his sister was intentionally keeping her presence on board quiet.

Aimee was a master at swaying people to her point of view. Even better than Millie when so inclined—and when it came to Reece, she would be highly motivated to extend her time on the *Sea Emerald* by any means possible. Chase hoped she was miserable and learning her lesson, but knowing his sister, she probably was in control of most of the crew, using her innocent looks and seemingly sweet nature to finagle a room, food, and as comfortable a life as one could get on a ship.

"Are you *very* certain, Mr. Greery?" Chase asked, his gold eyes boring into the older man's dark ones.

The Bow Street runner blinked. The task of finding out about the small rowing boat had been an odd request, and not until now did he realize how serious the lord felt about it. Fortunately, Greery did his job thoroughly and quickly, regardless of the task. "Aye, my lord. Most certain, if the description you gave me was accurate."

"Five quid is what we agreed, I believe," Chase said, and opened a drawer to pull out a small stack of paper. He thumbed out ten bills and placed them down on the desk, then pointed to it. "That's the five we agreed to, and another five for you to ensure your men remain quiet about all they asked and saw."

Greery eyed the money as it slid toward him on the desk, shocked that the marquess had just given him ten pounds. "Thank you, your lordship. They'll be quiet and I'll be keeping my ears open for news of your thief. If you ever be needing help again, you just find me."

Chase watched as the bulky man strode out of his study. He had an uneasy feeling that he would be calling again for Mr. Greery, and disturbingly soon.

Chase sat back in his coach as the driver departed for home. *Home*, he thought with bitterness. These days it felt more like an elaborate dwelling.

Until Millie left, he had thought it was his mother who had made Hembree Grove feel warm and welcoming. But she had left for Scotland nearly five weeks ago, and not until Millie's absence had he actually felt lonely. Even being among a crowd of people this evening had done nothing to relieve that feeling.

He had stayed at White's club for too long. Soon after Greery had left Hembree Grove, Chase immediately assigned guards inside every entrance, with instructions to capture and hold anyone who tried to go in, then send word to him at White's. He had also decided to retrieve the map that Reece kept at his townhome to study, and keep it with the three he had safely hidden away. Unfortunately, he was too late. The place had already been raided, most likely that morning. Which meant Hembree Grove was likely the next target.

Chase considered going back home, but the thief was most likely watching and waiting for him to leave. Chase wanted no more delays. More than anything, he wanted this mystery solved. He needed his life to return to normal. Chase wanted his wife back where she belonged—in his arms, his bed, and his everyday life. So he had headed to White's.

He had actually looked forward to the noise and people, which was unusual for a man who coveted his solitude. Upon his marriage to Millie, he had feared his home would become boisterous, filled with chaos. But he quickly discovered that he could enjoy the peace he so desired and her company at the same time. He had been quite surprised to learn how easily his wife became engrossed in a book, or writing letters, and a myriad of things.

Millie seemed to know when he needed companionship and silence, and helped steer his sister to other parts of the house when he needed to be alone. Likewise, he had learned to discern when to offer companionship when she needed it. After the way he had ordered her departure, Chase wondered if she missed his company as much as he missed hers.

Each day he half hoped, half expected her to defy his command to stay away, and return to Hembree Grove, ready to argue with him until he relented. If Reece's town house had not been vandalized so soon after the forgery had been stolen, he might have given in to his own desires and asked for her to return. But no longer did he intend to maintain the silence between them.

He had not meant to cause such a rift. By now, Reece was to have returned Aimee, and Chase had expected to have resolved the issue with the maps. Never was his separation from Millie to last this long. It was nearing two weeks and could possibly continue for two more. And he had yet to send her a letter.

At first, he had not done so because he knew Millie would want to know about Aimee, and he refused to lie and say that she was fine when he was not absolutely positive. He also did not want to say Aimee's whereabouts were unknown, when he was fairly certain she was with Reece. But just because he had not been sending her letters did not mean he had not been writing her. He had written every day. And in every letter he wrote the one thing that prevented it from going to the post. *Come home.*

Tonight, sitting alone, listening to all the random, inconsequential conversations around him, Chase realized she was just returning his silence. He had been a fool. By not sending Millie his thoughts and feelings about her, she had in return refused to send him anything regarding hers. He left White's immediately, having deciding the damn thief could wait another night to raid his home. He needed to write a letter to his wife and then *send it*.

He mentally urged the driver to go faster, eager to begin. He would tell her what he knew of Aimee. She deserved to know. He would convey just how much he missed her and that he would be joining her as soon as he could. Until then, there would no longer be this wall of silence between them. They would write with the understanding that soon she would be in his arms, where she belonged.

Chase closed his eyes and imagined Millie's expression upon getting his letter, delighted that he had been the first to give in. She would be relieved about Aimee and perhaps even decide to pack and return to London. He would send another letter to her father, stressing there was the possibility of danger and to do what he could to keep his daughter with him at Abileen Rose.

Reassured now that he had a plan to at least mend things between him and his wife, Chase smiled as the coach came to a halt. He hopped out, waved the driver to take care of the horses and retire, and then headed up to the front door. Instead of opening as customary upon his arrival, it remained shut. All the windows were dark.

Pushing open the door, Chase looked for the two guards he had assigned there, but found none. Neither could he see any evidence of a disturbance. He took another step inside and heard a scuffling coming from down the hall, near the kitchens. He paused, waiting to see if it was one or both of the guards returning to their post, but the soft noise stopped.

Frowning, Chase loosened his cravat. He rubbed his face, debating how to handle the guards when they returned from their midnight break, when he heard the scuffling noise again. This time it did not sound like it came from the back rooms, but his study. Immediately, years of trained instincts went on alert.

Moving quietly, he headed toward the study and nudged open the door. Reaching along the wall, his fingertips came into contact with the hilt of a sword. It looked decorative, but it was also deadly, for he had made sure it was regularly polished and honed. Once the long blade was in his grasp, he whirled his body inside, ready to attack whoever was there, but the room was empty. The thief had used the connecting door to the drawing room, near the front entrance.

Chase heard the soft click of a door opening and immediately pivoted to give chase. He made it outside just in time to see a hack, which must have been waiting, vanish down

North Audley Street. Going back inside, the open door to
the drawing room caught his attention, for just inside were
the bodies of the two night guards. Blood from their head
wounds was pooling on the floor, but thankfully both were
still breathing, if only just barely.

Servants appeared, most of them still dressed in their
sleep attire. Chase quickly gave orders to go for the doctor
and to send word that he wanted to see Bow Street runner
Randall Greery as soon as possible. Then he went into his
study and shut the door. The room looked untouched but not
his desk. Chase went over and simultaneously pushed down
on the desk's inlay and the Chaselton crest, freeing a secret
drawer. Inside, he had left several unimportant papers. They
were still there, but not as he had left them.

Chase grimaced. Closing the drawer, he pulled a pedestal
up close to the wall. Standing upon it, he reached up to un-
screw the end of the rod from which hung a large, heavy
portrait of his grandfather. It was the one place Chase
thought might remain hidden, even if the thief had ravaged
his study. From the rod he pulled out and unrolled three old
vellum maps: the one he had kept to study, the one dropped
when the thief had left the *Zephyr*, and the one he had
switched out on the *Tempest*.

He glanced at them once again but still saw nothing that
would tell him just why they might be so valuable to someone. They had nothing in common beyond their overall
appearance and origination. Only someone who knew and
studied maps might be able to discern just what it was that
made these particular ones so unique.

Chase rolled them back up and slid them back into the
rod. He then returned the pedestal and went over to collapse
on the settee to think.

As expected, the thief had come into his home, but Chase
had not anticipated the man would be able to overcome two

guards. The strikes had been precise and potentially deadly, which only someone with extensive combat training would know how to do. The attacker had also known about the secret drawer in his desk. But what concerned Chase the most was that the thief had known just how to escape. The thief was not a stranger but someone who had been in his home and in his study. Someone he trusted.

Any wavering thoughts he had about allowing Millie to return home vanished. Until now, the incidents had been benign, but now he was dealing with a dangerous villain. Tonight he had been unsuccessful in finding the three maps he knew Chase had in his possession, which meant next time he was going to get creative.

Only three things in Chase's life could be used as leverage against him. His mother, who was safe in Scotland; his sister—who, ironically, had placed herself in safety when she allowed herself to be abducted by Reece's men; and his wife—his greatest weakness.

He had almost lost Millie to a madman once. Never again. However long it took, she was going to remain safely away from anyone who thought to use her to force his hand.

In another part of the house, Elda Mae quickly lit a candle. She took out some paper and an inkwell and sat down. Taking a deep breath, she attempted to calm her excited nerves. For too many days, she had watched and listened for anything the master did, but he was just as silent as the house.

Visitors had stopped by for business, but only one had been summoned to handle the riddles of the thief and of Aimee. Elda Mae had told the rest of the staff to find her, for she must be present when the Bow Street runner came to call. But until today, her eavesdropping had resulted in nothing of value. More questions than answers. But much had happened this day.

Elda Mae did not know where to begin. What should she relay first? That Aimee was most likely safe and with Reece? Or that the marquess was in grave danger?

Chapter 11

October 19, 1816

Millie stepped out of her father's post chaise in front of a sizeable gray stone manor that was Jennelle's residence. It was just as she remembered, though she had only visited the place a handful of times in her youth.

"Should I get your bags down, my lady?"

Millie looked back at the questioning expression on the older footman's wrinkled but very expressive face. "Yes, please," she answered and returned her gaze to the manor.

Four days ago, she had initiated her plan and then waited for a reply. It finally came two days later. All Madame Sasha's note said was *Gent Manor, Saturday 3 p.m.*, but that was enough. She would have only a little more than two hours to spend with Jennelle, though her friend thought otherwise.

Millie had not seen her since the day they had departed London. They had written to each other twice, but all of their correspondence had been brief, as the one topic they were most consumed with neither wanted to discuss. It was too hard to sit and wait and know nothing. Soon that would end, for Millie was determined to find out what had happened to Aimee.

Squaring her shoulders, she walked slowly up the stone steps. For a moment, a twinge of guilt pulled at her, but Millie pushed the feeling aside and was about to rap firmly on one of the old oak doors when it unexpectedly opened. Millie jumped back, startled. There before her was a *butler.* If not, it was an exceptionally small man dressed like one.

Two dark and wizened eyes narrowed at her and Millie stared curiously back. She suspected she was supposed to find the gaze intimidating, but she was too caught up in the fact that she was returning his gaze without having to tilt her chin even remotely upward. The man was born to be a jockey, not a butler. And yet he most certainly was one, something Millie never thought to see at the Gent Manor.

Jennelle's father, Lord Gent, had a fairly substantial stipend, which he generously used to support his love of knowledge by acquiring an ever-increasing amount of books. To spend coin on servants might infringe upon his ability to indulge in his favorite pastime. Millie could remember him saying more than once that all he required was a good cook and a dependable housekeeper. Over the years, Jennelle had managed to convince him that a scullery maid to help in the kitchens, a couple more housemaids, one of whom could assist as a lady's maid, and a stable master were also necessary. He had finally agreed on the promise that they would help to keep his life peaceful and allow limited interruptions when he was doing his research and writing.

Seeing the improvement the handful of staff made to the quality of their living environment, Jennelle had then attempted to persuade her father to hire a butler and a gardener, but this time he had adamantly refused. "What do I need a gardener for, my dear?" he would ask. "We do not have parties. And neither you nor I is inclined to take turns about the hedges we have." Jennelle had often told Millie that she would have liked to walk in the gardens as she did so often when visiting her and Aimee, but could not, as hers were riddled with thorns.

The small man broke his gaze and gave a wide wave and bow for her to enter. "Lady Chaselton, please come in and I will see you to the salon." Once Millie entered the room, he spoke again. "I shall let Miss Perrin know you are here." And suddenly he was gone, leaving Millie to stare open-mouthed at the salon door.

Miss Perrin? she repeated silently, unable to make a sound. Granted, her friend *was* technically Jennelle Perrin, as her father was a baron. As such, she was supposed to be referred to as Miss Perrin in formal situations, but it had been years since anyone had called her that. Early into their friendship, Millie and Aimee realized that everyone addressed them as "lady," but not Jennelle. Thinking it quite unfair, they had decided everyone would call her Lady Jennelle. Mother Wentworth had readily agreed. It had taken some time to convince Chase, his friends, and all the servants, but they had eventually acquiesced to the girls' constant entreaties. The honorary title had been used for so long it had become second nature to use it. But it seemed Jennelle's butler was a stickler for the proprieties.

Millie was pulling off her second glove when double doors burst open and Jennelle rushed in. They embraced for several seconds before Jennelle finally pulled back. Her blue eyes studied Millie's, looking for any sign of hope that there was news of Aimee. Seeing none, she swallowed. "What has Charles told you?"

Millie looked down for a place to sit. "Nothing," she answered simply, deciding on the settee.

"Nothing about Aimee? Or—"

"I meant *nothing*," Millie repeated, making a slicing gesture with her hand.

Jennelle sank down beside her, shock filling her expression. "Nothing," she repeated.

"I have received not a single letter. Most likely for the same reason I have yet to send him one. We have nothing to say that the other wants to hear. He obviously has no news of Aimee, and I would only beg to come home and help."

Jennelle swallowed, once again thankful she was not in love or ever planned to be. "I suspect you are right. I doubt Charles realizes the pain he is causing by sending no word at all. But he will soon, Millie. We will have our Aimee back and she will be telling us all about her grand adventure, making us so jealous we all will forget these weeks of worry. I know it."

Millie offered Jennelle a smile when a soft cough came from behind her. Jennelle turned and gave the man a nod in acknowledgment. "Thank you, Mr. Wattkins."

Once the tray was settled, the butler bowed and left, closing the salon doors quietly behind him. "Who *is* that?" Millie asked quietly as she stared at the doors, waiting for them to spring open again at any moment.

"*That* was Mr. Wattkins," Jennelle answered before taking a sip of the hot tea. "He has been a godsend, and to think that I was worried the other servants would harass him when he first arrived."

"But however did you convince your father to employ another servant?"

Jennelle sighed. "It was not me, but Alice, our housekeeper, and Emmerick, our cook. Those two have bickered since I can remember. In many ways, I think they actually enjoy quarreling as long as everyone plays their assigned roles—and mine is that of the pacifier. But I have been gone much of this year, and the fighting must have gotten to untenable levels during my last absence. You know my father, he likes simplicity but demands peace and quiet to do his reading. I was not home more than a handful of hours when it started again between them. This time, however, Father looked at me and said, 'Jennelle, get someone in here to handle those two and do it immediately!'"

"But how did you select Mr. Wattkins—*Miss Perrin*?" Millie asked.

Jennelle waved her hand. "Oh, the man *is* dreadfully formal, but he is amazing at keeping peace among all the servants. Even more importantly, it was Mr. Wattkins who made it clear to my father that the manor was in need of a gardener. Without pause, my father agreed."

Millie twisted her hands together to release some of the nervous energy building within her. So much of her wanted this visit to be like the others, when she and Jennelle could just talk and enjoy each other's company, but with Aimee missing, it was impossible.

Jennelle eyed her for a long moment and then said, "Come. Take a walk in the gardens and tell me your plans to find our friend."

Millie felt her eyebrows arch in surprise and then shook her head. She should have known that Jennelle would recognize she was not here to commiserate but to take action. She had known Millie for too long.

Nodding in agreement, Millie followed Jennelle through the connecting doors to the back library, which had originally been designed as a small hall for dancing. Jennelle pushed the double glass doors open and stepped out on the stone terrace, pausing for Millie to join her. The stone veranda was much smaller than the one at Abileen Rose, which in turn was a fraction of the one on Chase's country estate. But it had a wonderful view, and the gardener had made several improvements. By spring, the area would be lovely. A place Aimee hopefully would get to see.

"You might as well tell me your plans now," Jennelle stated without preamble. "I know as a good hostess I should inquire after your father and you about mine. We could

make niceties all afternoon, but what I really want to know
is just what we are going to do about Aimee. And I know
you have a plan, Millie. Tell me now or I shall use every
means of manipulation and subterfuge to get you to admit
what it is."

Millie chuckled at the soft, semi-serious threat. She
stepped down the stairs into the sunlight. Bringing a hand up
to shade her squinting eyes, she wished she had not left her
bonnet behind, but was too lazy to go back and fetch it.
"Subterfuge will not be necessary, Jennelle, for there is nothing to say that you don't already know. When I became Lady
Chaselton, it was a little overwhelming. I did not feel worthy
of being the marchioness of such a substantial estate or to
such an important man. I have never desired to cater to what
those in Society think is correct and proper. I prefer to follow
my own counsel. Therefore, I've always known that the *ton*
would never really accept me. They might pretend, but not
truly welcome me. Chase, however, believes differently. The
moment we arrived in Town, he started trying to convince
me in various ways that I do belong."

Jennelle remembered Chase and Mother Wentworth
coaching Millie into hosting one of the first social events of
the Little Season. Jennelle's understanding was that the
party had been quite a coup. Millie had been a gracious,
stunning, and undeniably faultless hostess. Mother Wentworth had declared that Millie knew everything she needed
to make her Charles proud, and promptly left to visit her
friends the MacLeeries in Scotland. One week later, Aimee
had talked the Daring Three into one last adventure and
everything went wrong.

"If Mother Wentworth believes you are a fine marchioness, then you are."

"Unfortunately that does not make me a *wife* my husband
can be proud of. After what happened with Aimee, I wonder

if I will ever have the aptitude to be such a wife." Millie lightly kicked a stone and watched it tumble down the rocky path.

"It was not you or me who abducted Aimee that night. If she had done what you said, she would be here, with us, right now. It was her choice—not mine and not yours."

Millie crossed her arms but nodded her head. "You're right."

Jennelle took a step forward to stand next to Millie, looking skeptical. "I am?"

"Yes. All three of us can be extremely obstinate, and Aimee is especially so when it comes to Reece."

"Finally!" Jennelle exclaimed, throwing her hands up in the air. "The voice of reason is released from your lips."

"I am also aware that if I *had* refused to help her, Aimee would have just found another way to capture Reece's attention."

"Of course she would have. All you have to do is explain this to Charles now that he has had time to think and gather his wits, and make him understand . . ."

"But don't you see, Jennelle?" Millie asked. "None of that matters. Aimee is still missing and she will eventually need to own responsibility for the pain she caused. However, I too must own what I did to Chase by helping Aimee. And waiting at my father's for her to be found will not help right my wrongs. By now Chase must have exhausted his resources; otherwise he would have told us something. His ways, however, are not the only means to determine what happened to Aimee."

"I truly think she is with Reece, Millie. I might not have seen her being taken, but I was close enough to have heard a scuffle, a muted scream—anything that would signal she was in trouble. I heard nothing."

"I was there as well, and everything I saw tells me the

same—that Aimee *believed* she was being taken by Reece's men. But if that were true, she should have been home by now."

Jennelle nodded. "When we heard no news in the first few days, I became worried for the same reason. But unless those were pirates taking her—which I am positive they were not—the captain of *any* ship would have turned promptly around upon discovering her gender. Which brings me back to my original conclusion: Aimee is with Reece. Just as she managed to get aboard his ship, she found a way to stay. Aimee claimed she only wanted to talk to Reece, but what she really sought was time with him. Time to either convince Reece that he does love her, or for her to come to the conclusion that he is not the man for her. I suspect our clever friend found a way to keep that ship on its course, and it will be two months before we see her again."

Millie had not considered that possibility, but it only further supported the necessity of her plan. "Two months is a long time. If only we could be sure she was on the *Sea Emerald*, then we could all rest peacefully."

Jennelle nodded in agreement. "So what is your plan?" Jennelle probed. Before Millie could deny the existence of a plan, she added, "Was it not you who once told me that trying to keep you confined to a life of rules and restrictions was like me never reading another book? Simply impossible. And think again before you refuse my company."

Millie stopped walking and turned to look at her friend. "I do have a plan, Jennelle, but for me alone."

Jennelle's blue eyes simmered. "Why? Because I'm too practical and levelheaded? Maybe I am, but you underestimate how much I enjoy our escapades. You and Aimee do not have the monopoly on passion. I'll have you know that I possess quite a desire for thrilling activities. If I did not, there would have been no amount of cajolery that could have enticed me to join you on so many of your questionable excursions."

Millie sighed. "What I am about to do is far from an excursion. I am not going on a jaunt to Vauxhall Gardens. No one is to know what I am doing. There is an element of danger in my plan and I will not put anyone else—especially you—in jeopardy. Can you imagine how my heart would break if you too became injured or disappeared? No. Absolutely not."

Jennelle blanched. "Millie, just *what* are you planning? What are you thinking of doing that is potentially so dangerous? For I throw back your sentiments. Do you not think that I would be just as pained if something happened to *you* and I had not been there to help or prevent it? No! We must do whatever you are planning *together*!"

Jennelle threw her chin up and stepped around Millie as she headed toward one of the benches that used to be covered in moss. Jennelle was furious at the idea of being left behind. More so than Millie had anticipated. In the past, such fury would have been tremendously persuasive and would have convinced Millie to change her mind. But not today. Not with this plan. And yet her friend would never accept such a decision. Unfortunately, Millie needed Jennelle's support, even if passive and indirect.

Taking a deep breath, Millie joined Jennelle and sat down beside her on the stone bench. Looking around, she said, "In a few years, I suspect this will become one of the loveliest gardens in Tarrant Crawford."

"Distraction will not work, Millie. I am not taking no for an answer, and you *will* be including me in your plan."

"Your father would not like it."

"I highly doubt your father knows what you are about to do, and now that there is peace in the house, my father is so engrossed with his research he would not even realize I am gone."

Millie elbowed her friend gently in the side. "Your father loves you. He would notice."

"I *am* coming with you."

Millie pretended that she was beginning to acquiesce. "I *could* use your help."

Jennelle pulled back to study Millie. "I know you could, but are you really going to accept it?"

"It might be best if we first discuss my idea." Millie closed her eyes for a couple of seconds. She hated to misdirect her friend but promised herself she would come clean at the last possible moment. "But before I tell you everything, what does your cook have for us to eat? Dinner is hours away and I am starving."

Jennelle stood up to leave but turned around before Millie could rise to her feet. "I will agree to a slight delay and allow you to eat. But then, dear friend, I will know all that *we* are going to do to find our Aimee."

Millie was thinking about Chase again and remembering the last time he had held her in his arms, when she spied out the front salon window a dark hackney coach roll to a stop. She wished she could see him again and tell him that she loved him. She prayed Aimee was well and that by taking this bold step in finding her that maybe Chase would see she did understand what she had done and was willing to take responsibility in helping to correct it.

Millie looked at the mantel clock. It read five minutes before three. "God bless you, Madame Sasha," Millie whispered, not only for the seamstress's generosity but her punctuality. The woman had played many roles in their short acquaintance—seamstress, confidante, counselor, and matchmaker. Now Millie would add friend, for only a friend would answer such an unexpected and unorthodox call for help.

Taking a deep breath, Millie laid the letter to Jennelle on the table where she could not miss it, grabbed her bag, and snuck out the front door, hoping that she would be down the road before anyone realized she had left.

By the time she reached the carriage door, the coachman had hopped down from his seat. He was tall and widely built, with thinning gray and black hair slicked to one side. He also had small, dark eyes, which were openly assessing her. Millie got the distinct impression that he knew her, or at least knew of her and was trying to match what he had heard with what he was seeing. "*You* are Evette's cousin?" he asked pointedly.

Millie opened her mouth, staring at the coachman, then slowly closed it, nodding to the obvious lie. The man stretched his neck to glance at the manor behind her. With a huff of disbelief, he turned around and opened the door. Millie was about to hand him her bag when she heard Jennelle behind her, shouting her name.

"Mildred Aldon Wentworth, this is outrageous!" she bellowed as she marched down the drive, waving Millie's note in the air. "I won't let you!"

Millie swallowed. She looked back at the driver, but he was busy climbing back to his post, pretending he had not heard Jennelle calling out her name. When he gathered the reins, Millie pleaded, "Please don't leave."

"Door's open, miss. Can't likely drive till you close it either from the inside or the out. Don't care which you choose."

"*Miss!*" Jennelle hissed as she reached the coach.

Before her friend could say anything more, Millie pulled her aside. "Jennelle, please, please understand. I must do this."

Jennelle shook her head. "You are *not* leaving in a hack!

And certainly not *alone*! I'm beginning to wonder how all my friends could be so ripe for Bedlam and I so unaware."

At the accusation, Millie issued her friend a hostile glare. "I'm *not* alone, Jennelle, nor am I acting irrationally. I am doing what I must to protect not just you but me as well."

Jennelle was unconvinced. "He called you *miss*!" she said through clenched teeth, pointing at the coachman. "Which tells me that even if I have to get every servant out here *and* my father to sit on you to keep you here, I will do just that. Then I will send for your father and for Charles to sort out this lunacy. Just see if I don't."

"No, you will not," Millie said simply. "I would never forgive you if you did so and you want me to find Aimee just as much as I do. And if this is how it must be done, then you will let me go."

"But go where? With whom?" Jennelle pleaded, her voice cracking as tears began to fall.

Millie shook her head and gave her friend a quick peck on her wet cheek. "I doubt my father will come here in my absence, but if for some reason he does search for me, please tell him that I am safe."

"I will not lie for you!"

Millie pulled Jennelle into a tight embrace. "But I will be. I promise that I am not doing anything rash or unwise. I'm not alone. I'm with people who can help, and I vow not to take any undue risks. I'm just going to someone who can actually help find Aimee. I promise, once I have any information I will turn it over to Chase. I will not go after her myself."

"Then let me go with you."

Millie shook her head. "Jennelle, please stay here. This is how you can best help me. Keep my secret as long as you are able, to give me time. Please. I need to do this for Aimee, Chase, and you, but for me as well."

Jennelle pulled away, nodding as she acquiesced to what

she realized was the inevitable. Tears began to fall in earnest, slipping down her cheeks and onto her fingers, which were still tightly holding on to Millie's. She could argue with Millie for the next millennium, but it would not change her friend's mind. And just like Aimee, she would just find another, and more dangerous way to attain her goals.

"Fine, my fearless friend. We will do this your way, but promise me that if in one week you have not found the proof you are looking for, you will come back and get me. And *together* we will find a way."

"A fair compromise," Millie said, pretending to agree as she choked back tears of her own. She would most likely need more than a week for her plan to work, but hopefully nothing more to discover exactly which ship held Aimee.

Breaking away, Millie turned, quickly tossed her bag into the carriage, and climbed inside before she changed her mind. A small hand reached out from the shadows to close the door, and within seconds the hack began to move.

Millie leaned back and wiped her eyes free of her tears, forcing her mind to what was to come, not what she was leaving behind. "Madame Sasha, thank you so much for coming."

"Madame Sasha is in London."

Upon hearing the familiar voice, Millie leaned forward. "Evette? Is that you?"

A small, thin face framed in pale blond hair swept back into a bun moved slightly so that she was in the light. The girl looked young, but she was only a year younger than Millie. Millie did not know her well. She was Madame Sasha's assistant and had helped to make all of Millie's gowns last season, but kept to herself, unwilling to join in any conversations. It appeared she had been just as unwilling to make this trip and had done so only because Madame Sasha asked.

Brown eyes that normally would have looked kind and friendly, held no warmth. Their murky depths were instead cold and distant. "It is me, dear cousin. I've come to fetch you so that you may pay one last visit with your sick aunt, my mother, before she passes."

Millie sat back and absorbed the story and the crisp manner in which it had been delivered. She had told Chase many times that women had special ways of communicating, and Evette had been quite eloquent in her ability to convey that she was not happy to help and that Millie was to portray her cousin. "And what is my aunt dying of?" Millie inquired, making it clear in return that she would not be fazed by Evette's stony manner or sharp tongue.

"Does it matter?"

Millie took in a deep breath and exhaled. "Not in the least, cousin."

Evette pointed to Millie's travel case, made of stiff leather hinged in the middle. "My cousin doesn't own a portmanteau. Not a soul who is not from wealth owns one, and yet, Lady Aldon, you expect to become 'one of us'? I hope you are not serious. My life is not some experiment for you to try to improve. I did not ask for your help. Nor do I want it."

Millie's eyebrows rose to high arches. Madame Sasha had obviously told Evette only what she needed to know to make this journey, leaving it up to Millie to decide just what else to reveal. "I had no intention of helping you, as I did not think you desired or required it. It is I who am in need."

Evette's cold stare softened at the admission and her brown eyes warmed slightly. In doing so, her whole countenance changed. "How could anyone like me help you? You are educated, well-spoken, beautiful, and married to a very wealthy and important man."

Millie took her time in replying. "I am all that you said," she finally admitted, refusing to deny the undeniable. "But I am not wise about the world most people live and survive in. Madame Sasha is, which is why I asked for her help."

Evette pressed her lips together at the subtle reminder as to why she was there. "It won't work, you must know this."

"I know nothing of the sort. But I do know that I am determined and no one, even those who are predisposed to think that they know me and all that I am—or am not—will keep me from my purpose."

Hearing the well-aimed censure, Evette bit the inside of her lip, but a second later shrugged her shoulders. "We are stopping at an inn tonight. We are to pose as cousins because we are too dissimilar to pass for sisters. What shall be your name?"

Millie's head began to spin. "I had not thought we were to stop." The sooner they arrived in London, the sooner she could begin her task. "Could we not just hire another hack to continue our route?"

"This is Madame's own carriage. She rarely uses it, but Bernard, the driver, keeps it in good condition. We can switch out the horses, but we must allow him time to rest before we finish our journey."

Millie had not thought of that. She had planned to ride all night, but that was because she owned the carriages and dictated the length of the ride, not the driver.

"Your name?" Evette reminded her.

"You know who I am, but does anyone else?"

"Just Madame Sasha and myself, though Stuart will most likely recognize you," Evette answered, then quickly added, "However, I doubt Bernard believes you are my cousin. No one in the house will either, after one look at you. But we each owe Madame Sasha a lot. She has our loyalty, and therefore if she says you are my cousin, then that is who you are. But I and the others will need to have a name."

Millie's brows furrowed. The name was unimportant. "Just how many people live with Madame Sasha?"

A hint of a smile came across Evette's lips. "Why, nine of

us. You will make it ten. Six of them are men. Shall I ask
Bernard to turn around now?"

Millie flashed Evette a confident smile. "You really do
think I frighten easily. No need to turn around. And as far as
a name, you can call me Ellie. And since I am your cousin,
what is your aunt's last name?"

Evette bristled at the question, realizing Millie naïvely believed one could just adopt a name and inherit an understanding of another life. "It's Lefevre. She married a Frenchman
and now lives south of Paris," she answered, hinting that their
cover story would be easily discovered if someone did even
the simplest of inquiries.

"Why the sudden hostility, Evette?"

Evette did not look away, nor did she deny the implica-
tion. "Until two days ago, you were just another noble. But
then Madame Sasha tells me that you are to come live with
us and that I am to help you appear to be part of the working class. I remember your whim at Vauxhall Gardens. One
cannot just don a mask and dress to appear like a servant. I
would be surprised if you have ever tried to think about
life from a point of view like my own."

Millie was shocked. She had asked for the truth and received it. Getting angry would be pointless. She could explain that many times she and her friends had disguised
themselves as someone else to see if they would be recognized. Most times they were, but each venture had been an
eye-opening experience. "Your accusation is mistaken in
many ways, but unfortunately it might also be too true.
Evette, I do not wish to *appear* like I belong to the working class; I intend to become part of it. I must, if I am going
to work on the docks."

It was Evette's turn to be shocked. "The *docks*? Is Madame
Sasha aware of this?"

"She is."

"Then she is sending you to your doom. 'Twould never

work. It would be hard enough pretending to be a servant around nobles, but the docks? Nothing about you would persuade anyone to believe you belonged there. Your dress alone is going to make it difficult convincing the innkeeper we are related. The docks are dangerous and the men who work them even more so."

"I have no choice."

"Then find one. Go home and hire one!" Evette retorted. Millie's silence compelled Evette to lean forward, this time not from hostility but from genuine concern for another human being. "A decent woman doesn't work down there. Not safely, she don't. I know I wouldn't. And you being so little, well, there's no chance you'd survive."

True concern was staring at her and it rattled Millie, but it did not dissuade her from her cause. "Do you remember my friends Lady Jennelle and Lady Aimee?"

Evette nodded. Madame Sasha had never worked as a seamstress for either of them, but they had attended most of Millie's fittings. Like Millie, they had been kind and surprisingly respectful to everyone in the house. Even Stuart liked them, saying one time that Aimee was quite the flash for a noble.

"Well, Aimee's life may be in danger. The three of us went aboard one of my husband's ships one night, and before Jennelle and I could stop them, some men grabbed her. No one knows who has her or where she went. But I saw them and I saw the pinnace she left in. Someone on the docks has to know which ship it belongs to, but they are not going to talk to anyone who isn't one of them. It may be dangerous and hard, and I may have a lot to learn, but *I will do whatever I must to find my friend*."

Evette found herself speechless. Some seamen had taken Aimee? It was hard to believe, but it explained much. Why Madame Sasha had not only agreed to help, but expected

Evette to as well. But understanding the reason why Millie wanted her help did not make it any less of a hopeless mission.

"This is it," Evette said wearily as the carriage rolled to a final stop for the night.

Millie nodded and reached into her bag. Feeling cool metal beneath her fingertips, she pulled the small pistol out before concealing it under her cloak. Seconds later she heard a thump as Bernard hopped down from his seat. He opened the door and then moved to meet with the hostler to discuss the horses and where to put the carriage for the night.

Evette emerged from the carriage first, stretching her stiff limbs, uncaring of the rain, just thankful to be able to move. An hour into their journey it had begun to rain, slowing their progress. The muddy roads forced them to stop twice more than anticipated. They had seventy more miles before they reached London, and even if the weather improved, to-morrow would be a very long day.

Millie stuck her head out of the carriage and craned her head to look at the sign waving in the wind. "Inn" was all it said. Nondescript, just like the building as well as the rest of the small town it was nestled in. Millie gracefully stepped out of the hack and saw Evette staring at her, shaking her head. "What is wrong?"

Evette walked up close and whispered, "You cannot help it, can you? Being graceful. Even exiting a carriage you move like you are a duchess. No one with my background could ever walk like you do."

Millie shook her head. "With practice they could, but you are right to bring the discrepancy to my attention. What must I do to better conform?"

Evette grimaced. It would be impossible for her ladyship to shun the elegance she naturally exuded, just as it would be for her to change the way she spoke. Best they could do was to avoid people. "Step into the mud to cover your shoes and then shuffle your feet," she finally instructed, "and let me do the talking. Stay covered as much as possible. Your cloak is far too nice to belong to a farmer's daughter, but at least it has mud on it." Evette was about to head inside when she stopped and added, "And whatever you do, keep your head down. Keep your eyes on the floor. If someone gets even one glimpse of your violet eyes, they will remember them."

Evette went to the door and paused to square her shoulders. It was then that Millie realized just how nervous Evette was, and that she had reason to be. If anyone suspected any element of the truth, there could be trouble. Millie gave her an encouraging smile. "You will do fine, Evette."

Evette locked gazes with Millie. "I hope you are right," she whispered, and added sharply, in an effort to build her courage, "Remember, face and *eyes* down till we reach our room."

Millie pulled up the hood on her cloak so that it completely covered her dark hair and most of her face. She then tilted her head down so that she could only see the hem of Evette's dress and the heels of her moving feet as she entered the front room that also served as a dining area. Several tables were squeezed together, but only the ones closest to the large fireplace were occupied.

"Is Mr. Stokes here?" Evette asked in a crisp, businesslike voice.

Millie heard the footsteps of a heavyset woman approach them. "Eh? I'm Mrs. Stokes. What ye two be needin'?" Millie couldn't see the woman who owned the booming voice but envisioned a large-busted woman with yellow frizzy hair.

Evette looped her arm through Millie's and advanced a couple of steps. "My cousin and I are on our way to Bristol, and my father told me to ask for the best room you have available for the night." Evette's voice sounded earnest and held no hint of deception. Millie knew then that Evette might be nervous about lying, but she was also fairly experienced at it.

"Where are ye from, lass? Why are ye an' yer sister travelin' without yer father?" Millie heard Mrs. Stokes ask.

Evette squeezed Millie's arm and answered, "My *cousin* lives with me just outside of Portsmouth. Our grandmother is gravely ill and has asked for us to tend her during her last days. My father is busy preparing for harvest and has sent us on ahead. He told me specifically to stop at the Andover Inn and ask for Mr. and Mrs. Stokes. Said that you were really nice to him once and had excellent food and that you would take good care of us."

Mrs. Stokes took her time replying. "A room for the two of ye, plus the care of your animals, will cost ye a sixpence."

Evette hesitated just long enough to be believed and then pulled out a little purse. She dropped all the coins into her hand, making sure that the woman could see she held two sixpence, three farthings, and a single halfpenny. No half crowns, not even a shilling. Millie knew then that Evette wanted the woman to realize they could pay her demands, but they were not worth robbing.

Evette nodded and dropped the coins back into her bag. Then she moved closer to the woman and whispered, "He also bade me to tell you not to worry. We both sleep with pistols and are excellent shots, so you'll be getting your money when we leave."

Millie almost started coughing at Evette's brilliant performance. With one short comment, she had flattered the woman into giving them probably the nicest room of the establishment and then ensured their safety with her bit about being good with pistols. Millie almost thought they were free when she heard Mrs. Stokes snort in disbelief. "Excellent shot, ye say? Including this one 'ere? Yer cousin can't even lift an eyebrow up to greet me an' say 'ello. I doubt she could hit a pot if it was three feet in front of her."

Millie carefully pulled back a piece of her cloak and quietly aimed across the room at a large black cauldron hanging in the hearth. A second later a click was heard, followed by a clang and the hiss of steam as the bullet hit the heated pot, causing it to rock and spill some of its contents into the fire. The three men eating close to the hearth immediately jumped to their feet, but Mrs. Stokes waved for them to sit down. She swallowed loudly and Millie wished she could look up and see if the crotchety woman's eyes were popping out of her head.

"Right then," Mrs. Stokes said, clearing her throat before moving out of the front area and back toward the staircase. "Well, seeing as ye are together, I'll give ye girls the room at the top of the stairs. It's not me best. That one's on the other side an' already taken. But this one's clean an' it's the quietest. Breakfast will be served in the morning an'"—the woman paused midsentence to turn around—"I'm adding a thruppence to yer tariff for a new pot."

Evette reached out and stopped the woman before she continued moving toward the stairs. "As you can see, my cousin is not only a good shot, but very shy. I'll give you your thruppence plus two farthings more if you deliver dinner and breakfast to the room."

"Hmph," was all that Millie heard but assumed when Evette remained silent that Mrs. Stokes had nodded in agreement. A moment later she heard the creak of Mrs. Stokes's weight climbing the very narrow staircase. Then Evette went up and Millie followed.

They went up one flight and down a long hall, when Mrs. Stokes stopped at a door and opened it for Millie and Evette to enter. "As I said, it's clean. I'll send my girl up with some food and your bags."

Evette gave her a quick thanks before closing the door.

Millie waited until she heard Mrs. Stokes's heavy retreating steps before lifting her head. She immediately removed her cloak and began to twist her neck several different ways, surprised how painful it was to look down for such a long time. "Evette, however Madame Sasha found you, I can see why she never let you go. You are indeed a treasure."

Evette smiled, unable to pretend she was unaffected by the ebullient praise. "Your shot was most excellently placed and timed as well, my lady."

"Ellie." Millie sighed.

Evette pursed her lips and then nodded, removing her own cloak. "Ellie. That is very close to what your friends call you, is it not?"

Millie nodded, untied the laces on her once simple but pretty half boots, and then, using her toes, slipped each one off. "It is, but I am hoping that by keeping it close enough to my real name I will remember to respond to it. Besides, my middle name is Elizabeth. Somehow it seems less of a deception."

Evette raised a single brow at the rationalization but kept quiet. Instead, she followed Millie's lead and took off her own shoes and sat down to warm her feet by the small fire.

"Do you think we will still make it to London tomorrow?" Millie asked, joining her.

"Bernard will get us there, though it might be later than he had hoped," Evette said reassuringly.

Millie put her palms on the floor behind her and leaned back. "Evette, why is it that you rarely spoke to us when the three of us would come to Madame Sasha's?"

"Why speak if there is no need?" Evette countered.

Millie disregarded the question. "I think it is because as soon as you speak it is clear that you are educated."

Evette clenched her jaw. "Imagine, my lady, that if I find it challenging to hide my origins, how difficult you will find it."

"I have no intention to hiding my education. As you just said, it would be pointless."

Evette slowly turned her head so that she could stare quite pointedly at Millie. "How do you intend to be welcomed by *dock workers* who know that you come from a place of wealth?"

Millie held Evette's stare for some time before shifting her gaze to the fire. "I will tell them I was a governess."

Evette bit her tongue to keep from laughing, as it was clear Millie was serious. "Being a governess may explain your mannerisms and speech, but it would not explain why an educated woman would seek work near the docks."

"Then I will be a widow who once was a governess."

Evette shook her head. "The poor who make their home on the docks are going to devour you whole."

"Do not worry about me, Evette. I can defend myself, if necessary. But I am far more interested in your story. Where are you from? How did you receive your education? And how did you come to live with Madame Sasha?"

Evette rose to her feet. "My story is far from unusual and therefore quite uninteresting."

Millie was about to protest when there was a knock on the door. Evette motioned for her to turn around, then answered it. A girl, close to their own age, entered carrying a tray with a half a loaf of bread, two bowls of stew, and two mugs of port, a bitter-tasting dark beer brewed from brown malt.

The moment the girl left, Millie got to her feet and went over to the small table where the girl put the tray of food. Evette was already there, picking up one of the bowls and a mug. She went back to sit in front of the fire. Pulling off a piece of the bread, Millie dabbed it into one of the bowls of stew. After taking a bite, she went and sat by Millie. "Mmm, the stew is actually very tasty."

Evette was about to answer when there was another

knock on the door. With a sigh, Evette put her bowl back down and went to open the door, only to see the girl again, this time holding out two bags—one an obviously expensive portmanteau. Evette doubted the girl even recognized what she was carrying, for the thin face held an expression Evette knew overly well. Exhaustion. Closing the door, she put the bags down and then joined Millie again by the hearth to eat.

Licking her lips, Millie swallowed the piece of bread she was chewing and said, "I really am interested."

Evette shook her head and took another bite of stew. After a minute of silence, she exhaled and said, "If you insist. My mother was a governess. She was the one who taught me grammar and the little that I do know. My father worked in a shop that made the cast-iron pipes used to channel the gas to light lamps and burners. When I was thirteen, she got sick and died. My father took to the drink. He was not a mean drunk like some, but he was not a smart one either. He soon lost his job and it wasn't long after that we lost our home and were on the streets. One day I went to find us food as I always did, but when I came back he was gone. I haven't seen him since."

Millie sat quietly and listened. She offered no words, sensing Evette wanted neither sympathy nor condolences. "And Madame Sasha? How did you come to meet and live with her?"

"I heard rumors a great singer was coming to Manchester and snuck in to listen to her sing."

Shocked, Millie asked with her mouth partially full, "Madame Sasha was a *singer*?"

Evette nodded. "A very good one. Anyway, someone must have seen me, because I got caught. They were about to beat me and send me away for not paying, when Madame Sasha saw what was happening and rescued me." Evette smiled and let go a small chuckle as she remembered. "Told them that I was her new seamstress."

"Were you?" Millie asked, tearing off a piece of bread. "A seamstress, I mean."

"Oh goodness, no, and I said as much. But she just looked at me and said that I'd better learn enough to pretend the part if I wanted to keep it. I was starving, and for the first time since I could remember, someone was offering to help me. That was three years ago."

"It seems Madame Sasha makes a habit of saving lives. She saved yours, then mine, and now, with her help, I hope we can find Aimee."

"Your life?"

Millie pointed at the small revolver lying on top of her cloak. "She was the one who gave me that."

Evette stood up and took her bowl and Millie's back to the tray. "For some reason, she believes in you. She always has."

The tension in Evette's voice was unmistakable. It almost sounded like she was jealous. But that made no sense. Millie had known Madame Sasha for only a few months. Evette had known her for years. "Well, you have learned the part well. Have you your own clientele?"

Evette's back straightened and she pursed her lips. "Madame Sasha has said I have yet to prove myself." Millie wondered to herself, *How does one go about proving oneself?* when Evette answered her thoughts. "All I need is one client. Then I can show Madame Sasha what I can do and she will acknowledge that I really am a seamstress."

Millie decided a change of subject was needed. "I know others in the house will want to know who I am and why I am there, but please do not say anything about Aimee. It's one thing to risk my reputation, but I do not want to risk hers."

Evette motioned for Millie to sit down so that she could

help undo her braids. "I like Lady Aimee. I would never do anything to hurt her and I truly hope you find her."

Once her hair was undone, Millie gestured for Evette to sit and let her return the favor. They had both undressed to their shifts when Evette picked up a blanket off the bed. "You take the bed. I'll sleep in front of the fire."

Millie stopped her before she could take another step. "We will share the bed."

Evette measured her with a cool, appraising look. "You may be pretending to be Ellie, but you and I both know the truth. You are a marchioness, not my cousin, and I am not going to pretend that you are my equal."

Millie rolled her eyes, snatched the blanket out of Evette's hands, and tossed it on the bed. "Do not tell me *you* believe such nonsense. During most of the ride today you were either hinting that I am a fool for leaving my pampered life or making it clear that you consider me an idiot for thinking I could pretend to be part of the working class."

Evette blanched, but Millie continued, spreading the blanket out on the bed. "Now I must admit that most of Society would not appreciate such candor, but then neither would they have fought madmen, drowned a traitor, tended to their shot husbands, or sought to rescue their friend by attempting to work on the docks. I am not most women." Millie paused to look Evette in the eye. "You and I may have been born to different roles in this life and endured different burdens, but I have never thought myself above anyone. And as far as I know, neither have Aimee or Jennelle. We judge others by their actions, not their wealth or titles. I think you do the same, otherwise Madame Sasha would not trust you and sent you to help me. So choose a side. Left or right."

Evette stood motionless for several seconds. Finding her voice she said, "I . . . I prefer the left."

Millie smiled and pulled back the covers. "Then I shall enjoy the right."

Evette grimaced and joined her in the bed. "Enjoy? Not sure about that. Remember—these are the inn's sheets—not yours."

Millie wiggled her toes, feeling the coarse linen. She had slept outside, in caves, and many other uncomfortable spots. The feel of the rough sheets did not bother her overmuch, but they were a stark reminder that she was leaving her old world behind. A world with Chase.

Millie closed her eyes, and like every night since they had parted, she wished she were home, in his arms, and able to tell him just how much she loved him, knowing she was loved in return.

Chapter 12

Collins twisted his mouth humorlessly. His inability to find anyone he needed was getting to be more than just frustrating. It was damn infuriating. It was one thing for the seamen to be distracted, but now it was his idlers who had disappeared.

Tomorrow they would turn west and more than likely encounter at least one good storm before they reached Savannah harbor. They were not ready. He and Kyrk had completed a brief inspection of the sails earlier that morning and found some problems, one of which was going to need some help from the carpenter to ensure it was secured properly. Collins had no intention of waiting, and wanted the idlers to begin working immediately. With specialized skill sets, the two sailmakers and carpenter did not have to stand regular watches, but that did not give them leave to disappear.

When Collins had asked the bosun where they were, the man had been blunt in his reply. He had no idea where they were and it wasn't his job to know, but the chief mate's . . . something he thought Collins claimed to be.

Collins went down the companionway and prayed that what his gut was telling him was not true. That wherever he found his three idlers, he would also find a tall, green-eyed blonde. Turning right, he went down another set of stairs into the lower hold in the aft part of the ship where cargo was usually stored. He was almost there when he could hear Ray talking about something gruesome and sighed in relief. He had not only located his missing men—they were alone.

As a seasoned carpenter, most of Art Rayburn's stories dealt with woodwork, and all of them were full of grisly details about how some limb or extremity was mangled. The one he was telling now Collins had heard before, and was especially macabre. Something about how a doctor tried to sew a man's thumb back on, but did so backwards.

He was just about to step inside and ask how the story was going to end this time, when he heard a soft voice gasp. A second later, a familiar feminine voice said with far too much interest in the horrific story, "Alas, if only I had been available to help."

Collins clenched his fists and stared at the wood planks above him. *What was I thinking? Of course she would be with them.*

"You, miss?" Ray asked incredulously.

"Indeed, Mr. Rayburn. I am far from exemplary with a needle, but I am sure I could sew an appendage back on so that it faced the right direction."

Collins took in a deep breath. *Mr.* Gilbert, *Mr.* Miller, *Mr.* Willnon, *Mr.* Stuart, *Mr.* Solomon and now *Mr.* Rayburn. She spoke to all the men like they were fine gentlemen who had joined her for tea. And Ray was far from a gentleman.

He had spent most of his youth in Liverpool, but his Irish ancestry was evident in his dark red beard and the wild hair that covered his body. Collins had never seen a man hairier than Ray, and he hoped he never would. But the carpenter was not just Irish in looks, the man had a temper as well.

Strong, wide, and thickset, Ray loved a good fight. He had been kicked off more than one boat for onboard scuffles. Yet he had a rough but steady code of ethics. Once a man earned his trust and respect, Ray would be loyal to them until his dying breath.

Collins stood still, trying to think when he heard the distinct melancholic Scandinavian accent of Lamont Poulsen. "I tink te man was drunk."

"Probably not even a doctor."

Collins grimaced. That had been Lamont's brother Shiv Poulsen, the second of the *Sea Emerald*'s two sailmakers.

"Mr. Heilsen!" Aimee called out gleefully. "Please come look, for I do believe I found another one."

Just where am I? Collins asked himself. He felt as if he were frozen in limbo, where all people had mysteriously transformed into someone else. There was no other explanation. Kyrk Heilsen *never* allowed anyone to call him by his last name, except other Scandinavians because they were the only ones who knew how to pronounce it properly.

Unable to stomach any more surprises, Collins removed all expression from his face and walked into the room. He took in the scene before him and had only one thought. *I'm not about to lose control. I've already lost it.*

A large sail covered the floor and was draped high over the barrels and boxes that had been stacked in each corner. A Poulsen brother was at each end, moving in opposite directions to examine the sail's hem, inch by inch. They had been listening, but it was clear they were also focused on their task.

On the other side of the sail was Aimee, who was standing on an unstable barrel. To keep her from falling as the ship rocked, Ray was holding her hips. Right next to her, standing on another barrel, was Kyrk Heilsen, who was leaning in close to see what had made her shout out with joy.

Never in his imagination—never in his worst nightmare—could Collins have conjured what he was seeing.

Next to himself and the captain, Kyrk was the best sailor on board. He was young, but the Scandinavians had the sea in their blood, and Kyrk had known since childhood just what he wanted to do for the rest of his life.

His first job on the *Sea Emerald* had been cabin boy, during which time he began to idolize the captain, imitating him however he could. He kept himself clean, took pride in his work, was willing to learn, and had eventually become a highly skilled rigger. The men respected him and listened to him, making Kyrk an exemplary second mate. But most of all, he had been immune to Aimee's charms.

He had told Collins that he had a job to do overseeing the supplies, the sails, and the seamen while he was on duty, and he had no time for her. So it had seemed natural to put him in charge of the night shift, and it had worked. Kyrk kept his distance from Aimee and all had been fine . . . or as close to fine as Collins could expect under the circumstances.

Just what in the hell had happened?

Unable to see just what Aimee was pointing at, Kyrk stepped onto her barrel. His whole body was now practically touching hers as he leaned in close to take a better look. A second later, he stepped back and gave her an infectious grin. "Ah, Lady Aimee, are you sure you do not have Scandinavian blood in your veins? *Fan*, if you are not right. Shiv, come here and take a look. I need you to take care of this and any others she finds." Then Kyrk winked at Aimee. "I'm going to have a talk with the chief mate about keeping you around. As the only rigger, I could use some backup."

Aimee's grin grew even more devastating, and she was unaware of the captivating picture she made when she smiled. "Just remember, Mr. Heilsen, this makes the third one I've found. You promised."

Kyrk shrugged his shoulders. "I'll keep my promise, but only if you find something else to wear besides a skirt."

Collins stood there in shock. No one yet had noticed him, but he doubted it would have made any difference. He had no idea why Kyrk told this obviously genteel noblewoman to wear pants—at least that was what Collins hoped he meant. And he wasn't sure that he actually wanted to know the reason why, for he knew in his gut the answer would take years off his life.

"I already have something," Aimee promised, as Ray helped her to jump down off the barrel. "I'll leave now to find Gus and see where he put the things I wore aboard." She turned to leave. "Mr. Collins! I did not know you were standing there!"

Collins crossed his arms, hoping he appeared more authoritative than he felt. It did not help when all four men looked up but refused to look guilty. It confirmed what he already knew. He was not losing control. He had lost it a long time ago.

His whole crew had deserted every rule he had laid out. No longer did Aimee's injuries worry Collins. It was the men and her effect on them. Everyone who met her fell under her spell. When the captain finally did find out about her, it would not be the injuries to her wrists that would anger him the most—it would be his crew, the moment the captain saw how they looked at her. After all this, they might still find themselves stranded in Savannah, hoping to find a post on another ship.

"I thought you were going to have dinner tonight with Mr. Hamilton."

"Damn," Collins muttered. She was right. At least he could tell the captain that the idlers were already working on the sails, preparing them for the storms.

* * *

Reece waved at Collins to come in and sit down. JP had just dropped off dinner and tonight's fare looked to be a good meal. The cook usually waited a little longer before killing one of the chickens, but Reece was glad he did not delay this time. He needed the break from salt beef and hardtack.

Collins sat down and started in on his meal. He looked exhausted and no doubt was. Being chief mate was hard enough, but when it included the burden of keeping the men contained when there was a woman on board, it could seriously strain one's nerves. Reece knew he could step in, but he also knew that the chief mate was an able sailor and leader. If he did not want the men to ever bring aboard another woman, then Collins would prevent it from happening.

"Waves are picking up," Reece offered, hoping to spur some sort of conversation.

"Storm brewing. Bound to go through one this far south."

Reece nodded and swallowed the piece of meat he had been chewing. "We turn west tomorrow. There's a chance it will go south of us."

Collins scowled and stabbed a potato with his fork. "Trust me. We aren't that lucky."

Reece almost wanted to laugh at his chief mate's surliness. Nothing more needed to be said. Reece was now positive a woman was not only on board, but the source of Collins's irritable disposition. "Well, if you're right and we are not lucky, then in a few days it will finally get exciting on board. It's been a little dull around here lately. What do you think?"

Collins squirmed and kept his focus on his food. "Guess it all depends on your point of view," he finally muttered.

Reece knew he should give his second-in-command a break, but it was just so rare to see Collins—a man almost as unflappable as himself—fidget in discomfort. "Not just mine," Reece said, keeping his tone lackadaisical. "The crew as well. Or haven't you noticed how strange their behavior has been?"

Collins's face contorted.

"When was the last time men shaved in the middle of a voyage?"

Reece watched his chief mate's jaw grow considerably more tense.

"And I wouldn't say any of them smell good, but I noticed our onboard water level has dropped more than usual. Are some of the men actually bathing?"

Collins still kept quiet, but Reece knew that a woman on board usually inspired the men to take cleaning themselves a little more seriously than usual.

"But what has me really perplexed is the singing. I like my men to be happy, but I know something is up when the bosun isn't complaining about having to stop a continuous stream of fights, but about having difficulty getting men for the *day* shifts. Seems the night shift has become quite popular."

Collins's shoulders sank and he dropped his fork. He raked his scalp hard. The man looked like he was both relieved and panic-stricken. "You know."

Reece leaned back in his chair and crossed his arms. "God, Collins, I'm not a fool. Of course I know you brought a woman aboard. And she must be one hell of chit too. None of the others lasted this long before some kind of hell broke loose on the ship."

Collins lost all expression and it made Reece only more curious. "So who brought her on board?"

Collins snorted. "You wouldn't believe me if I told you."

"So what's she doing? By now the other females you took on board were getting pretty anxious to get back on land."

Collins rolled his eyes as if he actually wished he had that problem. "She's been trying to learn everything she can about the ship. She understands she cannot do the jobs, but she still insists on learning what there is to do and how to do it."

That information caught Reece by surprise. In a way it was refreshing to learn that at least one woman out there was interested in learning about ships and sailing, but it also was disturbing. Sailing was dangerous. There was not a job on the ship that did not carry some risks, and some of them were just plain perilous. "Why not send her to JP so she can learn about cooking? That's something women can do."

Collins looked Reece dead in the eye and shook his head. "You know JP."

"Couldn't even take a step in the kitchen, eh?"

Reaching back, Collins linked his fingers behind his head. "Oh, JP let her in. Let her cook a little while too. But as I said, her interests lie not with the domestic chores, but with the ship."

Reece sat immobile. *Just who was this woman?* He had not thought to meet her, but now he was more than a little curious. "Sure she is a woman?" he asked, thinking how some girls were unladylike, boisterous females who tended to look and act more like a boy than a girl. It was hard to believe a hoyden would entice one of the men to bring her on board, but then again it was not beyond the realm of possibility.

Collins broke out into chuckles that led to a coughing attack. When he could finally speak, he said, "Uh, no, Captain. She's many things, but she is *definitely* a woman."

Reece offered Collins a wry, tight-lipped smile. "Think I just might have to meet her."

"Just say the word," Collins whispered, leaning back in his chair.

Reece could have sworn he saw a shiver of fear go down Collins's back. The man was obviously at odds. "No need. Things are good with the men so far. Let's not mess with that, especially with a storm coming. Don't need another storm on the boat."

Collins rocked forward. "And just what about the storms we leave back at home?"

Reece blinked. Collins was not a man to pry into another man's privacy without reason. "Just what do you mean?"

Collins shrugged. "I mean the woman who drives you to leave your home so often. I like the sea as much as you—all the men do. But that don't mean we don't want to spend at least *some* time on land. A few of the men have homes . . . wives . . . families. Something you should consider starting."

Immediately, the image of Aimee swam before Reece. He had hoped avoiding her when he was in London would help him to forget, but even after ten months, he could remember every second of his last encounter with her, as if it had just happened. More than anything, he wished it were possible to have her as his own, but he was made for the sea. Aimee was not. She would never understand the pull of the open water. It left him no choice. He would stay away until Aimee was happily married to some nobleman with a title, a fancy home, and a pretty purse to match. Only then, when she was permanently out of reach, would he risk seeing her again.

"Then those men are lucky, Collins. My luck ran out with the war. I came out alive. I also was able to gather enough money to build this boat and start a shipping company. But that's where my luck ran out. Pretending otherwise is a fool's errand."

"You know, Captain, a lot of men in your position bring their wives on board."

Reece scoffed. The idea of bringing Aimee aboard a ship was ludicrous. He could not envision it. Beautiful women belonged in Society, not away from creature comforts. And his crew. Some of them would undoubtedly fawn all over her, but others would eat her alive. Aimee was no match for these hardened men. One hour in their company and she would be miserable. "If you knew the woman keeping me away, Collins, you would know how impossible that notion is."

"How do you know that, Captain? Have you asked?"

"I just do," Reece growled out. "You don't know her background, but trust me, she does *not* belong on a ship."

Collins refused to back down. "Women are a surprising lot. They are used to harder work than we realize."

Reece's laughter filled the cabin, but it held no joy. "You talk as if I am interested in a farmer's daughter. Hell, Collins, it would be unthinkable if she was the daughter of a gentleman."

Collins furrowed his brows. "I don't understand."

Reece leaned forward and rested his arms on either side of his dinner plate. "Then let me be clear. My best friend fell in love and became besotted—and when I say besotted, I mean completely incoherent. He thinks I don't understand, but he's wrong. I do. For I did the same damn thing just a few months before he did. I fell in love and every damn day I crave to be with her again, but I cannot. Even if I was willing to give up the sea . . . I cannot. She is not only the sister of my best friend but the daughter of the late Marquess of Chaselton."

Silence filled the cabin as Collins digested what he'd just learned. He had known most of what the captain said through snippets of earlier conversations. But *marquess*? That was damn close to a duke, and that was practically royalty. Hell, if she was the daughter of a marquess, Aimee probably had been presented in court and knew the royals personally.

"Lady Wentworth would no more set foot on this ship than the Queen of England," Reece continued. "If you ever saw her, you would realize I am not exaggerating when I say she could have anyone."

"But . . . but what about her? I had the impression that you thought she felt something for you in return."

"Even if she wanted to, her brother and I would prevent it. This way of life is dirty and somewhat dangerous. And as the second son of a lord, I have no title. I have nothing to offer. I'm just a man fortunate enough to be able to make money in a trade he loves. She is a dream that I hope will fade with time."

Collins stared into Reece's despondent blue eyes. He had thought to perhaps guide the captain into thinking of the possibilities—the positive aspects of finding Aimee on board—but the more the captain spoke, the more he made one thing clear: *He and everyone else on board his boat was soon going to be dead.*

And the deaths they were going to endure were going to make hell look like a welcome reprieve.

Sasha lit another candle to counter the dark shadows in the room. She had hoped Millie and Evette would have arrived earlier in the day, but with the uncooperative weather it was lucky they made it in at all.

"Did you get enough to eat?" Sasha asked. Tonight they'd had some leftover bread and meat, but it was not enough to feed three people. Thankfully, Bernard had volunteered to go out and get something.

Evette had taken her plate to her room, while Millie had sat in the front parlor laying out her entire plan to Madame Sasha in between bites.

"Yes. Thank you, and I know you are soon to tire of hearing the words, but I truly am grateful you were willing to bring me here," Millie replied. "But as you just heard, I need even more assistance. Will you provide it?"

"Not can I, but will I," Sasha murmured to herself. She

sat back and stared reflectively at the young beauty she had met a little over six months ago. Over the years, she had come to know of all three girls through one of her most trusted confidantes, the Dowager Marchioness of Chaselton. And like Cecilia, the current Marchioness of Chaselton had a wild spirit and a fearless soul. Last spring, being around Millie and her friends, Sasha had felt in many ways reborn, remembering her youthful and oftentimes foolhardy quest to experience all that life had to offer.

The Daring Three had been spellbound by her exuberant stories of life in the Russian court, unaware that not a one she had told was fiction but actually based on her own rich, unorthodox life. As a result, she might have indirectly as well as openly encouraged them to continue having adventures of their own—helping them with racy Vauxhall costumes, providing an occasional firearm, and enabling one of them to ensnare one of the Season's most eligible bachelors. Regrettably, the three young women were also learning, just as she had, that such inclinations sometimes had unfortunate consequences.

"Will you help me?" Millie asked for the third time.

Sasha tapped her fingers together, which—like her face—looked far more youthful than her sixty-one years. Her somewhat petite and rounded figure hinted at a previously curvaceous body, but only her graying brown hair reflected her true age.

"It is not that what you ask of me is difficult. It is that I'm not sure it is wise," Sasha began, her Russian accent more pronounced than usual. "Helping you come to London unseen is one thing, but what you are proposing is quite another. There are professionals for what you propose."

"And my husband hired them."

"And he has learned nothing in the past two weeks?"

Millie shook her head. "He has not written me one letter,

and I am sure he would have if he had any news." *And neither has Elda Mae*, she added to herself.

Sasha's expression went grim. If Chaselton had not written his wife, then far more was going on than Millie was aware of. Someday Millie would learn to recognize when he was keeping secrets, but until then, she needed help in making her husband realize that keeping such confidences was rarely rewarding.

"Your plan to find Aimee yourself is, well, simply put . . . it is dangerous. Those who make a living on the docks work especially hard, and they drink and play hard as well. Most are unfamiliar with the rules of gentlemanly behavior, and the rest have no interest in adhering to them."

"I'm not looking for gentlemen, Madame Sasha, and I am not trying to rescue Aimee. I'm only looking for answers as to who took her. There must be someone you know who might be willing to help me."

"There may be, *da*. But they would need to trust you, and that would take more time than you have."

Millie looked Sasha squarely in the eye and said without doubt, "But they know and trust *you*."

Sasha twisted her lips to one side. To deny Millie's assertion was pointless; Millie would never believe otherwise because it was true.

Sasha did have a rapport with several of the business owners who made a living along the docks. And as soon as she heard about Aimee going missing, she had conducted her own investigation. While she had been unable to confirm whether or not Aimee was safely aboard the *Sea Emerald,* Sasha did learn that there had been inquiries a couple of weeks ago concerning that same pinnace. After hearing the same tales that were told to Chaselton and his runner, she surmised Aimee was most likely safe.

The reason he had not told his wife what he learned was probably the same reason he had not written her. However, it was also unlikely he had written his mother, and Cecelia would want to know about her daughter's latest caper. Sasha would send word immediately, but until Cecelia returned, Sasha was going to have to act in her place. And she was not sure just how to proceed.

"I also must take into consideration the others who live here. This favor you are asking does not affect just yourself, but those in this house. And if something goes ill, then they will have to live with the consequences long after you're gone."

Millie tried one last plea. "Madame Sasha, I realize I am placing you in a difficult position asking for your help, but please understand that I intend to conduct this search even if I have to rent a place of my own."

Sasha examined the countenance of the woman sitting across from her. It was the same expression Sasha had worn when she made a decision that had changed her life forever. And while such willfulness and determination had brought her much heartache, Sasha knew that it had also enriched her life immeasurably. She would not go back and change her decision, even if she could.

Her original plan had been to tell Millie all of what she knew concerning Aimee and then persuade the young woman to join her husband. But now that Millie was here, Sasha no longer thought that was in the best interest of the couple. Chaselton would still keep his secrets and Millie would continue to take risks without considering him.

Sasha inhaled slowly and contemplated the problem before her. *What would Cecelia do?* she asked herself, and immediately knew the answer. Cecelia would say that more than one person could learn a lesson if this situation was handled correctly.

With a smile, Sasha exhaled just as slowly, as a new plan formed. It was not often one had the opportunity to walk in another's footsteps, and Sasha just might have a way Millie could do so safely. It would help assuage any misplaced guilt and give her something to focus on until either Aimee returned or Chaselton came to his senses. And living here, Sasha hoped her tenants would learn just as much from the marchioness as she would from them.

Having made a decision, Sasha rose to her feet. "I will help you, but on one condition. I know someone who owns a tavern on the docks and owes me a favor. If he likes you, he may give you employment. If he refuses, then you must return to your life as a lady and wait to discover the fate of Aimee."

Sasha studied the serious face looking back at her. She was actually proud of Millie for thinking about her answer before she spoke. For Sasha had meant what she said. There were lots of places for employment around the docks, but Sasha knew of only one where the owner looked out for the women who worked for him. It was not far and the route was well used and lit at night by the linkmen. Working there would still have risks, but life's best lessons were learned when one took uncomfortable chances.

Millie frowned and considered the proposition. She did not like it, but deep down she also knew Madame Sasha's offer was her best chance at having her plan succeed. She was entering a way of life that was completely foreign. To ignore the proposal of a person she had gone to for help would not be just reckless, it would mean failure.

Millie licked her lips and nodded once. "I accept."

Sasha produced a small smile, satisfied that Cecelia would approve of her solution and her decision to withhold what she knew of Aimee. Deep down, Millie knew the truth, but it did not lessen her need to be active, especially while estranged from her husband. "Clive Langdon owns a tavern frequented by dock workers. He usually has two women working for him at night, but Clarice married and moved back north to be closer to family. So he needs someone to take her place. While gruff and demanding, he is a good man and protects the women working for him. Dock workers know this, but they still frequent his place because Clive is honest and used to be one of them. But it's still a boozing ken and that makes it dangerous and open to a fair share of trouble."

"I understand. I'll avoid what I can, but I can defend myself if necessary."

Sasha exhaled, knowing Millie was not boasting but speaking the truth. She also knew that Millie had never had to defend herself against these kinds of men. They were rough, strong, and all too often single-minded when it came to their more carnal desires. "You will also have to lose some of the refinement that comes from being of Quality."

Millie grimaced. "Evette hinted at the same thing. I tried, but it seems I cannot erase years of habits just because I will it. I thought I would say I was a governess. That would explain my speech and mannerisms, would it not?"

"Then why are you not *still* a governess?"

"Maybe I could say that I was accused of stealing or—"

Sasha raised her hand to keep Millie from continuing. "When asked, just tell them you had no choice but to seek other employment."

"But won't people assume—"

"*Da.* Let them be curious and create tales about just why and how you came into their world. It is the only way they might accept you despite that you are unmistakably gentry," Sasha replied. She was about to open the parlor doors when she stopped and asked, "Are you sure?"

Millie outstretched her hand and placed it on Sasha's arm, giving it a slight squeeze. "I thought you believed in taking bold action, even if the risks were high."

Sasha cupped Millie's cheek in her hand. "This is no adventure you are planning, little one. And I do believe in taking bold action, regardless of the risks, when the reason is right."

"Saving Aimee . . . saving my marriage . . . are these not the right reasons?"

Sasha shook her head. Her young friend had much to learn, just as she had. "I cannot say. This is a path you alone must choose and follow. I once was in love. And like you and your Charles, we had to do and learn things the hard way. I wonder, though, if it was the best way. Now come, and let me introduce you to your housemates."

Sasha opened the doors and walked down to the end of the dim hallway. To the left was the back room, which housed a chaotic collection of materials. To the right, however, was another hallway Millie had never been down. At the end, Sasha waved her hand for Millie to push open the two old, dark, wooden doors that acted as the passageway to the rest of the home.

Millie's lavender eyes grew large as she crossed the threshold. On the other side was another world, one she never would have guessed existed. The building's true size was masked from the street with its narrow front and single large red door. Unlike the parlor and front hallways, which were lined in dark woods and deep maroons and navy blues, this large gathering room was decorated in bright colors, welcoming all who entered. The obviously well-used furniture was large and looked so comfortable that it invited one to come in, sit down, and talk. Millie felt the urge to truly smile for the first time since Aimee had left.

Touching Millie's arm to regain her attention, Sasha said, "One last promise between us, and this one is not just with me, but with all who live here. I want your solemn vow that you will not speak of this house and those who dwell in it. Their lives are private, as is yours. In return, I will guard your identity and your reasons for being here. Agreed?"

Millie nodded and with tears in her eyes, she gave Sasha a hug. "Thank you so much. This just has to work."

Sasha patted her on the back, returning the embrace. "It will be up to you, my young friend, to build goodwill with those in the house. Their friendship is not mine to give. It has to be earned."

Millie nodded. "I understand."

Sasha released her and with a wink said, "*Het*, I do not think you do, but neither did I when I was young."

Not understanding, Millie was about to ask for clarification when Sasha stared at a foot dangling off the end of a settee. "Stuart, is that you?"

A quick but grumbled reply came from the back of the room as a brown-haired figure pushed himself up to peer over the edge of the divan. "Who else would it be?"

Ignoring the saucy attitude, Sasha replied, "I believe you know . . ."

"Ellie," Millie filled in.

"That's right. Ellie. She's an old friend who will be staying in the upstairs spare bedroom across from Susan."

Stuart crinkled his brow and his hazel eyes took a long look at Millie. "*Bloody hell*, that banbury youse told me about her livin' 'ere now was true?"

"Indeed," Sasha answered crisply. "And from now on, you will know her only as Ellie. Understand?" Seeing him roll his eyes but give an affirmative nod, she added, "Please show her to her room."

Stuart scowled, but Sasha was unfazed. "Since you seem to be in the mood to help, why don't you show her the way to Clive's tomorrow morning as well."

Afraid of what else he would be asked to do, Stuart rolled off the couch and onto his feet. Grabbing a book off the cushion, he came around, ready to guide Millie but not hiding any of his displeasure in having to do so. Long-limbed and tall, his body looked older than his face, which only now hinted at the ability to grow whiskers. "She going to work at Six Belles? You must be cork-brained." Sasha issued him an icy stare. Stuart recoiled slightly before recovering, puffing his chest out. "I'm not wantin' to pull caps with you. I'm just voicin' me opinion is all. I mean, it's rather saucy to think of gentry workin' for Clive."

"Clive is not to know she's a noble," Sasha instructed.

Stuart looked Millie up and down and rolled his eyes again. "He's no flat. He'll know she's somethin'." Then with a huff he told her to come on.

Millie followed his back into the passageway and up a narrow set of stairs. In his hand, she spied the book he was carrying and finally made out the title. *An Inquiry into the Nature and Causes of the Wealth of Nations* by Adam Smith. Millie was surprised. Chase had the same book. She had looked at it once and it had given her a headache. Economics was a difficult concept, and she would not have thought Stuart educated enough to understand it.

"'Ere's the room. I'll meet youse in the kitchens in the mornin' to take you to Clive's."

He was about to leave when Millie asked, "Stuart, do the others know who I am?"

"Evette. Doubt anyone else cares much who ya are."

"Then please don't tell them or anyone."

For a young man, Stuart looked genuinely affronted. "Cry rope?" He sneered. "Nobles talk about honor, but we workin' poor live by it, 'cause it is all we 'ave. We don't 'ave titles, lots of blunt, and own more than one place to 'ide in when things go bad." He stopped in a huff and was about to walk away when he gave her an odd look. "Guess they must 'ave gone pretty bad to be willin' to work in a lushery."

Millie fought to hide the fear his words instilled in her and recapture her courage.

She had been chased by evil, survived nearly being drowned, and looked malevolence in the eye. Just how bad could a few dockworkers be?

Chapter 13

October 21, 1816

Millie grasped the doorknob to her bedroom and hesitated before leaving. Resting her forehead against the painted wood, she closed her eyes, took a deep breath, and once more suppressed the urge to go and see Chase. Her body longed for his touch and his comfort, but her heart suffered the most. If she looked at him and saw any pain, anguish, or proof that he was not sleeping or eating as he should, Millie doubted if she had the strength to keep from running into his arms. But would he welcome her?

"You know he would," Millie whispered aloud. Despite what had transpired that awful night, Chase loved her and she loved him. But she also knew he would just try to sequester her again using different means. No, she had to stay away, at least for now.

Millie took another deep breath, straightened, and opened the door. Pasting what she hoped to be a sincere-looking smile on her face, she began to make her way to the kitchen, unaware that she was nervously swinging her plainest bonnet by its wine-colored ties. She felt apprehensive about the day and asked herself what Mother Wentworth would do.

Though her mother-in-law had divulged only snippets of her own adventurous past, it was enough to know she had emerged from some rather scandalous schemes unscathed. But Millie wondered if she would approve of her plan. Any objection would concern the potential danger, but Millie deep down believed that Mother Wentworth would have supported her.

Deep in thought, Millie rounded the bottom stair and almost collided with Evette, who was headed in the opposite direction, carrying several yards of material. "Good morning."

Startled, Evette mumbled "Good morning" as she took a step back and cast an eye over Millie's appearance.

Millie arched a curious brow. "Is there something wrong with the way I look?"

Evette had no idea how to answer the question. Millie had fluffed and woven her dark brown hair into a large, broad chignon at the base of her neck, with one twisted lock wrapped around her head. While the design was significantly more modest than the styles she normally wore, it was far from a basic, secured knot. Her dress had similar problems. Though Millie probably thought it quite plain, Evette was at a loss for words to explain why it was not. The gold-tone, long-sleeved cambric day dress was plain—for a noble. However, the woolen, pleated, eggplant-colored pelisse that was hanging over Millie's arm made the outfit quite stunning. All together, it provided unmistakable evidence of her affluent background.

Evette sighed and shook her head, glad Millie was at least not wearing even the simplest of jewelry. She was about to continue walking, when she realized Millie had been coming from the stairs, not the kitchens. "Are you just *now* coming down to break your fast?"

Millie nodded, and with a smile proceeded toward the kitchens. Evette watched in awe. Then, with a roll of her eyes, she shook her head and continued on her way, wondering if all noblewomen were as clueless. Evette predicted there would be one less for dinner tonight, for if Millie survived the morning, it would be a miracle.

Surprised she felt so hungry so early in the morning, Millie made her way down the hallway to the kitchen area. Like the gathering room, it was surprisingly large. The majority of the space was dedicated to cooking, but near the far wall was an enormous square table. It was surrounded by wooden benches, which provided enough seats for all those living in the house to sit and eat.

Millie took a nervous step toward the table and told herself to calm down. It was not as if she had never eaten in a kitchen. She had snuck down as a child and asked to eat there many times, thinking it must be special as she was not supposed to do so. Just earlier that year, Chase had returned to England and found her scavenging for something to eat in the middle of the night. At home, the kitchen was one of the few servant places where she actually felt welcome. But this was not home, and she was definitely not feeling welcome.

One portly man, who looked to be not much taller than she, was standing by the stove, looking hot, sweaty, and very uncomfortable. The rest of the party was scattered around the table and, like the cook, they were intentionally ignoring her.

Determined to start the day on a positive note, Millie donned her most winning smile and straightened her shoulders. "Good morning, everyone. I'm usually not very hungry in the mornings, but I must say that today I am ravenous and really looking forward to whatever delicious food that is being prepared."

The man at the stove swung around and looked at her, his

wide hazel eyes moving up and down. With a snort, he thrust the large spoon that was in his hand toward her and said, "Ye think I am tae cook for ye?"

Millie stopped in midstride. She opened and closed her mouth, somewhat stunned. In her experience, flattery was the fastest way to gain the support of a cook. "I . . . I . . . assumed . . . I . . ." Then after a pause, finally blurted out, "Are you not the cook?" wishing she could remember his name.

The man let go another loud snort and turned his back to her. Plunging the spoon into the large pan, he vigorously stirred the contents. "I *was* till about an hour ago. Now I'm the man who is about tae leave an' go cook for others. Then I'll be the man who will come home and cook again *for them who show up on time.*"

Millie glanced at Stuart, who immediately looked away and hunched farther over his food. Like most of the other plates around the square table, Stuart's was almost empty. "I . . . I didn't know," she said in an apologetic tone.

Millie had stayed up late into the night, and had thought she *had* risen early. At home, people would have thought it a miracle for her to be moving, let alone dressed, at this hour. She quite firmly believed morning was best suited for sleeping. However, Millie was determined to appear to all as part of England's hardworking class and was prepared to lose many habits and adopt new ones. She just wished getting up at dawn was not one of them.

Spying some bread on the table, Millie sighed and slid into one of the empty spots on the bench beside Stuart. "I understand," she said. "This bread will be just fine."

She then counted heads; including herself, there were seven in the room. Millie smiled inwardly. Evette had said nine were living in the house, ten if they included Millie.

And as Evette was not there, nor Sasha, that left one person who was even later to breakfast than she.

"Good morning, Bernard," Millie offered the familiar face.

The driver paused to look up at her, his dark eyes assessing her before stabbing a piece of sausage with his fork and popping it into his mouth. *Well, at least he looked at me*, Millie said to herself. Pulling off a piece of the loaf, she took a bite and tried to remember what Evette had said on their way into Town about the personalities of those who lived with Madame Sasha.

Bernard was the age of most grandfathers, and though a fairly handsome man, he had never been married. He rarely spoke to anyone he was so shy, but somehow he could converse with Sasha, which resulted in a special arrangement. He still had to contribute money for food and drink, but his room was free. All it cost him was intermittent access to his carriage—the one thing he had of value. He drove it as a hack around Town for hire and had to rent a team to pull it so he did not have to worry about the cost or burden of stabling horses.

"There ye go, lad. Take this tae ye papa afore it gets cold," the cook said to Stuart, sliding a heaping plate of meat and potatoes on the table.

"All right," Stuart groaned.

Millie closed her eyes and stifled a sigh. Stuart's father was the one who was missing from the table, and unlike her, he was *not* late. He just wasn't coming to the kitchens to eat. She wished Stuart had said the cook's name, for she could not think of it. Strange, as Millie could remember quite a bit of what Evette told her about him—most of which Millie found hard to believe seeing the food the man had just prepared.

Supposedly he had been a chef at Palais-Royal in Paris and Grimod himself had praised his ability. The only reason Millie even recognized the name was that Jennelle had read about him and his achievements. Grimod had deformed hands and had learned how to write and dine using metal prostheses, eventually becoming well-known for his theater reviews and then as a restaurant critic.

Seeing the ill-prepared dish in front of Stuart, Millie suspected the man had spent most of his life in Scotland, never having set foot in France. But then neither had she, so if the small claim was his way of being important among these people, who was she to take it from him. Millie was just glad someone in the house was willing to cook for the rest of the group living there.

A scrape caught Millie's attention. Beside Bernard, a tall, very thin young man rose to his feet and was immediately followed by his twin sister. "Thank you, Henry," they said as they placed their plates on a small table for washing. *Henry!* Millie repeated the name to herself several times, hoping next time she would remember it.

"So, who do ye have today, Paulie?" Henry asked as he piled up another plate of food.

"Van Rangels," Paulie replied as he began to button up the worn jacket that also served as a coat.

"Och," Henry replied with a shake of his head. Then he put down a heaping plate of food and a full mug where Paulie had been sitting. Just before he sat down, he said, "Ye take care, and Susie, do nae mind her highness any."

Susie smiled and waved as she disappeared out the door after her brother.

As soon as they were out of earshot, Henry said gruffly, "The Van Rangels pay weel but nae weel enough tae put up with their insults. It's loondry!" Then, looking right at Millie, he pointed his finger and growled, "They should know that when they have a fight and throw their bottles of wine, things weel get stained. No' them. They think Susie should be able tae work a miracle just because they deem it so."

Millie swallowed, wondering if she were the only one to

realize how sweet Henry was on Susie. Then she mentally
chided herself. If it was so obvious to her after only a few
minutes, it had to be apparent to all.

A very tired young man sitting across from her yawned.
"Henry, just be glad their other house is nicer."

Henry snorted. "With nine wee ones, Tommy?" he asked
and then pushed another overloaded spoonful into his
mouth.

"At least it's more reliable income than being an enter-
tainer at Vauxhall," Tommy groused. "I made only a sixpence last night and had to spend nearly half of it getting
back here."

Henry took another bite of his food. "Can't imagine all
the washing, nursing, cooking, cleaning . . . they get paid
tae little for that amount of work," he said between chews,
still focused on Susie and her plight. Then, without any
warning or cause, Henry looked again at Millie and said, "I
suspect ye can't imagine it either."

Millie was not sure why she'd earned the man's hostility
and was unsure how to react. Stuart, probably acting out of
guilt for not telling her about when breakfast was, came to
her defense. "Insult the Toffkens all you like, 'enry, but Ellie
'ere won't deserve 'em after today."

Henry's eyes popped open at the rebuke for Stuart usually joined in when anyone disparaged the upper class. Yet
the lad had just defended the presumptuous interloper.
Henry's mouth stopped chewing and he stared openly at
Millie, trying to decide how to respond. But before he
could, the kitchen door opened and Evette entered. "Stuart,
your father is asking for you."

Stuart rolled his eyes but swung his leg over the bench
and grabbed the plate that Henry had fixed. Evette then
looked at Millie, the bread in her hand, and the vacant spot
where her plate should have been. "Henry, you're going to
send . . . Ellie off to Clive's with nothing but bread to eat?"

Henry swallowed and avoided all contact by reaching out for his mug. "Didn't ken she was working for Clive," he muttered after downing a swig.

Evette came up beside him and gave him a soft peck on the cheek. "Cook her some eggs, Henry, while Stuart takes care of his father and the pan is still hot."

Henry set the mug back down on the table with a thump. "If the lass is touched enough tae work for Clive, I suppose I'm touched enough tae feed her despite how she's dressed."

Millie fought the inclination to ask just what he meant. She was in her plainest, most modest day dress. Made of dark gold cambric, it was long-sleeved and high-necked, covering her throat and wrists. It had no elaborate trim and was practically devoid of decoration. Even her deep purple pelisse lacked the usual fastenings and braided hem. In her circles, many would have thought her a servant, dressed so plainly.

She was still puzzling over her dress when minutes later, Henry plopped a pewter plate holding two burned, barely edible eggs and a thick slice of beef down in front of her. Millie gave him one of her best smiles, and after saying some words of appreciation, she took a mouthful. Henry huffed something unintelligible and sat down to finish his own plate. It took a concerted effort to chew and swallow the badly cooked eggs, but Millie forced herself to finish every bite. From the remnants of what she had seen on the other plates, all of the eggs Henry had prepared had been burned, not just hers.

Millie glanced over at Evette, who had stayed to make sure Henry did not change his mind. Trying to use the same sweet tone Evette had used, Millie tried to start a conversation. "I once knew a cook who told me the secret to good eggs is that after you flip them, you turn off the heat. This way they don't become tough."

Bernard began to cough into his hand and stood up,

mumbling, "Should have already left. See you this evening, Henry, Evette."

Tommy immediately followed. "Thanks, Henry, Evette. Tell Stuart I'll catch up with him later." He tittered, barely swallowing the last of his food as he practically sprinted out the door.

Millie forced herself to take another bite as she wondered about the strange exit. Neither Bernard nor Tommy had said good-bye to her. Millie wondered if it was just an oversight or if they had felt uncomfortable around her, as she was still essentially a stranger. Turning to Evette, she shrugged and said, "I guess they are in a hurry."

Evette blinked. Did Millie really not understand what had just happened?

Henry, on the other hand, shook his head and muttered, "Sending this ninnyhammer tae work in a drinking den is like leading lambs to the slaughterhouse."

Before Millie could defend herself, Stuart returned to the kitchen and slammed his father's half-empty plate down on the working table, spilling some of the contents. Glaring at Millie, he said, "You ready?"

Seeing Stuart's frustration, Millie knew it had to be due to his father, but also realized that with little provocation, she could become the recipient of his anger. With a quick nod, she grabbed her pelisse off the bench beside her and said, "Have a good day, Evette, Henry," and then quickly ran to follow Stuart, who was already heading out the front door.

They walked one block to a very busy street, but before continuing, Stuart stopped and pointed back to Sasha's front door. "Know where youse are?" he asked, not surprised when Millie shook her head. "That," he began as he pointed one way, "is Rosemary Lane. Leads to where the Cits live. This," he said, pointing in the opposite direction, "is Cable Street, an' it's where you'll be goin'. It's busy, so watch yer step, but there'll be people about ter witness anythin', so youse should be safe enough. Once we're past Wellclose Square, look for Ollmanders. That's Pell Street. Clive's is at the end of Pell where it runs into Ratcliffe."

Without warning, Stuart started walking again, and not for the first time in her life, Millie cursed her short legs and sprinted to catch up. "Why would I need witnesses?"

Stuart stopped and crossed his arms. He was younger than she by several years, but the look he gave her made Millie feel like she was the youth and he the adult. "Not all blokes down 'ere are bad, but enough are. Youse gotta know that. So at night, down backstreets like Pell, just wait for the linkmen to light the alley up, is all."

Stuart resumed his pace, but this time Millie was prepared and managed to walk beside him. She had no idea what had happened back at the house to put Stuart in such a foul mood, but she knew from Evette that his father was an invalid and depended heavily on his son. From the few times they had met before, Millie knew the young man to be smart, impudent, and willing to exploit a person's weakness to take their money. However, she was also beginning to suspect there was far more to the boy than a sassy mouth and a constant eye for easy money.

"I saw the book you had last night. The one by Adam Smith."

Stuart said nothing and continued down the street, leaving Millie to try to keep up while avoiding people on the uneven sidewalk. "I . . . I can help you while I am staying with Madame Sasha. That is, if you are willing. I can help teach you to speak and act properly. You could then get work as an assistant, or in a shop—somewhere that would provide a good income."

"Givin' me a noose an' callin' it help," Stuart scoffed. "I've seen how gentry helps blokes like me. Youse make us servants an' then think ter own our lives day an' night. No, thanks. I don't wanna be ruled like that."

"That is simply not true, Stuart. My husband and I have the highest respect for those in our employ. Elda Mae—you met her—she is more like a mother to me than my lady's maid."

Stuart shrugged. He had met Elda Mae on occasion and had heard the old woman speak in an honest manner that would have resulted in her dismissal in most houses. Then again, Millie had proved only this morning that she was clueless how she oftentimes demeaned those around her. If anyone needed to be educated, it was Millie, not him.

"I'm not saying work in a house, or for a family," Millie pressed. "I'm only suggesting that with improved speech and an education, you could get employment that would allow you and your father to have a better life."

Stuart glared at Millie and increased the length of his strides. "That book was me father's, not mine. Neither one of us asked for your help an' that's cuz we don't want it. We have a home. We aren't starvin'. Just because the left side of his body don't work, don't mean *my father* can't be the one to teach me."

Stuart's anger was practically tangible, and despite his words and hostile stare, Millie could see that some piece of him longed for what she had offered. She would not push the matter right now, but neither would she give up trying to find a way to help the lanky youth.

They continued on in silence as the shops along the street took on a maritime flavor. At least one out of every four shops was stocked with gear either for a ship or for those who worked on them. The clothing stores were far different from those on Piccadilly. Here the attire was made to last and withstand harsh climates. Bright red and blue flannel shirts filled the windows, along with canvas trousers, pilot coats, large fur caps, and an occasional brass-buttoned jacket for naval officers.

Soon they reached the store Ollmanders, whose name

and a picture of a sail hung on a large sign outside their door. Instead of selling clothes or cases of tinned meat and biscuits, ropes and lines smelling of tar were stacked by the door and in the windows. Stuart pivoted right and headed down Pell Street, which was far narrower and less crowded. Suddenly, Millie fully understood what Stuart had meant about the safety of the crowd. The smells of the docks were becoming stronger, and she could see masts in the distance through the clouds of black smoke streaming from the tall chimneys.

Stuart came to an abrupt stop. Millie looked up and saw a faded sign with the words "Six Belles" painted on it. She peered inside and could see chairs on the floor, mugs everywhere, and a floor that would quickly make her dress hem look like she had taken a long walk through the mud. Millie licked her lips and wondered again about the wisdom of her plan. "Stuart, what should I do? What should I say? I must get this position . . . I . . . must."

Stuart inhaled and was about to say something very curt, but stopped himself. He had expected that as soon as they got here, Millie would demand to go back. But she was making no such requests, and yet he could tell she was truly scared. The woman must be in real trouble, though he could not imagine what could make a noblewoman run away from her rich man and work in a tavern. But then again, he never did understand the upper classes. She was just proof that all of them were a bit mad and such people should be avoided, not pitied.

"Listen, I likes youse and your friends. None of youse are 'igh and uppity like a lot of the gents I come across. But this ain't ever gonna work. Whatever your problems are an' whatever reason you gave Madame Sasha to convince 'er to let youse live with us, you gotta go back and tell 'er youse changed your mind. With what you're wearin', youse won't even get to speak before Clive is gonna know who youse are. And *nobody* crosses Clive. If 'e thinks that youse are lyin' to 'im, no tellin' what 'e is gonna do. You'll be lucky if 'e only throws you out."

Millie tensed her jaw. Stuart's speech was exactly what she needed. Unlike its intended objective, Millie felt her resolve to see her plan through gain strength. Stuart expected her to fail. Most likely, everyone in the house did. Little did they know that nothing ever quite motivated her like someone believing her incapable of achieving a goal she had set her sights on.

Millie jutted her chin in the air. "I'm wearing a day dress. It is simple and appropriate for any woman of any station. Now, will you please introduce me to Mr. Langdon?"

Stuart took three steps back and shook his head. "I ain't introducin' youse to no one, especially *Mr. Langdon*. Just bringin' youse 'ere is goin' to 'urt my reputation the moment Clive throws you out. You, *Lady Chaselton*," he quietly hissed, reminding her that he knew the truth, "are on your own." And with that he turned and left. In seconds, Stuart had disappeared into the crowd, which Millie suspected was intentional so that she could not follow him.

Taking a deep breath, Millie stared at the closed doors. It was now solely up to her. No more reliance on others for help. They had got her to this point, but now it was up to her to convince Clive she was somebody he should hire. But as soon as she learned of Aimee's fate, she intended to end this farce and get her life back. *And never again will I jeopardize it*, Millie silently vowed.

Brushing away a tear, Millie pushed the handle of the lopsided door and entered a public house for the first time in her life.

The large room smelled of smoke and spilled liquor mixed with the distinct scent of the pine tar worn by seamen. To her right, attached to the wall, was a large painted plank with a dozen large, worn circular nobs that served as hooks for sailors' coats and hats. Just beyond the rack was a serving area consisting of a well-used counter with several mugs lying haphazardly on its surface. Behind the ale-soaked surface were three casks, and on a shelf above them were several bottles of liquor. Millie noticed that to the far side of the serving area was the establishment's only other door. She suspected that it led to a room where most of the liquor was stored.

In the corner was a single padded chair facing a fairly sizeable stone hearth, and despite the chair's obvious well-used state, it appeared to be the tavern's only comfortable place to sit. To her left was a large bay window that let in a surprising amount of light considering the layer of grime covering every pane, which Millie decided was a good thing. For though she could not really look out and see who was coming, neither could onlookers glance through to see just who was within.

With the exception of six brass sconces, nothing ornamental was anywhere to be seen. The tavern's main decorations were the scars along the walls from brawls involving thrown furniture. The interior of the room was full of tables, benches, and scattered chairs, most of which were either skewed or toppled over.

A whistling sound caught Millie's attention and she took a step farther inside. Instinct told her to look down and see what had made her leather-soled boots stick to the floor, but Millie kept her eyes on the closed door beside the bar. A second later a massive bald man with wide-set eyes bounded through the doorway, carrying a crate of whiskey bottles on his left shoulder. He had several small scars scattered along his scalp and was smiling, which made him appear friendly—but only for a moment. That impression changed the instant he saw her. His whistling stopped and his face turned to stone.

Millie began to blink and felt her pulse race. "Are you Mr. Langdon?" she asked, returning his direct gaze. She straightened her back, suspecting any sign that she was either meek or mild would end any hopes of her being hired. Her height might make her look otherwise, but she was far from helpless.

A dark eyebrow rose upon hearing his rarely used surname. "Call me Clive," he instructed, praying the little thing he was looking at was not the woman Sasha had mentioned when she had stopped by last night. Damn woman looked like she belonged in Mayfair. "And ye better not be the chit I was told tae expect," he added, visibly raking her with his lapis-colored eyes. He had seen many pretty women in his time, but this one, with her delicate features, chocolate-brown hair, and unusual colored eyes, had them all beat—easily.

Clive set the crate down on the counter with a small grunt and reminded himself of the very firm rules he had about women working at his place. The first of those rules was by far the most important—no whoring in his establishment. He had allowed it at one time and every night had become a nightmare. Drunks he could handle. Thieves, angry dockworkers, disgruntled watermen—there wasn't a sailor he could not manage or find some means to persuade to behave when all he was after was a drink. But men lusting for a woman were pure trouble. And the woman standing before him was the complete embodiment of how Clive defined trouble. "Tell Sasha that I changed me mind."

Millie took a step forward, reminding herself that this gruff man ran one of the few public houses where patrons were not allowed to assault the women who worked there. Clive owned a tavern that seamen and dock laborers from all over the Thames frequented. Working here was her chance, probably her only chance, to learn just who had taken Aimee. "Mr. Clive, I understand that you may have reservations about hiring someone of my stature, but I assure you I am strong and able."

Hearing her fancy talk, Clive snorted and began taking bottles out of the crate and putting them on the shelf. He knew from the onset to be suspicious about Sasha's request, but she was impossible to refuse. Saying no to this female, however, was well within his ability. "I don't have reservations, woman. I would if I was offering ye anything, but I ain't. So take yourself back out that door and trouble someone else."

Millie removed her gloves and began to unbutton her pelisse, refusing to give up. "Mr. Clive, you are a businessman, and the fact is that while I admit to desperately needing this job, you are short a server. I can do the job and as a fair man, you should at least offer me the chance to fail."

Clive stared at her in shock. If he had not already been annoyed and squeezing his jaw, it might have fallen open hearing her little speech. No one he knew spoke like that, and certainly not to him in *his* place. He knew he needed to say something, anything, that conveyed those sentiments, but all that would come out was, "Not *mister,* just Clive."

Millie nodded her head and offered him a smile. "Clive then. And my name is Ellie . . . Alwick," she lied, laying the pelisse over the back of the chair that was near the hearth.

Clive grunted, repeating "Alwick" under his breath skeptically. The woman was a horrible liar and he was about to say as much when he realized the woman had taken her coat off and was starting to straighten up the chairs. Damn little thing believed he had actually agreed with her little speech. He needed to regain control and fast.

Straightening his shoulders, he said, "Fine. Don't tell me yer real name, as it don't matter. Ye can put yer coat thing right back on because, as I said before, you are *not* working here."

Millie used her foot to shove a bench out of the way and then began to organize the tables so that they were evenly spaced from each other. "Yes, Clive, I am."

Clive strolled around the counter to where Millie was working and stood right in front of her, preventing her from going to the next table. "Look, announcing stuff may have worked in whatever fancy house ye used tae live in, but *nobody* tells me how tae run my place."

Millie jutted her chin out, praying she looked more confident than she felt. "I am certainly not telling you how to run your place. *You* did when you promised Madame Sasha."

"Madame Sasha," Clive huffed, amazed that the old bird still got people to call her that. "I don't owe that convict nothing. All I promised was tae look at ye, and I've done that. The answer's *no,*" Clive stated unequivocally. Thinking he had finally made his point, he went back to the bar and his crate of liquor.

"But with Clarice gone, you need someone who is willing to work hard . . . and not on their backs." Millie paused upon seeing Clive's darkening gaze.

"Aye, maybe I do, but *not* the likes of ye," he said, refusing to relent. He pointed his finger at her and then the door. "So now take yer pretty arse out of here before someone sees ye in here."

Millie was undaunted. "Is that the basis of your refusal to hire me? You think I'm pretty?" When Clive refused to look at her, Millie moved forward to the bar. "But, Clive, that is a reason *to* hire me, for it will bring more business to your establishment. And if you are worried about someone becoming . . . let's say, friendly . . ." She waited until he looked her directly in the eye to finish her thought. "I can take care of myself."

Clive suppressed a smile. For a tiny female, the lass

showed spirit, and that was a quality he had always admired, especially in women. Too often the females who came to work in drinking dens were either timid and full of fear, or so jaded that they could no longer express feelings of any kind. But the idea of this petite beauty fighting off even the weakest of seamen was more than a little amusing.

Seeing his smirk, Millie leaned in closer and added, "*Without* it costing you any customers."

Clive stood bewitched by the sparkling deep purple hue of her eyes. The lass was serious in her claim. She truly believed that she could keep men away *and* keep them happy. It was almost worth giving her a chance just to see how she intended to do that. "What do ye know of serving ale and whiskey?"

Millie forced herself to remain calm. "Absolutely nothing. I am just as ignorant as you believe me to be when it comes to working in a public house. However, that does not mean that I am incapable of learning or hard work. I intend to earn my wages."

Clive let out a huge gust of air and folded his arms across his massive chest. Hard work, the woman said. She was as familiar with hard work as he was the waltz—and he couldn't dance to save his soul. So if this pretty little chit knew nothing about earning wages through hard physical labor, why would Sasha send her to work in a dockworkers' tavern? Why not one with gentlemen clientele?

Clive took another look at Ellie and tried to discern her background. A widow? He did not think so. She was unhappy, stressed, but lacked the telltale signs of grief. Governess? Perhaps, but doubtful. There were other, much easier forms of employment for someone like her. So if she lost one cully, why not just get another? Clive narrowed his eyes as he answered his own question. Ellie was here because she did not want to be found. "Why do ye want tae work near the docks?"

Millie licked her lips, somewhat unnerved that he had discerned that the locality of the job was essential to her. "I have my reasons."

Clive shook his head upon hearing his suspicion confirmed. She did not need *a* job. She wanted *this* job. "Now that makes me curious, and a man like me doesn't like tae be curious. Makes me think ye might not only *be* trouble, but might be bringing it here."

"M . . . Clive," Millie began, "I can assure you that—"

"No, it'll be me doing the assuring. Ye may be seeking a way tae make some money while avoiding those looking for ye, but I don't need a bailiff poking his head in me business."

Millie's eyes popped wide and her stance suddenly became hostile. "A *bailiff*? Why, I have never done anything illegal in my life! And I am offended you could think so when you know nothing about me!"

Clive flinched at her violent reaction to the accusation. Ellie might be beautiful and a mite small, but she was also fiery. He liked that but quickly scowled at her to hide his appreciation. "Hell, lass, how was I supposed tae know? Ye claim ye can take on a brawlin' bunch of seamen, when anyone can tell ye've only been around gentry. Don't deny it," he said, waving a finger in the air, drawing an imaginary circle around her. "It's written all over ye. Yer hair, yer walk, yer damn posture, and those hands . . ."

Millie looked down. "What about my hands?"

Clive reached out and grabbed one, touching the smooth, velvety palms. It was a mistake and he flung it back. "Just like I thought. Soft as a new bairn."

Millie's heart lurched. She clenched and unclenched her fist. It was strange, but only Chase had ever touched her in such a familiar way. She suddenly wondered if she could really endure this job.

Millie licked her lips and pushed the thought aside. She was about to lose this opportunity unless she gave Clive a compelling story about why she needed to work for him. She opted for something closer to the truth. "I admit I am having some difficulties disentangling myself from my previous life. It is possible—though very tenuous—that someone may make some inquiries about me. But I give you my word that I have done nothing dishonest. I only made a mistake, and it cost me . . . my life in a way. I am just trying to correct it and I *need* this job in order to do so. Give me one night, and if you still think I cannot do the job, I will leave and give you no more trouble."

Clive's deep blue eyes stared long and hard at the small, captivating woman standing in front of him asking for a job. He must be out of his mind to agree, but he knew that was exactly what he was going to do. "Be here at six. And don't dress up like ye're going to a party in Mayfair. Wear working clothes. That one's tae distracting."

Millie bit her bottom lip and Clive rolled his eyes as he realized that she was already wearing her plainest garment.

Millie returned on time, wearing the same gown. The place was empty. "Clive?" she called out.

A bald head poked up from behind the bar. A second later he stood up to his full height and tossed a cloth onto the counter. "Ye're back," he huffed.

Millie could not figure out if he sounded surprised or disappointed. "You did not think I would be?"

"A man's allowed tae hope," Clive groused. "But since ye are here, ye can prove tae me how good ye are at hard work."

Millie looked around. "But . . . no one has yet to arrive."

An unfriendly smile overtook Clive's face as he pointed to the dingy cloth on the counter and then at the bucket of water near the hearth. "But there is plenty tae clean."

Millie inhaled deeply as she picked up the cloth and went

over to grab the bucket. It was half full and its contents were
not just water. She wondered just how often Clive emptied
and refilled it and decided that she probably did not want to
know the answer to the question. Plunging the cloth in the
filthy water, she wrung it out and began to work her way
around the room, wiping off tables and setting the chairs
and benches back to their rightful positions.

Clive grimaced as she began to work. He had half hoped
the prospect of cleaning this place would send Ellie running
out the door. He had been serious about her hands. Based
on his brief touch, the woman had not done a hard day of
labor in her life. But Ellie surprised him as she continued to
straighten up the room, not uttering a single complaint. Realizing she was not going to, Clive busied himself in the bar
area, counting mugs and making sure that the used bottles
were stacked in front of the unused ones.

He did what he always did preparing for the night crowd,
but he also found himself spying every once in a while on
his new help, watching her tend to tables and chairs that had
not been cleaned for days. She had changed her hair to a
simple braided bun, but it had done nothing to hide her
beauty. Clive doubted anything would.

He also doubted she was recently let go of a paying position. No, whoever Ellie was, she had been forced out, and
based on her desire to stay away from the better parts of
Town, most likely it had been by some titled gent with considerable power. That explained how she came to be with
Sasha. The old woman made a habit of taking in strays, but
it still did not explain why Ellie wanted a job interacting
with the most undisciplined and roughest clientele London
had to offer. Not when she had the figure and the face to
find another man.

The only thing he did know about Ellie was that she had
secrets, and oddly enough, that was the one thing that *did*

make her fit in at Six Belles. Everyone had secrets. And when they drove someone to the docks, it created an intangible bond, where certain rules of privacy were considered sacred.

Every soul Clive knew, including himself, had a past that was nobody's business. And that included Ellie.

Bessie strode into Six Belles and threw Clive an apologetic look. "Sorry 'bout bein' late. Had somethin' I had to finish."

Clive arched a brow and shrugged his shoulders. Bessie was relieved he was not mad. With him being short-handed, she was expecting him to at least issue her an empty threat about making her stay late to clean up. Turning around, she was not surprised to find the place almost half full, customers shouting for someone to bring them a drink. She was about to holler back that she was coming, when she realized they were not just calling for anyone to serve them, but for one person in particular—and it was not her.

All eyes were on a dark-haired brunette. She was facing the other way, but Bessie could tell the woman was too small, too fragile, and based on her fancy gold dress, too pampered to be in a place like this. "Just who is *that*?" she asked Clive in a more shrewlike manner than she had intended.

"Ellie," Clive answered, unfazed by Bessie's glare. "Hired her this morning tae help out."

Bessie turned back around to assess her new competition, who was making her way around the tables and men. The woman was striking and young—the two things Bessie used to be, but was no longer. Ten years ago, her fiery red mane would have easily competed with the raven-haired beauty. Bessie's ample bosom could still turn a man's eye and she took satisfaction in knowing she was one of the better-looking women who worked around this part of London. Her figure was slim, she had all her teeth, and her eyes were the color of the sea. But none of those features could compete with the youthful curves of the petite woman standing across from her.

"What were you thinkin' hirin' her?" Bessie hissed, only caring slightly how jealous it made her sound.

Clive started filling a mug with ale and said, "Well, Bess, I was thinking I needed the help and that the men would like her. It looks tae me that I was right."

Bessie saw Millie's shoulders straighten, and when her purple eyes drilled into Bessie's blue ones, something inside her snapped. The little chit should have acted at least *a little* intimidated, but instead the missy actually thought to stare her down. Bessie fumed. "*Her?* That little girl ain't never served a drink before in her life," she said loud enough for Millie and everyone else to hear.

Millie finished taking the table's orders and began to walk toward Clive, stopping right in front of Bessie. "I'm actually quite well versed in serving an assortment of drinks in a variety of settings because, as you know, the rules of etiquette take into account minor details such as where, what, and who is being served. But I am sure that you possess similar knowledge or . . . oh my. My mistake. I did not realize you were only skilled in delivering mugs of ale and spirits to men whose only intent is getting drunk."

Millie did not wait for an answer but went over to Clive and said, "Five more of the same."

Bessie inhaled sharply. The saucy green chit might think she had won, but her flowery words had tipped her hand. Whoever the interloper was, she clearly did not belong here. Dockworkers and seamen might enjoy spying on a pretty, genteel face from afar, but not in their taverns and especially not when it belonged to the gentry and their judgmental ways. She was just about to say as much, but when the men eagerly hollered for Ellie's quick return, Bessie became so furious she could hardly speak.

Marching over to the bar, she snatched the mugs Clive had just put on the counter before Millie could get them and headed over to the table of customers. She issued each of them her most provocative smile and set the mugs down. "Here you go, men."

"Uh, thanks, Bess, but we was wantin' Ellie ter be bringin' us our drinks."

Bessie glanced around the table. Heads were nodding and several were stretching their necks to see around her and catch a peek at the woman who had just made her look like a fool. "But you get 'em faster with me, Mikey."

Mikey grimaced. "Maybe. Not goin' to argue that point, but we're payin' Ellie, Bess." He stared at her, letting her know without words that he was fully aware of her intentions to usurp Millie's tip. Bessie watched in shock as he waved to Millie, who must have started his way because a big grin took over his face.

Bessie took a step back, thankful to hear the doors squeak open, allowing another group of men to enter. She went over to see to their needs, but before she was done, four more men came in and Millie was already at their table. It went like this for the next several hours. And though the place was fairly evenly divided, with her serving one half and Millie assisting the other, Bessie was more than a little unhappy.

"It's just because she's a new face," Devlin said as Bessie handed him a glass of his favorite whiskey. The stuff was expensive and Clive kept it on hand just for his friend.

Bessie knew very little about the man, other than his name and what she could see. He had been coming here for as long as she could remember and he always sat alone, staring at the hearth, whether a fire was lit or not. He had plenty of blunt judging by the way he dressed and consumed liquor, but Bessie had no idea how he earned it. He was definitely not a dockworker or a stevedore for he lacked the specific odor that came from such labor. Tall, with dark, ominous features, Devlin was an odd one. He looked like he belonged at Six Belles and yet was not really one of them. Which meant Bessie trusted him only because Clive did.

Bessie glanced back at Millie and rolled her eyes when she missed the man's extended hand and almost tipped over another mug of ale. She let go a small, unfeminine snort. "Look at 'em fawnin' all over her. She could pour a whole drink in their laps and they wouldn't care." Bessie folded her arms and watched in disgust. "Didn't think Clive would get suckered in by a pretty face," she added under her breath.

In truth, Bessie had always thought she was Clive's type. He had never said as much, but she had just caught him spying on her every once in a while, especially when she was bending over. It was one of the reasons Bessie never thought to leave Six Belles. It would mean giving up the small fantasy that Clive and she might someday become more.

Devlin shook his head. "Settle down there, Bessie. I'm sure Clive still prefers redheads over brunettes," he reassured her. "But knowing his policy on women, I too am a little curious about his latest hire."

Bessie watched as one of the men's hands reached around to give Ellie's left cheek a squeeze. When she did not stop him, Bessie released a small smile of satisfaction. Clive was a tolerant man, but there were certain things he would not tolerate in his place. Bessie made sure the men knew she would serve them drinks and nothing else. If any refused to keep their hands to themselves, she gave them a painful reminder. It cost her tips and sometimes Clive customers, but it was the preferred alternative. "Tonight will be the last we see of her once Clive sees what's happenin'."

Devlin was about to agree when Ellie leaned forward over

the table, causing her small but attractive behind to rise higher and even more in reach. The men huddled close to her for a few seconds as she whispered something and then, inexplicably, they sat back. All were grinning, but the hand that had been touching her had released its grip and was slowly retreating. Devlin found himself surprisingly impressed—not that every man now had his hands visible and on the table, but that they seemed happy about keeping them there.

Bessie must have found it just as hard to believe. "What just happened? How did she do that?"

Devlin shook his head, smiled, and resumed his relaxed position in the chair so that he once again was facing the hearth. "Not a clue, and if I were you, I would play nice and ask. Because based on what I just saw, she's not going anywhere."

Bessie stole a sideways glance at Clive. He was not one to smile, but the man was wearing one now. He had seen the whole thing.

Clive arched a brow at Bessie as she marched over to him. He crossed his arms and leaned back against the barrels. "Makes you wonder what Ellie told them," he said with a smirk when Bessie got close enough to hear. "Maybe you should ask her."

Bessie shot him an icy look. "You want me back tomorrow, Clive, you tell me her story. What's a woman like her doin' here where she don't belong?"

"I too would be interested," Bessie heard Devlin say behind her. She was glad he had followed her, aware that Clive might be more apt to divulge what he knew to Devlin.

Clive took the empty glass Devlin handed him and shrugged his shoulders. "Never would tell me. Just that she needed a job. Pretty insistent about it. I suspect she's hiding from someone."

"She probably was spreading her legs for some cully who got tired of her and threw her out," Bessie mumbled.

Clive waved at Millie to get her attention and pointed at a group of men looking for her. He then handed Devlin a refill of whiskey and said, "I thought the same for a bit, but I've seen kept women—whether of quality or no—and there's a look about 'em that Ellie doesn't have."

Devlin took a swallow of the whiskey. "No, but she's no virgin either. Be careful, Clive. The way she handled those men, she's a clever one. Whatever trouble she's in, just make sure it don't fall back on you or Bessie."

Clive nodded. "If ye hear anything at yer place about her, let me know."

"I will."

Devlin genuinely liked Clive. One night while reminiscing about their Scottish homeland, they had become friends. Over the years, that friendship had solidified into trust, and Clive was one of the few who knew what he did for a living. And while Devlin was not ashamed of owning a prosperous gambling joint, he knew that such knowledge becoming widely known might make him a target in this part of Town. Clive understood that and respected a man's privacy. Which was fortunate, because there were many things Devlin wanted no one—including Clive—to know about himself and his past. Heirs to earldoms would never be welcome at Six Belles—even cast out ones.

Devlin downed the rest of his whiskey and stared thoughtfully at the brunette coming toward them with another order. She was a mystery and she was beautiful. Two things he found irresistible.

Millie had seen the exchange and felt the tall man's eyes on her. Walking past his blatant stare, she handed Clive a couple of mugs for refills and asked for two more. Then she turned and openly returned his assessment.

The man was no stevedore. He neither dressed nor smelled like someone who worked on the docks, loading and unloading ship cargo. His black hair was trimmed, and

though not of the latest styles, his clothes were tailored to
fit him, hinting at his athletic, Corinthian-like physique.
Millie was unsure just how old he was, but she suspected
that, like Chase, he was younger than he looked. Life had
taught him hard lessons, killing whatever innocence the
man had long ago. But there was something else about him.
A hardness that was almost frightening. His green eyes
were dark, cold, fathomless pits, yet she did not discern any
judgment within them. Just curiosity.

Millie broke the gaze and grabbed the mugs from Clive.
"You look like you have questions, Mr. . . ."

Devlin twitched his lips at the attempt at proper formality.
No, the woman did not come from this harsh part of London,
and yet she just might have enough spirit to survive in it.
"Name's Devlin. And, aye. I have many a question, but I do
not think you will give me any answers."

Millie could not help herself and smiled. "I promise that
I have none that would interest you," she said before walking back to her customers.

She could feel his probing eyes follow her. They had been
following her off and on all night. But they had not been the
only ones. Bessie had been shooting daggers at her whenever she had the opportunity. Then there was Clive. He had
never said a word, but Millie knew that his blue gaze had
caught all that she had done—the good and the bad—
throughout the evening and was determining if he would let
her continue to work there.

Millie set a mug down on the table and the man handed
her two farthings. "You already paid me for the drinks," she
said, handing him back the coins.

"Ah, but this, dearie, is for you."

Millie looked at the two coins. A halfpenny altogether.
The man had been one of the first she waited on. She had
spilled his drink, been slow, and he had been incredibly

patient and kind. He made so little money and she did not truly need it.

She opened up her palm and was handing the coins back when she heard Bessie roar "Bloody hell!" Less than a second later, the enraged redhead was at the table snatching the money right out of the man's hand. Before he could protest, Bessie glared at him and said, "Get out of here, Lem, and don't you think for a moment that you can come back in here and not pay for the service as well as the drink."

With a shrug of his shoulders, Lem got up, downed the mug of ale, and left, leaving Millie to face a furious Bessie alone.

Millie felt her jaw tighten. "Bessie, I did not want to take money for what I know was less than average service."

"Now, you listen, missy. *Never* give back any blunt a man gives you in here. *Never*. If they think they don't have to tip, they won't. You may not know it yet, little girl, but you ain't sleepin' between the legs of an aristocrat anymore. In this place, there's only one way to earn honest coin."

Millie put her hand out. "Then give it back."

Bessie snorted, her sea-blue eyes sparkling with victory. "Consider it payment for a much-needed lesson."

Millie watched in silence as the woman proceeded to take the tip and drop it in her bodice. She could argue it was hers, but then it was Bessie who actually had the wisdom to take the money. More mistakes like that one and people might start asking questions. Too many questions created rumors, and Chase frequented the docks too often to take the chance for rumors to take hold. Millie knew she needed to become a lot smarter, a lot faster.

Gathering two empty mugs in each hand, Millie proceeded back to the bar. She had tried three, but two were all her small hands could manage. She placed the mugs behind the counter and stretched her back, trying to ignore the dark-haired man watching her from the hearth chair.

She shook her head and squeezed her toes in her boots. Never had her feet hurt this bad, even after dancing with the clumsiest of men. She glanced up. The man was still staring at her and Clive was pointing to another group who had just entered. It was going to be a long night.

Chapter 14

October 22, 1816

For two days, Collins had been debating what he should do. His options were few, and yet he still could not decide how to proceed.

He had agreed to postpone announcing Aimee's presence on the ship to the captain, based on the hope her injuries would disappear given enough time. But her wrists were now for the most part healed. Unfortunately, evidence still remained of what she had endured. The white scars were not obvious, but they could still be easily seen. They might lessen with time, but Collins suspected they would never completely disappear. Aimee knew it too and was stalling for time. She was under some delusion that the captain's feelings about her would change based on how much she knew about ships. Collins could let her continue as things were, letting Aimee decide just when she was ready to reveal her presence, or he could do what his loyalty said he should, and inform the captain.

"Her injuries are healed, JP. That was the reason we waited, was it not?"

JP shrugged his shoulders and maintained his gaze on the

sea, listening to the water splash against the side of the ship.
The scattered clouds were thickening, but there was still
enough moonlight to see the waves, which were growing
stronger each day. "It was ze rationale, but not ze reason."

"Which was?"

"It's different for every person. Mademoiselle, she fears
rejection. I like 'er, and you know zat I do not like very many
people. As soon as ze captain sees 'er, she will be lost to us,
and I do not want zat. Neizer do most of ze men. You do not
need me to tell you your reason for delaying ze inevitable."

Fear, Collins answered nonverbally. Not of physical injury
or pain, but of losing his job. He was a good chief mate and
he had built a reputation, so he knew he could find another
position if needed. Problem was, he did not want another
job. He respected Reece both as a man and a captain. He
treated his crew well and did not meddle with those he left
in charge. He was fair and never used brutality as an initial
response to any situation. In short, he was someone Collins
hoped to become. He had hoped the captain also believed
in him and eventually would offer him his own command.
But those hopes and plans had just been trumped, and he
was powerless to do anything about it.

"Damn it, JP. She's the daughter of a *marquess*."

JP leaned one elbow against the ship's rail and turned to
study Collins with a sharp, assessing gaze. "And just why
does zat make such a difference?"

"Because it does. She should have said *something*."

JP turned back toward the sea, exhaling with agitation.
"Why? When she knew zis would be 'ow you would react."

For the first time in his life, Collins was frightened of the
power the noble class held. It did not matter that Aimee's
presence was thrust upon him and the crew by her own actions. He had helped to conceal her presence, and that alone
was enough to possibly get him incarcerated, if not killed.

"The damn woman knew I would have taken her to the

captain, and she didn't want that. She put me . . . hell, she put all of us in this position. Damn selfish of her."

JP nodded in mock agreement. "*Oui*, very selfish indeed. Troublesome too. Probably why zere 'ave been so many riots, like ze time *you* brought a woman on board." JP paused and when Collins said nothing, he continued. "I've noticed 'ow you 'ave to continually threaten the men to keep their silence as well."

"Sometimes, JP, you can be an ass."

"And you, Collins, wouldn't know anyzing about zat, would you? Just admit why you are mad. You zink she lied to you."

"She put the men in danger. Her being who she is, there could be hell to pay and she won't be the one who pays it. It will be the men."

"And you."

"Don't forget yourself, JP. Don't think you won't catch hell."

This time when JP nodded, it was in earnest. "But she doesn't know it."

"Or she doesn't care."

"If you really believed zat, you would 'ave dragged 'er to ze captain already. You, my friend, are trying to find a way to shield not just ze men, but 'er."

"Then I am trying to do the impossible."

JP's lips thinned with frustration. "Ze captain loves 'er, and no matter what you just said, you know Lady Aimee sincerely likes ze crew. She'll protect zem. You'll see. She'll even protect you."

Collins sighed. "If she does, then she is going to be hurt. Maybe not physically, but you and I have seen the full force of the captain's ire."

"His anger is inevitable, for zere is no way to successfully 'ide 'er until we get back to London."

Collins mused on the idea, wishing it were even remotely possible. "Maybe I should just wait until we are near the Savannah River to tell him about her. His wrath might be shorter-lived."

JP shook his head and leaned forward once more on the rail. "Unfortunately, I believe your first conclusion was ze right one."

"That I am a dead man?"

JP nodded.

"We all are," Collins said. "And that includes Lady Aimee."

"You would zink ze captain would be smart enough to realize just what a gift 'e 'as been 'anded. Maybe we will get lucky and 'e will."

The sound of rapid footsteps got their attention. They turned simultaneously to see a skinny man run up onto the afterdeck. As always, his dark brown hair was pulled back in a tight ponytail, making his face look more angular and severe.

"What's up, Mac?" Collins asked.

"You've gotta come to the main deck!"

Collins fought to keep from cringing. Ironlung Mac, the men called him, and it was appropriate because he always spoke louder than necessary. "Maybe in a while."

Mac shook his head. "Then it will be too late! The miss, well, she dared us and we couldn't deny the dare, now could we, sir? So we did it thinkin' she wouldn't, but damn, if she didn't start climbin' the thing. She got to the top even faster than the rigger!"

Collins glanced at JP, whose expression held the same foreboding his did.

No amount of luck was going to save any of them.

Chapter 15

October 24, 1816

Collins paused to look at the angry seas. The foul weather had finally caught up with them and the storm was going to make things very tense on the ship for the next several hours. The only person in their cabin and not working was Lady Aimee. Collins prayed she had believed him when he told her that she was not—under any circumstances—to leave her cabin. The men needed no distractions.

Aimee had nodded before calmly sitting down, but then that was how she responded to all of his instructions. The ship had already started rocking fiercely, but Aimee just sat there as if she was unaware of the storm and the nausea it should be creating. The damn woman did not even know when to get seasick.

He glanced across the upper deck, waiting for the captain to give him the signal that it was time to move the sails to the storm configuration. Just before the first gust hit, Collins had been in the captain's quarters, trying for the third time in the last forty-eight hours to tell the captain about Aimee's presence on board. But before he could, the storm had made its presence known. Immediately, Reece had gone topside to take over the wheel and Collins had gone to make sure Aimee was not just safe, but safely out of the way.

Another wave slammed into the side of the boat. Collins gripped the rail and watched the water recede across the deck and back into the ocean. The winds were growing in strength. The storm mimicked his mood, and both were growing worse by the minute.

"Collins!" Reece shouted, barely loud enough to be heard. He pointed to the sails and mouthed the words "heave to."

Collins nodded in understanding and gestured to Kyrk, who also had been waiting for the captain to give the signal to climb the rigging. It was time to change the sails and reduce the amount of canvas that caught the wind. It was important to leave just enough sail via the staysail and both fore and main topsails to minimize forward drift and the resulting strain on the vessel.

This balance between the force of the wind in the sails and the drag of the underwater keel was key to keeping a ship afloat. If the balance shifted and the ship turned its edge to the wind, it would be beaten by breaking waves. As an experienced rigger, Kyrk knew exactly what needed to be done. He and the Poulsen brothers had already taken down the jibs and were working on the foremast to get down the two highest sails—the royal and topgallant.

Once done, all three men quickly descended back to the deck and got ready to do it again. Shiv made his way back to the spanker while Lamont and Kyrk headed to the mainmast where Jolly George was untying the ropes to the main sails. Just then an enormous rogue wave crashed over the ship's starboard side. When the water slammed into them, they instinctively tried to grab ahold of anything nearby, but their efforts were futile.

The last thing Collins saw before grabbing ahold of the

companionway rail to anchor himself during the deluge, was the three men being swept away. When the water cleared and he was able to regain his vision, Collins scanned the deck. Near the capstan, an immobile heap of men's legs and arms caught his attention. The large, rotating machine was used to apply force to tighten ropes or pull up an anchor. To be thrown against one was never good.

Collins let go of the rail and made his way over to the scene. Both Poulsen brothers and Jolly George were injured but moving. Fortunately for Kyrk, he was unconscious because his right leg was seriously broken. Collins quickly ordered Turrell, Gilley, and Blackie to help him carry the men off the deck. JP joined him below. They did what they could for Kyrk's leg and then Collins headed up the stairs to the upper deck, knowing the captain would be impatient for a report.

"How bad is it?" Reece barked against the wind.

"They'll live. Jolly George is banged up. Shiv's hand is broken, and based on Lamont's inability to breathe without severe pain, his ribs are busted."

"And Kyrk?"

Collins swallowed. He knew that the captain already suspected the worst. "His leg is bad. It'll be weeks before he can walk again, let alone climb a mast."

"Damn," Reece muttered as he fought the wind trying to wrestle the wheel from his grasp. "Storm's getting worse and soon the last of the sun will be gone. We *have* to get those sails down."

"It's been years, but I can climb."

"Can't do it by yourself," Reece yelled, loud enough that his frustration was unmistakable. "Find me someone— *anyone*—who can climb the mast without breaking it and help you."

Collins returned Reece's stare. The *Sea Emerald* was not shorthanded, but it had a crew of just over thirty. They both knew that in that one wave, they lost their best chance at getting those sails down. In this weather, the weight of two large men on the mast would most likely snap it, leaving the ship even more vulnerable than it already was.

The boat listed severely and it was as if the sea and the captain were at war. Reece was using all of his strength and knowledge to keep the vessel pointed in the desired direction. But if those sails did not come down, he was going to lose the fight . . . and soon.

All Collins needed was someone who could help free the ropes along the halyard so the men on the deck could help furl the sail and keep it that way until Collins had enough time to tie off each sail. They did not have to be skilled in ships or sails, or even very strong. They just needed to be able to climb and help free knots. Only one person on this ship met all the requirements.

Could he ask a woman—a daughter of a marquess—to climb a mast in the middle of a serious storm? It was unthinkable, and yet Collins knew that was exactly what he was going to do.

The ship rolled and Aimee fell back against the wall that protected her from the sea. It was wet and leaking water, making Aimee wonder just how close the ship's side was to being in the water. Every instinct she had was to leave the room that felt more and more like a coffin and go topside. But she remained where she was.

Previously when Collins had threatened her about staying in her room, Aimee had known it was a tactic to get her to comply. But earlier that afternoon, he had meant what he said about her distracting the crew and how every man needed their full attention on their job to keep the ship afloat.

"Be careful of his knee!"

"Get JP!"

"It bloody hurts to breathe."

"Tie off that part of his leg . . ."

Aimee scrambled off the bed and unlatched the door to steal a look at what was going on in the hallway. It was hard to see and everyone was still shouting, but when Kyrk came into view, she nearly gasped aloud. His right leg was broken and a bone was protruding just below his knee. Her mind started to race. Had that happened when Kyrk was climbing? Were the sails still up or had he gotten them down in time?

The boat lurched and Aimee suspected that the injuries had occurred before all the sails had been taken down. She whirled around and went over to the small chest and pulled out the men's clothes she had been wearing when she tricked Gus and Petey into abducting her. Collins had told her not to leave, but he had said nothing about changing her clothes.

Quickly, she removed her dress and donned the shirt and breeches. She had just finished when she heard a knock on the door. Aimee went to open it, unsurprised to find Collins on the other side. He eyed her attire, his expression both surprised and relieved.

Aimee stepped out of the way to allow Collins entrance, but he declined. "I saw Kyrk being carried . . . his leg was bad. Will he live?"

Collins nodded, but Aimee knew from his brief glance down the corridor to the room where they'd carried Kyrk, that nothing was for certain. "None of us are going to live through this if we don't get the mainsails down."

Aimee's green eyes held Collins's blue ones. "I can do it."

Collins's jaw visibly tensed. "Do you know what you are agreeing to?" he asked. "Because this storm just severely wounded three men. Chances are it is going to take you out too."

Aimee kept her features deceptively composed. Collins was not trying to scare her into compliance, he was speaking the truth. Going out in this storm could mean death. But she also knew that it had to be done and the only reason Collins would be coming to see her was that he had little choice. "Just tell me what to do," she said as calmly as she could muster and moved into the corridor.

Collins pivoted and headed to the stairs that led to the main deck. Aimee followed, and as soon as she was out in the open her heart started to race. The wind was vicious and never had the main deck look so wide and dangerous. Lightning flashed and it lit up the scene just long enough for her to clearly see exactly what they were up against. The sails that remained unfurled billowed in the wind. Only the topsail was open on the foremast, but all four of the large sails on the mainmast were unfurled, becoming dangerous weapons. She did not need Collins to point out that that was where he needed her to climb.

Aimee nodded and followed Collins as they made their way to the mast and began to climb. Reaching the first square sail, she walked out onto the footropes under the first yard. Her fingers were cold as the ocean spray and wind beat at them, but she quickly released the knots, enabling Collins to furl the mainsail. Ignoring the tingling in her extremities, she headed back up the rigging until she reached the top, a small platform at the joint of the lower- and topmast. Following Collins's lead, she pulled herself across the ratlines that together with the shrouds formed a ropelike net. Each took one pair of backstays and together began to furl the topgallant sail. Relief flooded her when it freed and they moved on to the royal sail.

Once the last sail was collapsed, she waited until Collins, who was already on the mast, made his way down. Then she began her own descent. Never did she want to do this again. Climbing was not something she ever thought could be terrifying, but neither had she ever dreamed of doing it in a storm where the item she was climbing was constantly trying to throw her off. But it was not even the rolling boat or the wind that truly terrified her, it was the cold.

Aimee could hear shouts from below her, but the rain prevented her from seeing who it was or hearing what they were saying. All she knew was her fingers were so frozen, they barely responded to her demands to curl and hold on as she made her way down the mast. Her teeth could no longer chatter because her jaw and cheeks were unable to move. Only sheer will enabled her to take another step when she did not think she could.

She looked down. Her eyes grew large and then blackness consumed her.

Reece stood braced with both feet wide apart, to keep control of the wheel. A surge of relief went through him as he saw Collins and another man make their way up the mainmast. Collins was easy to make out despite the rain. Each time the lightning lit up the clouds, he could see that his chief mate's large body was not made for such work. Reece knew Collins hated rigging work, but every officer knew and could pretty much perform any role on the ship, whether they liked it or not. But furling sails was a two-man job, especially in this weather. Collins could climb up, but another, much lighter man had to make his way out onto the yard—the arm of the mast. And Reece was not certain who Collins had found not just willing, but capable of climbing like the lean figure making its way across the yard.

For a second, he thought it might be Carr, the bosun, but he was yelling out orders on the deck. The few others he might have guessed it to be were also working hard at the ropes, trying to keep the topsails up and in place. Reece was about to put it out of his mind when he realized that he was not the only one watching the thin figure work the ropes on the sails to get them free. JP—who never came on deck during a storm—was there, just past the companionway, staring into the dark sky. His body was tense as if seized with fear.

Reece looked around. JP was not alone. Practically his whole crew was watching the two people up on the rigging. It made sense in a way—if the sails did not come down, the ship was in real danger of not making it through the storm—but this was not the first storm this crew had seen, and Reece could not recollect any other time the men cared so much about those climbing the rigging. Just who *had* Collins found?

Several bolts of lightning lit up the sky and the little more that Reece could make out made his stomach churn. Surely Collins had not convinced the woman they had hidden on board to climb the masts.

A wave came, then another, but both figures held on. They were above the crashing walls of water, but each time one hit, the boat rocked, threatening to shake one of them off. Reece did everything he could to keep the boat pointing toward the oncoming waves. Only when he saw the final sail go down and the two figures start to descend did he realize that he had been holding his breath.

The men were shouting something, but from the little Reece could make out, they were smiling. Collins's feet hit the deck and Reece knew his chief mate was glad to be down. But instead of heading up to join him at the wheel, Collins pivoted and looked up, shouting. Reece still could not make out the figure still in the rigging, but he could see they were not holding on correctly. No longer were the men smiling. Shouts were coming from the deck, and suddenly the bosun bounded up the companionway and headed toward him.

"I'll take the wheel, Cap'n. You gotta go below," he bellowed.

Alarm shot through Reece. Collins had not come up but

Carr had, which meant the situation on the deck was even worse than he had been able to make out. Reece made sure that the bosun had a firm grip on the wheel and then made his way to the stairs. He crossed the deck where the shouts were even more frantic.

"Collins!"

Collins whipped his head around. Fear consumed his features. "Captain!"

Reece craned his head and could see that the mystery rigger was not caught, but frozen. Literally. The water, the wind, the nighttime cold, all had proven too much. With only twelve more feet to go, hands white with cold, body shaking, it was hard to believe that this person had just helped furl the sails.

Another blast of wind came. The storm was not over and Reece needed to get back to the wheel. "You're almost down!" he shouted, signaling the other men to be quiet. "Even though you cannot feel your fingers, you can still control them. Just force them to let go. A few more steps and you'll be down."

The climber did not move. Fear had finally caught up with the onetime rigger and Reece moved to climb up and help. If needed, he would carry the body down. But just as he grabbed ahold of the first handle, the figure started to move and was about to take a step. Just as the hand let go, the person looked down. Reece's whole world instantly imploded.

Green eyes, framed in an overly pale face that could only belong to one person, latched on to his for a brief second before another wave crashed over the rails into them. Reece instinctively held on, but when he looked up—Aimee was gone.

Chapter 16

October 25, 1816

Chase had learned to be a patient man when it came to solving problems. Almost always there were complications or peculiarities that required a unique approach, but that only meant one had to adapt. But all problems could be resolved *if* one was willing to do what was necessary. And right now, all three problems he was facing required him to go significantly beyond his comfort zone.

The first—his sister—was a quandary that only grew each day. After being alone on a boat with Reece for so long, her reputation was in danger, which had only one solution. But as he had little power over the outcome, all he could do was wait. In the end, it was a situation of her making and therefore a problem for her to address. And while he should feel for his friend, part of Chase also blamed him for ignoring her. Reece should have known that Aimee would go to extreme measures to keep from being rebuffed in such a way.

His second problem was less of a quandary and more of a predicament. As expected, the thief had gone underground. But the maps were secure, and until the culprit decided on his next move—if there would even be one—there was little Chase could do.

His largest dilemma—the ever-increasing wedge between him and his wife—was a result of how he had set upon resolving the first two. Millie had yet to write him back. He had even confirmed that she had not sent Elda Mae any letters asking about him. Nothing. And of all the mysteries he was dealing with, his wife's unexplained silence was the most maddening.

Did she not realize how much he needed to hear from her? Was she not reading the letters he sent expressing his concern and his regret, but most importantly, his love?

Like his father and his grandfather before him, Chase possessed a stoic personality. It enabled him to be patient, and in many ways tolerant, but it also caused him to appear apathetic and indifferent to the world around him. That he had found a woman whom he not only loved dearly, but who could also love a controlled, serious man like him had been a miracle. But Millie was more than just a loving wife; she had filled his soul with life. Until her, Chase had not known how empty he had been, and he knew he could not go back to the way he was. He needed her spirit to fill him—even if it was relayed via sentiments in a letter.

Five times he had written her, and yet he had heard nothing.

Chase had assumed Millie would be cross for being summarily dismissed, but she was neither subtle nor passive in nature. If anger was her chief emotion, he would be hearing from her multiple times a day, expressing those very feelings. So when he received no response to his first letter, Chase interpreted it as Millie's small way of retaliation against his being so overbearing. But after five letters, it was clear that he could write a dozen more only to be similarly dismissed.

It was obvious that she intended for him to come to her,

to seek out her company after so bitterly rejecting it. He had resisted because he feared that with one look, one touch, he would not be able to let her go. Bringing her to London was not an option, but he could take her home to Dorset. He would just tell those dealing with the aftermath of Sir Edward's betrayal that he would be unavailable to assist them for the next few months.

At the Chaselton estate, they would have time to be alone together, without the fanfare of Town. There would be no duty toward Society matrons, his sister, or even her friends. It would be just him and her. With enough time, they would mend what rifts had been created.

It would also be the perfect opportunity to calmly and patiently address her dangerous compulsions, the foundation of their current quarrel.

Millie leaned against the bar and tilted her head back slightly to stretch her neck. She had not anticipated how difficult it would be to work in a tavern. She knew the physical labor would be challenging and her tired feet and constantly aching back proved that assumption right. But she had not anticipated just how hard everything else would be. Remembering multiple orders and handling money exchanges were just not things done by noblewomen.

A man shouted out something unintelligible and Millie kept her eyes closed, ignoring him. Other than Devlin, only one group of men remained, and Bessie had laid claim to them as soon as they had entered the tavern. Their hollers belonged to her.

Millie had stopped trying to gain Bessie's approval and friendship by the third night. The woman was just abrasive to everyone, including those who frequented Six Belles.

And yet, most of the men did not seem to mind Bessie's saucy attitude.

On the second night, Bessie had arrived early and dictated that they would share the customers, but she would choose which were hers and which ones Millie would serve. After the first hour, Millie was unsurprised to learn that those who tipped or tipped well, Bessie claimed, the others she gave away. But as Millie got better at serving, more and more of the customers were requesting her to help them, overriding Bessie's initial claim. And each time, Millie braced herself for Bessie to explode, for it was not a matter of if, but when. And Millie suspected that if Clive were driven to make a choice between them, she would lose. She had little time left to execute her plan.

It was this fear that gave her the courage to begin asking questions about Aimee, the pinnace, and who owned the ship it belonged to. But she quickly learned that asking outright was the fastest way to learn absolutely nothing. Millie was fairly certain that not a sole she spoke to actually had the answers to her questions, based on their puzzled expressions, but she was just as certain that if they *had* known, they would not have told her. The men might enjoy having her serve them, but it would take a lot more than a fresh, pretty face to get them to part with any information.

With the direct approach not working, Millie shifted to a more indirect line of questioning. She asked about the men's work, or how their day went, trying to engage them in conversation. But each time she brought up the pinnace, they changed the topic back to her.

"Green and white dinghy? Never seen such a thing. Don't care to either, not when I have you to gaze at."

"Dinghy? Seen 'em all and none are painted, except maybe white. But if you want to go with me to check inside a few, I can promise you an enjoyable tour."

Millie sighed. She had promised not to return without

information on Aimee, and she intended to keep it. But she was beginning to wonder if working for Clive would ever yield results.

A clinking sound beside her brought her out of her reverie. Devlin had risen and was now beside her, placing his empty glass down on the counter. He plopped four half-crowns onto the wooden surface. Millie slid two of the coins into her hand and gave him a sincere smile but said nothing. Devlin always tipped Bessie and her equally, regardless of who waited on him.

Millie watched him turn and leave the tavern. There was something about the man that had her intrigued. On her second night, she had spied a handkerchief with a small emblem on it. It had taken her a solid half hour of cajoling to get Stuart to tell her what it meant. He would have told her outright for coin, but she was already paying him to keep his ears open for any news from Hembree Grove about Aimee. She refused to set the dangerous precedent of having to pay for answers to questions he would have openly answered for anyone else.

In the end, Stuart said he knew very little. Only that the emblem belonged to a gambling joint located near Goodman's Fields and that its wild reputation was often the tattle of the *ton* gossips. The joint itself brought in high-stakes gamblers because it had a reputation for being one of the more honest establishments of its kind. However, the owner was not a man to be crossed. If one lost his money, his livelihood, or even his home, then it was lost.

Though Stuart could not say who the owner was, having never been near the place due to his young age and lack of funds, Millie was sure it was Devlin. He dressed well and sat alone, but it was neither of these things that set him apart from those who came into Six Belles. It was something about how he spoke and comported himself. His Scottish accent had been softened by training and, she suspected, a good deal of effort. The way he moved spoke of confidence and ease, and something else she could not quite define. And yet, while he acted as if he belonged in this harsh side of London, Millie suspected that in reality he was as far from his true home as she was from hers.

As Devlin reached the door, he looked back at Clive and gave him a distinct nod. Clive bobbed his head in return, but watching the silent exchange between the two men made Millie's eyes open wide with realization.

Devlin, like her, was an aristocrat.

Without a doubt, the man had been brought up and raised among the titled, either as the backup heir, a cousin, or some other relation. Millie drummed her fingers on the bar, letting her mind race. Someone with Devlin's background and current occupation would have access to information. Of all the people in this tavern, she had never thought to ask him for help.

Could she trust him? Should she?

To know the answer, she first needed to learn exactly who Devlin really was.

Reece's head snapped up at the first sign of movement from Aimee. She moaned and her hand moved to her head. For a moment, he just stared at her, making sure that what he was seeing was not a vision he had conjured. Aimee was not just alive, but awake. He let his head collapse back into his hands.

In one second, he was seeing Aimee, frozen on the mast of his ship. In the next, a wave had overtaken her. As soon as it cleared, he had frantically scanned the decks, as had the rest of his crew—who knew that if she was not found, Reece would not be accountable for his actions. But he had spotted her. Her body was curled into a ball, her head against the gunwale just underneath the rail. And she was not moving.

He ordered Collins to take over the wheel from Carr and hurried to Aimee, gathering her in his arms. A myriad of questions pummeled his mind, but mostly just one thought kept repeating itself over and over again. *You will be fine. You will be fine. You will be fine.*

But she had not been.

He had taken her to his room and examined her body. Nothing appeared broken; however, on the back of her head was a large, angry welt. Reece knew that it was impossible to accurately discern the ramifications of such injuries until the person woke up—if they woke up. And he refused to leave her side until he knew she was going to be fine. Only then would he decide how he was going to kill her. And he was still debating just when and how to eliminate his crew.

"My head . . ." Aimee moaned.

Reece slid to the edge of his chair so that he was as close as he could get to the bed. "You hit it when you fell."

Aimee's eyes fluttered open. "I fell?" she asked, clearly trying to remember just what had happened.

"Do you know where you are?"

Aimee closed her eyes and nodded. "The *Sea Emerald.* There was a storm. Someone had to help Collins get the sails down. Did I?" she asked, opening her eyes again. "Get them down? Are we safe?"

It took everything Reece had not to explode at the idea of Aimee acting as one of his crew. His chief mate had already admitted to it being his idea for Aimee to climb the masts, but to hear her call him Collins, as if they were close friends, was making Reece's blood boil. "*Someone* had to get them down. Not *you.*"

Reece watched her, but Aimee did not even flinch at his words or his tone. "What time is it?"

"You mean what day is it," he gritted out. "You've been unconscious for nearly twenty hours."

Aimee turned her head and blinked as if she was just now

realizing to whom she was talking. She turned to her side and raised her brows inquiringly. "Reece?"

He pulled her hand into his and said, "It's me."

Without warning, Aimee sat up and threw herself into his arms, pulling him toward her. Reece's eyes shut and his face twisted. Unprepared, he allowed himself to savor the soft feel of her and immediately his body became aroused. Her smooth cheek nestled against his and he basked in its warmth. He wondered why something so wrong had to feel so right.

When he tried to set her apart from him, Aimee resisted, wrapping her arms around his neck. Then he felt her fingers delve into his hair, soft and full of promise.

He stared down at her—her lips, soft, pink, parted slightly—and every muscle in his body tensed. Reece knew he had a number of questions to ask her, but he could not think of a single one. All he knew was that he wanted so badly to kiss her he could not think straight.

Unable to continue resisting his growing desire, he caught Aimee's face between his hands and brought her lips to his. With barely any encouragement, she opened her mouth, allowing him access to her moist warmth. Reece groaned and let the full force of his own hunger break over her. He had been craving this—craving her—for so long. Aimee was everything he remembered, sweet and ripe and incredibly fresh. Never had anything tasted so exquisitely good as she.

He could not get enough of her. His hands soon became as undisciplined as his mouth, taming and exciting as he stroked a warm path from her shoulders to the base of her spine. She moaned softly and tightened her grip on his neck, moving evocatively against him. When he showed his pleasure with a low growl, she smiled against his mouth.

Then, acting on a mixture of instinct and need, he deepened the kiss. Aimee responded, sharing her own consuming desires as she mated her tongue with his. "Aimee . . ." Her name was a soft growl of swiftly mounting desire on his lips as he eased her onto her back. "I've needed you so." His mouth moved away from hers and he laid a trail of fiery hot kisses down her neck.

"I was so lonely," she whispered, craning her head to give him better access.

"Promise me to never do anything so foolish again."

"Never again. I swear to you." Her voice was muffled, her face buried against his chest as she breathed in his scent. "I was never so scared in my life. Nothing like before."

Summoning his self-command, Reece stilled his burning urges. Aimee's eyes were large, full of passion, beckoning him to kiss her already red and swollen lips. He pushed himself away from her as the word *before* still rang in his ears.

Reality crashed in on him. He closed his eyes, berating himself for nearly compromising her again. But whenever he was near Aimee, his mind and body forgot everything but his overwhelming need to taste, touch, and make her his. "*Before?*" he repeated, this time aloud. "Are you telling me that you've climbed the *Sea Emerald*'s masts *before* last night?"

Aimee sat back on her knees and tucked a lock of her hair behind her ear. Then, looking him square in the eye, she nodded her head. Damn woman did not even try to look innocent. Her large green eyes just stared at him, daring him to say something. It was as if she had known this moment was coming for some time and was not just ready, but quite willing to have this argument.

Reece narrowed his gaze and scoffed softly. "How many times?"

Aimee just looked at him with an arched brow. Anyone who thought Aimee Wentworth sweet and naïve was both correct and incredibly mistaken. She was kind and beautiful. And while in many ways inexperienced and trusting, there was an impishness about her that could try the most patient of men.

There was a reason she, Millie, and Jennelle had been named the Daring Three. Each of them had an indomitable spirit that could, without warning, become very dangerous. It was that side of Aimee that Reece was looking at right now. But she was forgetting that she was on *his ship*. Here *his* resolve ruled all, and his decision was final. "I'm waiting for an answer, Aimee. Just how many times have you climbed this ship's mast?"

"I thought our first argument would be about me sneaking aboard your ship."

"Trust me when I say that we will get to that, but first you will answer my question."

Aimee narrowed her eyes and after another few seconds, she answered, her tone challenging rather than conciliatory. "The answer is several times, but working with Kyrk as a rigger was only a fraction of what I've learned to do these past few weeks. Now ask me why."

Through an extraordinary act of will, Reece managed to control his rage. He very much wanted to know why, but he refused to play into her hands. Damn it, *she* was the one in the wrong, and he was not going to have her confuse that fact! "I'm not one of my men you can twist about with a smile," he said.

Aimee spied his favorite worn robe and reached over to grab it. Standing up, she put it on and then strolled over to one of the larger portholes to stare at the rolling waters. The sun was shining once again and the seas, while not calm, were back to being blue, friendly waves. "I've never been on a ship before I stowed away on this one. For years, I heard endless stories about ships being cramped, the awful smells, and the lack of food variety. I must say they were quite accurate. But what no one ever told me was how liberating it could be being out here, with no land in sight, only the wind and the water. I find it both peaceful *and* exhilarating. The sensation is"—she paused to turn around and look at him—"quite addicting."

Chase tensed. In just a few words, she had captured what he felt when he was at sea. But the last person he wanted to understand that feeling was Aimee. He did not want her to feel the same way. He wished she would complain about all the discomforts she had endured. He desperately needed her to hate the sea. "You loved it so much you wanted to become one of my crew. Is that what you are trying to make me believe?"

A momentary flash of light flickered in Aimee's green eyes. "I have no desire to become one of your crew. I never did," she said, annoyed. "I learned about these duties because of you."

"Me? You knew I would never approve."

Her face gave a slight wince, indicating the headache she'd had upon waking was still present. She squeezed her temples and then said calmly, "I also knew that just loving the sea would not be enough for you, even if you did believe me."

"Enough for what?" Reece heard himself ask and then mentally kicked himself. She was drawing him in, getting him to talk, when in the end all that was said would be meaningless.

"For you," Aimee said simply, as if Reece should have already understood her motivation. "It is incredibly difficult when the man who owns your heart prefers the sea over a life with you. I needed to understand your world, what you do, and just why you love it so much you could choose it over me. Never again would I have the opportunity to speak and interact with the men you work with, learn the complexities and experience firsthand all the challenges of running a ship."

Reece went cold. "If Collins let you run this ship, then I'll—"

"Do not make threats you don't mean," Aimee said, interrupting him with a wave of her hand. "It has been quite a struggle for Mr. Collins, determining just how to best be loyal to you."

Reece snorted. He grabbed her wrists and pointed to the scars. "This is not loyalty. What they did to you . . . is a death warrant."

Aimee licked her lips and then tugged her arm free from his grasp. "They told you?" she said, dumbfounded that the men would willingly put themselves in such trouble.

"Aye, they told me about how Pete and Gus tied you up for days. Waxed eloquent about how brave you were when they treated you so terribly. Even JP came to your defense. Unfortunately, my men have no such excuses for their own actions and deception."

Aimee sank back down onto the bed. She looked down at the white lines crisscrossing her wrists. They would most likely be with her the rest of her life. "It was my fault, Reece. Pete and Gus . . . they had no idea who I was or even that I was a female. Your men believed they were helping you. That was their motivation. You cannot hold what happened to me against them."

"You are no longer dealing with addlepated seamen or my softhearted chief mate. I've known you longer and am not vulnerable to your pleas," Reece lied. In his experience, the only way to ignore her entreaties was to not hear them.

Aimee looked up and her green eyes caught his blue ones. She must have sensed that he was doing his best to harden his heart. "I won't let you do anything to them."

His firm mouth curled, but there was no amusement in his smile. "You won't *let* me? Regardless of what you believe, every man aboard swore an oath to *me*, and on that oath they should have alerted me to your presence. They did not. And on my ship, a man who is not loyal isn't worth a damn."

"They're disloyal?" she said emphatically, jumping back to her feet. "In their minds, by taking care of me they were being loyal to you! I cannot believe you would punish your crew over that. If anything, you should be thanking them." She took a step forward. Reece refused to budge. "Tell me. If your crew *had* told you that I was on board, would you not have immediately turned around? Of course you would have. Just like when you are in port, you would refuse to meet with me or even share a handful of words. Then once we arrived in London, you would fire Pete and Gus and then hand me off to my brother, only to disappear again. And you and I would be exactly where we were when you left the first time."

Reece said nothing. He only folded his arms and glared at her.

Aimee glared back. "I am tired of letting you dictate the terms of our relationship, Reece Hamilton."

Reece could listen to no more. "We don't have a relationship, damn it! I am simply a childhood fantasy of yours! It's time you got over me, grew up, and sought a man who wants you in return."

"You *were* a childhood fantasy; and last Christmas, I *did* grow up. I was no longer dreaming of love—I was *in* love with you, and after the kiss we just shared, don't bother denying that you love me. I won't believe you."

"Not a wit of what you just said matters, Aimee. For nothing that happened then or now has changed who you are or who I am not. It certainly doesn't change who your brother is. And when I return you safely to his charge, I am going to tell him of your escapades and he is never going to let me or any other sea captain within a hundred miles of you. Nor should he."

"I can handle Charles," Aimee said dismissively and then

stepped around him to once again look out at the sea. "But you mistake my demeanor for something that it isn't. I am far from calm and my ire is just as roused as yours, I can assure you."

"*Your* ire?"

"Yes. How do you think it feels to love a man who plans and acts on fear and the opinions of others, rather than his own?"

Reece felt his mouth drop, but no words came out. His sky-blue eyes, however, had turned to ice. Aimee was unfazed. "I shall not endeavor to search for more palatable words to ease your pride. You know that you have been hiding and avoiding me every time you are in London. So, since you refuse to meet with me, I came to you."

Reece's nostrils flared and his breathing became forced. "You did not come to me. I *discovered* you, near dead and frozen after climbing . . . in a storm . . ." In an effort to regain some control of his turbulent emotions, he raked his fingers through his sandy-colored hair. "I cannot even think about it."

"Then I suggest that you do not," Aimee interjected. "And before you tell me never to climb the masts again, there is no need. I may have no fear of heights, but one terrifying experience on a ship's mast is enough for a lifetime."

Reece was not mollified at all. It mattered not if she was eager or unwilling to climb the riggings. This was not her decision. It was his. "You are never—I mean *never*—to climb any mast, on any ship, of any size, *for any reason,* ever *again*."

"I just said I would not."

Reece was silent for a moment. Her agreement was sincere, but it was also swift. "Nor will you do anything else that should be done by a crewman."

Aimee made a dismissive gesture. "Now you are being ridiculous."

Anger forced Reece to his feet so he could pace. His

expression was thunderous. "*Ridiculous* is finding my best friend's little sister as a stowaway on my ship. *Ridiculous* is discovering she's been living here for weeks. *Ridiculous* is learning that my entire crew knew you were on board and were teaching you how to do their jobs!"

Aimee ran her fingers through her messed hair, removing some of the larger knots, pretending to be undisturbed by his tirade. "What is wrong with you? Why are you acting this way?"

Reece threw his hands up in the air and turned away from her to grab the edge of his desk. "What way?" he asked sarcastically. "Mad? Furious?" he added, turning around to capture her gaze. His blue eyes could freeze even salt water. "Maybe because I don't like to be made a fool, and you made me one to my whole crew. Something I am not sure I will ever forgive you for."

For the first time, Aimee looked flustered. "I . . . I did no such thing. Your crew respects you just as they always have."

He pushed himself off the desk and walked toward her until she was pinned against the wall, his hands on either side of her head. "Do they, Aimee? Is it *respect* when two of my crew kidnap and beat a person without authorization? What about when they discover it was a woman they had nearly starved to death? Or how about a chief mate who decides to convince the whole crew to keep it all a secret? Because to me and to any other captain it looks like I've completely lost all control." With his lips almost touching hers, Reece added, "Every man on this ship owes his loyalty to me, and yet so easily they relinquished it to you. But when they did so, it was only at your peril and theirs."

Aimee stared at him. Her entire face was flushed, her mouth swollen, and her green eyes reflected regret. Then she pulled in a slow, shuddering breath and closed her eyes, unable to look at him. Reece inhaled, taking a big, deep breath of her. He could feel his composure slipping as a slow wave of lust washed over him. Despite everything, the need to lean just a little closer so his lips were against hers was enormous.

He pushed himself off the wall and took a step back. He would not give in to his desires again. "If anything happened to you, do you know what would have happened to them? Not their *jobs*, but their future? What that would mean for their families?"

The shock of what he said hit her full force. "But you . . . you would not have let that happen. Charles would not—"

"Lead the march to end every man's life aboard?" he answered for her. "And do not doubt that the first person he would leg shackle would be me."

Aimee swallowed. "You cannot believe that. Charles and you are friends." She shook her head and hugged herself. "No, you are just saying this because you are mad." She began to pace. At first her steps were hurried, but then they suddenly slowed. "That's it. This is about pride. Your pride," she said and came to a stop. "You are angry, not with the men, not even with me. You just have an insatiable need to be in control of everyone and everything about you. But you don't control everyone and you most especially don't control me."

Reece faced her without expression, without moving a muscle. "That's where you are wrong, Lady Wentworth. As long as I am captain of this ship, I absolutely control everything and everyone—*including* you." He glanced at the closed door. "Hurlee!"

Within seconds the large, fair-haired man entered. He sent a quick look of remorse to Aimee. The action only infuriated Reece more. "Take her next door." Then he turned to Aimee and said coldly, "You are to remain in the chief mate's quarters until we reach Savannah."

Chapter 17

October 26, 1816

"Mmm, this is very good, Jean-Pierre. You truly have a gift," Aimee said, putting the fork down.

"And you will not eat."

Aimee bit her bottom lip. "I will. I promise. Just right now my stomach is somewhat upset."

JP made a scoffing sound and crossed his arms. "Never before 'ave you complained of being seasick. Not when you were brought on board, not when we turned to ze open waters, not even during a bad storm. And suddenly you want me to believe you are not well enough to enjoy my food, mademoiselle—or am I supposed to call you some-zing else? Don't you English say Your Grace to someone of your rank?"

Aimee shook her head. "My brother holds the title of marquess. I'm no one, really, and certainly no one whom you need to address a certain way. In fact, it is you and the men who get the titles out here on the sea. And those are the best kind, for you earned them."

JP rolled his eyes. "Well, you are special to us."

"I doubt that I am to Mr. Collins. I think I have created quite a problem between him and Mr. Hamilton."

"Collins took a tongue-lashing, but if rumors are correct, 'e gave one as well. But I doubt you will be seeing 'im anytime soon."

Aimee bit her inner cheek at the thought of Collins being in trouble because of her. "I am so glad you came to visit me. Seems that everyone is very busy since the storm."

"Ha!" snorted JP. "Zey want to see you, my lady, but ze captain, 'e refuses to let zem. 'Urlee let me in because I was bringing you food and I told 'im zat 'e would only get 'ard tack if 'e did not open ze door."

Aimee looked worried. "If Mr. Hamilton finds out, you will find yourself at the mercy of his wrath."

JP shrugged. "Ze captain likes my cooking and knows zere are few wiz my skills willing to live on ze sea. And if I am wrong, zen I 'ave little doubt I would 'ave issues finding anozer position somewhere else."

"What about the Poulsen brothers? And Mr. Kyrk? How is he faring?"

A grimace overtook JP's expression. "Lamont and Shiv will soon be fine. Mr. Kyrk's injury was far more serious, but it looks like 'is leg is going to 'eal. But it will take time before 'e can work like 'e did before. 'E is actually much more worried about you, considering what 'appened. All ze men are."

Aimee's eyes widened in shock. "Mr. Hamilton surely told them that I am fine."

JP shook his head. "Not exactly. 'E just said zat you woke up. Nozing more, which is one of ze reasons I insisted upon seeing you today. Ze men are anxious to learn if you are truly recovered."

Aimee frowned at him in concern. "Don't they realize the

danger I've put them all in? That in less than a few weeks they could all find themselves unemployed?"

JP leaned in close and whispered, "I cannot say for certain, but I doubt ze captain will cut anyone for being nice to you."

"You did not see him, Jean-Pierre. The anger . . . the coldness." Aimee shivered at the recollection. "I've known Mr. Hamilton for many years and I've never known him to be so hostile to not just me, but everyone. He truly believes I've turned his crew against him, and if he is right, then his fury with me is justified. But he is *wrong*, isn't he? The crew are not more loyal to me than to him?"

JP took in a deep breath and then exhaled. "*Oui*, 'e is wrong. Ze crew is loyal to 'im, but zat is not what 'e is fighting against. Zere is somezing about a woman men will always rally to, my lady, especially when she appears to be in need or unhappy. Loyalty is not a factor, and zerefore it doesn't factor in our decisions."

"So then, Mr. Hamilton was at least partially correct. My being around the men is disruptive and I should stay away."

JP shrugged. "We all know you are 'ere and alone. It'll eat away at ze men, wondering 'ow you are. I'll tell zem of zis meeting, but unless zey can see for zemselves zat you are well and unhappy, zey will slowly grow agitated. What would be best is for ze crew to know ze captain was seeing to your needs."

"I'm not sure there is anything I can do. Mr. Hamilton has made it clear that I must stay away from the crew and from him."

JP sighed again. "Then let's just 'ope the men can last two weeks until we reach Savannah." He pulled open the door to let himself out. "I'll be back, my lady. Take 'eart. Maybe something or *someone* will convince 'im to change 'is mind."

* * *

Reece watched through the crack in the door as Aimee slowly tucked a lock of her hair behind her ear to reveal the delicate nape of her neck. The sight was both sensual and provocative. His body stirred and Reece grew annoyed. His reaction smacked of possessiveness. But she was not his and everyone on board now knew it, which left a man's mind to wander. And while Reece refused to claim Aimee, he detested the idea that he was at the same time giving up the right to challenge any man who desired her for his own.

JP turned to leave and Reece quickly took a step back from the door to avoid being seen. He did not doubt for a second that the crotchety old cook knew that he was in his cabin and able to overhear everything that was said next door. JP had made his point. Maybe the men's reaction to Aimee was not a question of loyalty, but rather human nature. And that nature made the men need to know Aimee was not just alive, but well. But what JP also proved was that Aimee was not just any woman.

The men had brought women aboard the *Sea Emerald* before, and though several of the crew had become smitten, a few never had. JP was one of them. So were Shiv Poulsen, Kyrk, Carr, and Afton Acker, an able-bodied seamen who didn't much care for women even on land. All five men were nearly hostile to women aboard the ship, JP and Kyrk being the most hostile of them all. And yet it was JP who risked all to check on Aimee and Kyrk who was more worried about her than himself.

Aimee was more powerful and addicting than opium, which meant one thing. He absolutely was correct in keeping her completely away from his men.

"Lord Aldon!" Chase called out, glad to have finally found where his wife was. The staff at the main house had been surprised, almost flustered to see him there at Abileen

Rose, asking about his wife. Finally, the housekeeper came and told him that he might not want to wait in the parlor, but go out to the stables.

Lord Aldon looked up from where he was crouched down, examining one of the legs of a prize horse. Getting to his feet, he said in a tone that matched his surprise, "Chaselton! What brings you here?"

Chase paused just inside the stable doors, trying to interpret his father-in-law's genuine shock to see him. He had left midmorning and had been riding nearly nonstop to get there by nightfall, and had not sent word ahead of his visit. Chase's letter would not have been delivered until the day after his arrival, and he had hoped to surprise his wife. "Well, Aldon, I suppose I came here for the reason you would expect—to see my wife and then bring her home."

Lord Aldon raised a single brow. Then he stripped off his gloves and pointed to the stable doors. Once they were outside and out of earshot of any stable hands, he said, "I consider myself a lucky man when some fathers would not. I love my daughter immensely and enjoy her company, as her interests and mine thankfully overlap to a large degree. And while I will always welcome her home, even for unplanned visits like this past one, can I assume that whatever unhappy circumstances led to my daughter spontaneously needing to spend time with me, will not be repeated?"

Chase inhaled. It had been a number of years since his father's death, but he knew he was being given a fatherly lecture. Lord Aldon was not a man of Town, preferring the country and his horses as company, but that did not make him any less sharp to the ways of men and women. Chase understood his meaning clearly, and while a part of him bristled at being lectured, he did appreciate its subtle and brief nature.

"I can assure you, Aldon, that the *unhappy* situation leading Millie to stay here with you was unique and shall not be repeated." Chase wanted to add, *if your daughter would just behave.* But he did not.

"That is good," Aldon nodded, clapping Chase on the back. The older man was of average height, but his wide shoulders and solid physique diminished the appearance of a difference in their heights. "Let's go back to the house and I will have Millie's things brought down."

Chase shook his head. "I did not come by coach, to save time. I just came to see my wife and if possible, borrow your coach to take us down to Dorset. Her things can join us whenever her maids can get them ready."

Aldon stopped in midstride. "You came *here* to see Millie?" he asked, clearly perplexed. Millie had left for her friend Jennelle's a week ago, and in all that time she had not informed her husband? Whatever had happened between them was far more serious than he had originally believed, for it was quite unlike Millie to hold a grudge for so long.

"This *is* where I have been sending my letters. They have not been returned," Chase said crisply. His father-in-law's question filled him with dread, for there was only one reason he would ask it—Millie was no longer at Abileen Rose.

Lord Aldon resumed walking, increasing the pace and length of his stride. "Millie must have given instructions to the housekeeper."

"And why would she need to give such instructions?" Chase pressed.

Not intimidated in the least by the bite in Chase's question, Lord Aldon answered him. "Most likely because you hurt her greatly and she did not want to tell you herself just where she went."

Chase scowled. Lord Aldon had shifted from intimations to actual accusations, and damn the man for being right.

"We had a . . . misunderstanding concerning one of her bolder pastimes."

Aldon nodded in complete understanding. He was well aware that his daughter was considered "undisciplined" in comparison to most well-bred young ladies. And for a nobleman's daughter she was positively wild. But he did not care. In his opinion, too many women were overly compliant and boring. It was his wife who had shown him that life was much better lived and enjoyed unreservedly and with passion. His wife was no longer with him, but she lived on through Millie. In her youth, he had refused to let anyone suggest her love for life and adventure be suppressed. But he had not always been so understanding. It took some painful lessons for him to learn to appreciate just why he loved his wife so and that if he tried to change her, subdue her inclinations, he was destroying the very essence of her that filled him with joy and love.

Regrettably, it was not a lesson that could be shared. One had to learn it firsthand. As he had come to learn it, so would Chase. A personality like Millie's required acceptance— not taming. In time, she would learn when to control her tendencies, but it would not be through instruction—and certainly not by sending her away.

Lord Aldon stepped up to the house and the door opened for him and Chase to enter. Handing his gloves to the doorman, he headed back to the library, his favorite room. He poured himself a small glass of port and then one for Chase, deciding the man needed one whether he realized it or not.

"I knew when Millie came that she was unhappy and that something had happened between you two." Aldon put up a hand to keep Chase from interrupting. "It happens to every couple, especially those who actually are attached to each other. I did not ask because I did not—*and still do not*— want to get involved. However, it did pain me to see her so unhappy day after day."

Chase swallowed. He had thought sending Millie away to Abileen Rose and her father would lighten her spirits, not further dampen them.

"So while I did not ask the cause of her depression," Aldon continued, "I did encourage her to take action. Eventually, she would have done so anyway, for Millie has never been the type to sit by and watch others tackle difficulties she considers to be hers. So I encouraged her, thinking it best to give her a little guidance and support, for *as you know*, when thwarted, she will take action anyway, and it always takes a far more precarious form."

Chase felt his body grow cold. "Specifically, just what guidance did you give your daughter?"

"Nothing specific. Just hinted that she should not wait for you but take the initiative to fix whatever issues are between you. In other words, I believed I had persuaded her to return to you in London."

"When did she leave for London?" Chase asked far too calmly. Most men would have begun to quiver in the face of Chase's ire, but not Aldon. The man had a phlegmatic air about him, but he was made of iron. There was no bend. And he had made it clear that he believed Chase, not he, was at fault for Millie's decision not to return home.

"She did not leave directly for London. A week ago, she left for Gent Manor to visit a friend. She was to depart from there."

Chase took the glass of port being handed to him and followed his father-in-law's guidance, downing it in one swallow. It stung the back of his throat, but it helped to revive his body, which had temporarily gone numb.

Millie was at Jennelle's. Jennelle had told him that she believed Aimee to be with Reece, and must have convinced Millie of the same. That left Chase as the sole topic of their conversations. And Jennelle had been so angry at his treatment of Millie that he would not be surprised to learn it was she—not Millie—behind his wife's silence.

"Aldon, I had intended to leave this afternoon for Dorset, but those plans have obviously changed. Do you mind if I stay and leave in the morning?"

"Think that would be best. You are going to need a good night's sleep before you tackle what awaits you in Tarrant Crawford."

Chase had little expectation of sleeping much, but his father-in-law was correct. Tomorrow was going to be a long day of dealing with two angry women, but he would recover. And most importantly, he would recover in the loving arms of his wife.

"Clive, I need a glass of the Glenturret," Millie said, trying to keep her voice low enough that only Clive would hear.

She looked back over her shoulder and sighed in relief as the second-to-last group of men rose to their feet and left the tavern. The remaining lot continued their focus on Bessie, who in turn focused solely on them in an effort to elicit a higher tip.

Clive slid a glass toward her and Millie cringed as she lifted it to inspect it. "Do you own any glasses that do not endanger men when they drink from them?" she asked, pointing to a chip in the side that looked exceedingly sharp and hazardous.

Clive gave her what he hoped to be a menacing glare and snatched the glass from her hand. He poured the contents into another glass and shoved it back toward her. "Here."

Millie's eyes stared at the obvious dirty smudge marks. Then with a small shrug, she offered him a sweet smile that caused Clive to smile back before he realized what he was doing. Millie then turned and caught Devlin openly studying her. Refusing to act flustered under his open stare, she walked over to where he sat and handed him his drink.

Devlin took it and placed it on the small table to his left. "Why don't you bring another drink over and join me?" he said, waving his hand to one of the empty chairs. "I'll cover the expense with Clive."

Millie looked longingly at the empty chairs haphazardly scattered about her. Her feet hurt and the idea of sitting down, even for a few minutes, was very appealing. Even the idea of a drink sounded good. From the moment they knew it was forbidden, she and Aimee and Jennelle had snuck down to their fathers' studies to drink scotch, brandy, and even gin. Millie had done so out of principle, Aimee had asserted it was to understand her dear Reece better, and Jennelle had proclaimed her actions to be in the interests of research. But whatever the reason, they all continued sneaking tastes whenever they could, until one day they realized they were not only acquainted with the flavors—they enjoyed them.

"Sit," Devlin softly ordered. "It's uncomfortable watching a woman make love with her eyes to a piece of furniture instead of me."

Flames erupted in Millie's purple gaze as it snapped to his, but she clamped her lips closed just in time. Instead of lecturing him on the improprieties of making vulgar comments to women, she marched over and grabbed the back of the nearest chair and turned it so that it was close to Devlin's, facing the fire.

Devlin chuckled as he watched her gracefully sink onto the hard surface. Under his breath, he said, "Try slouching a little."

Millie shot him another glare as she quickly caught his meaning. Just as she had deduced his background, he suspected hers. And now he was baiting her. With a slight raise to her right brow, she gave him a long, steady look. Then she reached down, pulled up the hem of her dress, and gave in to the urge to massage her calves and ankles—something no proper woman would ever do. Millie was lost to the sensation for several minutes, only to have her annoyance renewed at finding Devlin grinning at her when she at last reopened her eyes.

"You definitely need a drink," Devlin said firmly as he shifted in his seat in an effort to rise.

Millie eyed the pale liquid in the filthy glass on the table next to her and shook her head. "No, thank you, Mr. MacLeery. The glass is unclean."

Devlin sat back and gave her a saucy grin, amused by her propriety. "Take it. It's yours. I still have a bit left of this one to enjoy," he said, lifting another semi-full glass and swirling it around.

Millie smiled back, realizing that Devlin was assuming that she was curious, not knowledgeable about the taste of whiskey. She glanced at the drink but unable to help herself, she wrinkled her nose once more at the dirty glass.

"Ah, lass, that only adds to the earthy taste of a good scotch."

Millie's gaze shifted from the scotch to Devlin. He was toying with her. His eyes were a much more brilliant shade of green than she had previously realized. With his dark features and austere countenance, he was not a pretty man, but she suspected he could attract practically any of her sex without much effort. Oh, yes, he was definitely playing with her. Why, she did not know, but it removed all guilt about her decision to try to pry information out of him.

Millie picked up the glass and held it for a moment before saying, "A drink for a question."

Devlin sat back and intertwined his fingers. "I agree," he said readily.

To Millie, too readily, but nevertheless, she lifted the glass to her lips and took a long swallow, closing her eyes as if she enjoyed savoring the flavor on her tongue. "Mmm. This is very, very good."

Devlin sat back and let go a small snort, once again feeling surprised and more than slightly attracted to the woman who called herself Ellie. "Interesting."

"Many women enjoy scotch," Millie countered with a slight shrug. "Especially those who work in taverns such as these."

Devlin winked at her and shook his head. "But they cannot recognize good whiskey from average. Neither would a mere governess have knowledge of such things."

Millie took another small sip to hide the shot of anxiety that ran through her. "Alas, unfortunately for you, our agreement never included answering your questions."

Devlin smiled and pulled his left ankle to sit upon his right knee. He knew Clive suspected Ellie to have been a kept woman. And while it was possible, having been with several—including some who were quite expensive—Devlin was positive Ellie was not one of them. Ellie lacked the jaded look they all carried. And even if she had just begun her life as a courtesan, he just could not believe the petite beauty in front of him would settle for being kept on the side, receiving leftover affections as it suited someone else. So if she was not a governess, nor a courtesan, that left only one other option. Like him, she had not just lived among the upper class. She was one of them.

"Then ask your question."

He watched her purple eyes in fascination as she rehearsed the question in her mind before asking it. "Why do you own a gambling establishment when you despise the occupation?" Devlin knew that she had assumed much about him, but how she had come to such accurate conclusions was irksome. He looked back at Clive.

"Clive said nothing," Millie said, seeing where his mind

was heading. "It is the way you look at the emblem on your handkerchief—pride mixed with what appears to be hatred."

Devlin swallowed and forced his features to look relaxed and unconcerned. But he had not realized until now that just as he had been studying her, she had been scrutinizing him as well. "Perhaps I have a passion for gambling."

Millie squinted her eyes in disbelief. "Mr. MacLeery, an honest drink deserves an honest answer."

Devlin leaned forward, bringing him within a foot of her. He could see that such nearness made her uncomfortable, but Ellie refused to pull back. He wished it were because she was attracted to him. "You and I both know each other to be liars, but I will give you the truth. I am not a gambler, nor have I ever been nor will be."

That Millie did believe. Devlin MacLeery was not a gambler. His voice cracked with hatred at the very subject. Still, he had told her nothing more than what she already knew. "While I delight in free information, I am still waiting for the answer I purchased."

Devlin grimaced, acknowledging she was correct. He had not answered her question. He could lie, but untruths bothered him. He preferred dodging and hedging truths. "I do not like gamblers. But I need money and rather enjoy the idea of relieving foolish men of theirs."

Millie decided that she could drink a whole bottle of scotch, but nothing more on that subject would be volunteered by Devlin. "Did you grow up in Scotland? At your ancestral home?"

Devlin's face hardened and he closed his eyes. She had changed topics, but not for the better. "Aye," he answered, preparing himself for questions about his home, family, and place of birth.

"I always wanted to go there."

"We could go to Gretna Green tonight. Just give me a moment to call for my coach."

Millie rolled her eyes playfully. "Such a tempting proposal when put such a way, but I cannot."

Devlin licked his lips and studied her face. *Cannot* she had said. Not *will not*. He had called them both liars and he meant it. But they also loathed to lie, and therefore did it sparingly. Truth to Ellie's real identity just might be buried in every comment. He just needed to read between the lines and find the truth.

"I suspect if you came back home with a new English bride you met working in a tavern, your family would be more than a little upset."

"You're right about that," Devlin confirmed before taking a large gulp from his own glass. "Still, you would look good in Drumindaloch."

Millie blinked. She knew the names of the castles of only a handful of clans. And Drumindaloch was one. It was the very castle that Mother Wentworth had left to visit nearly six weeks ago. "You are not *of* the MacLeerys," she whispered, "you actually *are* a MacLeery."

Devlin froze. MacLeery was not a common name, but then neither was it uncommon. In all the years he had made London his home and spent time with nobles, not a one had ever deduced just how closely he was related to the chieftain of their clan. Then again, he had never mentioned Drumindaloch castle. Still, how many would know the name of a castle that was in much need of repair and belonged to a clan with little power? Very few—and that included the nobles who had known his grandfather, before his father took over and with his gambling ruined their family in every way thinkable.

His curiosity was shifting to something else. Just who exactly was Ellie? And if Ellie knew what hardly a soul outside of where he lived in Scotland knew of his clan and his home, just what else did she know about his family? Did she know his father tried to rectify his repeated losses by forcing a horrific marriage to a wealthy woman on his only son? She may know of his refusal, but whoever Ellie was, she did not know his real reasons. Devlin would have done his duty and married his wealthy neighbor's purportedly malevolent daughter, except he knew his father would only spend his wife's money as well. Only when his father was dead did Devlin intend to return.

There was noise in the background, but the silence between them was growing. Devlin finally said, "So if you know who I am, then you know why I cannot go home, but I cannot fathom why you cannot return to yours. Why is that?"

For a second, he saw her eyes grow large before they returned to their normal kind but curious expression. Still, it was enough for him to realize that he had guessed correctly: It was not that she did not want to; she could not. Ellie was afraid of the idea of going home, and it was that fear which kept her from going back. Fear of whom? Just who was she running away from? If she was gentry, an abusive husband would send her into the arms of friends and family—not here. Perhaps she had done something illegal. And yet Clive had relayed how she had been quite vehement in her assertion that the law was not after her. But that didn't mean the law was not involved.

Devlin swallowed as he realized just what could send a gentleman's daughter to this life. Ellie had not done wrong, but she was hiding from someone who had. There had been a lot of murders of nobles the past Season. Had she witnessed something that placed her in danger? Was that why she was here—a place no one from the upper class would look?

A rush of protectiveness suddenly overcame him. He wished he could take back his flippant comment about Gretna Green and propose the idea more seriously. He could protect her then. He could remove her from this life and give her one to which she was accustomed. He certainly had the funds. As the idea started to take shape, Devlin found it more and more appealing. Ellie was far more than just beautiful. She had a wild spirit that spoke to his.

"But I do go home. To a very nice one. Every night," Millie said, interrupting his thoughts.

It was Devlin's turn to narrow his eyes in disbelief. "We both know your destiny was not meant for the Thames."

"Neither was yours."

"Aye, but whoever cast you out should be shot."

Millie shook her head, then drank the last of the scotch and put the glass on the small table. "Unlike you, I deserve to be here. I doubt that you do. Otherwise you would not look so—"

"Defeated?"

"No," Millie countered softly. "I would say sad. As if the only way to preserve your honor was to leave."

Devlin looked into his empty glass, wishing it was full to the brim. Ellie understood him. It was as if their souls recognized each other. He thought his destiny had been ripped from him seven years ago, but had God sent him another? "You guess correctly. I was banished."

Millie sighed. Of all the things she understood, being cast out of your home was something she knew all too keenly. "I too was asked to leave my home."

Devlin blinked. Did he just hear her right? "You aren't hiding from someone?"

The idea that she was hiding from someone puzzled Millie and she shook her head.

"So you came *here*? You had no other options but working at a tavern?" he blurted out with obvious disbelief.

Millie felt the need to defend herself. "While I have no desire to be found, I came here intentionally, Mr. MacLeery. I . . ." Millie swallowed and decided that if she were ever going to get his help in finding Aimee, then he would need to know at least something about why she was there. "I . . . am looking for something."

Devlin cocked his brow, encouraging her to continue.

Millie swallowed again. "Do you know which ship has a green and white pinnace?"

Devlin blinked at the very unexpected and extremely odd question. Was that what happened? Did the man she love leave her? Was she trying to chase after him? He looked at her and realized she was waiting for an answer. "I do not."

The hope he saw stirring in her lavender eyes faded away and Devlin felt his heart wrench.

Millie rose to her feet and clasped her hands in front of her. "Thank you, Mr. MacLeery, for your time and the drink. If by chance you ever do learn of the ship's name, would you let me know?"

"Of course," Devlin responded, wishing he had something else to say.

He watched her walk away and begin to tidy up the near-empty tavern, vowing to learn exactly who owned a green and white pinnace and why such a fact would have great meaning to a beauty who was slowly taking over his heart.

Chapter 18

October 27, 1816

It was the early morning hours before Aimee realized what JP's parting comment had meant. *Maybe something or someone will convince the captain to change his mind.* He could have only been meaning her. She was the someone who needed to change Reece's mind about sequestering her for the rest of the trip. But how?

Aimee glanced at the door. If she truly put her mind to it, she suspected she could convince Hurlee to let her out. However, it would be her one and only chance. Reece would barricade her in and not risk using his men again as guards. So whatever she planned to do, the end result had better resolve things between them once and for all.

Aimee began to pace. How was she going to convince Reece to let her out and mingle with the crew? The idea seemed impossible in his current state of mind. Why did men have to become so soppy at the idea of a woman getting hurt? Chase was practically nauseating, the way he worried over Millie. Unfortunately, that was not the primary reason Reece was keeping her inside this cabin. Not fear of her getting hurt, but fear of her getting to his men—and most of all, to him.

Aimee stopped in midstride and began to tap her finger against her chin. She was thinking about this all wrong. Her freedom was a byproduct of what she had been seeking in the first place—a claim to Reece's heart. She did not need to convince him to let her out, but that he loved her. This voyage was her one chance. If she had not secured his love by the time they reached Savannah, it would never happen. For once they arrived, he would quickly put her on another ship, and any future opportunities to be alone with him would vanish.

Aimee began to pace again, this time trying to conjure up Millie and Jennelle beside her. What would they advise? Jennelle would tell her to have a well-thought-out plan. Millie would agree and say that it should be something shocking, in order to capture Reece's attention. Her mother, however, would tell her to think like a Wentworth.

Wentworths preferred order, and minimal disruption to themselves, friends, and family, *but* if something did threaten those they loved—then laws, rules, and conventions were ignored. Her brother had thrown Millie over his shoulder and marched out of Almack's when he decided that he loved her. Aimee had no intentions of throwing Reece over her shoulder, but she did have an idea about how to make him admit the truth: that he loved her and it was not his lack of title or choice of profession standing in their way, but his own stubbornness.

If she failed, her reputation would be ruined. But then, wasn't it already?

Jennelle entered the parlor and stared accusatorily as Chase rose to his feet. He had arrived nearly half an hour ago, and though it was unheard of for a baron—let alone a baron's daughter—to leave a marquess waiting so long, Jennelle had done just that. She was not just angry, but terrified, and had been for weeks. She had pledged to not say a word until she had to, but that had been more than a week ago. Now that Chase was here, she had no idea where to start.

"My lord," she said and followed it with a formal curtsy.

Chase raised a brow but followed her formality. "Miss Perrin." In truth, he had forgotten her real salutation, for Millie and Aimee had acted as if she were their titled equal since childhood.

"I assume you came with news of Aimee?"

Chase frowned and looked behind Jennelle to see if Millie would soon be following her. When she did not, he assumed she was waiting in the shadows for an answer.

"While I cannot unequivocally confirm her safety, all information that I have been able to gather—which is a considerable amount—leads me to believe that she is indeed with Reece on the *Sea Emerald* and not in immediate harm."

Jennelle closed her eyes and relief flooded her expression. "I *told* you that Aimee intentionally had herself captured."

Chase's jaw hardened at Jennelle's genuine surprise at the news. Not only had Millie not written back to him, she had not even deemed it necessary to read his letters. "It was in my correspondence to my wife," he growled.

Jennelle's blue eyes flashed in anger. "How would I know? I am not in the habit of opening mail that is not my own."

Chase was done playing word games and being patient. The time for retaliation was over. He wanted to see his wife. "Please send for Millie immediately. I wish to see her."

Jennelle glared at him. "I wish I could, my lord, but I cannot because she is not here."

His golden eyes suddenly went cold. "Explain."

"I have no more information to give you other than that, my lord. Your wife is not here. She left here over a week ago to London, *in a hack*."

Chase could feel his heart begin to pound so hard he suspected Jennelle could hear it from where she was standing. If so, she bore him no sympathy. Her unflinching stare frightened him more than anything. If she knew Millie was safe, Jennelle would be indignant; but she was not annoyed. Her bright blue eyes were full of fear. And she blamed him for it.

In two strides, Chase moved to stand right in front of her. "What the hell is going on, Jennelle? What do you mean, Millie is not here? *Just where in the hell is she?*"

"*I do not know!*" Jennelle stepped around him and hugged herself, feeling her composure begin to completely unravel. Finally, she could share this burden. But the relief she had hoped to feel was not forthcoming. If anything, she felt only guilt at seeing the same terror she had been feeling for days take over Chase.

Chase did not move. "You must have *some* idea."

"I have none. She made sure that I would not be able to follow and join her, for I would have done just that." Jennelle closed her eyes and shook her head. "I caught her just as she was leaving. The driver called her 'miss,' so wherever she is, it is under another identity."

"You let her go?" Chase growled out, half in anger and half in pain.

Jennelle whirled about. "No, I did not *let* her. It was you who practically forced Millie into whatever insane plan she has embarked upon."

"Me!"

"Yes, you!" Jennelle yelled back. "Just what did you think Millie would do after receiving not a single word from you when it was clear the *Sea Emerald* was not returning? She assumed you had exhausted all your resources and had nothing to tell her. And you *know* her! You know Millie would not be able to stay home waiting, if she believed there was even a small chance that she could be out there helping. So damn you for not telling her sooner and putting her in a position of believing she had to do things on her own."

Chase felt every accusation almost as if it were a lethal blow. He knew Jennelle was right, but at the same time his mind rebelled at the idea that Millie was alone and vulnerable and it was his fault. "I did not give her any such ideas. I sent her to her father's! If anything, I begged her to stop all this foolishness because of this very reason!"

"Oh, Charles, is it possible that you still don't understand your wife?" Jennelle asked as she collapsed on the settee and buried her face in her hands. After a moment, she looked up. "Do you not recall what you said to her? You told her repeatedly that Aimee's abduction was *her* fault. If Millie is told that she has caused a problem, what do you think she is going to do? Sit back and let others fix it?"

"Good God." Chase sank onto the settee next to her. The blood drained from his face. If Jennelle was right and Millie had left to discover what happened to Aimee, then she was more than just alone and vulnerable. If she was snooping around the London docks and anyone discovered her real identity, she was in grave danger. And they would. Millie might like to think herself wild and untamed, but compared to the poor who found work around the wharfs, she was a polished and refined diamond.

"You have to find her, Charles. She told me she would be back by now, and not only is she *not* back, I have only received one brief note stating she was close but needed more time. Nothing else."

"I will find my wife and I will find her well and unharmed," Chase announced, just before he shut all his emotions down. He instinctively shifted into the man he had been for years working as a spy in the war. Feelings were sometimes an asset, but in times like these, fear and worry drove men to poor decisions and actions. No longer was he Charlie, who adored his beloved wife, but the Marquess of Chaselton. There was no power, means, persuasion, or force he would not employ to find what he sought.

"Start from the beginning and tell me everything that you know."

Jennelle stared at him for several seconds and then began. "First, my lord, you need to know just who was behind the events of that awful night. For it was not your wife."

"Hello, Reece."

Reece closed the door behind him out of habit and then froze. His gaze moved over her body slowly before becoming riveted on her green eyes. There was no mistaking their dark look. Every nerve ending immediately responded to their unspoken message. "What are you doing in here?" he barely choked out as he visually devoured her.

Aimee lifted her arms to swirl the diaphanous material she was wearing around her. "And I thought I was being obvious. I intend to seduce you."

Damn, she sounded calm. Even confident. He felt neither. What he did feel was his lower body tightening to a painful level. His heart began to pound and he clenched his fists, determined to remember all the reasons why he did not want to do what his body was demanding.

As soon as they returned to London, the pressure for them to marry would be incessant, and it would come from everyone who knew either of them. But Reece fully intended to resist. He refused to be punished for the situation Aimee had alone created. He would look Chase in the eye and swear on everything that he valued that his sister had been returned untouched. But, damn, if she was not making it very hard.

Only that morning, Aimee declared that not only did she believe she was being treated like a prisoner but so would Charles, Millie, Jennelle . . . and her mother. He had pointed out that prisoners did not have quarters, beds, decent food, or many of the other amenities she had been allowed. And yet he also doubted many would think it tolerable that he had locked up a woman—especially the daughter of a marquess—without letting her see or speak to anyone. So he had agreed to let Aimee out of her room and waited for her to reveal her real intentions. And once she tried to enlist help from his crew, he would be well justified in locking her back up.

All day he had spied on her, waiting and watching for her to recruit his men into doing something he had forbidden, but Aimee approached no one. She had been friendly to everyone she encountered. Kyrk had been grateful to receive her company and Collins had been shocked when she had apologized, stating that he had been correct and she should have heeded his instruction about staying away from the crew. She also apologized for usurping his cabin. When lunchtime came, Reece had thought she would seek him out, and when she did not he had gone to look for her, only to find her *in the kitchen* with JP. Soon afterwards, she had retired to her cabin.

Aimee shifted her stance slightly and the material shimmered, once again drawing attention to her figure. His whole body instantly constricted with desire, remembering just what it felt like to hold her in his arms. He took a step forward and her hand went up. Without thought, he stopped.

Aimee tilted her chin up slightly. "My heart is yours, Reece, and I can say confidently that it will always be yours. Whether you are aware of it or not, I *have* met other men. I have fulfilled my social and familial responsibilities of being introduced into Society. I have danced, and conversed, and even flirted with the most eligible bachelors seeking a wife."

Every word Aimee spoke felt like a fist being driven into his stomach. But Reece refused to let anything in his stance or expression show what he was feeling at the thought of other men around her.

"Not all were titled, but most were," Aimee continued. "A few of the men were dandies, some disturbingly old, and a handful were idiots, unable to carry on even a dull conversation. But there were several gentlemen who were intelligent, witty, and unusually charming in both looks and manners. I was surprised to learn how many men of leisure are secretly ambitious, discontent to live off their inheritance. And yes, a few of these gentlemen have pursued my hand with remarkable persistence."

Jealousy. That was the root of the twisting pain eating Reece. Any sane man with means and a title would seek her hand, but he had told himself she had been ignoring them in order to cling to her childhood fantasy. He had not realized how much that belief had enabled him to stay sane, because deep down Reece suspected that once Aimee did meet some eager, witty, and available gentleman, he would become a distant memory.

"And while the *idea* of marrying tempted me after seeing Millie so happy with Chase, I realized something. When I looked into my future and envisioned the father of my children, I could see only you. Despite everything, I have wanted, and still want, only you."

Reece swallowed. It was not often he dreamed of being a husband and father. For the only woman he could imagine making a commitment to was Aimee—and she was an impossibility. Women like Aimee did not become sea captains' wives. They were not content to wait for weeks, sometimes months, to see their husbands.

Aimee stilled for a second, and only when their eyes were once again locked did she resume speaking. "But after tonight I am not going to pursue you any longer. I will refuse any attempts to force us into marriage and I will mimic your endeavors this past year to avoid each other. Or . . . you can take what I am offering."

Reece's eyes narrowed, but he did not move his gaze from hers.

"I will give you my love and a future with me by your side, either on this ship or at our home with our children. You choose. After tonight we will become either strangers or lovers. But either way, you will need to do something for me in return."

Reece's jaw clenched. The catch. There always was one when a woman proposed a deal or compromise. Did Aimee think he would confess his undying love? Was she going to demand that he swear off other women if he refused her? Did Aimee think she could persuade him by blaming him for her self-imposed spinsterhood?

"And just what is it that you expect me to do?" he finally managed to grind out.

"Either way, you must admit what you are accepting or refusing."

Stunned and perplexed, Reece creased his brows in confusion.

Aimee gave a delicate shrug of her shoulders. "Admit that my reputation is ruined, and as a ruined woman, I am now more of a risk to *you* than you are to me. Recognize that my love for the sea is sincere and acknowledge that I *could* be one of those rare women who could be happy away from family and friends for weeks at a time on a ship. Concede that my presence is *not* a problem for the crew. And . . ."

Upon her hesitation, Reece mentally braced himself. Everything she had said was true. If her brother had not been able to keep her whereabouts a secret, then she was right about her reputation, just as she was about loving the sea and being able to mingle with his crew. But just as he would never admit any of those things, neither would he acknowledge her final demand—to admit his love. Only he would be haunted with that information. Someday Aimee would change her mind about him and it would be a lot easier for her to find and commit to another without a past love.

"I want you to admit that last December meant something to you. That I was not a mere dalliance. That you would not have reacted the same way to just any woman who kissed you awake. I want you to tell me that I was not just a bit of muslin, willing and easily accessible."

He swallowed, rattled by her last request. "You know all that you said is true."

"Even December?"

"Especially December," he answered, his voice hoarse with emotion.

She closed her eyes and he spied a tear sliding down her cheek. "Thank you." Then, straightening her back, she asked, "What is your choice?"

He shook his head. "Aimee, I cannot be with you . . . I wish I could, but I just . . ."

She looked at him, and with a small nod of her head, moved past him to go to the door and leave. The moment she stepped around him and out of sight, his future, which had always been so clear to him, became blank. He could recall his dreams—growing the fleet, living on the water— but it was suddenly all meaningless. He could achieve every goal he ever set, but unless she was in his life, he would never be at peace, never be truly happy. And he would know that it was not Society, or titles, or circumstances of birth that were the cause of his loneliness. He would have only himself to blame.

Reece grabbed her arm and swung her around and roughly pulled her up against him. Aimee splayed her fingers across his chest and without any hesitation she lifted her face. He pushed all of the reasons why he was not the one for her out of his mind and gave in to his desire to once again feel her lips against his. Soft, warm, and inviting—everything he remembered and more.

Aimee closed her eyes and blocked out everything except Reece. Finally, he was kissing her. Not from shock or lack of self-control, but because he wanted her and he could not let her go. The moment his fingers curled around her arm, tendrils of fire licked every nerve in her body. When his mouth opened, she welcomed him and swept her own tongue inside, delighting in the taste of him. A deep groan of satisfaction escaped his throat and he crushed her to him, deepening the kiss. And still it was not enough. All Aimee knew was she wanted to be closer to him, to touch and be touched and know that he was finally hers and she was his.

Reece reveled in the small hungry sounds Aimee was making deep in her throat. She had ruined him ten long months ago. Before Aimee, kissing had been an enjoyable pastime, but not something that would ever cause his emotions to become involved. As with all things concerning the pursuit of pleasure and women, it was predictable, easily attained, and dismissed. But the touch of Aimee's lips against his was unlike anything he had ever experienced. She was everything he had ever wanted and never thought to have. He did not deserve her, but he had not been able to stop himself that afternoon. He just wanted more, and that one soft kiss had turned into something that had consumed him day and night. And now that she was in his arms again, he wanted to believe this was real . . . that she not only wanted him, but always would, for she was all he would ever want. Easing back, he cupped her cheek. "Are you sure?"

Aimee blinked her passion-filled eyes, but he could see she understood the question. "Only if you promise not to regret this—regret choosing me," she said, her green eyes boring into his.

Reece swallowed and dove his fingers into her hair, letting

her feel the tension in him. "I cannot change, Aimee. I will always be who I am now and nothing more."

Aimee closed her eyes and smiled. When she opened them again, Reece caught his breath at the love shining from the emerald depths of her eyes. "I know who you are, Reece Hamilton. What's more, I know that you *cannot* change. We have known each other for years, but while you were ignoring me, I was not ignoring you. I know you are loyal, passionate, patriotic, and so many more things. I also know that once you have committed to something, it's forever. And you've been torn because your heart is committed to me and the sea. You thought you couldn't have both. But you can."

All words came to an abrupt end as he took her mouth in a searing kiss. Reece had been completely unprepared for the flood of sensations her words would have on him. He wanted her to be his wife, to be the mother of his children, to do things right and in the right order, but he most desperately needed to make her his. And the way she was pressing her body against him, Aimee needed him as well.

Reece groaned and Aimee's eyes closed as the full force of his hunger broke over her. This kiss was not like the others. In those, Reece had held something back. Now, she could feel a new level of tension radiating from him. He was no longer trying to fight his desires. Instead, he was surrendering to them, and in return she was giving him everything she had. It was too late to retreat, even if she had wanted to do so. Her whole being was already committed.

A soft whimper came from deep in Aimee's throat and the soft, sensual sound nearly pushed reason aside. Reece was already tight and hard with arousal and he had to fight to remain in self-control. He refused to just bury himself in her. Aimee would know the beauty and all the pleasure of making love.

Reece's lips captured hers one more time before trailing to

her jaw and down her neck. Aimee could hear his breathing—harsh, uncontrolled, and ragged with need. It excited her almost as much as his touch did. His hands were gliding over the soft material, up and down her back until they cupped her cheeks. Remembering what those fingers had done to her in December, a frisson of longing rippled on the surface of her skin and Aimee moaned her pleasure into his chest.

Reece whispered her name. An aching hunger was growing in him that only Aimee could assuage. He needed to touch her, see her. Not daring to raise his mouth from hers, he started to slowly slide the gown down her shoulders. His lips followed, leaving a trail of sensual kisses along her collar bone. When he moved the material down her arms to reveal her chest, he stared in awe. Her skin was creamy and flawless.

Something fluttered in her stomach as she saw him taking her in. She drew in an unsteady breath and let the gown fall to the floor.

Slowly and seductively, his gaze slid downward. "You are so beautiful," he muttered, overwhelmed with emotion.

A small thrill shot through her, making her feel alive in a way she never had before. She was not going to retreat, but she suddenly felt lost. She had been pretending to be knowledgeable in the art of seduction, but the confidence she had mustered was disappearing fast. "I don't know what to do."

Reece's eyes darkened to an intense blue hue. "Just let me love you," he whispered, his concentration strained. She was so perfect that all he could think about was touching her.

Gathering her in his arms, Reece returned his lips to hers and instantly his body reacted to the touch of her naked skin. Need tore through him. He was on fire. His blood, his muscles, every fiber of his body burned for her.

Their lips embraced, moving hungrily against each other. Tongues teased, tasted, tantalized. Aimee was breathless and anxious and exhilarated at the same time. Never had she felt as beautiful as she did in his arms. Gone was any fear. She felt only passion and love.

Reece held her close, becoming intoxicated with the feel of her skin against him. His body was tight and so hot he thought he could breathe out steam. He knew he was in danger but fought to remain in control. He kissed her again and, feeling her quiver to the point she could no longer stand, he swept her up in his arms and made his way to the bed.

Aimee closed her eyes, basking in Reece's strength. He carried her as though she were weightless. Never having been petite like Millie, the thought of a man wrapping his arms around her with ease was one she had refused to entertain. But Reece was no gentleman of leisure. The arms encompassing her were taut with muscle, just like the rest of his body. Awed by such strength, Aimee began to stroke his torso through the opening of his shirt.

Reece moaned as the soft touch of her fingers brushed erotically over his skin. He was burning with desire. The feel of Aimee in his arms and her softness cradled against his chest was almost too good to believe. Reece still could not fathom why a woman so beautiful, generous, and passionate would want him, but he no longer had the strength to push her away. Not now. He no longer needed to justify what he felt. There was a rightness in being with her. Aimee felt like his soul mate, and only when he was with her would he ever feel whole.

When Reece slipped away, Aimee opened her eyes just in time to see him divest his final piece of clothing. Pressing her thighs together, she bit her lip as her hungry gaze wandered over his body. She had never seen a man fully naked before. Reece's muscles rippled across his chest and stomach, but unlike the other large, brawny men of his crew, there was a trained and controlled power radiating from him. She could have examined dozens of nude men before him, but Aimee knew that none would have compared to him.

His blue, watchful eyes never left hers as he lowered himself slowly on top of her, pushing her into the pillows. Every nerve ending in Aimee's body immediately responded. When she felt the unmistakable evidence of his desire pressed against her, she sucked in her breath and reached out to touch him, verifying he was real.

Reece shuddered as her fingertips began to trace the contours of his arms. He wanted to give her time, but he could not take his gaze away from her mouth. It was slightly open, beckoning him to kiss her. Powerless to stop himself, he lowered his lips to hers. The pressure against her mouth was deep and persuasive and undeniable, but Aimee did not retreat. Instead, she moaned with pleasure and stroked his tongue with her own. In return, he feasted on her, devouring the sweet interior she so willingly offered.

Aimee had been told by countless men and women of her beauty, but in Reece's arms she finally felt the words might actually be true. His hands were caressing her everywhere— her shoulders, her arms, her back, and she loved the size and warmth of them. Needing to touch him in return, she pressed her mouth to his neck, relishing the salt-tinged flavor of his skin.

Reece closed his eyes. Her breath felt warm and sweet on his skin. The agony of staying away these past few months was nothing compared to the torment of her touch. His hand slid over her thigh, and the shiver that raced through her set him on fire. He had been a fool to believe time and distance could cause him to forget how incredibly soft her skin was. But this time his naked body was touching hers, and it only intensified his pleasure.

Aimee moaned again and began to move under his touch. Every muscle in her body was tight with sexual tension and it was taking all Reece had to control the urge to pin her hips and possess her. He needed to stop her restless motions and trapped her legs between his muscular thighs. Catching her chin between thumb and forefinger, he turned her head so she met his eyes. Passion and love stared back at him. No hesitation. No hidden questions. No desire for delay. He shuddered in response and closed his mouth over hers for a long moment before his lips freed hers to trace her jaw and trail downward.

Head tilted back, Aimee sank her fingers into Reece's hair and gasped as he found the pulse at the base of her throat. His chest rubbed against her nipples and she arched her back, lissome and eager for more. Strong, powerful hands shifted to her waist and her breathing fractured as he began a sinuous, tantalizing glide upward along her body.

Aimee quivered again, and God help him, it only made Reece want to touch her more. He could not get enough. His fingers tightened about her slender form, momentarily pausing before he let them slowly slide upward until at last they found her breasts. His thumbs grazed across her nipples and she shuddered at the first rough touch.

A sweet, hot flame was scorching through her and Aimee realized she was holding her breath. The moment his hands found her breasts, she thought she would go out of her mind. The sensations Reece was creating were unlike anything she had ever experienced. He gently caught one hard little berry between his fingers and squeezed carefully, sending a shaft of longing racing through her. She wanted to touch him, to explore his body as he was exploring hers, but her body could only feel, not respond to commands.

He was so hard, Reece feared he might burst, but he refused to hasten toward his goal. Her throaty mews and lusty moans were the sweetest melodies, and he needed to hear more. Using his thumbs, he coaxed her nipples until they were hard and straining. His eyes were shadowed with dark excitement as he bent his head to kiss the side of her throat before moving down to capture one taut and throbbing bud between his lips. Firm and ripe, sexual tension seized him anew as the taste of it sent a shudder of excitement through him.

Aimee's breathing quickened the moment he took her breast into his mouth and ran his tongue across the tip. At first he did no more than flick his tongue over the sensitive flesh, but soon he began to suckle. The added stimulus was almost too much, and Aimee writhed beneath him. His tongue was blissful torture. The suction caused her to lose all restraint. She twisted and moaned. Her fingernails dug into his shoulders and the heat between her thighs grew even hotter.

Reece smiled and suckled again, finding immense pleasure in Aimee's uninhibited response. She was straining against his mouth and with each moan, her back arched and the innocent pressure of her hips against his groin caused the muscles in his abdomen to tighten further. Soon the sensation would be unendurable. Momentarily he raised his head, and upon hearing her whimpering protest, a satisfied grin spread across his handsome face. Then he switched to the other side, repeating his sensual assault while his kneading fingers possessively cupped and stroked her newly deserted rosy peak.

When Reece pulled away, Aimee heard herself cry out and arch upward. She was stunned by the degree of abandonment she felt, and yet she could not help but react so openly to his onslaught. Nothing had ever felt so wonderful. Running her hands through his thick, unruly hair, she pulled him closer. He answered her unspoken request and flicked his tongue over her hardened peak again and again, while gently rasping his teeth against it.

One hand continued its massage on her breast as he worshipped the other with his mouth, sucking until the nipple was a hard nub. He longed to taste all of her, know all of her, touch and caress her whole body, making it quiver in desire. Edging his knee more deeply upward, he lodged it between her thighs and gloried in the sultry heat that emanated from between her legs. For he was the cause.

The pressure of his knee sent shivers of ecstasy through her frame, which made her tremble all the more. The passion that had lain buried inside her since December had reawakened, and she wanted more. She began to kiss him wherever she could. Her hands drifted over his back, his sides—touching him in all the places her fingertips could reach. Desire continued to scorch through her, igniting needs for which she had no name. "Reece," she whispered against his neck, needing more but not knowing how to say it.

"Yes . . ." he half asked, half teased. Her soft entreaty was making him burn. When she leaned into him and tilted her head back for his kiss, he had no will to resist. Reece took her mouth hungrily. His tongue thrust into her mouth and she responded in kind. Undisciplined, untamed, and unre-strained.

Aimee pushed her head back against the pillow and opened her mouth to draw breath. His lips returned to her breast, where they gently tugged and his tongue rasped across the very sensitive tip, but she knew she was not alone in her growing desire. She could feel Reece growing ever more ready and Aimee ground her hips against him to encourage him into action. She remembered the sensations his fingers could create and so did her lower body. Aimee moved again and this time, his mouth let go of her as he moaned.

Leaving both breasts swollen and aching, Reece covered them with his chest again and captured her mouth in a long, searing kiss that made her cry out for more. "Please . . ." she begged.

Intensely aware of his own sensual hunger, Reece buried his face against her throat with a soft groan of desire. He was not sure how much longer he could last, but he vowed she would never regret choosing him. He drew his palm down between her breasts and over the small curve of her stomach. Her hands began moving up and down his broad back, encouraging him though he needed none.

He placed another soft, sensual kiss on the sweet, scented curve of her breast. Then with a low, husky groan, he closed his hand possessively over her, lacing his fingers through the soft thatch of hair between her legs. He paused and soon Aimee cried out softly as a deep tremor shook her. She clung to him. "Reece, please," she whispered.

"Please what?" he asked. "This?" Reece slid one finger across the small pleasure bud hidden in the soft hair and Aimee sucked in her breath and nodded. Watching her, he stroked her slowly, barely parting her with his fingers, teasing her opening. She shuddered beneath the sensual onslaught, but she did not pull back from it. Instead, she thrust herself against him, prodding him to tease her into something she could not name. He kissed her passionately and at the same time slowly began to move his finger deeper into her channel.

Aimee buried her face against his shoulder. He eased his finger back out of the snug passage and used her own moisture to massage her small, swelling button of desire. Reece had touched her before, but this time it was somehow different. This time it was possessive. He was marking her as his. She wanted to do the same to him but she was powerless to think, to do anything but drown in the sensations he was creating within her. He repeated the action slowly and deliberately, easing his finger into her and then teasing her flesh. Again and again he did it until she thought she would die. She wanted more, needed more, and began to writhe against his hand, demanding Reece give what her body so desperately needed.

She was melting for him, hungry for him and arching against his hand, begging for more. Never had pleasuring a woman provided such enjoyment. But touching Aimee, feeling her arch against his palm as he penetrated her, was unlike anything he had ever known. This incredible lady wanted him. All her heat belonged to him and only him, and that knowledge was close to pushing Reece over the brink of sanity. Soon he would lose what little control he had left, and she needed to be prepared.

He introduced a second finger into her and slowly began to separate his fingers, stretching her gently. Aimee bucked, and as she cried out, his mouth slanted over hers, swallowing her shouts of excitement. His tongue mimicked his fingers penetrating, stroking, taking, as they slid deeper, widening her slick, hot channel. He stroked and caressed, drawing forth the wet heat until she was half mad with desire, calling out his name. He wanted to hear more. God, he couldn't get enough of her.

Aimee was sure she was on fire and that burning flames were scorching her skin. She felt unbelievable and impatient, fulfilled yet wanting, elated but apprehensive. She wanted more of him inside her and again pushed her hips into his hand, seeking release from the tension suffusing her body. "Reece, I don't . . . I can't . . . oh God." Aimee was only half aware of what he was doing to her. The only thing she truly understood was that she did not want him to stop. A twisting sensation began to build swiftly inside her and in the next moment, she arched her back and cried out his name when the splendor erupted inside her.

The sight of her writhing naked in his bed, crying out in ecstasy while demanding more, was an overwhelming invitation Reece could not deny. With the evidence of her readiness on his fingers, and her hips pressing so eagerly against his own, it was all he could do to restrain himself from thrusting into her right then and riding her climax. But this was her first, and he would be her only. When women chattered about the laziness and selfishness of their lovers, Aimee would never know what they meant.

His sense of urgency was growing beyond control. Desire roared in him, for her body and all the things she could bring him. He leaned toward her and put his forehead on hers, cradling her face in his strong hands. He breathed in her scent and gently brushed his lips against hers. "Oh God, Aimee," he rasped, disclosing an undercurrent of doubt. "I should not . . . but I need you. God knows how much I need you," he whispered, afraid she might realize her mistake and resist.

He paused, his lips so close to hers she could feel his breath on her upper lip. His gaze held hers. Aimee could not look away and did not dare breathe. She doubted she would ever get accustomed to the intensity that Reece was able to channel through his eyes. The look of primal hunger in them now made her heart race. His knee pushed her legs apart and he positioned his hips above hers.

Reece saw the fear flash in her eyes and his heart seized. He pushed her hair off of her shoulders. "There's nothing to be afraid of." He placed soft, passionate kisses on her throat. "I swear it. I won't hurt you. I could never hurt you." Then he leaned down and kissed her again—hot and searing, melting any resistance.

His need had become painful, and he could no longer deny his own release. As slowly as he could manage, he settled himself between her silky thighs, lifted her hips, and began to penetrate. Upon entry, she began to twist, forcing herself forward against him. He had fully intended to enter her slowly, but when she arched her hips, he felt her warmth and could not stop. He drove deep, praying she wanted him as much as he wanted her.

A sharp stinging pain seized Aimee. She closed her eyes and gasped in astonishment. Reece distracted her with a kiss while he held himself completely still, filling her, claiming her, as her body adjusted. He was big. Opening her and stretching her, he was making a place for himself in the very heart of her. The hurt began to dissipate, and in its wake was something new. Surprisingly, her body welcomed him, both his size and length, and suddenly Aimee knew she was now in a position to offer him the pleasure he had given her.

The sudden sensation surrounding his manhood almost undid Reece. Entering her was like entering the gates of heaven. Warm and tight, he felt himself coming apart and had to remind himself to take it slowly. Carefully he eased out of her with torturous care and then filled her again with even more tormenting gentleness. Each time brought more pleasure, more pressure, until she lifted herself against him, silently demanding that he quicken the pace.

Reece balanced himself on his elbows and tried to control the depth of his steady thrusts. His jaw locked with the effort and his shoulders strained. The encouragement Aimee was offering was the undoing of all his good intentions. With the increasing urgency of her body's unconscious demands, she pushed against him once more and dug into his shoulders with her fingernails. "Reece," she begged.

"I'm trying to be gentle, Aimee," he rasped, barely able to talk.

She pulled back to look at him, their gazes locked. "Please don't," she moaned. "Be gentle later. I need you . . ."

Hearing her plea, Reece could wait no longer. He pulled back and thrust into her again, rejoicing in her cries of pleasure as her body contracted around him. He pressed his face into the curve of her neck and thrust again, this time harder and faster. Her legs wrapped around him, spreading herself wide, instinctively locking her ankles behind him to keep him there. Aimee clutched him and rode each thrust, hardly aware of the passionate moans she was making.

Reece's blood roared, wild and hot, through his veins. He was balanced on the dangerous edge between joy and agony. He could not recall feeling so intensely alive in his entire life. Rocking her against him, he kissed her mouth, her neck, her ear, listening to her heart pound and her fast, short breaths. Her hands had turned wild, stroking him everywhere they could reach. Again and again he buried himself deep within her. Hard and fast. Slow and tender, wishing he could make being with her last forever.

Aimee's body quaked, and burned, and throbbed. She inhaled with every gasping breath. The world was spinning away and taking her with it. She parted her lips to cry out her pleasure and Reece clamped his mouth tightly down over hers, joining her soft sounds of passion with those of his own. His tongue plunged into her mouth. Hungry and urgent, he demanded everything and she gladly surrendered to his claiming. With a tiny, muffled shriek of surprise, Aimee surrendered to the glittering storm that swept over her. Her whole body sang the song of release accompanied by Reece's gruff sound of masculine satisfaction.

She had climaxed with a shock of incredible pleasure that shook her whole body, and Reece felt it all. His fingers closed around her buttocks with urgency, for every muscle in his body had tightened almost to the point of pain. Although he tried desperately to still the surging of his hips, his self-control had completely escaped him. The sounds he emitted would have shamed him at any other time, but every sense, every thought was caught in a whirlwind of pleasure. And then a heavy shudder racked him as he felt his release welling up from the base of his spine, from his toes. It rushed over him like an immense wave, until in a surge of euphoric satisfaction, a triumphant exclamation escaped his lips.

Aimee cried out with joy, feeling his release and then his collapse. Reece was finally and truly hers, she thought triumphantly. From this moment, he belonged to her just as surely as she belonged to him.

Chapter 19

October 28, 1816

The beginnings of a commotion across the full room caught Clive's attention. He was relieved to see that it was not Bessie in the middle of it, but Ellie. With Ellie, he was no longer concerned with her ability to handle the men's grumblings. Bessie, however, was another matter. And that was a fact that mystified Clive.

It had been a week since Ellie had walked into his establishment, and in that short span, she had improved greatly. Then again, she had been so bad that any progress was noticeable. However, as she became more comfortable in her role, she had also started asking his customers questions—bizarre ones about ships and the colors of their pinnaces.

Clive had said nothing. Her direct inquiries were just more evidence that Ellie knew nothing of the men or the lives of those who grew up and worked on the docks. One just did not volunteer information—even to a pretty face. Nevertheless, he was a little curious as to why she was so interested in ships and their owners. Whatever the reason, he was fairly certain it was related to why she had been so insistent on working for him.

Ellie refused to give up though, despite the obvious futility of her efforts. Each time she started probing someone, they would interrupt and shift the conversation to a subject they considered far more interesting—her. And while Clive refused to allow anything but drinking in his place, he could not blame the men for contemplating other ideas. The damn woman always smelled like flowers, and if the idea were not so preposterous, he would have thought she bathed before each shift. Her fresh scent gave men ideas, which usually turned into a situation Clive had to control with his fists.

But not with Ellie.

Somehow, the wee thing was able to turn a man down without his needing to intervene. He could only ever hear a part of what she said, and from what he could tell, it seemed straightforward enough. Most smiled, and some even laughed, but not a single man ever got truly upset.

Clive knew that he was not the only one who noticed Ellie's confounding abilities. He had spied Devlin watching with admiration, but Bessie had the opposite reaction. She would glare at Ellie with obvious envy. And last night, her resentment had grown to new levels of hostility.

Ellie had admirers, but so did Bessie. She was not a traditional beauty, but with her busty figure and wild hair, she could capture a man's attention. Having always been partial to curvaceous redheads, Clive had hired her without a second thought. And he had never regretted it. Bessie was always feisty and oftentimes irritable, but he liked her that way. He just wished that she could learn how to handle the customers better when they wanted more than just a drink. Unfortunately, she had never acquired the ability to politely turn a man down. And to hope she would glean any of the persuasive skills Ellie effortlessly used was futile.

Still, things between the two women were calm, and they might have continued that way if he had just kept his mouth shut. But Clive liked Bessie and knew that she needed every halfpenny she earned. So he casually mentioned that she should try to be nicer to the men, thinking it would help increase her tips. Unbeknownst to him, his revelation came on the heels of a lost tip—all because Bessie had rudely told the man just what part of his anatomy he would lose if he should ever comment on her body again.

Clive's suggestion had been the last straw and Bessie had exploded. She focused all her anger and frustrations toward him. Clive considered himself a patient man and fairly tolerant of Bessie's mood swings, but insulting him in his own place while it was full of customers was not something anyone was allowed to do, ever. Consequently, he had overreacted. Loud enough for all to hear, he bellowed that it was time for Bessie to take a lesson from Ellie—who could not just deliver drinks but *keep the men happy.*

He had wished instantly that he could recall his words. Bessie might not look like a sensitive soul, but she was. And he could not have insulted her more. Clive grimaced at the memory.

"I'll never learn the one lesson that little girl could teach me. I've never been paid to open my legs for a man and only a whore would know the art."

Clive had never seen anyone move so fast, but suddenly Devlin was at Bessie's side, whispering something into her ear. Her blue eyes had grown large with fear as he took a firm hold of her elbow and escorted her out the door. He paused only long enough to say that Bessie looked a little hot and would be back after she had cooled off.

At the time, Clive had been stunned. Not just that Bessie could have said something so foul, but that Devlin would react in such a way. Even now, after a day to think about it,

Clive was still not sure whether he was grateful or angry at Devlin's high-handedness. Controlling Bessie had always been hard. Not because Clive did not know how, but because he never wanted to hurt her.

Ellie, on the other hand, was still a mystery. She was growing on him though. Kind and nice, the customers liked her. And yet, he still had no idea just who she really was.

Bessie, though, was like him. She had been through a lot of hardships in her life, and as a result trusted very few people. He was one of those few. That meant a lot to him, so if she wanted to hate Ellie, he was not going to intervene. He refused to see the disappointment and hurt in Bessie's eyes again.

Chapter 20

October 29, 1816

Aimee felt warm lips press against her cheek. With a sigh of pure contentment, she rolled over, thinking that nothing could be better than being woken up in such a way. For the past two days, she had been living not just *a* dream—but *her* dream. Finally, she and Reece were together.

He had not yet asked her to marry him, but that he would was a certainty with their current living arrangements. When he did, Aimee wanted Reece to have no more lingering doubts. She wanted him to be just as happy with their union as she was, which left her just a little more than a week to prove to him that they truly belonged together.

Smiling, she reached up and pulled his head down until their lips met. The kiss quickly turned hot, lasting for several minutes. When Reece pulled back, he saw her look of disappointment. Bending his head once more toward hers, he brushed his mouth lightly across Aimee's startled lips and whispered, "While I would love to continue this, I thought perhaps you might like to join me this morning when I take the wheel."

Aimee's eyes shot wide open. Reece was already dressed

for the day. Her hands gripped his shoulders to study his expression. "Shall I be watching or participating?"

Reece cocked a brow. "Perhaps some of both."

Seeing that he was indeed serious, Aimee gave him a quick kiss and threw the blanket off of her. Standing up, she pointed to the door and said, "Just give me twenty minutes and I will be ready."

Reece laughed. "No need to rush."

Aimee shook her finger once more at the door. "Leave or you will decide that the wheel can wait and convince me of it as well."

He took a step forward. "Are you sure you do not want to explore—"

Aimee gave him a slight shove. "I'm sure. Now go."

Reece laughed again and slipped out the door. He could not remember feeling so light in spirit. He was not sure he had ever felt this completely happy. And he was not the only one finding himself smiling for seemingly no reason. Practically all his men were wearing boyish grins as they did their duties—even JP.

Later, Reece felt someone step in close to him as he stood in the bridge behind the ship's wheel. He knew without looking that it was Aimee. Men plodded and could be heard long before they approached, and they certainly did not smell of flowers. Her fine-boned hand reached out and pointed to the man climbing the foremast. "Is that Mr. MacDarmid?"

"Who?" Reece asked right before he remembered her insistence on referring to his crew as if they were gentlemen.

Aimee pointed again. "The one with the dark brown hair pulled back into a ponytail. I cannot see his face, but Mr. MacDarmid is the one whose high cheekbones make him look angry, even when he's laughing."

Reece scrunched his nose for a moment at the description. He never really thought about it, but Mac did look annoyed most of the time. Reece had always assumed Mac was just easily irritated. "If you are talking about Ironlung Mac, then aye, that's him on the rigging."

Aimee leaned her head on his arm. "Why him?"

Reece shrugged. "He's one of the able-bodied seamen. He's thin and wiry but strong. Plus he can shout loud enough that everyone can hear him."

Aimee sighed. "But can he hear them? It's just that I wonder if he speaks so loud all the time because he is partially deaf."

Reece blinked. Again, he never really thought about *why* Mac chose to shout everything he said, but Aimee's theory could be right. Her knowledge about his men was both inspiring and disconcerting.

"Enough about Mac. I thought you wanted to take the wheel."

Aimee jumped a step back and clutched her hands together near her chest. "*Take* the wheel? I don't know anything about steering a ship!"

The corners of his mouth raised a fraction with inner pleasure. He had not realized until now how disappointed he was that he had been robbed of the chance to open his world to her. Of all the duties he most wanted to show her, he could not be more pleased that it was steering.

"Take the handles here and here, and keep your stance a little wide to enable you to keep your balance when fighting the rudder."

Aimee did as she was told, glad that Reece was behind her, his hands just above hers on the spokes.

"This ship has only one wheel, but on larger ones, sometimes there are two, to help handle her in bad weather or when too much seawater gets into her hull."

Aimee nodded in understanding. She remembered Collins explaining how during a storm, if too much water got down into the hold, sailors would literally be pumping for their lives. "How do you know how fast we are going?"

"A long time ago, men would watch how long it took to pass something in the water, and measure the distance. Now we use a similar concept, only it is far more accurate." Reece paused and called out to one of the men. "Deadeye! Fetch the log line and give me the knots."

The hardened-looking man quickly turned to do as asked. "Why do you call Mr. Harkle Deadeye? I mean, he tends to wrinkle his brow a bit, but both his eyes work perfectly well from what I can see."

Reece flashed her a grin. "Mr. Harkle? I bet Deadeye enjoys that." He chuckled upon seeing her annoyed expression. "Listen, seamen get nicknames. They like them because it means they've earned the right to have one. And Deadeye?" he asked rhetorically, feeling suddenly a little sheepish. "Well, we call him that because of the way he looks."

"He looks dead?"

Reece shrugged. "No, he looks like a pirate."

It was Aimee's turn to roll her eyes, but before she could say anything more, Deadeye had returned. Upon seeing the nod from his captain, he yelled out "Mark!" and tossed the line overboard. Attached to its end was a triangular-shaped piece of wood that caught or "dug in" the water, pulling the line from a hand-held reel.

"See those knots in the line? Each one is forty-eight feet and three inches apart. That's what tells us how many sea miles we are moving per hour. Now Deadeye is counting the seconds, but if we really want to be accurate, we would use the half-minute sand glass I have in my cabin."

"And knowing how far you've traveled tells you when and where to turn?"

Reece winced. "Unfortunately, it doesn't account for currents and winds and weather—all of which can push a ship off course."

"I've heard the men mention that we needed to go south and that you know the route's sweet spot."

Pride compelled Reece to grin. All worthy sea captains knew the route from and to the Americas. They used the current that made a large circle going from England down south to Africa, cutting across the equator, and up along the American coastline. It took four or more weeks to get to the Americas, but to get back to England, it took perhaps three. One just followed the Gulf Stream up to New York and then as it cut across the Atlantic. But Reece's knowledge and intuition on just when to turn westward off the African coast was what made the *Sea Emerald* so widely known for its exceptional speed. That the men knew the ship's reputation for speed was not just because of its style and build, but their captain's knowledge—that was like a salve to his injured pride.

"You getting tired?"

Aimee shook her head and held on. "This is better than any adventure I've ever embarked on. To think you get to do this all the time. I am going to look forward to the few times a year I can leave our home and sail with you again."

Reece waited for the panic to hit him as her words sank in, but it never did. He honestly never thought his and Aimee's worlds could be merged together. He knew that a handful of captains successfully brought their wives on board from time to time, but none of them had come from Aimee's upbringing. They also had always seemed more rugged and built for a ship's harsh environment. Yet Aimee was proving herself to be every bit as resourceful as any wife he had ever met—more so in many cases.

The most amazing thing was her genuine love for the sea. Everything about Aimee came alive when the salty spray came over the side and the wind whipped at her face and hair. It enabled her to understand *his* love for being a ship's captain. As such, she would never separate him from not just his career but his passion. Nor did she intend to be with him on each and every trip.

Marrying Aimee was a necessity. He had known that from the instant he realized she had been on board his ship for weeks. Her reputation had to be saved, and as the sister of his best friend, he would do his duty. But he had thought the initial benefits of their union would be fleeting. Between them in bed, all was bliss; however, he had assumed Aimee would not understand his responsibilities, which oftentimes forced him to leave that bed. But he had been wrong. And if he had been wrong about that, then maybe he had been wrong about their future.

Chase had told him marriage was the best thing that ever happened to him. Reece knew his friend was being earnest, but Reece had also witnessed how Chase and Millie were always trying to change one another. Reece had assumed all couples were like that. His laughter filled the air. Aimee had no desire to change him and he truly could not think of a thing he wished to change about her.

Suddenly, he could not wait until they arrived in Savannah. Friends and family would be disappointed, but when he and Aimee returned to London, it would be as husband and wife.

Chapter 21

October 30, 1816

Millie came up to the bar and set three empty glasses down to be refilled. The night was slowing down, but most of the men who remained would stay until Clive closed up Six Belles for the night. Clive reached down to get the bottle of rum to refill the glasses. He stood back up and sighed. "I need to go in the back tae get more. Stay here."

Millie nodded, but when she saw Clive go over to Devlin and ask him to help her out, a shiver of vexation shot up her spine. "That's right. Get a man to help the helpless woman watch the bar," she said mockingly and loud enough for Clive and Devlin to hear. "As if women—*especially weak little ones*—are helpless when it comes to telling a man no."

Clive rolled his eyes and muttered something about how men were doomed when it came to understanding women. Devlin pushed himself up out of his chair and sauntered over to where Millie was standing with her arms crossed. "Ye remind me of someone I once knew."

"The world is full of petite brunettes. I am far from un-usual," Millie retorted. She was still annoyed and was not in the mood to be charmed out of her anger. She had thought that with a little more time, the men would start opening up to her, but she was beginning to realize that it was going to take a lot longer than she had anticipated to gain their trust. More time than she had if she was to return to Chase with news before he became aware of her absence.

"The lass I refer to is neither short nor dark haired. But like you, her tongue is quite sharp when riled."

"You are not the first to remark on my harridan-like nature. I have been called many things . . . twig . . . sprite." She whispered the last two words, reminded of how much she missed Chase.

Devlin smiled. He liked the fact that she did not deny who she was. "Sprite. Aye, that works."

"You like sprites, do you, Mr. MacLeery?"

"Not usually. You are the exception."

"But what about this other woman I remind you of? Do you still love her?"

Devlin started to cough. "*Love* her? Not at all! I cannot stand the vixen. For a while, the *bampot* was the bane of my existence."

"*Bampot*?" Millie inquired, unfamiliar with the Scottish term.

Devlin frowned, somewhat embarrassed that he did often call the woman who wanted to marry him "unhinged," and usually to her face. "It matters not."

Millie did not pursue the subject, mostly because she did not need to. Devlin's expression reminded her of her own just a few months ago when she and Chase denied their true feelings, pretending they only felt irritated by the other. She still detested being called Mildred and probably always would, but Charlie had become an endearment.

A sharp cry from across the room broke Millie's train of thought. She turned around and instantly realized just why Bessie had yelped in pain. A man had caught her arm in a tight grasp.

He was neither tall nor short, but he looked strong and his unshaven face did not hide the sneer on his lips and the intent in his deep-set eyes. This man was not just randy—he was mean. And Bessie knew it too. Millie glanced at the three men still sitting at his table and knew without question that they were not going to intervene.

"Mr. MacLeery, I think it would be wise to find Clive and ask him to return immediately."

Devlin had been about to intervene but decided that with four men, it was best to get Clive first.

Once Millie saw Devlin head toward the back room, she made her way to Bessie. The man holding her arm looked to be from one of the ships that had just arrived. He was wearing galligaskins—loose pantaloons designed to cover knee breeches. Most men wore their "goin' ashore" clothes, but not the four strangers. They were also carrying cutlasses. The knife was typically used for cutting lines or tearing sails; sheathed on the small of the back, it was accessible by either hand, and therefore a formidable weapon.

Millie grew uneasy as she stopped just out of arm's reach. "Let Bessie go," she said softly.

The man laughed triumphantly. "Not likely."

Millie knew then that her normal method of dealing with men was not going to work. No amount of talking, flattery, or smiles would work on him or his men. What they enjoyed most was exerting power over others, especially in the form of physical pain. That was the language they understood.

Without additional preamble, Millie stepped forward and let all the years of training take over as she lunged for the man's Adam's apple. As a child, she had been small and a target for others. Charlie had ensured she learned how to defend herself as a child. Since the incident with Sir Edward, he had made certain that her fighting skills included tactics many would consider not just unfair, but deadly.

From the corner of her eye, Millie could see that one of

his companions was overcoming his surprise and was about to act. She let go and spun low, causing the man to miss his grasp when he came for her. Using his momentary lack of balance to her advantage, she punched her heel into his knee, causing him to crumple.

The man whose Adam's apple she had struck thrust Bessie away from him so hard that she landed on her hip on a nearby empty table. He was enraged, and for a second, Millie had no idea how to stop him. Then she remembered the one method she and Chase had never been able to practice. Just in time, she shoved the bottom part of her palm into his nose, pushing upward. She heard a crunch and he fell.

She was about to make sure she had not killed him, when she heard two chairs fall abruptly backward as the final two companions decided to come after her. This time Millie did not panic. One was coming from behind, the other from the front, both believing their size and strength a benefit. Millie, however, decided to make them a handicap, and just as they came at her, she did another low spin. Both being of similar height, they clashed heads, momentarily stunning each other. As one reached up to rub his forehead, Millie took his arm and used the momentum to twist it until the shoulder popped out of the socket. Seeing the damage she alone had caused, the fourth man turned and ran out of the joint, leaving his companions to follow as best they could.

Millie took a deep breath and closed her eyes, trying to slow the rapid beat of her heart. *Oh, Chase, you would be so furious and proud of me right now,* she said to herself, wishing she could rush home and tell him just what had happened. She would even enjoy enduring one of his lectures.

When she opened her eyes, Millie wiped her perspiring palms on her skirt and looked around. Only then did she realize not only how quiet the place had become, but that every set of eyes was on her.

Swallowing, Millie pasted on her sweetest smile and said

as nonchalantly as she could manage, "Just something I learned to do in my youth." Then she winked at the table of men closest to her and said, "Warn your sons, gentlemen, that this is what happens when young boys mercilessly pick on little girls."

The men took the cue and began to drink again, but Bessie, Devlin, and Clive, who was still holding a case of rum, remained motionless, staring at her wide-eyed. "Clive, do you need help with those?" Millie asked, but before he could answer, Bessie recovered enough to grab her wrist and pull her to the corner of the room.

"Listen, little missy, I don't know how you got so wise an' all about that punchin' when you know nothin' about other things, but that man . . . he would've hurt me bad if you hadn't done what you did."

Millie just blinked. Bessie's tone was not one of gratitude, but neither did it contain its usual venom.

"I don't want any debts over my head," Bessie continued. "Especially to you. So I'm goin' to tell you how to keep your tips safe. I notice you put 'em in your pocket where anyone here can—and probably has tried to—swipe a coin or two without you knowin'."

Millie licked her lips. Despite what she just did to four grown men, she did not want Bessie thinking that she could be intimidated. "Putting them in your bodice is highly uncomfortable and not much safer, in my mind."

"You're right," Bessie said, surprising Millie. "You only swipe at your chest as if you're dropping the coins inside. Then you put them in your pocket."

Millie was tempted to ridicule the value of Bessie's secret, when the woman continued. "Before tomorrow night, sew a long strip of cloth to the inside layer of your garment, about so wide." Millie watched as Bessie spread out her fingers to indicate between one and two inches. "That way you can slide the coins down for safekeepin'."

Millie's brow creased in confusion. Bessie shifted a little to the left to ensure no one could see her movement and picked up a piece of her gown for Millie to take a closer look. As Millie traced the outline of several coins, her mouth opened with understanding. The strip did not act as a standard pocket, which would allow money to jingle and create noise. Instead, it stacked the coins on top of one another. Millie watched as Bessie twisted from side to side. Her gown was well worn, but it moved easily and no one would know that she had any money on her.

Seeing Millie's appreciative expression, Bessie nodded. "I've got nearly three pounds down there. So you know it works. Now, we're even."

Not waiting for Millie's agreement, Bessie immediately turned and left.

Even? Millie thought. *Was there such a thing, after all that had transpired between them?*

No, Millie decided. It was close, but they were not even. But she knew just how Bessie could square things between them.

Chapter 22

November 2, 1816

Devlin drummed his fingers on the arm of the worn hearth chair as he watched Ellie clean up after the last of the patrons. In the past, he rarely stayed until closing, and though a frequent patron of Six Belles, it was only after his conversation with her that he had become a nightly customer—and a nightly stalker. At first, he had just been curious, wanting to know where she lived and who she spent time with when she was not at the tavern. Lately, however, he had become more protective. After yesterday afternoon, those feelings had seriously grown.

He had just left his own business establishment when a man with a handheld portrait of Ellie stopped him. He was slightly more muscular than most men of his height. Though his brown hair was cut a little shorter than was fashionable, the style was better suited for the thinning, wiry strands. It was his close-set eyes that had made Devlin wary. They observed everything, but more than that, they detected what people did not intend for him to see. The man was clearly a Bow Street runner.

Devlin had noticed him the day before, along with several

others canvassing the streets. Suspecting that he was the one in charge, Devlin had decided to purposely put himself in the man's path to discover which one of his more indebted gamblers they were looking for. Never had he dreamed he would flash Ellie's face at him.

Devlin had lied and done his best impersonation of boredom when informing the man that he had no idea who the woman was, nor did he care. The runner had shrugged and walked away, but this afternoon, the man had approached him again, asking once more if Devlin knew the whereabouts of the woman in the portrait. Devlin gave him the same answer, but it did not matter. The man did not believe him. He had seen something in Devlin's initial reaction—the split second of recognition that one cannot disguise when unprepared.

Devlin had walked away, but immediately doubled back and followed the runner to learn just who had hired him. They had reached the northern parts of Mayfair before the man realized he was being tailed and cleverly got swallowed by a crowd. Devlin then headed to Six Belles. Whoever was after Ellie came from a different world than the docks. A wealthy one.

Devlin glanced over his shoulder at Ellie, smiling and laughing with a longshoreman who made no attempt to hide his attraction. Even in a modest frock with her hair tied back in a simple knot, she was unusually pretty, but no man hired numerous runners just to hunt down a beauty. Ellie might claim she came to work at Six Belles because she was looking for something, but that did not mean she was not also hiding from someone. Realizing someone wealthy and most likely powerful was searching for her, Devlin no longer doubted the appropriateness of his nightly habit of following her home. Ellie may be able to fight drunk men, but that did not make her invulnerable.

"Ellie!" he called out.

A few seconds later, she arrived at his side. "Mr. MacLeery, what a surprise to see you here this evening," she said teasingly, her lavender eyes sparkling with humor.

For a second, Devlin was mesmerized by them but quickly recovered. "I do not want you walking home alone at night anymore."

Millie smiled. "Clive walks Bessie and me down Pell and ensures the linkmen have the lights on. From there, it is only a short distance. I am perfectly safe."

Not from people specifically looking for you, Devlin wanted to say. However, he suspected such a disclosure might cause her to go on the run and vanish from his life. "Then will you tell me why you are so curious about ships with green and white pinnaces?"

Millie's eyes grew large for a second. "I can assure you the reason does not put me in any danger. And if you know nothing of the pinnace, then why do you care about my interest?"

Because I think I am falling in love with you, Devlin thought. But aloud, he only said, "Just don't leave here tonight without me."

Chapter 23

November 3, 1816

"I'd say we have two more days at sea and should anchor sometime Wednesday morning."

Aimee heard Mr. Collins's voice just in time to keep from opening the door to the captain's quarters. The chief mate was inside, and to her knowledge it was the first time he and Reece had spoken privately. Until now, all their meetings since her accident had been in public because Reece had been so furious that he had not trusted himself to be alone with Collins. But as the days stretched into a week, an awkwardness had grown between the two.

Knowing she was the cause, Aimee had decided she had a responsibility in repairing the relationship. Confronting Reece had been more than a little unpleasant. Enduring several harsh, and not totally inaccurate, accusations about her being the reason behind the tension between the two men had been hard, but not nearly as challenging as keeping quiet. For too many times during his nearly hour-long diatribe had counterpoints to his barbs come to mind.

Yes, she had disrupted the way of life aboard ship, but unlike the way Reece made it sound, her disturbances had not resulted in catastrophe. From what she could see, all the men were happy. They had been friendly and cooperative while she had been avoiding Reece, but at the same time there had been a weighted veil of secrecy that hung over them. With it gone, their spirits were free and merry. Even Reece had felt the effects and had started to join the men singing sea songs—a pastime, according to JP, Reece had abandoned since last December.

When Reece had brought up loyalty again, a surge of resentment had gone through her and Aimee had almost interjected in her defense. She might not have been able to stop herself if Reece had continued to assert how he had lost the crew's trust—because he had not. Instead, he had made it very clear how it *could* have been lost and the problems that would have caused.

Through it all, Aimee had only listened, staying silent when she could have argued and corrected several of his claims. To do so would have defeated the real purpose of the lecture—the chance for Reece to release all the emotions and thoughts that had been festering inside him.

It was her mother who had taught her the importance of letting a man offload his thoughts and feelings. It was rare her parents quarreled, but more often than not, her mother would just sit and listen to her father rant about something or someone. One time, after her father expressed several fairly harsh opinions to his wife about being manipulated into activities he expressly disliked, Aimee had sought to comfort her mother. But when she went into her room, Aimee had been surprised to find her mother completely untroubled. Instead, she was in the process of deciding which gown she was going to wear to the event her father had just made clear that he was not going to attend.

It was years ago, but when Reece first started spouting all of his frustrations, it was the memory of what her mother told her that day that had enabled her to remain quiet.

"Aimee, never forget that men can be just as emotional as women. Now those who are strong in mind and conviction like your father will never weep about what is troubling them. Nor will they plead or whine about their problems. However, at some point, men—like all human beings—are compelled to express their vexations. So you see? That is all your father was doing. In a way, it was the highest of compliments he paid me. Of all those he knows, your father chose me to release the inner thoughts that had been burdening him. It's a form of trust, much like the one you have with Millie and Jennelle."

Aimee had kissed her mother and was about to run and play, happy once again that she really was the luckiest of all girls to have her mother and father as her parents, when her mother stopped her. "Aimee, before you go, I would like to clarify something important." Aimee had shuffled back, unsure because the tone in her mother's voice had gone from relaxed to quite serious. "A person can be frustrated and a good friend lets them release those frustrations, but it is never tolerable to belittle or cause another person harm, either physically or through words. And *never* let a man, even one you love, do so to you."

Not until Reece started detailing all of his frustrations did Aimee truly comprehend what her mother had been advising her about. For the first few minutes, Aimee had held herself still, listening, waiting for the personal attack, because she had given Reece many reasons to take that route, but he had not. He had just detailed every single aggravation he had experienced, beginning with how he thought he would go crazy hearing her sing all the time. In the end, his speech had just further convinced Aimee that she and Reece were right for each other. It also seemed to enable Reece to move past his anger and mend things with his chief mate.

Smiling to herself, Aimee pivoted and was about to give Reece and Collins more time alone when she heard Collins ask, "So, the crew believes you and Lady Wentworth are going to marry when we reach Savannah."

Aimee could not help herself and grinned at the thought.

"Don't have much of a choice," Reece replied brusquely. "From the moment we left London and she was on board, marriage was inevitable."

Collins cleared his throat. Aimee could not see him, but the muffled sound was one of distress. "You are a lucky man, Captain. The men and I know that, we just hope you do as well."

"Lucky? Any man *but* me would be lucky to marry Lady Wentworth, Collins. My biggest fear is regret."

Aimee heard shuffling feet, but before they reached the door, they stopped. "The crew will want to be there."

Reece immediately replied, "No. The men should not be wasting the little bit of shore leave they have watching me resolve a personal problem."

Collins snorted. "You don't know what you're saying, Captain."

"I did not recall asking for your opinion," came Reece's quick, clipped retort.

Collins said nothing further as he knew it would be a waste of time. When it came to most things, there was not a man he admired more than his captain, but when it came to love, the man could not see clearly. On one hand, Reece was opening himself up to a chance for happiness, but in the other, he was shoving it away. Collins feared the latter was going to win. He did not want Reece to be unhappy, but then if he was not wise enough to thank the heavens for finding someone who truly loved him, then maybe misery was what he deserved.

Collins turned and opened the door. What he saw wrenched his heart. Aimee was slouched down on the wall, crying. He knew without asking that she had overheard the captain. And while Collins knew deep down the captain did not mean what he said, it was clear Aimee did not have that same conviction.

Kneeling down, Collins whispered, "Can you stand, my lady? Perhaps you should go somewhere private."

Aimee nodded, but when he was about to push open the door to the chief mate's cabin, which had been given to her for the rest of the voyage, she refused. "I need air," she whispered and moved up on the deck and into the night air.

Collins was unsure what to do and decided to follow her, for his gut said she should not be alone. "He didn't mean it, my lady. The captain's just scared. All men are when it comes to getting married."

Aimee wiped one eye and then the other. "Is that why you are not? Married, I mean."

Collins scoffed and leaned his elbows on the rail, looking out at the moonlit waves. "You tell me where there's another lady like you in the world and I'll snatch her up in a heart-beat."

Aimee knew that Collins was just being kind. She appreciated it, but that did not change what she had heard. "Your captain does not feel that way."

Collins shook his head. "You're wrong. I doubt the captain even knows just how much he wants to marry you. He just doesn't want his crew—or even me—to know it. He's afraid that love will make him look weak or foolish, or in his case both, because he loves you so much it frightens him. You will see in time."

Aimee swallowed and jutted out her chin. "No, I won't."

Since the age of six, she had dreamed of marrying Reece Hamilton, and as a girl she had vowed to say yes only to him. But that pledge had been based on the belief that love—not a damaged reputation—would be the foundation of their marriage. The idea that she and Reece would marry as a result of her sneaking aboard the *Sea Emerald* had definitely been in the back of her mind, but not that he would feel forced into it. Marriage under these circumstances was inconceivable.

Despite her firm belief in what she and Reece felt for each other, love was *not* the only ingredient needed for a happy marriage. One also needed to have integrity.

It did not matter how much Reece actually loved her or if she knew it without his ever admitting it aloud. If he refused to acknowledge his feelings, at least to himself, then it did not matter whether he actually loved her or not. Reece would always believe that circumstances—not love—forced them to marry. And that was unacceptable. Reece might believe they had to marry, but Aimee knew otherwise. Shredded reputation or not, she would always have the support of her family and friends.

The simple tone of resolve in Aimee's voice was one that Collins had become familiar with in the past few weeks and his mind searched for an appropriate response. But before he could furnish one, Aimee reached over and touched his arm to get his attention.

"Mr. Collins, when we reach Savannah, I may have need for some assistance. Would it be too much to ask for more of your help?"

Collins listened as she quickly detailed what she wanted and why. His mind searched for a valid argument against her reasoning, but, in the end, he heard himself agreeing to aid her in the simple request. He would not have been able to live with himself as a man or as a friend otherwise.

At a loss, Collins stood and watched Aimee as she turned to disappear down the companionway. Once they reached Savannah, the past few days of peace would be over. And if the crew thought their captain a surly man before, they had not seen anything yet.

Chapter 24

November 4, 1816

Millie closed the door to her room and immediately slipped off her shoes and clothes, until she was standing in her shift. She then pulled out the pins in her hair and let the dark locks fall loose before climbing into bed. She knew she should comb it, but like the previous two nights, all she wanted to do was crawl under the covers and remind herself that she was safe—no one was after her. If Devlin had not decided to walk her the entire way home, she suspected she might have caved in to her fears and told Sasha that she was returning to her father's. But Devlin had been there and ensured she was safe. Unfortunately, his presence did not remove the uncomfortable feeling that something evil was lurking over her shoulder, studying her, mapping out her life so it could pounce when the opportunity came.

Millie curled up into a ball and reminded herself of all the reasons to stay and keep hopeful. Most recently, it had been Madame Sasha's crusty, extremely shy driver, Bernard. He rarely spoke to anyone, so when he had waited in the hallway just outside her room in order to ask her to join him for lunch in his room, Millie had agreed, despite it being very improper. For Bernard to conquer his nerves enough to ask such a thing, it had to be important.

All throughout their meal, he had asked question after question about Sasha. What Millie knew of her past, what she liked, what made her laugh, what made her sad, until Millie had divulged all the information that she had about her friend. It became clear Sasha's mysterious past was not just unknown to Millie but to all who lived in the house. Seeing Bernard's frustration, Millie explained that a man did not need to know all a woman's secrets to win her heart, he just needed to show a *willingness* to learn them.

After leaving him with several ideas on the next steps in his pursuit, Millie was stopped by Henry, who specifically asked what she would like to eat for breakfast the next morn. For several seconds, Millie was sure she just gaped at the man before telling him that her favorite dish was his ham and potatoes. It was the truth. While the heavy meal was not what she preferred to eat so early in the day, it was the best thing Henry knew how to prepare.

She and Tommy only saw each other in the morning at breakfast, and they were both so tired they only nodded to each other. Paulie and Susan continued to be aloof, but they at least moved down to make room at the table. Evette was her normal self, never shying away from pointing out when Millie was not acting the proper part.

The one person she could not quite figure out was Stuart. She had paid him to use his contacts and monitor Hembree Grove for any information on Aimee. To date, the servants only knew that runners were still being hired. Millie knew why: Charles was still trying to learn what had happened to his younger sister.

She had tried to push Stuart into learning more, but the boy refused on the grounds that to learn anything more, someone might get fired for divulging information, something of which Stuart refused to be a part. A piece of Millie admired him for it.

The boy was very smart but he also spurned anything that would enable people to see just how intelligent he was. When she realized Stuart read everything he could find, she told him about Jennelle's favorite booksellers, circulating libraries, and reading rooms. As expected, Stuart had shrugged her off, saying those kinds of places only catered to those with blunt. Instead of arguing with him, Millie had let Bernard know that he might want to take Stuart over to Hatchards off Piccadilly if he ever got the opportunity. Bernard had been quick to point out that he was too busy for such matters, but the next time she saw Stuart, he had been carrying a new book she highly suspected came from the bookseller she had recommended.

Even work had improved significantly. No longer did every muscle and joint ache for hours after she got home. She was growing physically stronger, and though she would never be able to carry as many mugs as Bessie because of her small hands, she could now maintain a quick pace when things got busy. And things had gotten more active, just as Clive predicted they would.

Even Bessie was nicer. Millie's guard slowly came down and as it did, she began to see things about her fellow server that she had not before. Most important was just how much Bessie needed every tip she made. Living on her own, she assumed the entire costs of coal, food, and shelter. She had only one dress, and when she washed it on rainy days, it was not quite dry when she arrived to work.

But mostly Millie noticed that Bessie was no longer trying to horde all the best tippers—so as Millie saw her income rise, Bessie's was going down. Something in Millie's mind found it incredibly unfair. Plus, she knew it would eventually create problems between her and Bessie again. So this evening, she had done something about it.

Before they left for the evening, Millie had called Bessie over to one of the far tables and dumped out all her tips. After some persuasion, she convinced Bessie to do the same. And without waiting to see if Bessie would agree, Millie combined the pile and began dividing it in half. As she did so, she explained her reasoning.

"No one would dispute the claim that you are the better server. It would take years for me to discover everything you have learned. Despite that, I've noticed that my tips are higher, but you and I both know it is only because of what happened the other night. Soon that memory will fade and my tips will quickly diminish. However, if we combine the money we earn, then who is more successful or why is no longer relevant, because we will both benefit."

Bessie cocked a brow and said, "Little missy, you use a lot of words to say very little." But then she had licked her lips, and after a couple of seconds, sat down and helped to divvy up the pile. "This here idea of yours just also might get me to help you more, now won't it, little missy."

Millie said nothing and instead just smiled. For the first time, Bessie's insult held no bite. If anything, it contained a little bit of respect.

Chapter 25

November 6, 1816

Aimee leaned against the rail and watched dockworkers load the colonial goods, rice, and other agricultural products onto a ship while off-loading English manufactured goods and Mediterranean wines. To her right, another large vessel in the narrow harbor began to pull up its anchor in preparation to cast off. The *Sea Emerald* had moored just a few hours earlier, just as the sun was beginning to rise. Reece had never made it to bed, as he had been up on deck to oversee the tricky navigation up the Savannah River. By the number of voices and footsteps she had heard, most of the men had been up on deck as well, either working at their assigned duties or just eager to be near land again.

Part of her wished she could spend some time in Savannah. The small city was so very different from London. The landscape was much flatter, and incredibly green. Aimee inhaled and closed her eyes, wishing that the heavy burden on her heart would be miraculously lifted. Her mind once again replayed incredible memories of the past couple of weeks with Reece.

Only this morning, he had returned to his cabin to retrieve something, but before leaving, he had walked over and kissed her gently, thinking she was asleep. It was a very loving, instinctive gesture and it had almost been enough to change her mind about leaving. It just proved in another small way that Reece did love her. If he could only admit his feelings, they would have an incredible life together. One that was pleasant during the day and wickedly playful at night. The past week had proven that. But such happiness would not last, not as long as Reece believed as he did.

A successful marriage demanded more than love. It required a deep bond of friendship, which was born from trust, loyalty, and acceptance. Too many of Society's marriages were based on status, money, or convenience. Husbands and wives were not friends, but acquaintances. Friendship between two people, however, was a mutual bond. It could not be forced. Aimee wanted her marriage to be the same, not just another arranged union based on propriety. What Reece wanted was to be left alone. In his mind, he already was married to the sea and it was enough for him. As a result, Reece was no longer enough for her.

Aimee looked down at the small bag by her feet. Besides the gown she was wearing, she had left all the feminine things Collins had given her neatly folded in his cabin. All that she was taking with her were a few of the drawings and a couple of the figurines the men had whittled for her.

She thought about the letter she had left on the desk in Reece's cabin and wondered what he would think when he read it. Would he agree with her decision? Be relieved? Would he feel a few pangs of regret? Aimee hoped so. She wanted Reece to know what he was losing. It was doubtful that he would anytime soon, but someday he would be on his ship and on his beloved sea and feel not the peace and joy he did now, but loneliness. And he would know that it was by his choice.

Aimee twitched her lip, wondering if such a yearning

made her a smaller person. She wished she could ask Millie and Jennelle their opinion. Not that it would change her decision, but it would help to know that she had their support.

Loud, rapid clomping up a ramp got her attention. Aimee turned to see Mr. Collins as he came over the ship's gunwale and stepped onto the deck. She waved to him as he sauntered over to her side. They both got a few sour looks from the crew, but no one said anything.

"It's all in place," Collins told her. "I've spoken to Captain Shay and he assured me that he and his wife would be happy to have you come aboard the *Sea Rebel*. They leave for London this afternoon."

"His *wife*?" Aimee repeated, caught off guard by the possibility of having female companionship.

Collins bobbed his head. "Aye. Mrs. Shay travels with her husband quite a bit now that their children are fully grown."

"And the crew doesn't mind?" Aimee asked, remembering the lecture Reece gave about how a woman could be extremely disruptive to a ship's order.

Collins let go a short snort. "Wouldn't matter if they did. The men on the *Sea Rebel* are just lucky Mrs. Shay is nice, but even if she wasn't, Captain Shay is not the kind of man I would ever cross. Not even by accident."

Aimee had not even thought about trying to familiarize herself with a new crew and having to overcome superstitions about having a female aboard. It was nice to know she would not have to.

"And, uh, I might have misled Mrs. Shay a little," Collins added under his breath.

Aimee's brows crinkled slightly. "How so?"

Collins's face turned bright red as the nervousness he was feeling became glaringly apparent. "I just . . . well, I told her that your clothes were ruined and how you were wearing some things left by um, uh, well, someone else. Mrs. Shay said that you could get a couple of ready-made dresses at Sarah Henderson's. Her place is off State Street near Greene Square. Mrs. Shay told me to let you know that she will meet you there in about an hour."

He paused and took in a deep breath, obviously glad to have delivered that message. He then pointed to a hunched-over man and a small girl sitting in a two-wheeled chaise-like cart that was designed more for carrying lightweight goods than people. Collins winced again, his expression one of regret. "I know you are used to traveling better, but I know the man and he owes me a favor. He will get you to the shop safely and without a problem. I'd take you myself, but—"

"No need, Mr. Collins," Aimee quickly assured him. "The transportation you have procured is more than adequate. Moreover, I appreciate you thinking about such matters, for I had not." Uncaring about propriety, Aimee reached out and squeezed his forearm. "You have been very kind to me."

Collins scowled. "I wasn't always kind."

Aimee let go and gave him a thoughtful smile. "I will only recall your kindness to me, Mr. Collins. You are a good man. I hope the next woman aboard your ship causes you much less grief and far more pleasure," she added with a wink.

Collins could not help himself and laughed out loud, ease replacing his tension. "Not possible, my lady."

"And Mr. Hamilton," Aimee said, realizing it was now her turn to feel awkward, "when he returns . . . you will not have to tell him about my departure or your role. I left a letter in his cabin explaining my reasons for leaving. I presume that he will be relieved, but if not, his anger will be directed toward me. Neither you or any of the men will lose their positions."

Collins sighed and shook his head. He was not sure how the captain was going to react to the news of her departure, but it was not going to be good. And when he learned of the role his chief mate played, it would be worse. But Collins refused to ever regret helping her. She not only gave the men hope of possibly finding a soul mate, but him too. "My lady, I have no doubt that the captain may make it uncomfortable for a while, but I doubt he'll be firing the men because he's in a bad mood."

Aimee nodded, somewhat relieved to be reassured that Collins did not believe the crew would be penalized once again because of her. "Then all is well and the quicker I leave, the sooner life will return to normal on the *Sea Emerald*."

Aimee reached down to pick up the small bag and when she stood back up, she glanced around. Since they had moored, the crew had been very busy and most of the men were not in sight. She was glad, for it would be hard enough walking away from the few she could see. "I already told everyone I could find good-bye. Please tell the rest that I will miss them and that my life is better for having known them."

Collins gritted his jaw. *Her* life was better from knowing a bunch of dirty old seamen? He never thought that meeting and spending time with a noblewoman would make him a worthier man, but it had. "No, my lady. I didn't realize it right away, but you being on board was a good thing. We men . . . well, feel like this—the ship, the sea, each other—that it is the only life we can have. That nary anybody but another old sea dog would ever take a kindness to us, but you did. You gave the men hope that there might be a chance for more."

Aimee blinked several times to keep the tears from falling, and then with a final nod, she headed down the planks to the awaiting cart.

Collins watched silently as she said hello to the man and then spoke to the little girl. He swore to himself never to repeat Reece's mistake. When he became a captain and found a woman willing to share the life with him, he would not be so shortsighted. He would thank the Lord profusely and never let her regret loving him.

A grunt came from his left side and Collins stole a peek to see who it was before returning his gaze to Aimee as she helped them adjust the cart to make room for her.

"She really is a lady, ain't she?" asked Swivel Eye Stu, his voice mirroring the sadness Collins felt.

"Aye."

Stu shook his head. "I don't think I really believed it until now."

Collins did not have to ask Stu what he meant. He knew. Aimee had walked no differently than she always had. Her mannerisms and interactions were the same, but now that she was leaving, he could see what he had previously ignored. Aimee had a gracefulness about her in the way she held her head and arms. No matter what she wore or looked like, she was elegant.

Aye, Collins thought to himself. *Our ship has just lost its lady and all aboard are going to feel her loss.*

Reece bounded down the stairs and down the corridor leading to his cabin, eager to find Aimee and depart for the church. He had left right after they docked, instructing Collins to oversee things while he was gone. The plan had been to be back within two hours, but nothing had gone right.

Another captain had cornered the harbormaster just as Reece arrived, forcing him to wait his turn to discuss the *Sea Emerald*'s cargo. When he was finally able to leave, Reece discovered that finding a preacher late Wednesday morning was far from an easy task. Few had residences near the harbor, and those who did were meeting with their parishioners or out conducting church business. With perseverance, Reece managed to locate one and was headed back to the ship when he decided to return to town for a wedding ring. Though an uncommon custom, Aimee's mother had worn one and Reece wanted Aimee to have one as well. He knew she would appreciate the thought, but it would also signify to anyone she ever met when he was away at sea that both her heart and hand in marriage had been taken.

Impatient to surprise her with all he had arranged, Reece opened his cabin door without knocking. Instantly he knew something was wrong. The room looked familiar—too familiar. It was once again like it had been before he knew she was on board. Nothing of Aimee's was in sight.

He was about to leave when he spied a piece of paper folded on his desk. Tension flooded his body. Reece forced himself to walk over and pick it up. Bringing it to the window for more light, he read the contents, not skipping a single word until he was done.

Anger and fear raced through him, and for several minutes he could not think. He could only feel. Not since the war had he needed to compartmentalize strong emotions. Slowly, cold determination replaced the turbulent feelings. Putting the letter down, he walked brusquely to the stairs and then to the upper deck. "Collins!" he barked.

Smiley heard the shout first and elbowed the chief mate in the ribs. Taking a deep breath, Collins went to meet the captain on the upper deck, deciding this particular reprimand was going to be in front of the crew and not in private.

"Where is she?" Reece hissed, the only indication of his inner turmoil.

Collins stood poised and unapologetic. His brown eyes locked to Reece's blue ones. "I helped her ladyship safely depart this morning."

Reece took controlled breaths. "*When* did her ladyship make this request of you?"

"Three days ago."

"And you did not think to tell me?" Reece exploded.

Collins stood, refusing to move or give any sign of remorse or even guilt. "At the time, Captain, you were expressing concern about being forced into a marriage and later regretting it. Lady Wentworth believed she was doing you a favor by leaving, for now you will not have to worry about either."

The words hit Reece full force, and the coldness that he felt before once again washed over him. "I have a mother, Collins. I don't need another. Neither do I need a confessional or guardian angel."

"And I have no intention of being any of those things for *you*, Captain, but Lady Wentworth?" Collins said tersely, making it clear that Reece was not the only one riled over the situation. "She needed someone to turn to for help, and asking the man who didn't want to marry her didn't seem like an option. Now I ask you, Captain, if you had been me, what would *you* have done?"

Reece bridled furiously. "I *never* said I didn't want to marry her!"

Collins shook his head and then looked Reece in the eye, remembering the conversation clearly. "You said you did not have a choice. That you feared regret. Perhaps Lady Wentworth misunderstood what you meant, but then so did I."

Collins's anger-laced sarcasm and unhidden disgust were unmistakable, and again Reece felt like he had been hit full force. This time in both the gut and the heart. "Not to *her*," he countered, shaking his head. "I never said any of that to Aimee."

"Aye, it was to her." Collins's tone changed to one that was less sharp and more what it should be as a chief mate. "She was at the door that night when we spoke, Captain. I found her outside your room crying. Her ladyship overheard it all. And you had said quite a bit."

Understanding overcame Reece and he could feel the blood drain from his face. The conversation itself was vague in his mind. It was when he was still struggling with not just his feelings but appearing to be a love-whipped boy in front of his crew. What he did remember, however, was Collins and his reaction. Normally, his chief mate was sympathetic to woman troubles, having had his share in the past. But not that night. Collins had not said so, but his aloof mannerisms had made it clear he thought Reece just one step shy of a fool.

It had spurred Reece into reassessing his situation. He considered the men and truly watched as they and Aimee interacted, waiting to see what would come of it—jealousy, obsession, resentment, arguments. But none of those occurred, nor, from what Reece could see, were they going to occur eventually. The crew was happy, and if he was being truly honest with himself, for the first time so was he. He wanted Aimee. He needed her. He wanted her in his life and had been impatient to get to Savannah, where he could irrevocably bind their lives together.

"What inn is she at?"

The question was calmly put; however, refusing to answer was not an option. Based on Reece's reaction to learning of Aimee's departure as well as his current look of determination, Collins was relieved. The captain was finally going to do what he should have done weeks ago, if not back in December. "She's not at an inn. I found her safe passage on a suitable ship that was leaving immediately for London."

Reece quickly began to mentally catalogue all the ships in the harbor. The *Albatross* had arrived after them and would not be leaving so soon. He had seen the *Ella Marie*, the *Bonnie Star*, and the *Longview* in dock preparing to go, but none of them had been taking on foodstuffs, so time of departure was questionable. In town, he had exchanged curt nods with the captain of the *Miss Charlotte*, who was working out an unwelcome change in his cargo. From what Reece had overheard, the unexpected goods were causing the *Charlotte* to head directly to the London Docks before going to Spain. And these were just the ships he saw, for there were many more up the river.

Any captain on his way to England would have agreed to transport Aimee without hesitation. However, her being unmarried and having no chaperone made her extremely vulnerable. Nobility would not protect her. If anything, it would only enhance her appeal. "She had better be safe," Reece growled dangerously.

"She is on the *Sea Rebel*—"

The first fragments of relief broke over Reece. The *Sea Rebel* belonged to W & H Shipping. It was one of his own and he knew it well. It was much older and larger than the *Emerald*, equipped with a larger crew and more cargo area for bigger hauls. Its captain had also fought in the war and had been handpicked by Reece to manage the bulky ship. Shay was a real hard-ass, but fair and honest. And, blissfully, he was also very married. The man would have no issue with Reece coming aboard, getting Aimee, and leaving with her.

"—with Captain Shay and his wife," Collins finished.

"His wife?" Reece repeated.

"Aye—she travels with him now and then. Mrs. Shay met Lady Wentworth at a seamstress's shop where she purchased some new clothes. I would expect they are back aboard the *Rebel* by now."

Reece blinked as he assimilated the information and looked up as he began to deliberate on his next move. Only then did he realize most of his crew was lurking around, pretending to work in order to listen to his and Collins's conversation. Even JP was among them, only he was openly staring at the upper deck with his arms crossed, doing nothing to hide his obvious curiosity.

Reece looked behind Collins and waited for his bosun to stop whistling and sneak a peek at him. "Carr, go to the *Sea Rebel* and tell Captain Shay that he is not to leave until I get there if he wants to continue working for W & H Shipping."

Carr's eyes grew large as he realized that Reece was serious. Anyone who had ever gone to see Shakespeare performed in one of the cheap, unlicensed theaters, knew the saying "don't shoot the messenger," but no one ever thought their life would truly be put at risk by delivering a simple message. Then again, no one was reckless enough to deliver a threat to Captain Shay.

Recognizing he was a dead man either way—refusing Reece or doing what he asked—the bosun finally murmured, "Aye, Captain," and then left.

Seeing Carr needed no additional motivation, Collins asked softly, "What are you planning?"

Reece took in a deep breath of air and exhaled. His gaze fell over his crew and then, loud enough for all to hear, he said, "I am going to go fetch my soon-to-be wife and remind her of just why she snuck aboard my ship. To catch a husband. Well, she caught him *and a crew* and she is now going to have to live with the consequences."

Cheers erupted from the deck. Reece smiled and waved for a few moments before going belowdecks. Men started shaking hands and slapping each other on the back. A few even broke into a brief jig. Only Collins refrained from joining the crew's merriment upon hearing the captain's decision.

It was not that he was not supportive of the captain's plans. Just the opposite. Collins just feared that it might be too late.

The captain may now want to marry, but *both* parties had to be willing before a preacher would agree to perform a marriage ceremony. For that to happen, it was going to take a lot more than charm and some passionate kisses. The only way Collins could envision Aimee accepting Reece's proposal was if she became convinced that he did not just want her, but truly and absolutely loved her.

And for that to happen, the man would first need to admit those feelings to himself.

Reece stepped out of Captain Shay's cuddy. He clenched his fists and forced them to relax. It was rare he found himself covetous of any ship over his, but having a designated room to converse with officers—or unexpected visitors like himself—had advantages. What was even rarer was confronting a man whom Reece could not intimidate in the least. It was the reason he had hired Shay. He just had never anticipated their being on opposing sides.

After an hour of explanations and arguments, Reece had not gained any ground when it came to Aimee. Though tempted, he had not threatened Shay's continued role with W & H Shipping. Good captains were hard to find. Honest ones were damn near impossible, and Shay was both. His morals were so strong that an ultimatum would not have worked. If anything, Reece's demands were pushing the man toward quitting.

Not until Reece revealed his and Aimee's whole story did the old captain begin to understand the real reason Aimee had come to be aboard his ship. Only when Reece had fully admitted his blunder was the captain swayed to let her leave. But only if certain stipulations were met. The four of them would go directly to the chapel. There, Captain Shay and his wife would be present to witness the happy nuptials.

At first, Reece resented how the man was trying to act like his father, but then realized that Shay had no interest in him. The fatherly role was for Aimee.

Reece took another deep breath and reminded himself that he had achieved his goal. He and Aimee would soon be married.

He then proceeded up the gangway, which led to the poop deck. Just before he moved out of the shadows and into view, he heard Aimee's voice.

After thanking Captain Shay profusely for his offer to take her home and the lending of the wardroom for her to stay in, Aimee had wandered up on the highest deck in the far aft portion of the ship. She was determined to stay out of the crew's way and not make Captain Shay regret his decision.

The *Sea Rebel* was at first glance similar to Reece's ship, mostly because of the number of sails and masts. But once on board she realized it was noticeably wider, and had more deck levels, which meant there were more rooms and interior space. Aimee remembered Mr. Linwood explaining how the *Sea Emerald* was made for smaller cargo and speed, while most of the other ships in her brother's shipping business were built to transport large amounts of goods.

With the augmented space and cargo came more work and a larger crew. Like those she had come to know and care for, the men on the *Sea Rebel* were working side by side, some singing shanties to ensure the rhythm was maintained and to synchronize their efforts. On the *Emerald*, the crew was smaller, so it was rare to hear more than one song at a time, but not on the *Rebel*. Some of the songs were sung with one group singing the verse and another the chorus.

Aimee leaned against the rail and hummed softly to the one being sung in D minor. Its melancholy tone reflected her current state of mind.

"How do you like your stateroom?"

Startled, Aimee jumped and then quickly apologized.

"Mrs. Shay, pray forgive me for my reaction just then. I did not see you. Oh, and the room is more than lovely. I feel quite spoiled."

"Good." The older woman laughed softly and joined her at the rail, smiling. "I always love coming ashore, but it's nice to be going again."

Aimee sighed in agreement. Mrs. Annabelle Shay had been like a godsend at the dress shop, helping her to navigate the world of ready-made gowns. Aimee had found herself enjoying it far more than she did going to a modiste for a new dress, where she would see the material and the accessories but would not know how the dress looked until it was delivered. It was rare her modiste made something she did not like, but there was something about selecting dresses that were already made that was refreshing. None of them fit as well or were of the quality she typically wore when home, but at sea, such things did not matter.

"Thank you again for your help today at Miss Henderson's."

Mrs. Shay patted Aimee's arm. "My pleasure. To my husband's delight, we had three sons. All of them are now grown and on ships of their own, but how I longed for a daughter. Helping you gave me the chance to know what it would be like to have one."

Aimee squeezed the older woman's slender fingers. She had instantly liked Annabelle. Though in her late forties, Mrs. Shay was still a stunning woman. Her red hair was turning a beautiful white around her temples, perfectly framing her oval face and large dark brown eyes. She was neither tall nor short, and her figure was lovely and feminine. Her nose and cheeks had several freckles and her skin had browned somewhat from being in the sun and wind. Aimee wondered if her own face had taken on the loathed brown color. She secretly hoped it had; then maybe Society would discount her as an eligible marriage choice and allow her to be alone with her misery.

Annabelle pointed to a group of men who were singing near the mainmast as they adjusted the halyards. "I was wondering how my men would do with you around."

"I . . . um . . . I am not sure that I understand. Your men?"

Annabelle shrugged. "I travel with Henry in the spring until it becomes too hot, and again in the fall until the weather turns too bitter to enjoy being on deck. Spending so much time on board, I have developed relationships with the crew. From what I saw of Mr. Collins this morning, you have done the same in a relatively short bit of time." She pointed again. "I think you might have already started to enchant some of my men."

Annabelle was teasing her, and despite Aimee's worry that she would not find anything to smile about for a long time, she found her lips curving upward. "Sailors are unique in personality and demeanor. I am not sure everyone I know would appreciate their good qualities, but they do have them."

Annabelle nodded in agreement. "I'm glad you think so, for my husband tells me that the crew is trying to make a good impression. Have you not heard all the songs they are singing?"

Aimee threw her head back slightly and laughed out loud. "I thought it was because this is a big ship and singing helped to ensure things ran smoothly."

"True, but until today I am not sure that I have ever heard four tunes being sung at once."

Aimee shook her head in amazement. "But why would these men care about my opinion? They do not know me. If anything, I am an additional burden."

"Hmm, well, the crew of the *Sea Emerald* did not consider you such. I was with my husband when the chief mate came to visit him and ask about berthing space. That young man spoke incredibly highly of you. Even mentioned that you climbed a mast and saved their lives, something that notably impressed my husband. And that is very hard to do."

Aimee shook her head and turned around. Crossing her arms and leaning back on the rail for support, she said, "It may sound courageous, but I assure you it was far from it. Did Mr. Collins add that I took so long getting down that I became the target of a wave, scaring me and terrifying half the crew?"

"No, your Mr. Collins was intelligent enough to keep that to himself," said Annabelle softly, laughter still laced in the sound. "So then the sea does *not* agree with you."

Aimee stood straight up and moved to face the woman, shaking her head. "Oh, very much the opposite. Though this was my first voyage, I immensely enjoyed being out in the open with the wind in my face and hearing the splashing sounds of the waves. No, Mrs. Shay, I love the sea."

"I believe you. It is just that very few women, including captains' wives, feel the way you and I do. They are tolerant, but this life does not inspire them. But there are some of us who have a passion for the water just as strong as any man's. It is a shame women with your family connections are discouraged from ever getting the chance to develop a love for the sea."

Aimee took a deep breath and after several seconds, exhaled. "I did not realize you know who I am."

Mrs. Shay curtsied and habit drove Aimee to return it. "You are Lady Wentworth, brother to the Marquess of Chaselton, who oversees London management of W & H Shipping, and is a co-owner of this ship." Then she flashed Aimee a wide grin and gave her a wink. "Mr. Collins made sure that Henry and I were very much aware of who you are."

Aimee stood perplexed. Annabelle Shay's actions varied from the mannerisms and demeanor of a lady, taught the courtesies demanded by the *ton*, to a relaxed friend, comfortable doing and acting as she pleased. Aimee wanted to assure her that she did not wish to be treated differently because of her title. "Please tell no one. Believe me when I say I neither require nor want all the formalities that come with my station."

Annabelle waved her hand, dismissing the notion that she would believe otherwise. "My father was a lord. Not wealthy like your family, and he had three sons and five daughters. I cannot remember a time my father was not stressed financially, but I still understand in a way. I was the sixth child and not the first daughter to wed an untitled man, but you would have thought I was the only one to defy expectations. Marrying non-gentry was not done. And yet I married Mr. Shay anyway and never once regretted it."

"I would have felt the same as you," Aimee stated without equivocation. "Moreover, I am fortunate that my mother would have been supportive of my choice. It is the man I attached my heart to who has issues with my place in Society."

"Ahhhhh," Annabelle said, drawing out the word.

"And though I am unsure what lies in my future, Mrs. Shay, I cannot imagine it not involving the sea in some way."

Annabelle shrugged her shoulders and took Aimee's hands in hers. "You never know. Maybe your future is on board this very moment."

Aimee exhaled sharply. "Even if he were, he would not want me. I practically threw myself at a man this past month, and despite everything I did or said, I was not enough. I may be a curiosity to seamen, but I am not what they are looking for in a wife."

The intensity of Aimee's words and the honesty with which she spoke them astonished Annabelle. She considered telling the young woman that after years of experience in meeting captains and their officers, she was exactly what they dreamed of finding for a wife. Annabelle was somewhat thankful she was not twenty years younger and having to compete with the tall, blond beauty. And yet Aimee's heart had undoubtedly been broken. To contradict her notion that she was undesirable would be a waste of air, for she clearly believed that nonsense.

Annabelle wanted to ask if it was Reece Hamilton who had broken her heart, but decided she did not need to. She had seen him board some time ago to meet with her husband. There had been time for only a quick glance, but it was enough to tell her that Reece had not come to pay a mere visit. She stole a glimpse at Aimee. The young woman was again leaning over the rail, trying hard to hide the tears that were falling. At that moment, Annabelle decided Captain Reece Hamilton did not deserve Aimee. And as soon as she saw her husband, she would make her opinion known.

"It sounds like you fell in love with what my mother called a ninnyhammer. Thankfully there are precious few of those aboard the *Rebel*. Take our chief mate, Mr. Haskin." Annabelle pointed to a tall, dark man standing in the shadows. Even from a distance, it was easy to see that he was self-confident and comfortable with authority. "Many women think he is very good-looking. Even myself."

Aimee cocked her head to one side and studied the officer. The man definitely exuded masculinity. He was also tall and had an air of confidence that undoubtedly would attract a fair share of eligible women. "If Mr. Haskin truly desires to be married, then why is he not?"

"I'm not sure exactly. Henry hired him over a year ago, but Mr. Haskin has yet to reveal his many secrets and I am sure he has several. Still, if I were to guess, it is because he has not found someone who awakens his soul and makes him eager to meet the next day." Seeing Aimee's disbelieving look, Annabelle shrugged her shoulders and tried again. "Perhaps it is because he has not found anyone willing to live this way of life—either here with him or at home and alone much of the time. As I said, there are very few women who are. But now that you are here, maybe he will not have to search much longer. You are surrounded by eighty men. One of them is sure to catch your eye, as I told you before. I know you have already caught theirs."

"Maybe you're right," Aimee replied noncommittally. Then with more conviction added, "I have spent my entire life believing there is only one man for me. He is now in my past. Perhaps it is time I finally start looking to another possible future."

"Good," Annabelle said encouragingly. "I'm going back in to find out just what is causing our delay and when we are going to leave."

Aimee waved her good-bye, and when she was alone once more, she turned to the water and made a private vow. "By the time I reach London, I will have forgotten Reece Hamilton ever existed."

Before Annabelle had reached the stairs, Reece was back in the cuddy, speaking with Captain Shay. After overhearing the two women, he realized his original idea of finding Aimee and going to the church was not going to work. In fact, nothing about his plan was going to work. He had to abandon his thoughts of quickly resolving the mess he had created and develop a new strategy to claim Aimee as his own.

"Hurry," Shay said. "We will be leaving the moment everyone returns."

Reece thanked him and disembarked, being careful to remain unseen by Aimee or Mrs. Shay. He was surprised he had received no resistance from the captain, considering their earlier heated conversation, but Reece suspected Shay could see that there was nothing that would sway him from his new objective.

He had little time and much to do. First, he needed to let

Collins know that his chief mate was temporarily in charge of the *Sea Emerald*. Reece intended to return to London on the *Sea Rebel*. Meanwhile, Collins was to work with the harbormaster to get the shipment of goods headed for Spain on board as quickly as possible. The change in destination would soothe all the merchants Reece had irritated this morning when he declared that England—not Spain— would be his first stop. But for the next few short weeks it would be Collins—not him—in charge. Once Collins finished in Spain he was to meet Reece in England.

Once Reece finished with Collins, he had to grab a change of clothes. Then he needed to find Gus and retrieve an item Reece had carelessly given away. Last, he needed a new plan. One that would eventually include marriage, but only after he reminded Aimee that she loved him. Her little pledge to forget him was never going to happen.

Reece smiled. The approach was obvious.

He would plague her thoughts and dreams as she had done to him.

Chapter 26

November 7, 1816

When Millie started to turn down yet another narrow backstreet, Evette grabbed her arm, forcing her to a stop. "Would you please explain to me again why I let you convince me to come with you?"

Millie sighed and shifted the large bag she was carrying to her other shoulder. Then she hooked her arm in Evette's thin one and began walking once again, coaxing her friend along. "As I told you before, someone I work with is highly sensitive to the idea of an imbalance of kindnesses. I need you to help correct any perceived inequity."

Evette's blond brows creased. She understood Millie's convoluted explanation, but it really did not answer her question. "Do you not already owe *me* several favors?"

"I do," Millie agreed. "I have found that in most cases a direct approach is preferred in handling situations, whether they be serious obstacles or the repayment of debts, monetary or not. However, I'm sure you would agree that to be locked in to such an approach and never consider other possibilities would be a foolish mindset. Fortunately for you, I have decided to take a circuitous path to settling any *favors* between us."

Taking the long-winded hint, Evette sighed and allowed herself to be led down another alley, wondering anew at Millie's ability to sway people to comply with her wishes. She was confident, but most of all she was persistent. Millie just wore down those around her until they had no choice but to follow her lead. It was a skill Evette had at first disliked; now she just wished she could emulate it. Maybe then she could get Madame Sasha to believe in her abilities as a seamstress.

"I do not trust you, *my lady*."

Millie decided to ignore the intentional reference to her real identity. "I know you do not, but you really should reconsider your opinion of me. I'm an excellent ally."

Evette rolled her eyes and Millie gently nudged her side with her elbow. "Fine. Then come with me because you are curious. I am quite aware that you and the others in the house wonder where I having been venturing to the past several days."

Evette said nothing, but both knew Millie was right.

Millie grinned and suppressed a chuckle. If anyone had told her a week ago just where she was going every afternoon, she would have found it not only difficult to believe, but impossible. And yet, here she was on her way to visit Bessie's home for the fourth day in a row.

The night Millie suggested they pool their tips, Bessie had practically demanded they meet in front of Ollmanders four hours before their evening shift. Millie had first been wary of the idea, but curiosity had compelled her to go. Bessie was there waiting, and before a hello barely passed between them, Bessie had begun to lead Millie back through several narrow alleyways to the place she called home. The structure was cramped, but it had three small rooms—a bedroom, front room, and a kitchen—a fact of which Bessie was quite proud.

She made them a small meal, which was astonishingly tasty and far better than the fare Henry typically served. But only after helping clean up the dishes did Millie learn just why Bessie had invited her over.

"I am goin' to show you how to make a pocket that'll hold your tips," Bessie announced. Then she went over to a box and pulled out a rolled strip of thin cotton Millie guessed had come from a worn-out shift.

Immediately she had put her hand up in protest. "I cannot sew."

Bessie searched the box, found a needle and some thread, and handed them to Millie. "I'm not talkin' about makin' clothes. I only wish I knew how to do that."

Millie stared at the needle and the thread for several seconds. Shaking her head, she tried to hand them back. "I truly mean what I say, Bessie. This is one of those intricate feminine talents that I could never perform, even poorly."

Bessie stared at Millie disbelievingly. "*Everyone* can sew. Even longshoremen know how to darn holes in their clothes, and that's all we're doin'. I promise we'll keep it simple."

Millie wanted to argue, to explain that it was not for lack of trying, but that she *really* could not sew. Needlework, for a mysterious reason, was a skill every gentleman's daughter had to not just learn, but master. Unsurprisingly, Aimee was good at it. Jennelle much preferred to read, but if forced, her embroidery was passable. Millie, however, had been deemed a hopeless case. Even Mother Wentworth had announced that a needle in Millie's hand was a danger to others.

"All you have to do is tack the material to your inner skirt. You can pull it up in your lap so you don't have to take it off. Then I'll help you attach the strip to your pocket so you can drop the coins in."

An hour later, Millie had given up sewing the material

to her inner skirt. What little she had done was far from straight and nowhere near the pocket. Bessie swallowed and said, "I guess it's nice to know there's somethin' you're bad at. Tomorrow, come again, and this time *I* will do it."

Millie nodded. "But I will bring the food."

Bessie snorted. "I'll even let you cook." Seeing Millie's stricken face, she slapped her knee and began to laugh. "You can't cook either?"

Millie shook her head, embarrassed. "My mother died when I was young, and while I loved the woman who tried to help raise me in her stead, I was not always the best pupil when it came to domestic things."

Bessie crossed her arms and smirked. "You liked learnin' how to fight."

Millie shrugged. "Much to everyone's dismay, you are correct. I much prefer physical activity over being sedentary."

"There you go again," Bessie said as she picked up the hem of Millie's dress and fingered the expensive silk. "Talking like that. No one I've ever met speaks the way you do. You just can't help yourself, can you?" she asked, narrowing her eyes at Millie.

Millie raised her chin slightly and stared back.

Bessie dropped the garment and shrugged. "Don't guess it matters how a body ends up at Clive's. We all have our stories."

"Including you?"

"Everyone," Bessie repeated.

The next couple of days, Millie had brought meat and bread and they talked while Bessie sewed a thin strip of lining into Millie's dress. When it was done, Bessie looked disappointed. There was no longer a reason for them to meet, and both women had been secretly surprised to learn how much they enjoyed the other's company.

"Bessie, thank you so much. I know you said we were even just by giving me this suggestion. However, I could not have done this without you. I feel I owe you something in return."

Bessie looked uncomfortable and glanced back at the kitchen. "You brought food. 'Twas no favor I did."

The small gesture confirmed Millie's suspicions. The food she had been supplying was helping to offset Bessie's living expenses. "I disagree, as you had to do the cooking for both of us. If you could partake in just one of the meals being prepared in the house I am staying in, you would realize that dining with you benefited me far more than you."

"Little missy, you can make a head spin using all those fancy words. I said we were even, and I meant it."

Millie shook her head. This time she refused to let Bessie dictate the terms of their developing friendship. "Then I will simply say that you may believe we are even. I do not."

Bessie's pride surfaced and her chin rose in the air. "I won't accept coin."

"Excellent, because I have too little to offer you," Millie lied. "However, tomorrow I would like to return, if you would agree. And when I come, I shall bring you a surprise. One you cannot refuse."

Bessie had crossed her arms and tried to look intimidating. "Well, if you are goin' to force it on me, it better be somethin' I will like."

Millie smiled and knocked on the door with her free hand. Her other arm was still hooked with Evette's, and she had no intention of setting it free. The battered door opened and Millie smiled as she saw the shock on Bessie's face upon seeing Evette. "Don't tell me that *she's* my surprise."

"I'm a what?" Evette murmured.

"Indeed she is," Millie told Bessie, ignoring Evette's question.

Bessie pulled in her chin and looked Evette up and down.

"What? You're leaving and she's going to take your place at Clive's?"

Evette sharply turned her head toward Millie and said, "That *better* not be your plan."

Millie rolled her eyes and walked inside, dragging Evette with her. "Evette, this is Bessie. Bessie, please say hello to Evette. She also rents a room in the house where I am staying."

Unhooking the bag from her shoulder, Millie went into the kitchen to put the food she had brought onto the table. Bessie followed and immediately took the meat and prepared it for the oven. Meanwhile, Millie offered Evette the one seat at the table and went to grab a wooden crate from the other room to use as a stool.

When she came back, she saw Evette helping Bessie chop vegetables. Both women stopped, wiped their hands, and turned to look at Millie. "I think we deserve to know why you asked me here," Evette said without preamble.

Millie grinned at them before diving back into the bag and pulling out scraps of material. They were Madame Sasha's discards and were going to be thrown away until Millie had intervened. All the cloth was of quality, but Millie had done her best to select only the more durable, less fancy materials.

Bessie swallowed and walked over to the table to take a closer look. "Where did you get these?"

"From a seamstress who was going to throw them away."

Evette narrowed her eyes, but Millie ignored her. "Bessie, Evette has been training with one of London's best seamstresses, but needs the opportunity to prove to her mentor and *herself* that she is more than capable of designing and sewing a dress on her own." Evette opened her mouth to protest, but Millie continued before she could utter a word. "Evette, I've seen what you have done on my gowns."

Bessie's mouth gaped. "You did hers?" she asked Evette while pointing at Millie.

Evette pursed her lips together. "Not really."

Millie clucked her tongue. "You did. In addition, you have made all your own clothes, and I am fairly certain I have seen Susan wear your handiwork. And even if I am wrong on all accounts, it does not matter. You are talented and your services are needed, not just by Bessie here, but I believe by many in this community."

Bessie lifted the hem of Millie's dress and looked at Evette. "I was never taught how to make much with needle and thread, but I know enough to see that whoever did this— and I know for sure it wasn't Ellie here—is very good." Then she dropped it and stared at Millie, but her gaze was far from friendly. "Even if your friend is half as good as you say, it would cost me a year's pay to afford a dress like yours. And you bringing her here, offering me something you know I cannot accept . . . well, now I know your heart isn't as kind as everyone thinks."

Evette crinkled her brow and picked up a larger piece of the cloth Millie had dropped on the table. None of the pieces were large enough to create a complete outfit, but if designed right, she could create something that blended several pieces. "Bessie, seamstresses can be costly, but the majority of the expense is in the material. You have that."

Millie could see Evette was starting to design something in her head. She had asked Sasha why Evette had never created something on her own, and Sasha's reply had been crisp. "Fear and lack of confidence. The girl's biggest difficulty is herself." Millie did not say it out loud, but she could definitely understand just why Evette would have a lack of confidence around her mentor. Madame Sasha was unusually gifted. Most garments would seem deficient in comparison to the ones she created.

"I implore you to consider this offer, Bessie. Evette owes

me a favor, and if she could make something for you, it would relieve several debts."

Bessie looked at Evette. "You would truly do this for no coin?"

Evette glanced at Millie. "Like Ellie said, I owe her a favor."

Bessie could not bring herself to say the words "I accept" aloud, but she did nod her head.

Millie grinned and started gathering the material to take into the other room. Evette followed her. "So what do you think? Should I do two dresses? One for every day and one a little nicer? And her hair . . . It's a beautiful color, but we need to tame it somehow."

"Agreed," Millie said. "By the time we are finished with her, Clive will—"

"Clive will what?" Bessie demanded.

Millie looked back and saw Bessie standing in the doorway. "Why, he will realize that others will be able to see just what he has known all along."

"Which is?" Bessie snapped.

Millie reached over and clasped her hand. "Just how beautiful you are."

Evette nodded. "Your hair really is pretty. It just needs styling."

Bessie's fingers flew to her hair in an effort to smooth back the numerous wayward tendrils.

Millie waved her hand, dismissing Bessie's apprehension. "My hair can be difficult too, but I have learned a few secrets over the years. Why, Jennelle could—" Millie stopped midsentence. Jennelle should be here right now, as should Aimee. The Daring Three should be doing this together. Would they ever be together again?

Bessie did not know who Jennelle was, but she could see that just mentioning the name was upsetting Millie. Never having been comforted much in her life, she really had no idea how to offer sympathy to others. So instead she tried to redirect the conversation. "I have a secret wish. I know we all do, but this dress is prob'ly the closest I'll ever get to havin' it come true."

"How so?" Evette probed softly.

"One night I was comin' back from a market near Dawsons Gardens and I looked up and I saw two people on a balcony eatin'. And I thought just once I'd like that to be me. Eatin' a fine meal made by someone else under the moonlight."

Evette sighed in agreement. "Mine is similar except that it is daytime and I am in the gardens."

Millie listened as Evette described her secret wish to Bessie, who was nodding beside her in agreement. The two were already on their way to becoming good friends. Millie was glad. For while she had come to know both women and enjoyed their company, they would not understand who she really was.

Evette looked at Millie and then Bessie. "Maybe we should eat."

Nodding, Bessie got up and headed into the kitchen area to see if the meat was ready to eat. When she was out of sight, Evette asked softly, "Are you feeling ill, Millie?"

Millie shook her head. "No, just a little discouraged. I miss my friends."

"You have made others. I know the people at Madame Sasha's can be distant, but they have grown to like you. Even Stuart grumbles less, and Bernard actually convinced Madame Sasha to go on a drive with him. Everyone knows he would never have done so without your influence. In their own way, they have missed you these past few days."

Millie sighed. "I've grown to like them as well and it makes being around them much harder because I am forced to deceive them. They deserve better, just as Clive and Bessie do. But if I told them the truth, I would be imposing my burden on them. It is hard enough that you know the truth. I will not ask anyone else to lie for me."

"My lady, it has been no hardship, and the reason behind your current pretense is of great importance."

"I never believed it would take so long to learn the answer to such simple questions, but until I am sure Aimee is not in danger, I have little choice."

Bessie hovered just out of sight, listening to all that was said. She had always known Ellie was not who she claimed to be, but Evette had called her *my lady.* Just who was Ellie?

Old questions resurfaced along with several new ones. Were her lies really in an effort to protect them? If so, from what? And what had really driven her down to the docks—a man? Or some friend named Aimee?

Chapter 27

November 8, 1816

"Did you get his name?"

The question was direct, but Randall Greery could hear the faint sound of hope within it.

"Devlin MacLeery," the runner answered, glad he could finally relay some good news to the powerful marquess in front of him. Randall knew he was a good investigator, and when in the vicinity of the Cit or the docks, he was darn near exceptional. And yet it had taken him nearly a week and a half to find out even a sliver of information about the lady the marquess had hired him to find. He was almost beginning to think his lordship had been wrong to believe she was in that area until he had by chance asked Devlin MacLeery if he had ever seen the woman. Randall knew immediately that he had finally gotten a break in the case.

"His name's MacLeery. He owns one of the more successful gambling joints just north of the docks. Caters to a wide variety of clientele, from the poor to the rich. He doesn't seem to care how a man gets his blunt as long as he has it."

"And you say that he recognized the portrait."

Greery nodded without hesitation. "Absolutely. He denied it, but I am certain he knows who she is. The man's adept at hiding his thoughts, but I surprised him that day. During those first few seconds of looking at the portrait, he not only recognized the face, but he was surprised at what he was seeing. As if she looked different somehow."

The marquess tapped his fingers on his desk. "Did you follow him?"

Greery inhaled. "Aye, but he knew I was doing so and he returned to his place. I've hired men to follow him. We'll learn where he goes. If he knows the woman, we'll find out how and where."

"As soon as you know anything, Greery," the marquess said in a low tone, "come and find me."

Chapter 28

November 10, 1816

"Here you go, sweetness," Burt said, catching Bessie before he made his way out the door. "And here's a little something more for yer lookin' so pretty tonight."

Clive's blue eyes darkened like storm clouds before a heavy rainfall. Of medium height and brawny with muscle, Burt was built very similar to himself. But he was also five, maybe even ten years younger and still had his hair. Clive was not a man who normally heeded how another man looked, but he suspected that, to a woman, Burt was more than just a little good-looking. And for the past few nights, he, along with several others, had had become regular patrons. None of them had hidden their appreciation of the changes in Bessie.

The first night, Clive had wondered why they were not eyeing Ellie. Oh, they glanced her way and enjoyed the vision, for the lass was in many ways the prettiest woman they had ever seen, but for most of the night, it was Bessie who had had their attention. She was one of them. She was from this part of town and understood how it worked and its people. Ellie, no matter how much she tried, was not of the docks and never would be.

"So first a new hairdo and now a new frock? What's gotten into you, Bessie?" Clive finally asked as Bessie stopped to hand him some empty mugs.

Bessie raised a single eyebrow. "I didn't even think you noticed."

Clive gave her a smirk. "Aye, I noticed. Just as every man who has ever been here has noticed. So what makes ye think ye need tae look pretty tae work here? I already got one lass doing that and causing me problems. I don't need two."

Bessie looked at Clive, trying to decide how to interpret what he just said. "Ellie is not causin' you any problems, so don't be blamin' her for stuff that's got nothin' to do with her. And as for my new dress, well, I think a woman deserves a new garment every once in a while. And I was certainly due for one."

"Ellie shouldn't be making ye things like that. Gives men ideas. And not good ones."

Bessie suppressed the huge grin she was feeling inside. "You can blame Ellie, but you'd be wrong. The little missy can barely thread a needle. It was someone else entirely who reminded me that at one time I was rather nice lookin' and could be again."

Clive watched Bessie turn and sashay back to a group of eager men. "Women," he muttered underneath his breath. "I'd be better off running this place alone," he added, knowing even as he thought it, it was a lie.

"I think it's working," Bessie whispered over her shoulder to Millie.

Millie waved her hand at the two men who had just entered and were sliding into chairs at the table nearest the front window. Then she glanced at Clive and then back at Bessie, nodding. "Oh, it most definitely is. When old Burt stopped you, I thought Clive was going to order him out of Six Belles and tell him never to come back again."

Bessie sighed. It had been so long since she'd had any hope for the future, she had forgotten how wonderful it felt. So much had changed in a week. She and Ellie had put aside their animosity, and while Bessie could never see them ever becoming close friends, a mutual respect had grown between them.

The afternoons had gone from laborious and lonely times to the part of the day she looked forward to the most. Ellie always brought Evette, who was someone Bessie found herself growing to like more and more each day. They had much in common and similar personalities. Their growing friendship, in addition to the new dresses, made Bessie once again feel indebted to Ellie. Owing the little missy was just something she refused to do, and it occurred to her just how she could settle things between them. The one thing Ellie wanted most was the one thing she could not do for herself.

Bessie hustled over to Millie to stop her before she was able to reach the two men and take their orders. "I don't know what's so important about some green and white pinnace, but those two men . . . well, they know somethin'. They knew it the last time you asked them. I heard 'em say so when they didn't know I was right behind 'em."

Millie stood transfixed, feeling both naïve and surprised that someone would lie about such a simple question. "But why did they say they knew nothing? What could it cost them to tell me who the pinnace belongs to?"

Bessie sighed and answered her honestly. "No matter how much you try to fit in here, little missy, you never will. Otherwise you would know people in these parts don't like questions, aren't ever goin' to ask them, and they certainly won't answer any. Goes against our nature."

Millie looked deflated. Bessie was right. Her speech, her walk, even how she moved her hands, all set her apart;

something Evette and Bessie had taken turns pointing out to her the past few days. It was done in good humor, but it was clear that she could be there a year . . . maybe even longer, and it would still be obvious to all that Millie had not experienced the same difficult upbringing as those who lived and worked along the docks. "Then it's hopeless."

Bessie shrugged. "Doesn't have to be. Ask those two about the pinnace again and this time tell 'em that if they tell you, it'll be as a favor to me."

Millie stared at Bessie. "A favor?" she asked, hinting at Bessie's dislike of being indebted to someone. This time she was volunteering.

Bessie refused to look at Millie. She gathered the empty mugs from a deserted table and said over her shoulder, "Consider it payment for helping me with me hair."

Bessie exhaled when Millie did not argue and turned to go and speak with the men near the window. Then she walked over to the bar and handed the mugs to Clive.

"Why are ye all of a sudden trying tae help Ellie with the pinnace?" he probed, keeping his voice low so that only Bessie could hear.

With a small shrug of her shoulders, Bessie replied, "I have me reasons."

"And just what reason do ye have tae be wanting tae help Ellie return tae a man and a life she's running away from?"

Bessie bit her bottom lip. She had decided the very night she had overheard Evette and Ellie talking that she would not divulge to anyone—even Clive—what she had learned: that it was not a man, but someone named Aimee who had driven Ellie to this life. So Bessie told him something he would understand. "I owe a debt and I'm payin' it back."

Clive waved for Devlin to join them. Devlin did so, but his pained expression made it clear that he wanted to know why he had been summoned. Clive casually pointed at Bessie before crossing his arms. "Did ye know that our Bessie has decided tae help Ellie find out about the pinnace?"

Devlin stared at Bessie coolly for several moments. "I don't think that is a good idea," he finally said.

Bessie returned his gaze. "If you're thinking that, it's because you've already gone and found out about it. Yet you've never said anythin' to her. And I thought you was a real gentleman, not just dressed up like one."

The accusation hit its target and Devlin felt the sudden need to defend his actions. "*All I know* is which ship the pinnace belongs to, and that the information is meaningless. The company, ship, owner, captain . . . even the crew have done nothing in the past or present that would generate the least bit of interest. There is nothing suspicious or unusual about them in any way. They're successful but no more so than several other shipping companies. And from what I've learned, the captain of that ship is hard but fair, with a loyal crew. So until I can figure out how that pinnace is involved with Ellie, I'm not telling her a bleeding thing. And neither are you."

Normally, Bessie balked at such orders, but instead she just pointed over to where Millie stood. "Too late. See those men Ellie is with over there? They know about the pinnace and are telling her about it right now."

Devlin's head shot up and he began to march over toward Millie, but as he did, a familiar figure came into view. The Bow Street runner who had been following him was across the street. He was heading toward the tavern, and with him was a tall, dark-haired man whose clothing was impeccably tailored.

Running a place for gamblers, Devlin had learned to be something of an expert at assessing people from afar. And it only took him a few seconds to know the man coming toward the tavern was not just determined to achieve his goal, but lethally so.

Suddenly small fingers flew to his arm and squeezed tight. Millie sucked in her breath and whispered in fear more to herself than anyone else, "He's found out that I left. Oh, good Lord, he cannot find me. Not here. Not now."

Then his arm was free and she was rushing over to where Clive and Bessie stood. Devlin quickly joined them. "There is a man coming. He is looking for the same thing I am, but he *cannot* know that I am here. If you know anything about the pinnace, please tell him. He has a right to know, but I beg you to tell him *nothing* about me."

Concerned, Bessie reached out to clasp Millie's hand. Millie looked pleadingly into Bessie's blue eyes. "If he learned I was here, he would be very, very angry. My life would be over."

Clive coughed into his hand. "He won't learn of you from us. Devlin, take her out the back way."

Millie scrunched her brows but was given no explanation before Devlin grabbed her cloak and whisked her into the back room where she thought only extra liquor and spirits were stored. As soon as they disappeared, Clive yelled out to the room. It wasn't often that he used his booming voice, so when he did, it got everybody's attention quickly. He knew Ellie had not told him the truth as to why she was there and working for him, but at the moment it did not matter. Six Belles was his family and she was now a part of it. And he protected his own. "Anyone says a word about Ellie, knowing about Ellie, seeing Ellie, or anything about her working here, I'll make yer life hell."

While the order came as a surprise to everybody in the room, not a single soul considered disobeying it. No one had more contacts along this part of the Thames than Clive.

His network was unparalleled, and getting on the wrong side of a man with connections was a death sentence.

Thirty seconds later a dark, stern-faced man entered. He was clutching a small portrait in his hand and walked straight up to Clive. "I'm looking for a man named MacLeery, who I have been told comes here every night."

Though not as quick to read men as Devlin was, years of owning his own place and having to predict the actions and attitudes of men both sober and drunk had enabled Clive to see that the man staring at him was not one of the pampered, soft-brained gentry. He exuded an air of command. His mouth was set in a firm, unyielding line, which should have implied a total lack of emotion. For some reason, Clive got just the opposite impression. If Clive had to guess, the man was afraid, and unaccustomed to feeling that way. But just what did a wealthy man like him have to be afraid of? And what did he want with Ellie?

Clive pointed to the empty chair Devlin normally sat in. "He was here, but he's already left."

The man held out a hand-sized portrait, but carefully kept his thumb over the name at the bottom. "Have you seen this lady?"

The question was more of a challenge than an inquiry. Again, Clive felt strong emotion from the man and gazed at the picture as if he were seeing the person for the first time. In a way, he was. The woman in the portrait was definitely Ellie, but she was dressed in finery and jewels and appeared more like a heavenly angel than a woman. No wonder Ellie thought her fancy working gown was plain and unexceptional.

Shifting his gaze back to the tall man's golden stare, Clive said without any waver in his voice, "I've never seen a lass who looks like that in my life. Why would ye think a fancy woman like that would be here?"

Clive saw the man's jaw tighten upon hearing his response. "Knowing her," the man answered through gritted teeth, "she believes she has good reasons, but I promise you they are not."

Arguing, Clive knew, would only give away the fact that he knew Ellie. So he just looked at the dark nobleman and shrugged his shoulders, pushing back the niggling feeling that he would be protecting Ellie better by letting the man know where she was. But he had made a promise, and a man was worth nothing if he could not keep his word. "If ye say so. But in my experience, that is the way with most women. Don't know why fancy ones like her would be an exception."

The man looked at the door to his storage area and then back at Clive. "Mind if I take a look in there?"

"I do, but I don't think that is going to stop ye."

The man gave him another pointed look and then went into the back room. A couple of seconds later he came back out. This time he addressed all those in the tavern. "I've been told a woman works here. She is about this high and has eyes the color of wood violets. If any of you can tell me where she is staying, I will give you a hundred pounds."

Clive smiled inwardly as the men, one by one, went back to their drinks. The upper class thought the poor cared only for coin and naught for pride and respect. And while two to three years' salary was a lot of blunt, it was not a permanent way out of their poverty. Eventually it would return when the money ran out. Squealers would not have a life to return to.

"I think, gentry, ye got yer answer," Clive said calmly. "I have a woman working here and she is short, but the lass has *never* looked anything like that."

The man's gold eyes shifted to the figure standing near the door. Clive guessed he was a runner. Never had many dealings with them, but very few were unaware of their existence. The runner crossed his arms. "Can't say for sure if the barkeep knows her or not. All I know is MacLeery is a regular here. I never got a look at the other girl. Just know she has dark brown hair and is shorter than her," he said, pointing at Bessie.

Without another word, the man walked out of Six Belles, leaving the runner to follow. He never looked back.

And not once did he ever mention a green and white pinnace.

Edward crouched low into the shadows and watched Chase enter the tavern. Tagging along was the Bow Street runner he had hired.

Edward had not expected locating the maps to be difficult. In truth, he had thought to find them all in one place at the office. His initial plan had been to take them, use them, and return to Society, not as the broken man he was, but transformed into a man with unmeasured power. And yet, despite all his efforts, he still had only four of the nine maps. He needed the others and had resolved that it would take time to locate and procure them. But a week ago, fate had offered him another solution.

The first time Chaselton had hired Randall Greery, it had been to find him—the elusive thief. Evading the runner had been more difficult due to his current physical condition, but not impossible. When Greery was hired for a second time, Edward surmised he was again the target, but could not comprehend why the runners were focusing their efforts on the London Docks.

A puzzle Edward was determined to solve, he decided to conduct his own inquiries. Greery was honest and loyal to Chaselton, but one of the younger men the runner had hired to help was not as scrupulous. When cornered, he had revealed everything he knew for a single quid.

Edward had nearly laughed out loud upon learning who the runners were after. Not him—the mysterious thief—and not pathetic Aimee, but the very woman who had turned his life into a living hell. The runners were unfamiliar with the woman they sought, but Edward was intimately familiar with the woman in the portrait.

He savored the idea of Lady Chaselton running away. Shunned by her perfect husband, she had disappeared to one of the most dangerous places in London to look for her simpering, foolish friend.

Pulling back farther into the shadows, Edward waited to see if his one-time protégé had found his beloved wife. Several minutes later, Edward had his answer. Chaselton had left unaccompanied. Edward sighed in relief. He still had time.

Chaselton had no doubt bribed the people and the owner for information. The working poor were often misunderstood and the titled too often thought that all things in life could be purchased with enough coin. Most failed to realize respect was something that had no price and therefore could belong to any man. The small, beautiful hellion must have earned the loyalty of those inside. Chaselton failed to understand that he was not buying information, but their self-respect—something that was not for sale.

Edward would not make the same mistake.

He would wait no longer. If chance refused to offer him the opportunity for retribution, he would just have to create one. A face-to-face meeting with Lady Chaselton was long overdue.

Meanwhile, it was enjoyable seeing Chaselton in a near state of panic. To those who passed by, the marquess looked cold and distant, but Edward had trained the man to be a spy. He had honed the marquess's skills and taught him how to mask his emotions. Edward knew by the length of Chaselton's gait, the clip of his heels, and the hardness of his jaw, just what deep emotions truly ran through the marquess.

Fear.

And Edward could hardly wait to use the overwhelming love behind that fear to his advantage.

Chapter 29

November 12, 1816

Aimee stopped midstride, pivoted, and came back to the man who had just spoken. "Can you please repeat what you just said?" she asked, trying hard to appear only casually interested, though her heart was pounding.

For the past six days, she had thought herself either ready for Bedlam or close to it. Whenever she was alone, she had heard the whisper of Reece's name. Even at night, as she tried to sleep, it was as if her pillow came alive, reminding her of who she had left behind. To make matters worse, the whispers had been in his husky voice.

One morning she had woken up with a quill in her hand and his name scribbled multiple times on a piece of paper next to her bed. That had shaken her to her core, so much that she had finally agreed to let Mrs. Shay introduce her to the *Sea Rebel*'s chief mate, Mr. Haskin. Up close the man was even better-looking than from afar, which was not something Aimee could say about most men. He had midnight-black hair, strong cheekbones, and his eyes were an unusual color of blue, reminding her of the lighter hues of a shallow sea.

At first, the evening had been surprisingly enjoyable. The four of them had sat down to dinner and the first course was served. The soup was very good, though it lacked JP's scrumptious flavor. Then, just before the second course, Mrs. Shay professed a headache and requested her husband's assistance, leaving Aimee alone with Mr. Haskin. The idea of eating with an unmarried man was unheard of in London, and Aimee had almost risen to her feet to follow the captain. But the memory of the voices and note caused her to remain seated. She had requested a distraction and Mrs. Shay had provided one. Besides, Aimee thought, after all she had done, what was the harm in breaking one more rule of propriety?

Thankfully, Mr. Haskin had agreed to stay as well, and soon they were engaged in pleasant conversation. Unfortunately, the man must have consumed something that disagreed with him, for the room had begun to reek of rotten eggs. Aimee remembered looking at him, trying in vain to think of something to say to put him at his ease. His expression said that he was trying to do the same, but was equally unsuccessful. As with all human smells, the odor had eventually dissipated and they tried to resume their previous discussion. Then, the smell returned. The third time, Mr. Haskin politely excused himself, to Aimee's relief.

When he approached her on deck the next afternoon, she had been glad, for one bad night could happen to anyone. His hair was wet and slicked back and he smelled of soap, hinting that he had just bathed. Aimee thought the gesture extremely flattering, as she knew sailors washed themselves only when it became necessary. It was nice to know a man considered she warranted such an effort.

Again, their conversation was interrupted prematurely

when Mr. Haskin began to twitch. It had started with his shoulders moving as if he had an itch in the middle of his back. Soon after, he was rubbing his legs. He kept shifting his weight in such a way that if he were a little boy, Aimee would have asked him if he needed to be excused to the privy. Instead, she suggested they sit on a nearby bench, and Mr. Haskin hastily agreed. But being seated offered no more relief. If anything, it was even more uncomfortable to watch him rock back and forth with his hands fiercely gripping his legs. Then, without warning, he had stood up, quickly bowed, and began to scratch himself all over as he disappeared below the main deck, shouting for someone to get him some water.

She had not seen Mr. Haskin since, and the incidents that had incited her original request for distraction had only grown from annoying to worrisome. The worst was just moments ago.

She had been standing out of the way at the back of the ship on the poop deck, watching the crew work, when an eerily familiar blue scarf caught her eye. The man was near the forecastle, securing the ship's bell on the belfry. Being so far away, it was hard to see just who it was, but before she could even get halfway across the main deck to call out for him to wait, the seaman had disappeared below. Disheartened, she turned back to resume her earlier, unobtrusive position.

That was when she heard a nearby seaman say something to a fellow sailor that made sense of every incident, every whisper, *every single odd thing* that had happened to her.

"Miss?" the lanky sailor asked when she approached them. His brows were up and his hazel eyes stared at her with concern.

Normally, Aimee would have assured him there was nothing to be distressed about, but her mind was focused on only one thing. "Please repeat what you just told this gentleman as I was passing by."

The second sailor froze, and his eyes twitched, wondering just what they had said to upset her. After a moment of hesitation, he licked his lips and said, "Goodfellow, here, um, well, he just mentioned that Friers really likes the blue scarf the new guy gave him."

Aimee stared hard at both men. "Please describe this scarf for me."

"That wasn't you?" Haskin asked, his tone one of disbelief.

Aimee looked horrified for a second at the thought of ever being able to produce such a foul odor. Then she broke into laughter. "No! I assure you that, well . . . I thought it was you!"

"Bloody hell," Haskin said under his breath. "What you must have thought. I tried, Miss Wentworth, I did try to be a gentleman and stay. I kept waiting and, well, hoping, that you would excuse yourself, but finally I could stand the smell no more and had to leave."

Aimee rubbed the back of her neck. "I am so glad that you did. Not until you left did our prankster stop and leave me to finish my meal in peace."

Haskin wiggled the note in his hand and asked, "I understand why you would want to tell me in private, but why did your missive include instructions on how you wanted me to get here? There are easier ways to get to the cuddy than via my bosun's cabin and the council chamber."

"The cuddy was the only place on the ship I was sure we would not be overheard."

Haskin crinkled his dark brows, still not understanding. "The captain's stateroom is below us, and from here we can see who comes and goes on the deck above. I can assure you we are alone."

"And that is why it is safe for us to speak. No one will be introducing foul smells through the floors below us."

Haskin cocked his head and his turquoise-blue gaze increased in intensity. "So you honestly think it was intentional?"

Aimee gave him an exasperated look. She needed Mr. Haskin's help, and it was important that he be just as committed to her plan as she was. "Do you normally fidget and squirm around women as you did yesterday?"

Haskin scowled and Aimee knew he was finally starting to believe her. The man before her was healthy, well trained, and possessed the power of self-control from years of practice. It had to have been humiliating to act as he did, and she suspected few men could have endured the discomfort for as long as he had.

"My clothes," Haskin growled. "Something about them made me itch. I could not tell what, and just assumed I had foolishly laid them on some powder or . . . are you telling me *that* was intentional?"

Aimee repressed her desire to flash him a large smile and nodded. Mr. Haskin was hers. "I am fairly certain I know who the culprit is and was hoping to elicit your help in teaching him a lesson."

Haskin's eyes narrowed. "Tell me who he is and I will find him and then will be just as creative when I discipline him, Miss Wentworth. I assure you nothing more will happen to you on this ship."

Aimee bit her inner cheek. She did not think Mr. Haskin would cause any permanent harm or make Reece disappear, but the chief mate did believe it had been a low-ranked crew member who had humiliated him. On a ship, such things could not be permitted. And yet, Mr. Haskin had no idea she was referring to Reece—someone who may not be his immediate employer, but his employer nonetheless. She knew very little of *Sea Rebel*'s chief mate, but she suspected that Mr. Haskin's level of pride could rival Reece's. The man also had to be incredibly intelligent to have so quickly gained the respect and admiration of Captain Shay. This did not bode well. Moreover, having Mr. Haskin confront Reece was not what she wanted. Aimee fully intended on being the one to teach Captain Reece Hamilton a lesson he more than deserved to learn.

"Mr. Haskin, I think that might not be the best way to resolve the situation. I was hoping for a little bit of retaliation. Let him learn a lesson about what it is like to be on the receiving end of one of these little pranks. I mean . . . you could always do your disciplining later, could you not? It would mean a great deal to me to have your support."

Haskin crossed his arms and thought about it. "Normally I am not one who would encourage any vengeful activity. It rarely leads to anything positive. But I do believe that this is one of those rare times."

The grin Aimee had been suppressing came to life. "I say we find out where he sleeps and begin there."

Haskin inhaled, finding himself once more ensnared by Aimee's charms, and shook his head. "Miss Wentworth, you look like an angel, but you have the cunning of an imp. I cannot decide if I am appalled or if I rather like it."

Aimee rocked onto her tippy toes and came back down, something she rarely did because it accentuated her height. But she could not help it. Millie was always the one people thought of as the imp. It was finally her turn to be the mischievous one.

Chapter 30

November 14, 1816

Clive knew from the start that he should never have let Ellie convince him to hire her. His world had been predictable a month ago. It had been comfortable, and not once did he lie awake worrying about those he cared about. But that was before Ellie Alwick. That was when he could look danger in the eye, assess the size, skill, and weapons of the man, and attack him straight on. But now that he knew the danger hunting Ellie was neither imaginary nor feeble, an awful feeling had begun to grow in his gut. A feeling that said whoever was after her would stop at nothing and no one to achieve his goal. And never could he remember feeling so helpless.

Part of him wished that he were the sort of man who could just cut her loose. It was not as if the lass had provided an explanation for what that nobleman wanted from her, nor ever planned to offer one. Clive knew Ellie thought she was protecting him, Bessie, and everyone at Six Belles. So, if they needed protecting, then didn't he have every right to take one look at her when she walked in the door tonight and tell her to turn around and never return? He did, but Clive knew that he would not . . . could not do it. That left him few options, and continuing as he had been doing the past few nights was becoming less and less a viable one.

The night the nobleman had come in looking for Ellie had changed things. When Devlin returned after seeing her home, he had divulged some disturbing information.

Clive had known that Devlin was smitten with Ellie; half the men were. But lately his mind had been more focused on the other half who were more than a little taken with Bessie. So just as Devlin had been trailing Ellie home, Clive had begun following Bessie, intent on protecting her from any drunken men who mistakenly believed the women of Six Belles were available for some additional service. However, Clive had not known about the runner or that Devlin was no longer content with staying in the shadows—that he had been at her side until she reached her front door. Devlin did not want to tell Ellie, but somebody was following her and he did not move like a runner. After learning that, Clive made some decisions.

First was limiting those who entered his place to only men he knew. Almost all of the clientele at Six Belles were regulars, so of all the changes, it was the least difficult and cost him very little in the way of sales. Stopping in the middle of the afternoon to go fetch Bessie and Ellie was an imposition, but as the women were already together, it was not too big a burden.

At night, instead of accompanying each woman home individually, he and Devlin decided to double their strength. Clive was at their side while Devlin lurked behind to see who, if anyone, was following them.

The first night had been uneventful. A couple of runners skulked in the shadows, but they left them alone. Ellie had worn her cloak with the hood, and looked down as much as possible to hide her face. She was being unusually quiet, and Clive had caught her fingering something in her pocket.

When he asked what it was, Ellie had pulled out an object just far enough for him to see that it was a gun.

"Why are ye carrying something dangerous like that?" he had half whispered, half barked in shock.

Ellie stopped, looked up at him, and said simply, "Because someone is following me."

Clive waved his hand at the nearly deserted streets and buildings surrounding them. "If they are, lass, they cannot harm ye. Not with Devlin and I close at hand."

Ellie had given him a look of appreciation, but she had not been totally convinced. He should have taken that as a warning, but instead he had dismissed her concerns. "'Tis a small little weapon ye have there. Do ye even know how tae shoot?"

Ellie resumed walking and said in a low, deadpan voice, "With deadly accuracy."

It was not a boast, and consequently Clive had not doubted her. It only added to his curiosity about her. He should have been more concerned with why Ellie was so nervous with two men to guard her and a gun that she felt comfortable using.

But the second night, Clive learned that Devlin's and Ellie's fears were not as unfounded as he had initially believed. The runners were there as before, but there was also someone far more stealthy, sliding in and out of the shadows. Every time Devlin neared, the lurker would slip out of sight. The only two things Devlin could discern were that the man was of average height and extremely nimble despite a slight limp.

Last night, he had followed them again, but this time the runners had as well, and maneuvered the shadowy figure into a trap. But when Devlin had gone to see who the culprit was, he discovered that it was not the shadow who had been caught; it was the shadow who had caught one of the runners. And the runner had been beaten severely by a master in the arts of combat, for no normal man or soldier could cause such damage in such a short amount of time.

It was when Devlin had relayed this latest news that Clive knew that he could not continue doing nothing. Walking the women home, waiting for an attack that he could not prepare for, was not an option. Neither was remaining vulnerable.

But most of all, Clive was done with being ignorant. It was time everyone in their small group started talking.

"I've just done something I've never done before," Clive began, "so make it worthwhile."

A crash of thunder exploded outside just as Clive finished. Millie swallowed. The moment Devlin arrived, Clive had made everyone stop drinking and leave Six Belles. It had cost him in doing so, because he did not make one of them pay for their drinks, even though some had finished at least one mug of ale and were working on their second or even third round.

"Every one of us is keeping secrets, and while I normally hold firm tae keeping information tae oneself, a man nearly died last night and it could have been any one of us."

Devlin waved his hand toward his chair at the hearth. Clive nodded and the four of them went and sat down in a semicircle. "Where do you want to begin?" Devlin asked.

Clive had thought his friend would volunteer to be first, as the man was the most eager to protect Ellie, but then realized that was the very reason Devlin would *not* go first.

"It's me tavern, so I'll speak me peace first," Clive offered, just before lightning lit up the sky. He waited until the thunder subsided before continuing. "I've been keeping what I know tae meself for yer benefit," he directed at Millie. "I had hoped that whatever problems ye had when ye came here would go away with some time. That was when I thought ye just needed tae learn tae believe in yerself and realize that whoever forced ye in tae this kind of life was not someone ye should ever go back tae."

Millie was about to come to Chase's defense when Clive raised his hand. "I've come tae believe now that my supposition was wrong. I think ye chose tae come here. And in doing so, ye brought danger with ye."

Millie shook her head no. "I did not. I swear I did not."

Devlin shrugged his shoulders and pulled his ankle onto his knee. "Not intentionally, but obviously you are not the only one interested in this green and white pinnace."

Millie's mouth gaped open for several seconds. Then her brilliant eyes turned dark. "Do you *know* who owns it? Have you known all along?"

Clive coughed. "Not all along. I only found out after Bessie started helping ye. Whatever trouble ye were in, I wasn't going tae let it touch her just because she felt an obligation tae ye."

Bessie said nothing. But with her crossed arms and piercing blue eyes, she did not need to. Clive ignored her and continued. "It belongs tae a ship called the *Sea Emerald*."

Millie gasped and her hand flew to her mouth. Tears sprang from her eyes. "She's *safe*!" she whispered. "Thank the Lord, she will come home unharmed." Then, though she tried not to, Millie broke down in tears, crying into her hands with obvious joy and relief.

Devlin and Clive just stared at her in astonishment. Bessie, with the benefit of having overheard Ellie's and Evette's conversation, was just as surprised by her friend's abrupt reaction, but not as confused as to the reason why. "Your best friend was on that pinnace, wasn't she? That's why you're here. To learn what ship she got on."

Millie nodded, wiping her eyes. "Since we were kids, Aimee, Jennelle, and I were never content to stay home and be proper. We were out looking for a thief when she was abducted by some men in a green and white pinnace."

Devlin's mind was spinning. "Who's Jennelle?"

Millie nodded. "She was with us. People call us the Daring Three. I always thought it a compliment and sought out ways to look for adventure."

Devlin rolled his eyes, chiding himself for not realizing it sooner. A noblewoman who *enjoyed* adventures. How else could she have made it this long working at Six Belles? "And the nobleman who was looking for you?"

Millie licked her lips and brushed away tears, despite the fact that new ones kept falling. "He's Aimee's brother," she said, trying to be honest while protecting her husband's name. "He blames me and he should. Aimee would never have gone if I had not agreed to go with her."

"So it was her idea?" Devlin prodded.

"Yes, but . . ."

Clive threw his hand up. It was nice to know why Ellie was there and that it truly was not for nefarious reasons, but nothing she had divulged explained just why a dangerous man was following her. "You mentioned a thief," he prompted.

"Yes. Nothing very serious. The man was taking insignificant items. Aimee's brother actually thought it might be his friend playing a practical joke. We discovered it wasn't when we snuck aboard and saw the thief sneaking off the ship."

"Do ye think that man saw ye? Recognized ye?" Clive impatiently probed.

Millie shook her head. "I don't see how. We were hidden the whole time. And even if he did, he could see us no better than we could him. And I could only tell you his height and that he had a slight limp."

Clive immediately turned to look at Devlin, who stared back. Thunder again cracked overhead, filling the silence. Then Clive shifted his gaze to Millie. "I don't know how, but I'll bet a week's earnings that whoever ye saw that night knows ye work here."

Millie's heart stopped. Fear had been her companion for days now, despite her constantly telling herself that she was being ridiculous. "What do you mean?"

"When I was walking ye and Bessie home, Devlin followed us." Both women's eyes grew wide and settled on Devlin in surprise.

Devlin returned Millie's pointed gaze. "Clive and I expected your friend's brother to send some Bow Street runners to determine just who you are. We were right. But there was another person among them, and last night he nearly killed one of the runners for interfering. I have no doubt that this thief of yours is going to try again."

Millie rose to her feet. "Then I have to go. If I remain here, everyone is in danger."

"Why is he after you? Just what did you see?"

"Nothing. I . . . I . . . took something he dropped. He must think I still have it, but I do not. I swear." Millie moved over to Clive and looked him in the eye. "Are you *sure* the pinnace belonged to the *Sea Emerald*?"

Clive nodded his head. "It left for America on a scheduled trip and is expected back next week or the week after."

Unconsciously, she reached out and gripped his hand. "Thank you."

Bessie heard the finality in Millie's voice and leaned forward to catch her arm. "You cannot be thinkin' of leavin'."

"I must."

"Whoever this man is, he's after you. Just where do you plan on goin'?"

Millie stood there and stared for several long seconds at Bessie and then Clive and Devlin. She had money and that meant she had options. But she knew that she was never going to be able to leave there tonight unless they agreed she was in a position to protect herself on her own. "It is time I told you who I really am."

"A real marchioness?" Bessie hissed. She had come to doubt her theory of Ellie being a cast-out mistress, but it still seemed more plausible than the explanation she had just heard. "And I suppose your father's a powerful duke," she added under her breath.

"Actually he's an earl," Millie quipped defensively. Then immediately wished she had not and knelt down beside Bessie's chair. "You've always been correct in believing that I came from a life far different from the one here. I wish every governess I ever had could have seen you teach me some of the lessons I learned under your . . . style of tutoring."

Bessie produced a small smile, but Millie knew the news of who she was would take more time to digest. Even in her world of titled people and gentry, being married to a marquess was no small thing. Millie glanced at Clive, who remained unmoved. She knew his mind was whirling with all the repercussions of hiring a marchioness, and no doubt feared that Chase would return and retaliate by ruining Clive's business and livelihood.

"I promise you the only person my husband will hold accountable for my being and working here is me. And while he will threaten to be angry with me for the rest of his life, as soon as he realizes that I am safe and was only here trying to correct the wrongs I did, he will calm."

Clive snorted, then stood up and went to pour himself a drink. "I should have known," he finally said. "As soon as he walked in and he held out yer portrait, I should have known what could make a man like that afraid. I should have told him who ye were."

Millie felt her heart clench with guilt. "If you had, then I would not be able to tell him that his sister is safe and begin to mend what I did. You must understand, the three of us—myself, his sister, and Jennelle—have never been content to follow Society's rigid rules." She looked directly at Bessie. "Imagine never having any say in what you do or with whom. That embroidery and gossip are the highlights of your day. Work is deciding the evening menu and what outfits to wear. You have good food and nice jewelry, but in return you must dance until your feet are swollen and sometimes even bleeding when men stomp on them. You have to pretend to enjoy singing and playing for others even if the sound of your voice makes them want to leave the room screaming."

Bessie looked up at Millie, and while not an unkind look, there was little sympathy in her eyes for her titled plight.

Millie stood up then, letting her anger show. "I've lived your life, Bessie. You have not lived mine. You dream of the benefits wealth brings, but you do so from a man's perspective, not a woman's. For my and my friends' independent natures, the constraints are too often stifling."

"And so you get into men's clothes and search for thieves in the middle of the night. Makes sense," Devlin huffed, and took the glass of whiskey Clive brought him. He downed it in one swallow.

Millie took a deep breath and exhaled in frustration. "It was not a whim. There were other reasons. Good reasons. But in my husband's mind, every excursion the three of us undertake ends up in disaster. If you had heard Charlie that night, ordering me to go and stay in the country while he resolved another one of my mistakes, you would better understand why I had to fix this one on my own."

Devlin felt a shiver run up his spine hearing Millie refer to her husband so informally. It just dug the knife in a little deeper. He had wanted *his* first name on her lips, to hear the love in her voice when she referred to him. Now Devlin knew he never would. "You both are fools," he said, standing. "Your husband for thinking that putting you in a cage would work, and you for not understanding why he sent you away in the first place."

Devlin walked over to the hook holding his overcoat and slipped it off. Putting it on, he said to Clive, "I need to get out of here, but I will send you a hack for Lady Chaselton."

Clive grimaced in understanding. He had known Devlin liked Ellie. The news she was married had to be somewhat of a shock. "I'll make sure her ladyship gets home safely tae her husband before I go home tonight."

Opening the door, a cold blast of wind blew in just as another lightning bolt lit up the sky. Any minute the rain would begin to pour. Devlin looked one last time at Millie.

She stared at him, confused and angry over what he had said. Damn if she did not look even more beautiful. It was no wonder the marquess fell in love with her. Her spirit was infectious and no doubt a constant nuisance, but it could warm the hardest of souls. Devlin had let it thaw his, and it hurt to know that this would be the last time he ever saw her. What had he expected? Had he really thought he was going to somehow whisk her away to his home? That by gaining her love and support he could solve all his problems? She would have only caused more.

Just like him, Ellie—*Lady Chaselton*, he corrected himself—had only temporarily escaped from her real life and responsibilities. Just as she needed to go and reclaim her identity, it was time for him to do the same. He had gathered more than enough funds to recover what his father had lost. All he needed to do was go home and face what he had to do.

* * *

Millie wanted to scream out of frustration. She was standing in a tavern, her hair in a simple bun that she herself styled, wearing a dirty garment with tips hidden inside, looking *nothing* like a woman who had any wealth, let alone a titled husband. And yet, the moment she had revealed who she was, all three of them had begun to treat and talk to her as if she were some fragile piece of china. They no longer saw her, but her title.

Devlin MacLeery had not asked if she wanted to go home. He and Clive just decided to send her there. Could they not understand that Chase would be furious for bringing yet *another* problem for him to resolve?

"I will leave, but I won't go home," Millie announced unequivocally. "I will not give my husband another reason to believe I have brought nothing but trouble into his life when he married me."

"I have no doubt that ye are as much trouble as ye say ye are," Clive said softly. Millie's head whipped around to glare at him, but he just shrugged it off. "But there's something ye should know about yer man. The night he came in here looking for ye, he was in pain not knowing where ye were. And a man who can feel that amount of loss over a woman is never going tae change his need tae protect her. That's just a fact."

He pointed at Bessie and continued. "Bloody hell, if it were Bess, I would be doing the same thing. And, aye, she's trouble. Lots of it. Damn woman is either insulting the men who come in here or making them crazy with lust. But that wouldn't have anything tae do with why I would be hiring every runner I could tae bring her back tae where she belonged."

It was Bessie's turn to jump to her feet. "Who says I *belong* anywhere?"

"I do. Ye belong here and ye belong with me. Something ye and I have known for a while now." After realizing all that he just said and what it implied, nerves claimed Clive. Both women were staring at him in shock. Suddenly he felt the need to disappear. Ducking down, he grabbed an empty crate and announced, "I'm going in the back tae get some more whiskey."

Bessie's mouth was open in shock. It was Millie who found her voice first. "I *told* you that Clive was far more interested in you than you believed."

But before Bessie could respond, another huge gust of wind blew the front doors open. With it came various pieces of material that had been flying around in the streets. It was a miracle nothing had hit and broken the main window.

Bessie headed toward the door. "I gotta get the shutters closed."

Millie nodded and grabbed her cloak to help, but Bessie stopped her. "That wind will throw your ladyship all around. You best stay inside."

Millie thought about arguing, but she did not want to distress Bessie any more than she already had. She handed Bessie her cloak and said, "Then wear this."

"I'm not puttin' that on."

Millie ground her teeth in frustration. Bessie would have taken the thing from Ellie, but now that she was Lady Chaselton, the pride-filled woman was refusing. "Bessie, I remember someone giving me a thorough scolding for not accepting tips because I did not think I had earned them. That woman would have snatched this cloak when it was offered, regardless to whom it belonged. She would say only a fool would be cold when they did not need to be."

Bessie's mouth twitched and a second later a smile overtook her lips. "I'm nobody's fool," she said. Then, taking the cloak from Millie's outstretched arms, she put it on and headed outside.

Millie heard Bessie close the shutters over the window as she started to pick up the muck that had been blown in.

Several minutes passed and Millie worried when Bessie had still not come back in. Thinking that it was just taking longer to tie the shutters in the unusually fierce wind, Millie went outside to help her.

She was no more than two steps out the door when a bolt of lightning flashed, illuminating all that was around her. Immediately her heart stopped.

"Lady Aldon. We've been waiting for you."

The man was holding a dagger to Bessie's throat with one hand and had another hand over her mouth. He was hunched and disfigured, but Millie recognized the voice. It was one from her nightmares. "It's Lady Chaselton now, Sir Edward. Or perhaps I should just refer to you as what you are. A traitor."

Fury erupted on his face and he squeezed the blade closer against Bessie's skin, causing her to yelp in pain. "Call me what you like. It doesn't matter. But unless you want to say good-bye to your friend, you will get into that carriage."

Millie looked at the black vehicle behind him. The single driver on top looked straight ahead, refusing to intervene. Whatever happened once she was inside, she would be at Edward's mercy.

Millie reached down for the gun in her cloak pocket and inwardly cursed. Her hooded coat was probably why Edward had grabbed Bessie, thinking that she was Millie. "Let Bessie go, Edward. She is no one important."

"Ah, but she is to you," he snarled. "So she comes. Now, get in before anyone else comes out here. Otherwise, their death will be on your conscience."

Millie swallowed. Fear swirled inside her and she forced it down. Clive was not a small man, but he would have been caught unawares, and Edward was not the type to make threats he would not keep. Unable to think of what else to do, Millie stepped into the carriage and was barely inside when Bessie was thrust in behind her.

The door closed and the carriage immediately lurched forward. Using the end of the long knife, Edward pointed at the seat across from him. "You sit there. And you there, next to her."

Bessie whimpered and did as she was told. Millie did the same, cursing her luck. Her gun was not in the pocket closest to her.

"Just what do you intend to do?" Millie asked, amazed her voice was so calm.

"You and Chaselton," he snorted, "ruined *everything*. You even thought you had destroyed me, but you were wrong. I'm alive. Something you won't be come morning."

Bessie squeaked and grabbed Millie's arm in fear. But Millie sat composed, staring at the long thrusting dirk in Edward's hand. She could fight, but with her size, there was really no way she could offer any resistance against someone who knew how to wield the weapon. "I might be dead, but you would soon join me. Charlie would find you."

Edward produced a laugh that chilled her bones despite her effort to remain unaffected by anything he said. "He doesn't even know I'm *alive*."

"Then does that not remove a large portion of the thrill in killing me?"

Edward twisted his lips. "For a time, perhaps. But he will eventually learn of my resurrection. The thefts, the actual prize I seek, your death . . . all will become clear and he will realize I was behind it all. But by then it will be too late. I will be unstoppable."

All three of them bounced unexpectedly as the road became extremely rough. They hit another hole, and then another, and Millie realized where they were. When she, Aimee, and Jennelle had left Hembree Grove that infamous night a month and a half ago, they took this road. Right before it converged with Piccadilly, Grosvenor Place was in serious need of repair, but there was a dispute about when it should be fixed. Some who were in Town for the Little Season had wanted it done immediately, but most gentry opted to wait until the spring, after more of Society had arrived and could share the expense.

Millie waited what seemed like forever for another major rut to cause the carriage to heave. This time she was ready and gave in to it, allowing herself to be flung over Bessie. Immediately, Edward grabbed her shoulder and flung her back into place, but it was too late. Millie had managed to snatch her pistol out in time. Fearing that Edward would see the pistol and grab it in the time it took to aim, Millie fired the weapon. She was rewarded when Edward yelped in pain.

She had no idea where she hit him but was not going to take the time to find out. Kicking the door open, she shoved Bessie out of the moving vehicle and then lunged after her. She made it out and landed with a thud, but not before Edward had stabbed her with his dagger.

Millie forced herself to ignore the pain and forced her eyes to open to see if the carriage had stopped, but the sound of the gunshot must have made him want to disappear. Bessie was screaming, but this near the park and at this time of night, there were no linkmen around to hear her. The only one who knew where they were was Edward, and Millie could not be certain she had injured him badly enough that he wouldn't be coming after them.

"Stop screaming," she managed to get out, loud enough for Bessie to hear her. Immediately Bessie did, which both surprised and relieved Millie. "The blade. It's in my shoulder. Take it out."

Bessie swallowed and crawled near where Millie lay on the road. She hesitated. "I don't know if I should."

"Tear off a piece of your shift. Then pull it out and tie it as best you can, tightly around the wound."

Bessie's hands were quivering as she did as she was told. By the time she reached for the blade, they were seriously shaking, and Millie almost told her to stop. But when Bessie grabbed the dagger, white hot pain shot through Millie's body, causing her to pass out. When she came to, she felt a sharp pain as Bessie tied another knot in the material binding her shoulder.

Millie considered telling Bessie to leave her there and go for help, when she heard the sound of a carriage coming toward them. Forcing herself to look around, Millie quickly discerned that she was right. They were at Hyde Park Corner. "Help me up. We have to hide before that carriage gets here."

Bessie's blue eyes flew wide open as she understood what Millie was implying. They could not assume whoever was coming would help. Worse, more than likely it was Edward coming back for them.

Going to Millie's uninjured side, Bessie helped Millie to her feet and asked, "Where should we go?"

Millie pointed to the park. "Inside. We'll have to stay near the trees, but I know a place where we won't be found. The good and the bad news is that it is not close."

An hour later, Bessie half dragged, half carried Millie into the hidden clearing. She fell down next to where Millie lay. They were safe from their attacker for now, but in a few hours it would not matter. Lady Chaselton would be dead from her wound.

"My lady?" she asked, praying Millie was still conscious enough to tell her what to do next. But she feared otherwise, for she was looking very pale and her breath was extremely shallow.

"I'm still here," Millie whispered.

"I need to go for help, but I can't leave you alone."

"I'm safe here," Millie said, trying to reassure her. "Get the money from my dress." Bessie immediately did as she was told and was surprised to find not the pennies and farthings that filled her own pockets, but a couple half crowns and several guineas. It was more than she made in several months. Swallowing, she clutched the coins in her fist and said, "I have it."

"There's a ranger. Stays here. Should be near the lake. Look for a lodge. Tell him—" Millie paused to catch her breath. She was running out of energy. "Tell him to take you to Hembree Grove. Providence Court. Let Chase know . . . I'm waiting in our spot . . . and that—"

But before Millie could finish, she went limp, leaving Bessie to do as much as she could.

Only years of practice enabled Chase to hide all the anger he felt inside as he listened to Randall Greery tell him about yet another failed attempt to verify whether or not the woman at Six Belles was his wife. He was about to go against his initial instincts and look for Millie himself, even if his presence did stand out.

When he looked at the situation intellectually, Chase knew the barmaid could *not* be Millie. To live and work that way *for weeks* . . . he just could not fathom it. It was hard enough imagining his sister Aimee enduring the discomforts of being aboard a ship. To think of Millie living by the docks, assimilating into the lives of people who worked and barely survived there, he just could not accept it. But Randall Greery was sure of it. That confidence, mixed with Jennelle's fear and his own firsthand experience of dealing with Millie's determination regardless of the danger it put her in, gave Chase reason to think the runner was correct.

But after what Greery just told him, the situation had become far more than just unfathomable, it had become terrifying.

The night following his visit to Six Belles, he had sent Greery to personally follow the barmaid in question. What neither he nor Greery had anticipated was that the tavern's owner would start escorting the women home while another man followed, watching for anyone like Greery who might be tailing them. Chase had made it clear that on the next night, Greery was to do whatever he had to, including barging into the tavern. But Devlin MacLeery had been waiting. He had recognized Randall and had a few men escort him far from Six Belles.

The third night, Greery again had waited, this time with several other runners. He had intended to waylay the women and delay them just long enough to verify their identities. But before Greery could do so, he saw yet another figure following the group. And from the way the shadow limped as it moved, it was not just anyone, but Chaselton's thief. In an effort to trap and capture the elusive felon, one of Randall's men had nearly been killed. The boy was still unconscious and it would be a while before he would be able to describe his attacker.

Chaselton had reached the limit of his tolerance and that was *before* Greery told him that both women had just disappeared. No one knew where or how, but the tavern's owner was frantically calling the constable, who was being far from cooperative. Without evidence of a problem, he was not eager to actively search for two missing barmaids in the middle of the night.

"Leave," Chase ordered.

Randall Greery turned to do as instructed. He had been given no more instructions and he had no advice on what to do next. And while Chase had not given him any reason why Lady Chaselton would be pretending to be a barmaid near the London Docks, both knew she was.

Just before he opened the study's doors, a cry from the front hall pierced the air. "Lord Chaselton! You need . . . you need to come here right now!"

Chase stood momentarily transfixed at the shrill-sounding voice screaming for him from the entranceway of his home.

It was nearly five in the morning. Few souls were up and not a person he knew or knew of him would ever call for him in such a manner.

Randall Greery opened the door for Chase and then followed him out of the study. At the end of the hall was a woman. She was filthy and her clothes and chaotic hair looked to be matted with blood. Behind her stood a sleepy servant, looking perplexed. "I tried to send her away, my lord, but you heard what she did when I tried."

"Who are you and what do you want with me?" Chase demanded, trying to recall how he recognized her.

"Edward . . ." Bessie stammered, out of a mixture of fear and exhaustion. "Your wife told me to . . ." Bessie collapsed onto the marble floor, unable to stand any longer.

Chase knelt down and grabbed her arms. "Millie! Where is she?"

Bessie shook her head. "She . . . she shot him and we jumped out, but that man, one she called Edward, stabbed her. Please believe me there was nothing I could do!"

Hearing her words, fearing what they meant, Chase shook her. "She is not dead! Tell me she *is not dead*."

"Not dead," Bessie said, still gasping for breath. "Least not when I left. She told me to find you."

Chase let Bessie go. His eyes caught the shocked look of the servant. "Go get the doctor. Greery, you get your men." Then he looked back at Bessie. "Where is she?"

"I . . . I . . . I really don't know. We were somewhere in the park. Said to tell you she's waiting at your spot."

That was all Chase needed to hear. He flew out the back door toward the stable and minutes later, the sounds of a horse being urged into a gallop could be heard.

Chapter 31

November 15, 1816

She knew.

Dripping wet from a brief, cold bath—his first since they left Savannah—and feeling damn close to naked, there was no doubt in Reece's mind that the current state of his clothes was *not* an accident or a coincidence. Lady Aimee Wentworth knew he was on board and what he had been doing. The woman had obviously decided to retaliate and no doubt begged the insipid Haskin to help.

Reece should have recognized the signs two days ago when he kept falling out of his hammock. The slight change in one side's height had not been enough to visually detect there was a problem, but it was more than enough to be very disruptive to sleep. He had been so frustrated that he almost announced his identity and demanded a real bed. But Reece had not wanted to see the I-told-you-so look on Shay's face.

Reece had initially thought his idea to play the role of a carpenter working directly under the captain's supervision a clever one. It gave him the freedom to be where he wanted to be and when, without having to explain himself to Shay's officers or bosun. Unhappily, he had not considered what it would be like living as one of the men. He had told himself that bad food, no baths, and an uncomfortable hammock would all be worth it once he and Aimee were together again. Of course, that was when he still thought her to be a heavenly vision and not a fiendish sprite taking joy in making him miserable.

He should have seen the truth upon Aimee's sudden interest in Mr. Haskin. And yesterday, each time he had tried to return to the cramped area he slept in, Aimee had mysteriously appeared in or near every convenient entry point. Eventually, he had no choice but to go down into the foul-smelling hold and crawl up the base of the mainmast steps to avoid being seen.

Now that he knew Aimee was aware of his presence, Reece suspected sleep was not the only thing she had been depriving him of, for he had not been able to finish a meal either. Each time he sat down to eat, some kind of interruption occurred, resulting in a mishap that rendered his food inedible. One time it had simply disappeared. He had sat down, placed a large slice of bread and a chunk of meat next to him, and hearing a scream, he looked up. When he glanced back down, the bread and the meat had vanished. At the time, Reece had thought it a prank being played on him as a new crew member, but now it seemed much more likely Aimee had put someone up to the task. Damn woman was using the same charms on Captain Shay's crew as she had his own.

It was the only thing that made sense.

The difference was, *his* mischief was aimed at keeping her mind *on him* while driving the trite Haskin away from her side. *But this*, he thought to himself as he put on his shirt and pants, *is going too far*.

Lady Aimee Wentworth had wanted him. Well, she got

him. And even if she was a ship captain's worst nightmare, she did not have the option to throw him back.

It was time she realized it.

"Mr. Haskin, I am just fascinated by ships and all that is required to run them. The big tall poles with the sails—" Aimee remarked as she put her fork down to break off a piece of bread.

Haskin arched a dubious brow, not at all deceived by her wide eyes and green-chit remark. "They are called masts, Miss Wentworth," he finally replied, wishing Miss Aimee Wentworth was as interested in him as she pretended.

Aimee formed an O with her lips and tried to avoid the puzzled looks on the faces of Captain and Mrs. Shay. Collins had told them about her little foray as a rigger, but per her request, they kept it to themselves. She would have to explain to them at some point the reason behind her deceit, but at the moment, she needed to focus on Mr. Haskin. If Reece was loitering about, she wanted him to know that his mischiefs were not going to work. She just wished that there was someone else aboard with whom she could flirt.

It was not because she was not attracted to Mr. Haskin, for she was. Any woman would be. He was pleasant, unquestionably good-looking, and had a mysterious element about him that one desired to expose. Unfortunately, Mr. Haskin was also incredibly reserved. He made her brother Charles seem carefree and outgoing. Aimee was still amazed she had convinced the chief mate to help in some of her efforts against Reece.

"Ah—masts," Aimee said, drumming her fingers on the table as she tried to think of another engaging question that would irritate Reece. "Um, how does it feel to climb so high? Is it frightening? Is there a lot of wind?"

Haskin opened his mouth to tell Aimee that such ploys were never going to work but before he could, Reece stepped through the doorway. His blue eyes pierced her green ones. "Aye, tell us, Lady Wentworth, *just how did it feel when you climbed a mast*? Do not tell me you forgot! You only did it *yourself* just a few weeks ago and during a storm at that!"

Haskin jumped to his feet and was about to come to Aimee's defense and throw the intruder out when the words sank in. "*Lady* Wentworth?" he murmured, clearly looking at her in a different way.

Aimee swallowed the guilt she was feeling and pursed her lips. Feeling intimidated, she rose to her feet as well. "There was no choice. I am an excellent climber and the three men who could have unfurled the sails were seriously injured. So I did what was required to stay alive, just as anyone at this table would have done."

"You almost *died*, Aimee," Reece hissed, taking a step forward, but Haskin's large hand whipped out, stopping him from coming any closer.

Haskin snapped, "You, seaman, are out of order and . . ." Then his eyes grew wide as he took in Reece's state of dress. ". . . you have been for some time," he mumbled, finishing his thought. Then finding his voice again, Haskin barked, "*Just what the hell are you wearing?*"

Reece crossed his arms, and the tension emanating from his body filled the room. His light blue eyes had turned icy, and danger radiated from him like an aura. Haskin was tall, but Reece had at least two or three more inches on him. Other than that, the men were similar in physique and strength, and it was not exactly clear who would win a brawl between the two of them.

"I'm *wearing* what that angel-like hellion over there gave me!" Reece yelled back.

From the corner of her eye, Aimee could see Mrs. Shay assess her handiwork and raise an eyebrow at her. Aimee bit her bottom lip, but deep down she did not feel guilty for cutting his pants off above the knees as well as leaving him only a couple of inches for sleeves on his shirt. She had done nothing else to any of his other clothes. It was not like he had nothing else to wear, and besides, she had spent weeks in garments that did not fit. She had made do. So could Reece.

Haskin, who was used to being in constant control of his crew, looked back and forth between them. It was clear that he no longer saw her as innocent and sweet, which was fine with Aimee, as she was neither. But Haskin's expression also was one of disgust that she would desire to be tied in any way to a lowly, unmannered seaman. Unfortunately, Reece was seeing it too. He was mad at her, but his anger toward Haskin had increased exponentially. Soon he was going to lose his self-control and fly into a rage.

To Aimee's relief, Captain Shay stood up and said in a low but commanding voice, "Haskin, stand down and wipe that look off your face before Hamilton here removes your good looks and feeds them to the sharks."

Haskin remained transfixed but did look at his captain. "You know him?"

Shay nodded. "He's the co-owner of W & H Shipping, *and* he's also engaged to Lady Wentworth."

Mrs. Shay, feeling left out, stood up, hooked her arm in her husband's, and said in a tone that indicated she thought the whole scene quite entertaining, "I believe our Mr. Haskin is in shock and could use some time to digest everything, my dear. Shall we take our leave and let these young ones have some privacy?"

Captain Shay gave his wife a wink and pointed to the

bottle of wine on the table. "Grab it, Haskin. You need it, by the looks of you."

Haskin did as told, and without a word turned and left. The Shays followed him but on their way out, Aimee could hear Captain Shay say to his wife, "'Twould be a shame if the two of them worked it out. They were actually quite entertaining the past few days, weren't they, my dear?"

Reece could only stare at her. His anger could not be squelched, but neither could his desire. For days now, he had been getting only glimpses of her from afar or had only been able to hear her voice. Now that Aimee was standing in front him, her green eyes blazing, all he could think of was that she was even more beautiful than he remembered.

"Why are you here, Reece?" Aimee finally asked, breaking the silence.

"You missed our wedding and I am here to correct that."

"I did not *miss* our wedding. I canceled it."

Reece tilted his head and pursed his lips. "And I am uncanceling it."

Aimee's jaw tightened and her spine straightened. "I will *not* marry you."

Reece took a step back, shrugged his shoulders, and leaned against the doorframe.

Aimee waited for him to say something, start an argument, or just bark out an order, but he infuriatingly remained silent. "I mean it, Reece. I do not want to marry you. It's not going to happen. I don't know what drove you to follow me . . . injured pride, misguided sense of decency, a need to right a wrong that doesn't exist—"

"More like obsession."

That caught Aimee off guard. "Obsession?"

He nodded. "Mixed with quite a bit of possessiveness, as it turns out." He shrugged his shoulders again. "Who knew that I was the jealous type? But I am. Haskin may not know it, but he's lucky to be alive. For if I had thought for even one instant that your interest in him was real, I'm not sure what I would have done."

Aimee swallowed. Reece's tone came off as lighthearted, but there was something quite serious about it as well. Then realizing just what he was trying to do, she shook her head. "Charming words will not work this time. I know the truth, Reece."

He pushed himself back to a standing position. "And just what might that be?"

Taking a deep breath to steady herself, Aimee replied, "You fear that you will regret marrying me."

Reece cocked a brow, took a step forward, and said, "I fear regret. Still do. But it was not mine that causes me concern . . . it's yours."

Aimee licked her lips. She could remember his words to Mr. Collins as if they had just been spoken. It was much more than just fear of possible regret that had caused her to turn her back on their future. "You feel forced into marrying me. That you have no choice."

Reece took another step forward. "Again, what you say is true. The situation demands we marry. And since you are not leaving this ship until we *are* married, you now can sympathize with my initial reaction. *But*, if I did have a choice about marrying you, it would be an easy one to make. I'd choose you."

Aimee could feel her heart pound. She instinctively took a step back and pointed her finger at him. "You are just saying that. You . . . you think anyone *but* you would be lucky to have me. For you, I'm a tragic mistake you made."

With a roll of his eyes, Reece argued, "Those are your words, not mine. And only for a short while did I think I was unlucky. Can you imagine the hell of being married to a person you want but who does not want the real you? But I've decided you are more than worth the risk."

Taking another step back, Aimee's back came up against

the wall. Reece was only a couple of feet away. Part of her wanted to flee, but part of her wanted to stay and give in to her heart's desire. But that was something he had yet to give her. She had given him her heart, but he had never given her his. "You want me."

"I do," he said, inching forward.

"You may desire me."

"Beyond imagination." Another step.

"But I want more, Reece," she whispered, looking into his eyes boring down on her. "You were right. What we have is not enough, and I will regret marrying you."

Undeterred, Reece leaned down until his lips were inches from her own. "Don't you know? You have captivated all of me, body and soul. Not even my love for the sea can compete with how I feel about you. I don't just desire you, Aimee Wentworth. I love you. And without you in my life, I will never again be complete."

His love for her shone in the depths of his sky-blue gaze. He meant what he had said. He loved her. More than that, he loved her in the same way she loved him. Completely. Aimee felt the wound inside her start to close. Happiness had found her. "I love you, Reece. I always have and I always will."

With a groan, he pulled her into his arms and kissed her. The volatile emotions that had been raging through him suddenly became a wild, desperate hunger. Lifting her in his arms, he carried her down the two flights of stairs to the wardroom, kicking the door closed behind him. Without lifting his mouth from hers, Reece eased her back onto the soft bed.

Finally alone with no fear of being interrupted, his long fingers delved into her hair, loosening the pins that held it. "Tell me you are not a dream. That I really do have the most beautiful woman in my arms," he mumbled against her lips before brushing a kiss across them once more.

Aimee basked in his loving attention. "I am real and I am yours," she whispered softly into his ear. Her warm, caressing breath flooded him with hot images of their nights together, sending another rush of desire through his veins.

Reece devoured her lips with another slow, seductive, mind-numbing kiss to which Aimee submitted willingly, eagerly. His hands splayed over her back, pulling her against him. Aimee clung to him, reveling in his power and his need. Hot little ripples of pleasure slid down her thighs as she felt the hard bulge beneath his cropped pants and moved sensuously against it.

Wrapped in the haven of her love, for the first time Reece could feel his mind at peace. "I need to be inside you. I need to feel you around me, shivering in pleasure. I need to know exactly how much you need me."

"I do. Reece, I do need you." She said no more as he cut off her words with another kiss.

His fingers tangled in her hair, crushing the silky strands as if he couldn't get enough of the feel of her. Her fingers worked at the buttons of his shirt until his torso lay exposed, powerful, well muscled, and perfect. Aimee sighed and bent her head to flick her tongue in smooth strokes over his skin.

Reece's arousal surged higher into insistent fevered pulsations. He nuzzled her neck. The scent of her filled his head. As he slid her gown off her shoulders, his lips followed, wondering anew how a woman could be so warm and soft.

He slowly made his way down to the valley between her breasts, pausing for short moments to remove the rest of their garments. "You're so beautiful," he murmured as his mouth found the first ripe berry. He laved it with his tongue, taking the hardened nipple into his mouth and teasing it until she squirmed with want of him. Turning his attention to the other breast, his hand lowered, parting her thighs.

Aimee moaned. Reece was kissing her with exquisite passion and touching her in all the right places. She arched her back, desperate to feel his lips glide farther down her body. When he finally lifted his head, she reached for him, but he caught her hands and guided them to his shoulders. He grinned as he slid slowly down her body, bringing his hands up the insides of her thighs.

Aimee's heart began to pound. Her body burned and clenched as she trembled with anticipation. Reece leaned down and kissed the inside of her knee. Then he moved forward and kissed the inside of her thigh.

Her fingernails dug into his shoulder blades and her hips bucked. That was all the invitation Reece needed. Bending down, he took her in his mouth, his tongue hot and rough and insistent. Aimee moaned a soft whimper. The primitive erotic sound nearly drove Reece insane with desire. He cupped her hips and lifted her tighter against his mouth as his tongue plunged into her in an almost savage quest to mate with her.

Aimee thought she was going to die from the pleasure. His mouth was urgent, demanding everything, and she gladly surrendered to his claiming.

It had turned painful holding back, and Reece could no longer wait. He needed to be inside her. To fill her body and her soul completely. Aimee moaned his name and begged him with her hands and mouth to end his torment. Rising up, he lifted her hips and thrust into her with one powerful surge. She was more than ready for him.

Aimee gasped at the feel of him. His size and girth shocked her as he filled her, but as always she reacted primitively to his bold, aggressive hardness and surged to meet his thrust. Reece urged her into a passionate rhythm. He made love to her until his back was slick with sweat and his muscles trembled beneath his skin. Aimee felt her body clench around his with each stroke. She could not seem to get enough of the hot, thick feel of him inside her.

She wrapped her legs around his waist. Then, suddenly,

her whole body was pulsating with erotic release. Reece tried to pull out a short distance but ended up surging back into her hot sheath, unable to resist the pull of Aimee's climax. It sparked his own, a bolt of lightning shot through him, and he gave a shout of exultant satisfaction that echoed against the cabin walls. Reece then collapsed beside Aimee, too exhausted, too satisfied to apologize.

Long minutes passed before either was capable of speaking. He had taken her, possessed her, claimed her, as he had never done before. By giving himself so completely, by trusting her, he had made her his own. He had imprinted himself on her heart and on her soul. Aimee did not think it possible to love him more, but she did.

She settled her head on his shoulder and stroked his chest, loving the feel of his crisp hair.

Reece captured her hand and brought it to his mouth. He kissed her palm. "So I guess you think your little scheme of sneaking on board the *Emerald* a successful one. The Daring Three win again," he murmured against her hair in a playful but sarcastic tone.

Curled in his arms, Aimee nodded her head against his chest. "Our schemes always work. Maybe not the way we plan, but in the end, we figure out a way."

Chapter 32

Chase heard the door open but did not turn around to see who had entered. For the past day and a half, maids and servants had been coming in to check on him and bring him food, though he ate very little. The doctor had agreed to stay, but had just left to take a nap in the guest room. Chase refused to fall asleep and was not sure if he could, even if he tried. Staying by Millie's side, holding her hand, praying for her recovery was all he knew to do. Everything else within his power had been done.

He had no recollection of how he arrived at the hidden clearing in Hyde Park. He could only recall seeing Millie, unearthly pale and unconscious by the bench. Her body had been cold and limp, but she was breathing. He rushed her home and the doctor was waiting for him. The wound had been treated and it was decided that bloodletting would not be necessary since she had already lost a significant amount.

As expected, Millie had developed a fever. She called out for him, for Aimee and Jennelle, so often that he sent word to Jennelle to come. He told her only that Millie had been found but was injured. Part of him knew he should have explained just how dangerously near death Millie was, but he could not do it. It was as if putting it down on paper made it even worse . . . and anything worse would mean death.

The fever had finally broken early that day, but it had now been several hours and she had yet to wake up. When the doctor mentioned that she might have become too hot during her feverish state and might never wake up, Chase had ordered him from the room. He had to be wrong. Millie was his soul, his life. She had to remain in this world, for if she did not, then he would soon perish as well.

"Me . . . lord?" The voice was not one Chase recognized, which caused him to turn around. A tall, thin youth who was in that stage where he was neither boy nor man stood before him.

"Who let you in?" Chase demanded, but its normal bite was missing.

"The one seein' to your front door," Stuart replied, as if the answer was fairly obvious.

Chase grimaced and returned his focus back to his wife. He pulled her soft hand into his and kissed it. He was exhausted and he had little energy to care just what else was going on in the house. "I assume you and my wife crossed paths during these past few weeks."

Stuart stepped closer and took a look around the room. To him, it matched the palatial quality of the rest of the house. He had not realized just how many luxuries Millie had given up while staying with Madame Sasha and her tenants. "Me name's Stuart. She sure must have loved her friend a lot to leave all this."

Chase looked at him pointedly. "Say what you came to say to her and leave."

Stuart was not ruffled by the brisk tone. He had honestly not expected to be let in the front door, and was probably pretty lucky that the doorman answered. "Didn't come to talk to her. Her ladyship looks in a bad way, but I came to say don't let anyone tell you that she won't make it. They said it to me when my father was ill, but they were wrong and they're wrong about her ladyship too. She's too pushy to allow death to take her if she don't want to go."

With a furrowed brow, Chase reassessed the young man standing at the end of his wife's bed. "Your father was ill?"

Stuart shrugged. "Some say he still is, but he's alive." He handed him a bound book. Chase reached out and took it. It was *Waverley* by Sir Walter Scott. "I thought I might come to read to her. My father woke up when I read to him and this is one of my favorites. But perhaps you should be doin' the readin'."

Chase opened it up and saw that the novel had been borrowed from Hatchards. The boy obviously had no idea that he had a library twice the size of the bookseller. But it did not matter. The book was not of any import, it was the idea of reading to stimulate thought. Chase swallowed. "Thank you. I will do just that."

Stuart exhaled the breath he had been holding. "I'll be going now, my lord. But when her ladyship awakens, can you tell her I came by?"

Chase nodded. "Is there anything I can do to help you? Do you need a job? Income?"

Stuart's eyes narrowed and he backed up a step. His demeanor instantly became defensive. "I did not come here for a job, and I certainly don't want to work for any man who thinks to change me. I told that to her and now I'm tellin' you."

Puzzled, Chase asked, "What do you mean, change you? Why would I do that?"

"Like you don't know," Stuart scoffed. "First it would be me clothes, then me speech. Titled men like it when blokes like me copy you and such. You get an idea in your head about someone becomin' a thing and then you go and start tryin' to change them. I don't want no part of it."

Chase sat quiet for several seconds. "I never thought about it like that."

"Didn't expects you would."

"I don't necessarily agree with you, young man. There are a myriad of reasons why people choose certain positions and lifestyles, but I do agree there should be some choice in the matter. Someday you may set yourself a goal and *you* will want to change and take my offer. Know that it will still be there if you do."

Waving one hand to dismiss what he obviously thought an impossibility, Stuart headed for the door. "I do hope her ladyship gets better. She was nice to me and my kind, even when we weren't so friendly to her."

Chase nodded and said, "I will tell her you were here when she awakens."

Stuart pointed at the book. "It's a good story. I'd wake up to hear it." And then he was gone.

Chase fingered the worn copy. He suspected he had at least one leather-bound version downstairs somewhere in his library along with the other novels Sir Walter Scott had written. But instead of going to get them, he opened the cover, turned to the first page, and began to read.

Chapter 33

November 17, 1816

"Edward wants far more than just the maps," Millie said, leaning back against the pillows. "He wants revenge."

Chase stood with his arms crossed, looking out the window. "He won't have it and I won't discuss it any further. You are still weak and are far too fragile to be worried about such things."

Millie sighed audibly. Though she did not consider herself fragile, Chase was right. She was tired and weak. She had woken up last night to him reading, and at first had trouble believing she was really alive and back home. But seeing Chase cry—something she had never seen before—was enough for her to realize that she was finally where she truly belonged.

He had told her his conclusions concerning his sister. He assured her that Jennelle was aware she was now safe and would most likely be arriving in another day or two. He had even told her about Stuart and what he had come to say. But the one topic Chase refused to discuss was Edward.

"I am tired," she admitted. "And I will only grow more weary if you continue refusing to tell me what I need to know. Is Edward alive? Are you close to apprehending him? Do you know what he wants?"

Chase pivoted and ran his hand through his hair, rubbing his scalp. "I offer a compromise. I will tell you briefly what you want to know and then no more until you are completely healed."

Millie twitched her jaw. Compromising was something Charles Wentworth never did. And if it did not work this time, she suspected he might never offer another concession on any topic in the future. "I agree. But only if you will tell me *all* I want to know. Not just the parts you want to tell me."

Chase dropped into one of the chairs close to her. "The parts I want to tell," he grumbled, "are none."

Millie clasped her hands in front of her and looked at him pointedly.

"Did you kill him?" Chase began. "I doubt it, as we have not found a body. Are we close to finding him? Unfortunately, no, and we have no leads as to where he was staying or where he went. I doubt we will until he resurfaces to get what he wants."

"And just what does he want?"

"What you already know. Some old maps that Reece and I purchased along with several other items. And, no, I do not know what they represent or why they are important. I am waiting for Reece to return to help, which hopefully will be before the end of the month."

"I want to see one of the maps," Millie said, hoping that he would concede but prepared for him to say no.

Chase rubbed his temples. "Millie, you are ill. You were *stabbed*. You do *not* need to be getting involved with something with which you cannot possibly help!"

Millie felt a tear slip down her cheek and wiped it away, praying that another did not follow. "So, I am assuming you intend to send me away again to keep me from even *seeing* what it is Edward wants so badly."

Chase shook his head. "I admit that I want to do that very thing—not to keep you from seeing the maps, but to keep you safe. Can you blame me? I almost lost you for the *second* time."

"I don't know . . ." Millie began and then stopped, hesitating before trying again. "I do not know if I can be what you need in a wife. I understand what you want—even why—and while so much of me wants to be that for you, at some point I will revert to my nonconforming ways. I love you more than I will ever love anyone. But I am not sure that I am capable of changing . . . even for you."

Changing. There was that word again. Why did everyone think that he wanted them to change? Minor adjustments perhaps, but he did not want Millie to be anyone other than who she was. He *needed* her to be herself. Did she not understand that?

"I never wanted you to change who you are, Millie. It's more about wanting you to accept me and who I am."

Millie's jaw went slack. "I have *never* given *you* lectures about how to act as a proper husband. Not a single conversation have we ever had about what is expected of you as the Marquess of Chaselton now that you have a wife."

Chase rolled his eyes, something he could not recall doing a year ago. "Maybe not in *those* words, but you have not been quiet about your thoughts on my 'rule-loving' ways."

Millie winced as she heard him parrot one of her favorite descriptions of him.

"I wonder how you would feel about me if I did change, became some carefree husband, indifferent to your whims. Do you truly want me to just shrug my shoulders when I am told that you are doing something that might put you, Aimee, or Jennelle in danger?"

"No, I wouldn't but—"

"But what, Millie? You want to remain yourself, but cannot I ask the same? I *like* rules. I like the clarity they bring. In general, they generate security, which is something I desire for those I love. And while I might not always agree with every rule, I understand the consequences to those that I break—and I *do* break them from time to time."

Millie felt another tear fall and then another. This time she did not try to stop them as it would be pointless. "Is it hopeless then? Are we just to accept that while we love each other, we cannot be together and be ourselves?"

"Who says we cannot be ourselves?" Chase countered, rising up to his feet. "We just proved that we can compromise when we decide to, even on serious topics. Why can we not on other things?"

Millie bit her bottom lip and considered the question. In her mind, she had been compromising for months now, but after hearing his point of view, so had Chase. But had they really been *compromising*? Compromise consisted of concessions by both parties. What she had been doing was surrendering to what she thought he wanted. Giving up all for him, and based on what Chase just said, he had often felt the same. But if they compromised, it would be acknowledgment of the other's desires and an agreement on just where those desires could be tempered. "I want to try. More than anything, I want to try."

Chase walked over to the side of the bed, sat down, and pulled Millie into his arms. He held her for a long moment before pulling back to kiss her. His lips were tender and full of the love he held for her. It filled Millie with hope, for she did not think she could live without him in her life. She had to be herself, and yet too much of herself now included him.

"I love you. We will find a way to make things work," Chase said. "But know this: I will work with you on any topic save one. I will never, ever compromise on your being in my life. I need you too much, Millie. More than I should have ever allowed, but it is too late. You are my soul, and I shall perish without you."

Millie leaned over and brushed her mouth across his. "That is one compromise I can live without."

Chapter 34

November 20, 1816

Clive lifted the glass up so that he could see it better in the light. With a scowl, he took one of his cleaner towels and wiped it down to remove the dirt. "Even now that damn woman is making me do things I don't want to," he muttered and lifted the next glass.

He had almost three dozen more to go through before he opened up the place. Something he was still dithering on doing. Ellie had sent the cases with a note.

> I have instructed my husband's man-of-affairs to give you a hundred pounds, but you must do two things. You have to keep the new glasses and use them. And secondly, you must close down Six Belles for one evening.

Pride had almost caused Clive to bellow at the man who delivered the cases to take his damn glasses *and* Ellie's money *and* get the hell out of his place. And if he were ten years younger, he would have, but Clive had learned too many painful lessons from being hasty. Denying Ellie's offer would not have been hard, but one hundred pounds was a lot of money. It was enough to enable him to make some changes that he had always longed to do.

"She said I had to do *two* things," Clive had snorted at the polished, unfazed man standing in front of him. "Tell her that I'll take the glasses *and* I'll use 'em. But I'm not shutting down my place on some woman's whim."

The man had merely nodded and said, "I will convey your message. I am sure that her ladyship will be saddened by your decision, but she will understand."

And then the man had left.

"Why would she care if I open my place or not?" he asked himself aloud.

The answer suddenly came to him. Was Ellie thinking of coming here? A marchioness? She had been here for weeks, but not as herself. That would be different. Clive had no doubt that her husband—a *marquess*—would be at her side. Both of them would be in all their finery and he had no way to stop them. If he was open, he would never live it down. The men would chide him for years for rubbing elbows with the titled. It would ruin him.

He put the glass down and headed out the doors. Several boys were across the street playing a game with rocks. He called out to them and gave them each a penny for spreading the word that Six Belles was closed for the night. If they made sure not a single man came up to the door the whole night, they would get an additional sixpence. Seeing their faces go from skepticism to belief reminded Clive once again why he was so glad he always kept his word.

Then he turned to go back inside and waited.

Just after eight o'clock, he heard the sound he had known was coming. A few seconds later, the carriage stopped just outside his doors. Clive held his breath. He wanted to reprimand Ellie for being so shortsighted, but with her husband there, that would be an impossibility. Clive doubted he could have done it anyway. He had a hard enough time dealing with her when she had been just a simple, infuriating lass.

The door opened and Clive felt his mouth go completely slack. And for the first time since Ellie forced her way into his life, he felt absolutely and completely grateful that she had.

"I cannot believe you are not right there watching the whole thing."

Millie smiled. "How I want to be there, but a piece of me knows that even if I want to, I'll never see Six Belles again. While I would love to see everyone again, it would cause problems."

Jennelle nodded in understanding. "Not to mention that Charles would never let you go."

Millie smiled, wondering if she could get him to compromise on the topic. Perhaps, if she would agree to let him go with her. Either way, it did not matter. For a few brief weeks she had crossed over and lived in another social class. Miraculously, her reputation had not suffered. But if she were to even visit that world again, it would not just risk her and Chase's reputations, it could seriously debilitate Clive's— and therefore Bessie's—livelihood. No, it was better she sent her thank-you in the form that she had.

"Bessie sounds like she can be difficult. Do you think that she went?"

"Oh, she went," Millie declared. "Bessie is many things, but she is no fool. She would be unable to refuse the opportunity to live out a secret dream."

Lying in bed every day had been torturous. Chase had been there most of the time, and it was during her detailed stories about the people she had met and worked with that the idea of how to thank Clive and Bessie occurred to her. Millie had been uncertain how Chase would react, as it was another unorthodox plan that in no way resembled the actions of a marchioness. But he had surprised her and readily agreed—just as long as it was his man-of-affairs and neither of them doing the actual delivery.

And so the next day a large selection of materials was sent to Evette along with payment for a cloak, a new working dress, and one evening gown. Once complete, she was to deliver them to Bessie along with a note.

> *My dearest Bessie,*
> *Unknowingly, you, Evette, and Clive helped to make my dreams come true. It is only fair that I repay the debt and help make yours a reality as well.*
>
> > *Best Regards,*
> > *Millie Chaselton*

Millie sighed. "I only wish I could have seen her in Evette's creation."

"Not me," Jennelle said, shaking her head. "I've never met either of them, but based on all that you have told me, it is *Clive* that I would like to have seen. I bet his eyes popped out of his head when Bessie arrived."

Millie laughed. "If they did not, then I am sure they did when all the food and the waiters came in wanting to set up a table for them on the roof of Six Belles."

Jennelle joined her. "Oh, it is too sad that you cannot communicate and find out what happened."

Millie winked at her. "We'll find out. I am thinking that I might be in desperate need of some new clothes before we leave Town. While we are at Madame Sasha's, we will find a way to corner Evette and learn all the details."

"After Madame Sasha grills you."

Millie grimaced. "Unfortunately, you are right. She is not

going to be happy learning what happened. I just hope she will be somewhat mollified when I tell her that I was truly unaware of the danger regarding Chase and the thief."

"Well, you have another week to think of what to say, for I expect it will be at least that long before Charles is willing to let you leave this room."

Millie scoffed and threw off the covers to let her legs swing over the bed's side. "Not if I have anything to say about it."

Jennelle watched as Millie stuck her feet into some slippers and then put on a dressing gown and tied it around her waist. "What will Charles say if he finds you out of bed?"

"Not a thing. I've agreed to all the security he deems necessary, and he ignores my need to sneak downstairs several times a day, just as long as I don't try to leave the house. This way I can be myself and break some rules, while he is no longer worried that I'll break the ones that truly bother him. This way we are both happy," Millie finished with a shrug of her shoulders.

No longer tongue-tied, Jennelle murmured, "I'm never getting married."

"I remember saying that once," Millie said, chuckling. "Meanwhile, there is something you need to see."

Chase entered his study and paused when he saw his wife and Jennelle hovering over his desk. Millie being out of bed when she should be in it, resting, was almost expected. That she was in his study was also not surprising, but seeing her studying the maps that were supposed to be cleverly hidden was not what he expected to find when he came home.

"I did not show you where those items were hidden for you to remove them at your leisure."

Millie rounded his desk and went over to give him a light kiss on the mouth. "Do not worry. I did not stress myself by getting them down. It was Jennelle who put forth the effort, and we have only now just begun to study them."

"I told you before—"

"And I heard you. But truly, Charlie, is there any harm in Jennelle and I looking at the very thing that is making us live with all this additional protection you have hired?"

Wanting to throttle and kiss her at the same time, Chase gave in to his second inclination and pulled Millie in close. With Jennelle in the room, it was a far less passionate embrace than he would have preferred, but every day Millie grew stronger. It would not be long now before he could truly show Millie just how much she was loved.

"Then look at them if you must, but when you realize you can understand it no better than I, will you agree to keep them concealed until Reece arrives?"

Millie nodded happily.

Jennelle sat down in the chair that Chase normally occupied, quite engrossed in what she was looking at. "Charles, just what do you think this is a map of?"

Chase went over and said, "I do not know, and outside of Reece, I do not trust any man who has enough knowledge of the sea and its charts to decipher it."

Jennelle shook her head and looked up, her eyes bright with excitement. "Charles, these are not islands, and no sea captain is going to be able to tell you what these are."

Millie went over to stand next to Chase. "Jennelle, what do you mean?"

Standing up, Jennelle fingered the large mark at the top of the map. "This symbol," she said, "is one that I have studied a great deal. I have written and debated with experts in recent years on whether these maps even existed. And now, standing here, I find it hard to believe that I am actually looking at something that is almost eight hundred years old."

Millie sucked in her breath. "How old?"

Ignoring the rhetorical question, Jennelle looked up and stared intently at Chase. "And if I am right and these are what I believe they are, then I know what Sir Edward is looking for . . . and it isn't on an island. And it most certainly is not treasure—at least not in the way most people define the word."

Chase held her gaze. "Then just what is he after?"

"Something that should not be in any man's hands. Something so powerful, it could potentially give Edward the power over, well . . . everything."

Epilogue

November 21, 1816

Reece watched Captain Shay from the corner of his eye pretend to amble along the deck acting as if his intentions were to quietly check on the work of his crew. Reece had no doubt that in just a few moments the balding old man would just "happen" to spy him leaning on the rail, when in reality it had been Shay's primary purpose of stepping onto this part of the main deck. Worse, the aging captain probably suspected that Reece knew of this and was enjoying making Reece wait by prolonging his stroll.

At long last, the sound of a satisfied sigh joined the wind on Reece's right.

"You took your time," Reece drawled.

"I did, didn't I?"

Though Reece refused to look and verify his suspicions, he knew the old man was grinning. Reece recognized the pure delight that rang in Shay's voice. Such happy sounds usually came from Aimee or another of the Daring Three, but nonetheless, it meant the same thing. The man was scheming.

"Glad our weather's being cooperative this trip." Shay

patted his protruding stomach and inhaled deeply. "Outside in the afternoons is the best. Don't you agree?"

The weather? Reece huffed to himself. Shay was obviously eager to talk to him about something and it certainly was not about climate conditions during the day. "Mornings are a little chilly," Reece carefully agreed, "but if the seas remain calm, we should make London a day or two ahead of schedule."

"Aye. The *Sea Rebel*'s a mighty fine vessel. You have five ships now, if memory serves. Your company must be doing well to afford expanding like it has."

Reece searched for the hidden meaning in Shay's words. Unable to come up with one, he remained silent.

Undisturbed by Reece's lack of willingness to participate in conversation, Shay pulled out a small telescope from the inside pocket of his outer coat and scanned the blue horizon. "Your reputation as a sea captain during the war was akin to dictatorial. I wondered if you could accept being on a ship you owned but did not command. It seems the rumors were overblown or untrue."

Reece risked a brief glance over to his right. Captain Shay had a reputation during the war as well and it always involved three words—cunning, brilliant and thorough. It did not take long to know his reputation was accurate, if incomplete. Cunning should have been in there twice. The elder captain was steadfast to those he served and always spoke the truth but one could count on there being more than one meaning to whatever he said. "Do not overly concern yourself, Shay. I fully intend to be off the *Sea Rebel* and back on the *Emerald* as soon as I am able."

Shay waved his hand dismissively. "I never was worried in the least about that."

Reece drew in a deep breath and exhaled. He was battling between the urge to leave and his gut feeling that he should just yield and ask the infuriating man what he wanted.

Normally, any prospect of being manipulated would have been enough motivation to walk away, but it would be another week before they were back in London. If Reece did not take the opportunity Shay was providing him now, then whatever topic the old man wanted to discuss would almost certainly come up tonight at dinner—and not to Reece's favor. Though vexatious, the creative control Shay had of the situation was to be admired.

Turning to face the man directly, Reece gave in and said candidly, "Speak your mind, Shay, for behind that nonchalant smile of yours, you have concerns and questions. And since they are not about W & H shipping, my reputation as a captain, me being on this ship, or the fair weather we have been having, that leaves only one more topic. Lady Aimee Wentworth."

Shay shrugged his shoulders and clasped his hands together. "Annabelle and I just want to know what your intentions are."

Reece quirked an eyebrow. "Same as they were when I came aboard. I had planned for Lady Wentworth and me to marry prior to our journey back to London, but her stubbornness delayed such wiser notions. So we are now forced to wait. However, the sleeping arrangements regarding myself and Lady Wentworth, which I suspect is contributing to some of the anxiety and the motivation behind your line of questions, are *not* going to change. All I can do is assure you that at the first opportunity, we *will* be wed."

Shay chuckled and clapped Reece on the back. "Ah Hamilton, any changes to *your* sleeping arrangements on this ship would undoubtedly create changes in *my* sleeping arrangements. Annabelle has grown quite found of Lady Wentworth and angry women tend to stick together. But that is something that you will learn in time."

Reece was about to remind Shay that he had known Aimee and her two best friends since childhood and was well aware of the close bonds that female camaraderie created when he stopped himself. If Shay's purpose was not to convince Reece of spending the next several days apart from Aimee, then what was it? "Then, damn it, man, what is it that you and I need to discuss? What has you filled with mirth and me uneasy to find out the reason?"

"Why, Hamilton, I have no idea," Shay professed less than innocently. "I'm fully content. At least I am now." He threw one of his arms around Reece's wide shoulders and despite only being of average height, maneuvered Reece so that he looked out toward the deck versus the sea. Letting go, Shay pointed at the upper deck. "I think right there will be the best spot. That way all the men could see the ceremony since Lady Wentworth's friends will not be able to attend. And while I know you said the *first* opportunity, our women will be wanting several hours to get ready and you agreed that the afternoon was preferable when being out on deck."

The knot in Reece's stomach became a lead weight as he digested just what Shay was saying. "Tomorrow?" was all that he could manage to get out.

"I'm quite looking forward to it," Shay said with a large, unapologetic grin. "Everyone is, with the exception of Haskin. I haven't exactly approached him about it. Maybe you and I should do that together this evening over dinner. Though I doubt he holds the same view as Annabelle and I. We were hoping that you and Lady Wentworth would continue your antics for at least another week. Quite entertaining, you two. Never knew what to expect and it made the voyage go by so much faster." Shay paused and lightly elbowed Reece in the side. "We were hoping that Haskin would get involved and help delay things, but the lad is just too reserved. Anyway, now that you and Lady Wentworth are blissfully happy and the crew knows one of the owners of W & H Shipping is aboard, everyone is acting and behaving their best. Things have become dull I tell you, even the weather has been cooperative."

Reece held up his hand. "I'm not getting married tomorrow."

"I thought you and I were of the same mind on certain matters. . ."

Reece shook his head and tried again. "We are of the same mind, Shay, but as a captain, you can only command a ship. It takes an ordained priest to marry two people. You lack the qualifications."

"Indeed I do. But I know someone who does not," Shay said with a playful smile.

Miles Haskin's fork hung in mid-air as he mentally translated just what had happened. The wiliness of Captain Shay was known to anyone with whom he came into contact for more than a few moments. He was famous for his double entendre and as a result, Miles had taken great care to successfully sidestep and avoid being caught in any of the man's traps. Unfortunately, tonight Miles had let his thoughts meander elsewhere instead of remaining focused on the seemingly inconsequential path of conversation.

His thoughts had been on Lady Wentworth.

Not actually on the lady herself, but on the *idea* that a woman like her actually existed, for until now, Miles had not believed it possible. In his experience, noblewomen or daughters of gentlemen of any stature resembled more like the grating creature Aimee had pretended to be the night her true identity had been revealed. It had been bad enough listening to her ask senseless questions about sails and masts, but when Hamilton barged in, indecent, and lacking proper clothes, it had taken everything Miles had to follow Shay's advice and walk away. Even today, Miles somewhat wished he hadn't. He would have enjoyed punching Reece Hamilton in the jaw a few times and blackening those blue eyes of his Lady Wentworth so enjoyed. Not that Miles thought such an action would win him her affections, but mostly just to ensure Hamilton knew there was a cost to treating another man as a fool. The only thing that *had* kept Miles from decking him then, and since, was knowing a true fool was ruled by his emotions—something he would never be. On the other hand, when it came to Lady Aimee Wentworth, Captain Reece Hamilton was definitely ruled by his. And that knowledge pacified Miles, but it also left him wondering . . . were there other women like Lady Wentworth out there?

Miles knew the luxuries of wealth having grown up not as a nobleman, but as the third son to one of the wealthiest gentlemen in England. His father was one of the most prosperous men in England in the textile industry—a true rags-to-riches story. As a result, he spoiled his wife and seven children quite abominably. They wanted for nothing and always went to the most fashionable balls and eateries and had the latest in fashions and transportation. As a result, women constantly swarmed his older brothers, Alastor and Leland. It did not take long for them to pass on their knowledge to Miles—enjoy a woman's beauty but do not become enamored by it. By the time he came of age, he quickly realized his brothers were right. Women simpered, plotted, flittered, blushed, and some even fainted. Those who were intelligent incomprehensively pretended they were not. Those who were not, men wanted to avoid altogether. Simply put, Miles, like his brothers before him, had decided that women brought up in the upper class of Society were not worth his time and effort.

Then he met Lady Aimee Wentworth, daughter of a marquess. Similarly spoiled in her upbringing, she understood how Society worked to control all those in its domain. And yet just as his father had mysteriously been able to instill in Miles and his siblings a sense of independence, Aimee had a streak of unconventionality about her that appealed to Miles's oftentimes too reserved soul. He had not realized how much he longed for someone like her in his life. Someone who could play the part of a Society duchess if required, but also was full of passion, enthusiasm, and ironically—someone he could not control. But until meeting Aimee, he truly had not thought a woman like her existed.

As a young man embarking into the world, he had resolved to keep his wealthy lineage a secret, thinking anonymity would enable those he encountered to focus on him and not on his family name and wealth. When it came to men, Miles had been correct. Unfortunately, God had given him highly-valued physical traits. So even without his inheritance known, he attracted a train of insincere females with the same boring personalities as their wealthier counterparts—they just dressed and smelled less appealing. So again, Miles followed the footsteps of his older brothers and focused on his career.

Knowing eventually his eldest brother would inherit the family business, Miles knew the textile industry would not be where he would invest his energies. His second eldest brother Leland had chosen law, a field Miles eventually tried as well. The law suited him in a way. He liked the idea of executing justice; however, sitting behind a desk for days leading up to a nearly-just-as-boring session at court was more tedious than his first chosen path—the church. But studying law had caused Miles to cross paths with Sir Robert Peel once again.

Robert Peel was an old family friend as both of their fathers had made their fortune in the textile industry. Robert was the same age as Alastor and was just leaving Harrow School and Oxford as Miles entered, but Alastor had made sure Miles was included in some of their more venturous antics. As they grew older, Peel and Miles realized they had much in common, including execution of the law. During the next few years, Peel held a series of positions in the government, one in which he established the Royal Irish

Constabulary, Ireland's first major police force. He hoped
to establish a similar police force in London and wanted
Miles to be a part of it, but Miles first needed to broaden his
understanding of the world in which he lived. This included
the London Docks.

With Peel's encouragement, Miles had gone to work on
a smaller ship that belonged to a friend of his father's. He
had quickly moved to a larger vessel and then after learning
all he could, Miles knew he needed to expand his knowledge even more by working for someone who had years
of experience commanding numerous ships in various
conditions—both war and commercial. After several discreet inquiries, Miles had chosen Captain Shay. Peel had
agreed and used his influence and connections to get Miles
on board the *Sea Rebel*.

What never occurred to Miles was that before ever being
hired, Captain Shay had done his own research on him.

"So what do you say, Haskin? Will you agree to offici-
ate the wedding of Lady Aimee Wentworth and Mr. Reece
Hamilton tomorrow afternoon?" Shay posed the question
again, this time far more directly than he did the first time.

Miles ignored Aimee's big green eyes and pretty mouth,
both of which were open in honest surprise. The tall, lanky
man she intended to marry, however, was sitting back with
his arms crossed. And he was smiling. Reece Hamilton was
far from shocked to learn of Miles's first choice of career.

Miles studied the smirk on the face of his soon to be
ex-employer, licked his lips, and shifted his gaze back to
Shay's. "I will," he answered.

Aimee fingered the ivory satin embroidered trained gown
she was wearing, unable to temper her disbelief at its beauty.
Scattered down its front were embroidered gold sprigs that
grew more elaborate toward the center of the gown. The

hem was adorned with two rows of intricate gold beadwork, but between them was a wide row of pearls stitched in the shapes and patterns of the sprigs yet with a flower that was in full bloom. Delicate ecru lace embellished with pearls and gold thread lined the satin puffed sleeves set just off the shoulders and in the front was a simple bow that offered just the right amount of adornment. The empire waist was hidden, defined by cut and shape, rather than by lace or ribbon, enabling the back of the gown to be more daring than found in the fashions of typical London Society. This, above all of its other features, made the dress perfect in Aimee's eyes, who saw herself a lot like the garment. Seemingly beautiful and delicate, but when one looked a little further . . . much bolder than one originally supposed.

"However did you find anything so beautiful already made?"

Annabelle gently nudged Aimee's chin back up so that she could finish pinning the last few coiled locks of hair into place. "You are fortunate that we were in Savannah and not one of the many other ports we frequent. Young Americans are many things, but among them is an eagerness to improve and outdo all that is English. You and I know their social climb is an impossible one, but when I saw this dress last winter when I was in port, I thought those colonials just might have done it this once, though the seamstress certainly priced this garment as if it were one of her children."

Aimee once again petted the satin, thinking in a way, it probably was. She had worn fine materials all her life, but somehow this one seemed more special. She wished it was hers, and not just borrowed for the day. "I'm sure Mr. Shay believes it was more than worth the expense."

Annabelle leaned down to whisper, "Don't tell him I told you, but he said not to spare any expense and I didn't. And in doing so I never had so much fun shopping, even if I was all by myself. Though I expect your brother might be more than a little displeased when he gets the bill."

Aimee swiveled in her seat to look at Annabelle, looking very puzzled. "You mean you *just* bought this gown for *me*?"

Annabelle nodded, twirling the comb in her hand for Aimee to turn back around. "Who else would it be for, dear? Not me, surely. The reason we were so late leaving Savannah was that the hem had to be let down another inch to allow for your height."

Aimee looked down and could now see that the hem had indeed been let out. Though beautifully stitched, it was not of the same level of quality as the rest of the gown, most likely from being rushed. "But . . . but this means that you and Captain Shay knew Mr. Hamilton and I would marry when we came aboard. You *knew* all this would come to be," Aimee murmured in a soft, confused voice.

"Of course we did, Lady Wentworth. Never would either of us have allowed Mr. Hamilton to remain aboard otherwise."

Aimee shook her head, remembering the day they left quite well. "I understand how you could be confident of Mr. Hamilton's desires to marry *me*—"

Annabelle smiled at the memory. "You should have heard him demanding that he be allowed to haul you to the church. Mr. Shay finally decided to let him, fully believing you would say 'no' once you got there."

Aimee furrowed her eyebrows trying to remember how hurt and angry she was those days after she had overheard Reece's easily misunderstood confession. "I suspect you are right. But what made you think that I would change my mind? If I recall accurately, that day you thought him to be a . . . a . . . ninnyhammer."

"I certainly did. But remember me stating that I was going to share those sentiments with my husband? Well, it seemed I was too late. Your Mr. Hamilton was there before me, explaining that he realized that he made several grave errors and needed time to make amends. That he loved you, cherished and needed you and always would. Well, after learning how much you loved him, I had no choice but to agree to Mr. Shay's decision to allow Mr. Hamilton on board, knowing you would marry once all the misunderstandings were settled. I, of course, was immediately sent out to find the perfect gown and make sure we had everything necessary for the ceremony. You have to admit that I do have the finest of husbands, Lady Wentworth. What other man would think of such a thing, especially when he had no daughters?"

"Perhaps a man with a similarly wise and cunning wife, who plants such a suggestion in his ear?"

"Perhaps," Annabelle agreed with a smile and shrug.

Unable to stop herself, Aimee rose to her feet and clasped the woman to her and held her close for several seconds. "Thank you, Annabelle. I cannot tell you how much my dress—the hassle of the wedding—ensuring the happiness of my future—all of it means."

Annabelle waved a hand in front of her face in an effort to stop her tears. "Truly was a pleasure, my lady. And regarding the fuss of the wedding, I had to do something. Captain Shay and I were finding ourselves rather lacking for topics of conversation at night after weeks of the non-stop entertainment provided by you and Mr. Hamilton."

Aimee shook her head and bit her bottom lip. "And one wedding is going to provide enough material? Reece tells me there is at least another week before we reach London."

Annabelle twitched her lips, unable to suppress a mischievous grin. "Perhaps Mr. Shay might wish for something more in time, but for me? I'll always have the story of how I helped a daughter of a marquess secure the admission of love from her sea captain, and then tricked them into being married at sea by none other than a famed Haskin. It is just

too delicious for words and what makes it more delectable
is that it is all true!"

Reece kicked the door to the stateroom closed with his
foot as he pulled Aimee tightly to him. His lips crushed hers
in a fierce, white hot embrace. "You are mine, Mrs. Hamilton.
Now and forever," he purred against her lips.

Aimee smiled and gave him a quick peck, but not doing
anything to try to leave the embrace. "And you are mine, Mr.
Hamilton. I've known it all my life. It is you who is finally
aware of how things were always meant to be."

Her smile tugged at Reece's heart, but he needed her to
know that he was serious. "You are my life, Aimee. You are
more important than anyone or anything."

Aimee said nothing. She only let go a sigh of pure bliss,
and rested her head against his chest. Reece loved the feel
of her body as it melded against his. He closed his eyes
tightly, knowing he held his whole world in his arms. "Mine
forever," he breathed again, close to her ear, his voice in-
credulous.

After several seconds, Aimee lifted her head, kissed the
tip of his nose and then wiggled a little, hinting for him to
give her a little space. As soon as he did she pulled off her
gloves and began searching in her hair, plucking out what
looked to be miniature weapons and laying them on a
nearby table. "While I would love nothing more than to fall
immediately in your arms, Mrs. Shay must have used every
hairpin she had on board in doing my hair. I'm afraid I
would be in danger of wounding you, myself, or us both if
I did not first remove these things."

Reece chuckled and came up behind Aimee to nibble on
her neck. "Take your time. I'll just enjoy what parts of you
I can get to as they become available."

Aimee rolled her eyes, but also loved the feel of his warm

lips against her skin. No matter how many times or ways Reece kissed her, it always sent shivers down her spine. She knew it always would. "I cannot believe Mr. Haskin actually married us," she remarked breathily, trying to distract her mind from the sensations Reece was creating with his mouth.

"I must admit to being more than a little surprised that he did not pull some type of prank to delay things," Reece said as he unhooked the back of her gown so he could continue his onslaught on her senses. "I honestly thought he would," he added right before bending his head once more.

Aimee removed a pin and a large lock of hair fell down her back. "We would have deserved it. We are fortunate that he has been so forgiving."

Reece made an inarticulate sound and began running his fingers through Aimee's freed hair, relishing its silkiness. "You mean we're lucky the man is so damn reserved. Probably has no idea how to generate a passionate response from a woman."

"Be nice," chided Aimee playfully as she pulled out the final pin, letting the rest of her thick curls fall free. "Mr. Haskin was very hospitable and I'll have you know there is something about his *reserved* demeanor that is quite compelling. If my heart had not already been claimed, I might have been caught by the allure of his mysterious nature."

Reece growled, spun her around, and covered Aimee's mouth with his own. His kiss was voracious, filled with longing as his tongue claimed hers over and over until she was weak and trembling with need. "What was that about finding another man compelling?"

Aimee lifted her passion-filled eyes to meet his. "Never. No matter how long you are gone—months or even longer—never will you have to worry. There has been and only ever will be one man for me. You."

Reece's large hand came up and gently cupped her cheek. "Who says I'll be gone for such long periods?"

Aimee pulled back slightly. "But I thought . . . won't you be?" she finally asked.

Reece slowly began to slip her gown off one shoulder and leaned down to kiss the soft skin its vacancy revealed. "I will have to leave from time to time, but I don't *always* have to be at sea. I am partial owner of the company and there are things that I quite miss about living on land."

Aimee threw her head back both unwilling and unable to stop Reece from what he was doing physically to her. But she was afraid she had just misunderstood what she had just heard. "But. . . but you love the sea. You never wanted to stay home before."

"Aye, I do love being on the water," Reece murmured against her skin. "But I was at sea for so long due to the war and then when it was over, I could not come home."

The second sleeve slipped down her arm and Aimee felt the gown slither down her frame and fall to the floor. Reece's mouth did not slow its exploration as he turned her around. Aimee could feel herself becoming more and more lost to his sensual attack. "Why not?" she finally managed to ask.

"I was in love with a blond beauty who could not be mine," Reece answered as he removed the last of her undergarments and began to lave one pink beckoning nub. "I knew if I spent any time around her at all, I would whisk her away and make her mine despite her family, my lack of status, and my best friend—who undoubtedly will kill me for falling in love with his baby sister."

Aimee felt her control slipping and decided to switch roles. Sliding out of his embrace, she stepped behind him and began to repeat the erotic torture he had begun on her. "So what about your ship?"

Reece swallowed as he felt her hands slip under his shirt and lift upward. A moan escaped him as her lips pressed against the middle of his back. "The, um, *Emerald?* Collins deserves a ship of his own. And, um, uh, and . . ."

Aimee delighted in his response and it encouraged her to continue downward. "Then which ship will be yours?"

"The *Emerald* will, um, always be mine. But this way . . . uh, I can relieve each captain for a trip, giving them a, uh . . . Good Lord, a uh, break and me a chance to check on the health of the ship and the crew and . . . good God woman, I can stand no more."

Reece spun around and buried his face in her neck with a guttural sound. He could feel the bed against his calves and fell back against the mattress, pulling Aimee with him. The moment the bed felt the impact of their weight, the frame shifted and immediately crashed onto the floor. Down feathers from a busted seam in the mattress flew into the air causing Aimee to roll over and cough, waving her hands in front of her face. "What . . . what *happened?*" she half coughed, half choked.

Reece remained lying on his back staring at the planks above him. Right above those planks were the captain's quarters, housing an old man and his wife—both of whom had to be behind their current predicament.

Aimee saw where Reece was staring and sighed in resignation. "We *should* have expected them to do something. I mean they each told us quite openly that they were bored."

Reece laid the back of his wrist on his forehead and muttered, "Aye, but what are we going to do for a *bed* for the next week?"

Hearing the loud boom and sharp scream, Annabelle froze for a second before putting her brush down and turning around to seek her husband's expression. Seeing a lack of alarm, she calmed and asked, "Whatever could that have been? If I did not know better, I would think that two or